lost in the
MOONLIGHT
THE MATHERTONS
LJ EVANS
WRITER'S DIGEST AWARD WINNING AUTHOR

# LJ EVANS

Where Music & Stories Collide

LJ EVANS BOOKS

www.ljevansbooks.com

Cover Design: © www.riverbriardesigns.com

Cover Images: © iStock | NaokiKim; rifatp; Praewpailin; kasimasimik; Natalia Lukiyanova; D-Keine; © FWStudioPhoto.com | Werachai Sookruay

Chapter Title Images: iStock | Svetlana Yaroslavskaya; Antonina Maslova

Developmental & Line Editing: Evans Editing and Michelle Fewer

Copy Editing & Proofing: Jenn Lockwood Editing, Karen Hrdlicka, Stephanie Feissner

Library of Congress Cataloging in process.

# Playlist

https://spoti.fi/3Sw7jjX

Chp 1 – Ghost Story by Carrie Underwood
Chp 2 – Crazy Angels by Carrie Underwood
Chp 3 – I Can Barely Say by The Fray
Chp 4 – Lessons Learned by Carrie Underwood
Chp 5 – I Know Where I've Been by Elle King
Chp 6 – Breathe by Kenzie
Chp 7 – Hold My Hand by The Fray
Chp 8 – Keep On Wanting by The Fray
Chp 9 – Crazy Dreams by Carrie Underwood
Chp 10 – Play On by Carrie Underwood
Chp 11 – Corners by The Fray
Chp 12 – So Small by Carrie Underwood
Chp 13 – Same As You by The Fray
Chp 14 – Sway by Danielle Bradbery
Chp 15 – The Wind by The Fray
Chp 16 – Happiness by The Fray
Chp 17 – Collide by Howie Day
Chp 18 – Love Wins by Carrie Underwood
Chp 19 – Turn Me On by The Fray
Chp 20 – Twisted by Carrie Underwood
Chp 21 – Electric Touch by Taylor Swift
Chp 22 – That's Where It Is by Carrie Underwood
Chp 23 – Keep Holding On by Avril Lavigne
Chp 24 – Guilty As Sin by Taylor Swift
Chp 25 – Never Say Never by The Fray
Chp 26 – Only Us by Carrie Underwood w/ Dan + Shay
Chp 27 – Look After You by The Fray
Chp 28 – Look At Me by Carrie Underwood
Chp 29 – Singing Low by The Fray
Chp 30 – I Dare You by Kelly Clarkson
Chp 31 – Heartbeat by The Fray
Chp 32 – You Better Believe by Train
Chp 33 – Superman (It's Not Easy) by Five for Fighting
Chp 34 – Your Guardian Angel by The Red Jumpsuit Apparatus
Chp 35 – Inside Your Heaven by Carrie Underwood
Chp 36 – Love Don't Die by The Fray
Chp 37 – Magic by Kelly Clarkson
Chp 38 – Changing Tides by The Fray
Epilogue – You Picked Me by A Fine Frenzy

# Dedication

*To all the ones who lead us out of the dark and into the light.*

*To the love of my life, who never lets me stay lost in the moonlight for long before bringing me home.*

# Part One

An unstoppable fury consumed me at the news. The messenger took a step back, gaze darting to the door, but it wasn't him I was imagining gasping for breath.

I would demand blood as payment.

I would exact retribution with my own hands.

We'd find hell together.

# Chapter One

## Lincoln

**GHOST STORY**

Performed by Carrie Underwood

**MY GHOST HAD RETURNED, AND THE** shock of it sliced through me with a brutal force. But instead of talking to me, instead of pushing me to acknowledge her as she once had, she moved away as if she didn't care that I was watching. She trailed through the ancient cemetery next door on light feet, looking more real than she ever had.

My pulse spiked, drumming itself through my limbs and making my stomach lurch.

I placed a palm on the window, and cold shot through me, reinforcing the fact I was awake. Awake and alive. The waxing moon flickered through the shifting fog as the spirit weaved between tombstones over frost-covered earth. I would have harshly rejected the clichéd image if an artist had dared bring it into my gallery.

Nothing unique about it. No new story being told.

A tired visual that was as old as death and cemeteries themselves.

Hair the color of the moonlight flowed behind the woman as she moved slowly amongst the decrepit graves. A translucent white skirt swirled about her ankles, echoing the spin of the mist. As if finally aware of me, she turned toward my house, lifting a sharp, narrow chin to the window where I stood shadowed in darkness.

Her hand grasped something at her neck, tugging nervously. The fine bones of her fisted fingers were echoed in sharply angled cheeks and a narrow, upturned nose. I'd once kissed those full lips. Ran my palms along the smooth skin of her face. Lost myself in the periwinkle-colored eyes.

The pain I'd thought was buried seeped into me.

And yet there was something slightly off about the image. The reality of her didn't quite fit on top of the memory. A copy that hadn't quite lined up straight.

She disappeared behind a family mausoleum, leaving me to stare at nothing but an aging façade. The granite was cracked, moss creeped over it, and the archangel atop its peaked roof was missing a wing.

I finally forced myself away from the window.

One step. Then two.

It wasn't until I'd put half a dozen paces between me and the glass that I finally began to breathe normally. My lungs burned painfully after being denied a full inhale for a heartbeat too many. I tugged at a thick, dark eyebrow. An old habit that would leave my brows different shapes if I wasn't careful.

I'd been free of Sienna since opening the gallery in D.C. Starting her dream business had finally allowed her ghost to move on. Or, as my therapist insisted, once I'd accomplished our shared goal, it had allowed the guilt causing the hallucinations to begin with to disappear. Regardless of which was the truth, her ghost had vanished from sight six years ago and never returned.

Until now.

A chill passed over me, and I finally registered the ache seeping into my bare feet from the wooden floors. I hadn't turned on the heater last night, and the house was now an icy tomb. I pushed my way past the boxes stacked in the center of the renovated bedroom suite to the walk-in closet. The cedar scent from the built-ins was almost overbearing, but it would settle. I had to give it time. Give myself the same.

Change was never easy. It always disrupted my barely held-together routines.

I scanned the labels on the boxes, annoyed to find some of them were my sister Katerina's. The moving company had mistakenly grabbed hers along with mine from our family storage unit, and now I'd have to figure out what to do with them.

It took me several minutes to find the boxes with my clothes in them. When I finally pulled out a sweatshirt, I wasn't at all surprised to find it was from the Kreeger Museum. It had been Sienna's favorite place in the world at a time when my favorite place had been wherever she was.

My jaw cracked, the frustration carving through me growing another notch.

What right did Sienna have to return to me now?

The truth whispered back that she'd earned it the hardest way possible.

She'd died, and I hadn't.

I'd finally laid her to rest, hadn't I? Replaced her ghost with new guilts and then buried those as well. Moving to Cherry Bay was supposed to be the last shovel of dirt tossed on the grave of my past. I was turning the corner my parents, and the entire world, had expected me to turn more than a decade ago. Turning the corner my ex, Felicity, had screamed at me for not taking.

I pulled the sweats and a pair of socks onto my freezing body before returning to the king-sized bed to retrieve my cell phone from the nightstand. A single glance at the twisted wine-colored sheets proved I hadn't been sleeping even before I'd been drawn to the window and the quiet tombstones that complemented the heavy, Gothic furniture of my bedroom. I'd made this room mine specifically because of its neighbor, hoping the solitude would bring me restfulness and never suspecting it would return Sienna instead.

I maneuvered around more boxes to get to the door. The only thing I'd unpacked so far was a crate of artwork that now rested in the sitting area of the suite. A stack leaned up against the dresser, practically hiding the flat-screen television sitting atop it. Some of the art was finished and framed, while others were barely marked canvases waiting to be completed. The painting at the front was a poorly designed imitation of Sienna's that hung in my D.C. gallery.

We'd created the two pieces together as teens, laughing and snickering behind our art teacher's back. Mine was full of amateurish lines because I'd been distracted by her, while Sienna's was a masterpiece made by a sixteen-year-old. Her art now welcomed people to the gallery as she might have if she'd lived, with vibrant colors, strong strokes, and an eye-opening look at our world.

The hallway was dark, but its parquet floors shone in the moonlight as I made my way down the circular staircase. The white marble columns and mother-of-pearl inlaid ceiling had called to me the instant the realtor had shown me the two-story Colonial. With its silvery satin wallpaper and white woods, walking in the front door felt like entering a dream instead of a nightmare. Hopeful instead of hopeless. And I'd needed the hope. The escape.

Slipping past the antique door with its stained-glass panes, I headed straight back to the kitchen, where I glanced out the bay window to the graveyard. When no sign of my ghost greeted me, I flicked on a single drop light, turning incandescent moonlight into warm sunshine.

I'd saved as much of the original artistry of the house as possible while enlarging rooms, hardwiring technology, and hiding solar panels amongst the gray tile roof. But it was in the kitchen I'd done the most work. When my family came to visit, I wanted them to see something here, something in me, they hadn't seen in a long time—happiness. In this vibrant room hinting of flowers and cheerful meadows, I'd started to convince myself I could achieve it.

Here I'd found a respite from the ugly rumors. Peace from the nonstop barrage of media making me into a monster and Felicity into a saint. I'd started to step into the light of day.

But I should have known better.

I'd never truly escape the dark shadows that had chased me long before gossip, trauma, and ghosts. I'd forever be a figure shrouded in the night with my idiopathic insomnia causing me to rise after mere hours of sleep. A move to a town and a house that looked like it had stepped from the pages of a fairy tale wasn't going to prevent my sleeplessness any more than the drugs the doctors had once prescribed—drugs I now refused unless I'd gone weeks without rest.

The phone I'd stuffed into my sweats' pocket buzzed, jarring me from my brooding. One glance at the ridiculous text from my youngest sister eased the heaviness in my chest.

> *KATERINA: Perchance to dream my brother sleeps while I was out dancing amongst the strips of black and spotted stars.*

Two in the morning in Virginia meant it was only eleven in LA, early for a Saturday night in Hollywood.

> *ME: Dare you torture me this early with your Shakespearian-inspired drivel?*

> *KATERINA: A sister can hope you wouldn't respond because you were ACTUALLY SLEEPING. I thought things were better lately?*

> *ME: Maybe I was and your text woke me?*

> *KATERINA: You'd have 'Do Not Disturb' on if that was the case.*

> *ME: Which stars were you dancing with? Anyone I've seen on screen?*

> *KATERINA: I don't kiss and tell.*

I snorted into the silence.

> *ME: I didn't say kiss. I said dance.*

*KATERINA: Don't try to pry information out of me without answering my question first. How have you been sleeping?*

*ME: I've had several good nights in a row.*

*KATERINA: I guess that's decent for you.*

*ME: Before I forget, the moving company sent some of your boxes with mine. I'll stuff them in a guest room until you can decide what you want to do with them.*

*KATERINA: I can't even remember what's in them. You could probably toss everything, and I wouldn't even know.*

*ME: Fat chance of me doing your dirty work. The ones I've opened are full of clothes. If I toss them, you'll claim there was a one-of-a-kind Dior dress in there, and I'll have to cough up an unseemly amount of money to try and replace it.*

*KATERINA: You're such a cynic. But you're probably right. Plus, it gives me an excuse to come see your new place. Are you coming with Dad and Mom to California?*

*ME: No. With everything that went down with Felicity, it's probably better for me to keep off the campaign trail. They don't need me anyway. Dad's numbers are good. He's a shoo-in for reelection at this point.*

*KATERINA: No one is ever a shoo-in these days. But his numbers are good.*

None of us would say aloud what we were all thinking, but the *thank God this is the last campaign we'll ever have to live through* still hovered unspoken between my twin sisters and me. The bulk of our childhood had been spent surviving one election after another. Now, as our dad's first term as President of the United States wrapped up, we caught glimpses of the end to the excruciating political process we'd lived through. Dad had achieved the mountain top, stayed there for as long as possible, and would soon be taking the easy road downward. While I admired him for choosing the difficult and unforgiving job of leading a country that seemed one step away from falling to pieces, I'd be grateful when it was finally behind us.

*ME: Are you tagging along with them for any of the stops out West?*

*KATERINA: Just a couple events in California. We start shooting on a new film week after next.*

*ME: What about Juliette?*

*KATERINA: She'll pop in when her schedule allows, but she's so close to finishing her residency she can taste it. You'd know that if you texted her yourself.*

It was a well-used but gently tossed rebuke. Texting was nearly impossible when I didn't even know where my phone was half the time.

*ME: Stop throwing shade and go get some sleep. You're not as young as you used to be, and those nasty bags under your baby blues are becoming permanent.*

*KATERINA: I do NOT have bags, Mr. Grouchypants. You're the one who needs to drink some tea and slide under the covers for a few more hours before you turn pale and pasty like the vampire you really are.*

I snorted at the Mr. Grouchypants nickname, pleased I'd needled her enough to use it.

I turned the electric kettle on, and while I waited for it to boil, I slit open the top box in the stack next to the island. I pulled out the contents, setting them on the rustic table I'd bought with thoughts of future dinners with my parents and siblings in mind. I'd dreamed of us eating, teasing, and playing cards at the roughhewn planks as a normal family once Dad's career was behind us. Except a normal family would never have the Secret Service hovering at the doors and windows as ours always would.

While the Secret Service would forever be a part of my parents' world, I'd had my fill of them. I'd sent my detail packing, and I wasn't sure yet if it had been the smartest or stupidest thing I'd ever done. Only time would tell, and I had plenty of it to spare. Plenty of privacy to go along with it.

I wasn't foolish enough to believe the privacy would last. Eventually, my presence in this tiny town would be discovered, and the media would swarm, especially once I opened a new gallery on Main Street. But for now, I could pretend I was just a regular man building his life in a quiet village where nothing bad ever happened and where the paparazzi weren't watching every move.

By the time my tea had been steeped, stirred, and grown cold again, I'd put away half the kitchen boxes. Thanks to my insomnia, in a few days the house would look like I'd lived in it for a lifetime. Then, I could turn my attention to the gallery.

I was still stumbling to find a direction there. The right vibe. But it would come into focus.

It had to.

While everything I'd done in the D.C. gallery had been for Sienna, the one here was for me. It was a chance to find my own footing, my own happiness. I just had to keep Sienna's ghost away long enough to make sure it happened. Because Felicity had been right about one, and only one, thing in our time together—I had to drag myself away from the dead and find my way back to the living.

# Chapter Two

## Willow

**CRAZY ANGELS**

Performed by Carrie Underwood

**THE SCENT OF CITRUS FILLED THE** air as I spread the icing in quick strips over the last batch of lemon-poppyseed scones. The motion was automatic, leaving my mind to explore the ideas I had for combining my miniature desserts with images of an old mosaic I'd taken this morning. Something about creating edible art was floating just out of reach. I itched to finish my shift so I could go home and play with it.

I dropped the frosting bag into the sink and shouldered the tray of scones, pushing through the swinging door between the kitchen and the café. The hiss of the espresso machine and soft chatter of college students greeted me. Hector's voice boomed out a name as I slid the tray into the display case alongside a variety of other pastries.

No miniatures in sight here…at least not yet. Just the possibility of The Tea Spot carrying my miniatures sent my heart cartwheeling around in my chest.

Hector's café was a favorite amongst residents, students, professors, and tourists because of its homemade goodies, unique teas, and specially blended coffees you'd never find at the average chain store. Not that Cherry Bay had any chain stores lining its streets. The town council adamantly refused to budge on the zoning laws preventing anything but locally owned businesses from existing inside the town limits.

When I'd first moved here with Mom almost six years ago, not finding the familiar shops and brands I was used to had been just one more loss. Now, I loved that the town supported their businesses and how the locals acted like one big family, watching out for each other. It was why, after finishing culinary school, I hadn't hesitated in returning to Cherry Bay.

I was happier here than I could remember being since before Dad had died. Every day, I had a hand in making the pretty treats sitting in the case, got to live in a town that felt like a fairy tale, and had people I called family welcoming me through the doors.

Hector joined me, examining the new set of scones. He had a few inches on my average height and was boxy all over. His arms and chest were muscled and contoured from years of pounding dough. Because he was in such great shape, he looked younger than the flecks of white in his black strands might have otherwise insinuated. The corners of his chocolate eyes crinkled when he grinned, which he was almost always doing, but they also told a story of heartbreak. I recognized the lines because they mirrored my mom's—grief had marked them both. The fact Hector could so easily smile even after all he'd lost was one of the things that had encouraged me to find my own happiness again.

"Those look perfect," he said, bumping my shoulder with his. "You're better at making my creations than I am now."

The pride in his words shed a warm glow over me, but before I could respond, he was called over to the register by our latest new hire. Ted was a college freshman who was there simply for the paycheck. When I'd first gotten a job at the café, five years ago, it had been for my love of baking as much as for the money. The Tea Spot had given me an outlet for my creativity, but more importantly, Hector and his daughter, Shay, had brought friendship back to my life.

I grabbed a dirty dish tub from the back counter and rounded the room, collecting empty cups and trash. I hummed along to the pop song drifting through the speakers. The lyrics were about today being a fairy tale, which fit the café perfectly.

From its eighteenth-century sideboards, white-washed tables, and gold marble counters to the hand-painted artwork, The Tea Spot practically shouted magical stories. The heart of the café was the mural taking up an entire wall. It was of a woman dancing amongst woodland creatures as a younger version of Hector, dressed like a prince, rode a white stallion across the flower-filled meadow toward her. It had been added to the café by Hector's late wife before cancer had taken her.

With the tub full, I twirled around, chatting with a customer here and there on my way back to the counter. I was still chuckling at the yoga instructor and his wife when a voice interrupted me, slithering through my good mood.

"Hey, Willow. Can I get a refill?"

I kept my smile fixed in place as I turned toward Poco. Perhaps it was the narrow slit of his eyes spaced too far apart or the slant of his nose with its tiny nostrils, but I often imagined a forked tongue flicking in and out of his too-wide mouth. Of all the regulars who came into The Tea Spot, he was the only one who made my skin crawl.

Not even his boss, Tall Paul, who everyone in Cherry Bay knew was involved in all sorts of criminal activities, made my fight-or-flight instincts spike to a fever pitch the way Poco did. It was ridiculous, considering the man had never been anything but nice to me. Plus, he tipped well whenever I helped him, and that was good for everyone.

"Absolutely, Poco!" I responded cheerfully, placing the tub on the counter before reaching for his reusable tumbler. "Traditional medium roast, like always?"

He nodded. I felt his eyes on me the entire time I topped off his drink from the large carafe. When I returned, I set the cup on the counter so I wouldn't risk touching him. Whenever I did, all my alarm bells jangled even stronger.

Poco's gaze slid down me, and I was grateful the apron I wore covered most of me. When his eyes returned to my face, they glinted with an interest I'd never take him up on—and not just because my skin prickled around him or because he was at least fifteen years older than me. I'd simply never take anyone up on that look unless they could accept the possible limitations of my life. While I saw nothing wrong with other people losing themselves in pleasure for one night, I wanted more than that for myself, and Poco certainly wasn't offering forever after. No matter how short of a time I had on this earth, I was determined to have what my parents once had—the kind of love that included dancing in the kitchen, tender touches, and doe-eyed looks.

"You've been back in town, what, a year now?" Poco asked. His tone seemed friendly, as if he was simply making chitchat, so why did it make me want to run?

"Ten months," I told him.

"Ten months and I haven't heard a whisper of you going out on a date with anyone. I think we should change that. You deserve a good time," he said with a smirk.

I bit my lip, trying not to snort at the knee-deep innuendos.

"I'm not really in a dating space, Poco, but thanks for thinking of me."

He shook his head, lips sliding wider, showing off those tiny teeth and making me imagine the slide of a forked tongue all over again. "I'll wear you down eventually."

I barely stopped myself from rolling my eyes and, instead, gave him my best pacifying smile, saying, "Eventually isn't today."

He rapped his knuckles on the counter, dropped a couple of twenties into the tip jar, and then strolled out, whistling an upbeat song that somehow sent a chill over my skin.

"Need me to set him straight?" Hector asked, coming up behind me with a frown forming between his heavy brows as he watched Poco leave.

His protectiveness chased away the clouds Poco had brought with him. My smile was genuine this time when I pushed at the crease between his brows. "Not unless you feel like starting a war with Tall Paul." When he didn't relax, I added gently, "It's harmless, Hector, really. I can handle turning him down once a month from now until eternity if it keeps the peace. I'm rarely out front anyway."

Since I'd returned from culinary school, I'd taken over the baking of the pastries five days a week, which meant I rarely left the kitchen. I no longer had to put Poco off every day like I once had. It also meant coming to work when the skies were still dark, but I loved the quiet time spent creating. Plus, I was off by noon, leaving plenty of time to play around with my own ideas at home.

When Hector still didn't look convinced, I eased up on my toes, kissed his smooth cheek, and said, "Thanks for offering to defend me. Mom will be singing your praises when I tell her."

And that finally did it. His entire face softened, and a faint blush stole over his face.

My heart squished.

Now, if I could only maneuver them into finally going out on an actual date.

It had been almost six years now since Dad had been killed, and the dark of those first few years was finally leaving us. These days, I caught more and more glimpses of the laughing, upbeat Mom I'd grown up with rather than the sober, serious human who'd barely survived day by day.

It was time for Mom to reach out and take what was in front of her. I wanted to do the same, but I hadn't found *my* Hector—a man who would completely dote on a partner. I'd heard enough stories from Shay about her parents to know he'd do just that. Sophia had been gone fifteen years, and Hector was still as single as my mom. They both deserved to have love shine in their lives again, and Shay and I were determined to make it happen.

I went back into the kitchen, my mind whirling with ways to thrust Hector and Mom together as I cleaned up my mess from the last batch of scones. After I took the garbage out one more time, I stepped into the office and stuffed my apron into the bin of linens before heading to the small set of lockers lined up on the wall for employees.

I pulled the clip from my long hair and let it swing down below my shoulders, reveling in the freedom after hours of having it pinned tight under a plastic cap. I grabbed the white chiffon maxi-skirt I didn't need but loved and pulled it on over my leggings. Gauzy fabrics always lifted my spirits, and if they hadn't been a hazard in the kitchen, I would live in them.

As I slung my patchwork bag over my shoulder, I caught sight of myself in the mirror behind Hector's desk. My cheeks were flushed, emphasizing the line of freckles over my nose, but the upward curve of my lips finally felt natural instead of forced. Even my pale, gray eyes seemed brighter. Like Mom, I was finally letting myself be happy again.

Our nightmare was over. For six years, no one had found us here. I was living the dreams I'd promised myself I'd make come true and marking off the joyous experiences on my bucket list one at a time. The heaviness of our past had slid away.

I ducked my head through the swinging door to the café and hollered goodbye. Hector's returned volley followed me out the door.

When I'd walked to work that morning, the fog had been thick, but now the sunshine had finally broken through, and the gentle warmth coasted over me. The quiet, damp of the predawn hours had been replaced with the noisy rush of lunchtime in a small town. The heady scent of cherry blossoms filled the air. The pink-and-white petals lined the cobblestone streets from Bonnin University to the far end of Main Street where the asphalt took over.

A fragrant petal twirled from the sky and landed on my skirt, blending in with the sheer fabric and making me feel like I was actually wearing spring. This was my favorite time of year in Cherry Bay, when the soft lights and vibrant colors shimmered over the old stone, brick, and iron buildings.

Founded in the seventeen hundreds, the town had existed in near anonymity until the college was built on the bluff overlooking the Potomac in the 1940s. Now, the charming little haven ballooned each fall from several thousand permanent residents to nearly ten thousand as students and academics from around the globe filtered in.

I inhaled the scent of the flowers mixing with the scent of coffee from the café and garlic from the Italian restaurant across the way before strolling toward home. I passed the yoga studio Mom and I kept swearing we were going to join and crossed the street at The Prince Darian Tavern before rounding the corner onto our street.

Here, the cheery hum of downtown disappeared, allowing another fairy-tale image to take over. Once thatched-roofed cottages faced rectangular Colonials of shiplap and warm red brick. It was like someone had drawn a line along the cobblestones and declared one side of the road belonging to the Elizabethan times and the other to the Southern gentry.

Mom and I lived in the last cottage at the end of the street where it butted up against an old cemetery. The down payment on the house had been made by the U.S. government before the mortgage had been tossed in Mom's lap. She'd scrambled to make the payments while building a new career for herself after the Marshals had declared her old one off-limits. Giving up nursing had felt like one more loss, but now she loved teaching science at the high school.

I stopped at the iron gate in our stone wall, turning my face toward the sun, closing my eyes, and letting the rays dance over me. The song of the birds and the buzz of the bees flitting around our haphazard garden only added to the glow I felt deep inside.

When I opened my eyes, my gaze landed on the manicured yard across the street. At least the construction on the white-and-gray Colonial had finally stopped. Whoever had bought the house had all but gutted it. For six months, hammers and saws had rung out, making my daytime nap more difficult than usual. With my alarm going off at two each morning, I often needed a few hours to catch up on my sleep when I got home. It was that or I drifted off before dinner, which was the only time I got to see Mom during the school year.

As I pushed open our gate and stepped onto the river rock path, the door of the Colonial opened behind me. An old habit I'd mostly shaken had me ducking into the shadows of our willow tree where I could watch and not be seen.

A man in his late twenties emerged from the house. He was tall and lean in a way that screamed corded muscles and tight control. His wide shoulders were pulled back straighter than I'd ever seen anyone hold themselves. He had deep brown hair with just a hint of a wave that caused the edges to curl over the collar of his gray jacket. The dark locks glistened with undertones of black and silver in the sunshine.

He twirled a set of keys around a long finger, a baseball cap in his other hand, as he jogged down the brick path to the sidewalk, where he jerked to a quick stop. He looked both ways along the street before finally sending his eyes in my direction. I had a quick impression of a strong nose and square jaw before a penetrating gaze landed on the shadows of the willow tree.

While I knew he couldn't see me, my heart still skipped a beat and I retreated farther. Something about the intensity of his look caused my pulse to thunder in my veins. It wasn't the fight-or-flight instinct I experienced with Poco. This was…tantalizing. A quiet dare. As if he could tempt my soul right out of my body if I let him.

For several long seconds, he stayed as still as I was, a strange mirror of opposites, before sliding the baseball hat on, tossing his keys from one hand to the other, and striding toward downtown. His denim-clad legs ate up the cobblestones at a pace even my long ones would have had a hard time keeping up with.

As my pulse slowed from its frantic beat, something tickled at the back of my mind about him. It was as if I knew him, and yet I was positive we'd never met. I would have remembered that soul-luring gaze.

Was he living in the Colonial or visiting? Did he have a wife and kids who'd moved in with him, or was he staying in that big house all alone? Was he working at the college?

I stopped my runaway thoughts. It was none of my business. If there was one thing Mom and I were good at, it was respecting people's privacy, because we needed the same in return.

I shook off the wild tumult his appearance had caused and made my way down the path to the cottage. The flowers needed watering, and the weeds needed to be pulled, but thoughts of the mosaic and my miniatures were calling to me.

I'd decided to start by printing an edible photo of the mosaic onto a layer of fondant, and then I'd stack carefully crafted miniature tarts and pies and other treats along the top until it became a three-dimensional version of the original. It would be a challenge, and I hadn't worked all the details out yet, but anticipation had me itching to begin.

I loved working for Hector and was grateful that he'd encouraged me to attend culinary school, but these days, I found myself craving more from my career. I didn't want to spend the rest of my life only making Hector's recipes, only creating treats gobbled up with barely a momentary glance.

I wanted to create art in the form of food.

I wanted it to be appreciated viscerally—with all your senses.

Desserts that would be remembered months after seeing and tasting them. I wanted people to tell stories about them to their friends, as if reliving a beautiful memory. A mark that would be left behind even if I no longer was here.

# Chapter Three

## Lincoln

**I CAN BARELY SAY**
Performed by The Fray

**MUSIC FILLED THE HOUSE FROM THE** built-in speakers, ranging from classical to country to pop. While the volume wasn't loud enough to wake my actual living neighbors at two in the morning, it was enough to keep my mind occupied so I wasn't fixated on seeing Sienna again.

Over the last two nights, I hadn't seen a glimmer of her, and I'd almost convinced myself the upheaval of the move had simply brought her back temporarily. After dwelling on it for much too long, I wasn't even sure it had actually been Sienna. Even as a ghost, Sienna had always been loud, demanding her presence be acknowledged, whereas the spirit the other night had simply slipped through the tombstones as if skimming through calm seas. A beacon of light rather than a black hole.

Still, I'd barely been able to claim three hours of solid sleep since then, which only hinted at worse to come if I didn't get more soon. The upside to my sleeplessness was that the house was nearly unpacked.

In the next few days, I'd hang the paintings on the walls, and the house would be done. As putting up art was usually a two-person job, I'd try and convince Lyrica to come down from D.C. to help me. I'd have to bribe her with something good because my gallery manager found the ambiance of the small town I'd moved to an affront to her city-girl senses.

I pulled a photography book from the box, adding it to a stack on the shelf alongside a smiling gold Buddha I'd snatched from Dad's gift pile before the State Department had shuffled it away. Everything in the study was bright and cheerful, from the paisley drapes in shades of bright blues to the robin's egg-colored arm chairs. The desk made from an antique white door and the white-washed bookshelves only added to the sky-like vibe that had me nicknaming the study my *Walking on a Cloud* room. It had the same light energy as the *Sunshine Meadow* kitchen. All the rooms of the house were purposefully upbeat except my bedroom, otherwise known in my head as the *The Vampire's Lair*. It was the only place I allowed myself to retreat into the darkness—where the gloom felt welcoming.

When my insomnia woke me, I didn't have to leave the shadows to keep my rules about using my bed only for sleep and sex to keep my brain programmed correctly. I could simply slip into the sitting area of the suite and watch television or read a book, letting the shadows keep me in their embrace a little longer.

In the quiet between songs, my laptop pinged with a notification, and I moved over to find a dozen messages in the secure chat app. Some of them were from my mother. Most were from Katerina. A single message from Felicity sat like a poisonous snake waiting to strike. Just seeing her name sent a chill down my spine while the subject line of *I need help* caused panic and then anger to rush through. The hate she'd spewed had dwindled to a stop since the beginning of the year, so what the hell could she possibly need now? How could she possibly think reaching out to me, of all people, was the way to get what she needed? I should have blocked her, but I'd learned from Dad's career that sometimes it was better to know what was coming at you rather than have it hiding and biding its time.

My jaw tightened, and even though I knew I should read it, I simply reached over and deleted the message before opening my sister's.

*KATERINA: Mom's going ballistic because she*

*hasn't heard from you in days. Don't be surprised if she's already pinged your location and sent a Secret Service detail to do a welfare check. Where's your phone?*

I tapped the pocket on my sweats only to find it empty.

*ME: Tell her I lost it in the sea of boxes but that I'm fine.*

*KATERINA: I've been a gofer for long enough in Hollywood. I don't want to be yours too. Tell her yourself.*

*ME: Who's the Grouchypants now?*

Even as I teased, concern coasted through me. Katerina was rarely snippy. Determined and full of energy, but not usually waspish.

*KATERINA: Please talk to her so she stops harassing me. I have a lot of work to get done before I'm back on set. As the assistant director, a lot is riding on my shoulders and I don't have time to keep on top of you.*

A twinge of remorse filled me for making her my regular go-between.

*ME: I'm sending her a note right now. But do me a favor?*

*KATERINA: Haven't I done you enough?*

*ME: Go get laid. I miss my relaxed sister.*

*KATERINA: Sometimes getting laid is the problem not the answer.*

Her answer only spiked my worry.

*ME: Hey, all joking aside, what's wrong?*

It took Katerina a beat too long to respond for me to be sure it was the truth.

*KATERINA: Nothing is wrong. I just need this film to succeed so I can get the gig I really want. Go back to your boxes. I have work to do.*

Maybe it really was just her working too hard, but something felt off. I'd call her later. She could never lie to me when we talked, I'd hear it in her voice.

I turned away from the computer and back to the cardboard stacked in the middle of the office, my thoughts drifting once again to the message from Felicity. I was furious she could still get to me. She'd played on my fears in our relationship. Not just about the women in my life who'd experienced tragedy, but about the coldness that had filled me since my friend Leya had been kidnapped and returned unharmed, thanks to the Secret Service.

I'd thought giving Felicity what she'd wanted, handing her some of my secrets and the pieces of me I kept hidden, would shed the numbness that had taken hold. I'd thought it would allow me to feel close to another human again. So I'd made the mistake of telling her not only about my insomnia but about seeing Sienna's ghost after she'd died. Instead of bringing us closer, it had given her ammunition to use against me. Grenades she'd launched without a second thought to what it would do to me or my family.

I stopped myself just as I reached up to tug an eyebrow.

The media had been relentless last fall. All my failings had been replayed with a new viciousness. The college images of me drinking and partying were smattered with articles about my supposed abandonment of Lyrica that had led to her getting shot and the car crash that had left Sienna dead. Those old stories turned into new rumors of drugs and alcoholism, encouraged by images Felicity had taken without my knowledge while I'd been pacing a darkened room in a sleepless frustration. My parents and their PR teams had struggled to keep the worst of it at bay. We'd all known that if it had lasted further into the new year, it would have haunted Dad throughout the election.

So I'd tried to make it all go away by disappearing. I'd taken off from D.C. last August, winding up in Cherry Bay, and found the town working a bit of magic on me. My shoulders had relaxed, and my breath had come easier. After three nights in a row with six hours of sleep, I'd shown up at a realtor's office, looking for a house I could buy immediately. It had taken mere weeks to close on the Colonial but another six months to complete the renovations.

All I wanted now was for the peaceful magic that had surrounded me while I'd stayed here in the fall to return to me. I had to find stable ground. I needed this or I might just drift off for good into that dreamless sleep Katerina was so fond of quoting.

I took my irritation out on the empty boxes, using the pearl-handled switchblade passed down from my great-grandfather to slash through the packing tape and flatten them. I pocketed the knife, filled my arms with cardboard, and headed for the back door through the kitchen.

As I stepped into the frigid air promising fog and rain, I cursed myself for not adding an enclosed walkway from the house to the detached garage as part of the remodel. I punched in the code on the garage door, and as I waited for it to roll up, my gaze drifted to the cemetery. My feet froze, and my body stiffened as a lone figure slipped through the swirling mist and tombstones.

She was pale and graceful with her long hair whipping about in the fierce wind the spring storm had brought with it. She looked completely real. Vivid and alive.

Just as she had the other night, the ghost ignored me.

Maybe that, more than anything, should have told me it wasn't a hallucination. That it wasn't Sienna.

My grip tightened on the cardboard. I dragged my eyes away from the pale figure and forced my legs forward into the garage. I dropped my load onto the pile already filling the space where I'd eventually park my Range Rover. My former detail would have had a field day with me leaving my SUV in the drive where anyone could screw with it, but it had given me a sort of twisted pleasure to live outside the bounds of the Secret Service rules after years of following them.

As I left the garage, the wind bit through my sweatshirt, its sharp teeth sliding into my skin. I refused to let my eyes journey to the graveyard. Instead, I kept them pinned on the back door.

I was two steps from making it inside when the sound of raised voices halted me—a man and a woman. I couldn't hear what was being said, but the male's tone had an edge of ugly to it and hers a hint of panic that had me spinning around and jogging toward the stone wall dividing my property from the graveyard.

As the argument grew even more heated, my urgency increased. With no time to walk to the gate, I used a hand to brace myself and hopped over the waist-high wall. As I rounded the corner of the mausoleum with the broken-winged angel, my eyes landed on the woman I'd thought was a hallucination and a man in a beanie who hovered over her while the fog churned around them.

He was dressed all in black, blending in with the shadows, and she was in soft pastels that glowed like a rainbow even in the broken moonlight. The epitome of angels versus demons. Goodness versus wickedness.

His gloved hand clamped down on her arm encased in a cotton-candy pink coat Sienna would never have been caught dead in. He yanked her closer, and the woman's sneaker-clad feet slid along the dewy grass. She lost her balance and had to catch herself by placing her free hand on his chest. The man leered at her, and the look on his face was ugly in a way that made my insides twist.

"I said, let go." The woman's voice was breathless but strong, full of a command I wanted to applaud her for as I hurried to close the remaining distance.

"I won't ask you again. How long have you been here, and what exactly did you see, Willow?" the man snarled.

"I didn't see anything. Now get your hands off me." She pushed on him, and her struggle made his eerie grin grow wider.

"Maybe you saw me and came crawling. I told you I'd wear you down eventually. Now there's no distractions. No Hector. Just you and me and the dead."

If he'd expected to scare her, he hadn't achieved it. At least, she didn't show it. Instead, she raised her chin in a defiance that made me feel proud when I had no right to it. "I told you. I'm not interested."

"Hey!" I called out. My voice startled them, and two pairs of eyes darted my way. "I think she said let go."

"Who the hell are you?" he demanded.

"No one you care to mess with."

He looked me over, sizing up my lean frame in nothing but sweats and beat-up tennis shoes and clearly not feeling impressed. While he had several layers of muscle on me, I had a couple inches of height and a determination backed with years of martial arts training he wouldn't know existed until he crossed the line.

As his eyes narrowed in on my face, I counted the seconds, waiting for him to recognize me, and was relieved when he didn't.

"Mind your own business," the man said, jerking again on the woman's arm. A moment of panic drifted across her face so white it matched the gravestones.

The wind whipped through the trees, but I no longer felt the cold biting me. Anger heated my veins until they roared with flames. I wouldn't stand by and watch while another innocent woman got hurt…manhandled…killed.

If I'd still had my detail, they'd have backed me up, or more likely, one of them would've taken care of the situation entirely. Instead, I was the only person who could stop what was happening.

As I stalked over the damp grass to the woman, my hand bumped against the switchblade I'd placed in my pocket. I pulled it out, flicked it open, and pointed it at the man.

"You're the one who needs to mind your own business," I insisted.

The woman's eyes widened, darting now between me and her captor. As she struggled to free herself from his grip once again, I reached for her opposite arm. The puffy jacket collapsed under my hand until my fingers collided with a thin rod of muscle and bone. It hit me all at once that she was actually real. Not a ghost or a guilt-filled hallucination. Real.

The man yanked at her one more time. The poor woman was now a tug-of-war rope between two equally hostile men staring each other down. When I didn't look away from him, when I angled the point of my knife in the direction of his face, he finally dropped his grip.

She stumbled toward me, and I wrapped my free arm around her shoulders. The tremble I'd expected in her voice coasted through her body, showing just how much he'd shaken her regardless of her brave tone. I admired the control it had to have taken to only show him a fierce calm.

"Do you want me to call the cops?" I asked.

The man stepped back, blending into the shadows. "Don't be stupid, Willow. You don't want the police involved. This was just a little warning to keep your nose out of things that don't concern you. Don't turn this into something Paul has to straighten out. Understand?" When neither of us responded, his eyes narrowed. "Let's keep it to ourselves, and everything will be fine."

Then, he disappeared completely in the dark and mist. Only a sickly, cheery tune he whistled let us know he was moving farther and farther away.

I closed the knife, pocketed it, and then looked down into the face of the woman tucked up against me. Her eyes were wide and dilated as she watched the shadows where the man had vanished.

"Let's get you out of here," I said. I slid my arm from her shoulders and took a step away. When she remained frozen, I placed a gentle hand on her elbow, encouraging her to move and then guiding her through the tombstones.

Warmth crept through me with her nearness, more than the light touch could account for. A fizzle of attraction that spoke of kisses and tangled limbs. Things this woman certainly wouldn't want after what she'd just experienced. I told myself the feelings were just because I was relieved to know she was real.

Wanting us out of the cemetery as quickly as possible in case the whistling asshole came back, I avoided the gates once more and headed for the stone wall and my house. I slid over first and then turned to offer her a hand.

At first, she didn't accept. She just stood there, chest heaving, taking me in.

The light from my back door glowed across the drive, shining on her face, and I finally realized why I'd thought the hallucination had been off the other night. It wasn't just the pink coat she wore that was a marked difference from the all-black clothing Sienna had favored. It was a thousand other tiny details. They shared the white-blond hair, fine-boned frame, and heart-shaped face, but the similarities ended there.

This woman was soft colors and warm lights versus Sienna's dark and broody. Her eyes were larger and much paler than Sienna's—a soft gray that almost blended in with the whites—and she had a dusting of freckles along the tip of her nose, whereas Sienna's skin had been completely untouched.

She *was* a copy that had been slightly altered.

Not less. Not worse. Just different.

It was the difference that stole my breath away and flamed the fires whispering of tangled skin, taunting me with whispered words of passion and adoration and unyielding joy.

Things I didn't want because they stirred up strong emotions I was trying to leave behind. I was damn happy to revel in the silent charm I'd found in my new home, and I was irritated it had been disturbed, frustrated that I'd been drawn into something ugly when all I'd been asking of the universe was for a few weeks of solitude and anonymity.

Why the hell had she been in the graveyard at this hour to begin with? And why the hell did I have to be the one to get involved? Where were the people who should have been looking after her? My irritation grew, morphing into anger at her for not only disrupting my peace but also for making me think Sienna had returned. For tormenting me with all my past failures, leaving me no option but to insert myself into whatever this situation had been about.

My resentment bubbled and boiled until my eyes landed on her tentative gaze resting on my outstretched palm. The sheer uncertainty in that look made my annoyance suddenly feel wrong, which only proved to anger me more. Except, this time, it was all self-directed. She'd had a terrible scare, and I was an ass thinking only of myself.

So I pushed my hand forward once more, offering even more help instead of less.

# Chapter Four

## Willow

**LESSONS LEARNED**
Performed by Carrie Underwood

***MY HEART WAS POUNDING SO VICIOUSLY*** I thought it might explode. Simply shatter into a thousand pieces like peppermint candies hit with a kitchen mallet.

I'd never expected to encounter another living soul in the middle of the cemetery tonight. Usually, I was only surrounded by the energy of those who had left this world and their memories that had embedded themselves into the stone and earth. I certainly hadn't expected to find Poco carrying a shovel or my stunning neighbor with his penetrating gaze. The stare that was right now burning me from the inside out rather than providing a soothing balm.

What would have happened if he hadn't shown up?

*No.* I knew better than to go down the road of what-ifs. They'd dragged me onto a dark path after losing Dad, and I wouldn't go there again. I would simply leave the heavy fears and questions about what had happened with Poco in the dark of the cemetery.

I shook my head, trying to wipe the thoughts away and push aside the tremors running through me. My neighbor took the motion as an objection to the hand he'd offered. So when I reached out to take it, a flash of surprise crossed his face followed by something that I thought just might be annoyance.

Sparks shot through me the moment our fingers touched. They were almost painful, like a palm placed near an open flame. If I let it any closer, it would leave a mark that might never fade, and yet it tempted me to touch it anyway. I'd felt the same scorching heat when he'd put his arm around me after jerking me free of Poco, but I'd thought it had been adrenaline. The fear and then pure relief of having escaped.

But here it was again, screaming a different kind of danger.

I inhaled sharply before bunching my long skirt in a fist and using his hand and his strength to help me scoot over the wall. When I landed on the other side, we were standing so close our noses almost touched, and the blaze ignited again, flickering down through my entire body. Our eyes locked. His were wary and almost angry. I wondered if mine showed my longing for all the things I'd previously denied myself—physical connection, lust, desire.

I pulled free of him, stepping back from the tantalizing blaze.

The light from his back door shone on his face, lighting up irises a brilliant shade of blue. A color so perfect it only existed in nature. One strand of dark hair had dropped over his brow, and even after he shoved it back, it fell forward again in almost the same place.

"You're shivering," he said. It came out raspy and annoyed, as if I'd offended him with a bodily function I couldn't control. "Come inside. I'll fix you a cup of tea."

For some strange reason, the pure grumpiness of his tone made my lips tilt upward. Even growling, his voice was dark and smooth, like melted ganache. A temptation I should step away from, just as I would the temptation to lick frosting from a spoon. The unexpected strength of the desire to do just that— to taste him like an intoxicating sample—had my feet rooting to the ground.

When I didn't respond to his offer of tea, his jaw clenched, and he spun around, heading for the door. As his heat dissipated, leaving the cold to latch on to me again, the lock on my limbs broke. I followed him on legs unsteady not only from what had happened in the graveyard but from him. Shaky because of the strength of the pure *want* curling through me. An unexpected and enticing experience that had me thinking of all the beautiful possibilities rather than fear of the last few minutes.

It was the music that hit me first as I stepped inside his house. Slow, sultry, and almost dangerous, it seemed to come from every corner. While it matched the mood of the situation we'd just escaped, it didn't quite fit the cheery yellow kitchen I instantly envied. It had top-of-the-line, professional appliances and an oversized, granite island so big I could lie on it and still have room. The glass-fronted, upper cabinets were lit, shining on brightly colored dishes as if they were flowers blooming amongst the vines painted along the roof line. The green of the leaves was echoed in lower cabinets, making it feel as if I'd walked into a sun-filled meadow at the height of spring.

"This is…" I shook my head. "Wow. It's incredible."

My neighbor frowned at me, and it crinkled the space between his brows in a way that made me want to brush the lines away as I did with Hector. I was so desperate to see a smile curve over his face that I had to stuff my hands into my pockets to make sure I didn't actually touch him.

He pushed a button on an electric kettle before grabbing two mugs from a cabinet above it.

"Mint? Chamomile?" he asked, waving toward a small apothecary chest on the counter that had a dozen drawers all labeled in gold paint.

I stepped closer, drawn to him as much as the antique. I examined the labels before turning my eyes to him in surprise. "That's a lot of tea."

"I'm up at night a lot. Tea relaxes me." His eyes narrowed after the grunted admission, as if I'd somehow tortured a secret out of him, and I bit my lip, holding back a giggle at his grouchiness.

"The Sweet Nothing is a Tea Spot special. I must recognize you from there," I said more to myself than him before pointing to the lemon verbena drawer.

He didn't respond, the frown between his brows just

continuing to grow, and yet I felt certain the scowl didn't fit him any more than the shadows clinging to him. For some reason, in my mind, I kept seeing him laughing, happiness wrinkling his face rather than a glower.

"Do you go to the café a lot?" I asked, beaming at him again, hoping my ease would rub off. He stared at my lips for several seconds before that intense gaze of his flicked up to my eyes. The look there hit like a dart somewhere deep in my chest. An echo of my own emotions. Longing. Desire. The complete opposite of the disgust and fear I'd felt in the graveyard.

Instead of answering me, my neighbor asked, "What were you doing in the cemetery at this time of night?"

The way he said it sounded like an accusation, as if I'd asked for Poco's attention and his hands on me. The momentary enjoyment I'd managed to capture slipped away.

"Definitely not encouraging Poco!" I tossed back, barely repressing a shudder as I remembered Poco's strong grip on my arm and the leer in his eyes. My stomach churned nastily until I reminded myself that he was gone, I was safe, and the moment was behind me. I didn't need to dwell on it. No need to obsess. No need to retreat to the panic that had kept me locked in the cottage that first year.

Moving forward was always the right answer. Leaving the bad behind. Concentrating on the good. Mom. My baking. My pleasant life.

I needed to leave, get to the café, and start the scones.

Even as I stepped away, attempting to break the wave of strong emotions winding around us, I felt called to do the opposite. To get closer instead of farther away. It was as if those dark minutes in the cemetery had somehow bonded us.

Maybe it had simply been a counterreaction to the fear I'd felt as Poco had tried to drag me away, but when this man had rescued me, when his hand had drawn me close, I'd felt safe. More than that, I'd felt special. As if I was dear to him. As if my well-being was important.

Which was utterly ridiculous. It would be better to leave now with relief and attraction still sizzling in the air rather than stay and do something completely embarrassing. Better to leave before his wariness and irritation squashed this experience of dancing with heady desire and left only a bad taste that couldn't be rinsed away.

I whirled around, moving toward the door, only to have my feet stall and my heart leap as he called out, "Don't go." When I looked back at him, his eyes were hooded as he added, "You don't know if he's waiting. Have a cup of tea, and give it a few minutes."

The way his tone and his words kept warring with each other was confusing. One second, he was all kindness and sweet pleas, and the next, anger and annoyance filled the air. It was almost as if he thought I'd purposely arranged to thwart his quiet night, and for the first time since he'd rescued me, I felt irritated too. My shoulders went back, and my chin came up. I wasn't going to let him make me feel bad just because Poco was an ass. I hadn't done anything wrong. And I hadn't asked for him to step in, even though I was grateful he had.

"I'm sorry I interrupted your night," I snapped. "I'm sorry you felt the need to interfere, but I certainly didn't ask—"

"No," he interrupted, shaking his head. "I'm the one who's sorry." He ran a finger over his brow, let out a deep breath, and continued, "My attitude has nothing to do with you or what happened. You said no. He didn't listen. That's all on him."

Our eyes locked again, pulsing with not only attraction but the heaviness of the night's events.

When I didn't respond, he grunted out, "Stay."

My body reacted to that single-syllabled command. It caused all sorts of delicious tingles to zing through me, whispering about things I'd wanted and never had. My fingers found the necklace buried underneath my jacket. I tugged at it, closing my palm around the ring for several seconds.

When I still hesitated, he added, "Please."

That quiet plea ate away any lingering hesitation because it sounded as tortured as the admission he'd given me about his lack of sleep. It made me curious. Thrust me right back to those feelings of wanting to soothe and calm.

When I didn't make any further attempt to leave, he turned away to spoon loose-leaf tea into two strainers and drape them over the edges of the mugs in a practiced move. After, he stepped toward me, stuck out a hand, and with wary eyes said, "I'm Lincoln."

As soon as he said his name, it was like a kaleidoscope turned, and my mind filled with images of him. The laughing one that had pricked at me earlier along with a multitude of others that had been plastered all over the television screen, magazines, and online sites.

"Holy bejesus," I said softly, glancing around quickly as if expecting the Secret Service to come running into the room, bundle me up, and send me on my way.

His face shuttered, he dropped his hand, and I immediately felt sorry my response had caused him to shut down even more.

The kettle whistled softly, and he retreated to pour the water into the cups.

"I didn't recognize you at first. I…" I shook my head, trying to clear it. I was in a kitchen with the president's son! *His* kitchen. The son of the president of the United States not only lived across from me but had saved me from Poco—personally. No muscled man with an earpiece and a sidearm had done it. Where exactly was his detail? I hadn't seen any men in suits lurking around. It would have alerted me days before if I had. A thousand new warnings flew through me. But the only thing that escaped was a croaked, "Where's your detail?"

"Sent them packing," he said as if it was no big deal. Instead, he offered me a cup with a face that remained blank. "You want sugar? Cream?"

A dozen more questions swung through me, including why he'd let go of the detail and what he was doing in Cherry Bay. But instead of asking, I simply responded to him, saying, "Sugar, please."

He offered up a blue-glazed cannister, and our fingers collided, sending a new round of aftershocks through me and reminding me the attraction I'd felt was real—and yet even more ridiculous now that I knew who he was. He watched as I scooped sweetener into the tea and swirled it around. I wouldn't be embarrassed by using the sugar to offset the bite of the tea. After all, the art of cooking was about balancing one flavor against the other.

I placed the spoon in the sink, and when he continued to just stare, I blurted out, "Why did you send them away? Isn't that dangerous for you?"

"Danger comes in a lot of different forms," he said almost wearily. "I needed some privacy and some normal before I forgot what it felt like to have it."

A pained understanding flew through me. Hadn't I'd wished for normal for years? For a past I couldn't get back? But then, I'd realized whining and complaining only hid the daily pleasures waiting around each corner, like the way a recipe came together perfectly or the joy tucked inside a laugh. But if I told him I completely empathized with him, it would likely come across as some sort of come-on rather than the truth.

And wasn't that even more ridiculousness? The idea of me coming on to the president's son. Even if, for a moment, I'd felt a brief and enticing smattering of hope that I could experience another of the joyous items on my bucket list, it had been dashed away with the knowledge of who he really was. But I could still cherish the thrill I'd had from simply touching him. The loveliness of this moment next to him in a sunny kitchen with citrus-flavored tea bursting on my tongue and the vibrant and spicy scent of him drifting through the room.

Tonight, when my day was over, when work was behind me, I'd add these memories to my journal, relish them a bit longer, and savor the pleasure of them. But for now, I needed to leave. I needed to put this stunning man behind me and get to work. If I wasn't at The Tea Spot by three, the first batch of scones would be late.

As if sensing my impending departure as I set the teacup down, Lincoln said, "You didn't tell me your name."

The words were accompanied by a wry half-grin that didn't quite reach his eyes and made me ache to see his full smile. Made me long to tease and taunt until a real, brilliant one emerged. Like the one captured on the cover of *TIME* magazine as he'd danced with his sister at the President's Inaugural Ball. His laughing face had been all over the media after that, dozens of GIFs sprouting out of that singular moment.

"Is your name a state secret?" he asked, lips twitching again.

My breath caught, not only because I was still waiting for that real smile to emerge but also because he was closer to the truth than he could ever know. The silence drew out as I fought for the air to answer him, and the longer I went without responding, the larger and more real his smile got until it creased the corners of his eyes and danced across his cheeks. It dazed me in a way that had me forgetting any ideas of leaving and nearly stuttering out my old name.

"W-Willow. Willow Earhart."

His lips tipped upward even more. "Any relation to Amelia?"

I shook myself out of the stunned stupor caused by his perfectly shaped mouth and dazzling white teeth. "No. But my mother wished there was a connection."

Hadn't that been the reason she'd chosen our new last name?

"You were pretty brave back there," he said, head tilting toward the window and the graveyard.

My stomach flopped. I reclaimed the teacup and took another sip, trying to steady myself while repeating, *It's over. Nothing bad happened. Everything is fine. You're safe.* I didn't need to tell Mom or Deputy Marshal James about it. This wasn't the Viceroys. This was some handsy local who could be shaken off.

"I didn't expect to see anyone there this early," I said. "Poco caught me off guard."

"You know him, then?"

"Everyone in town does. He works for Tall Paul," I said as if it was a known fact. Lincoln simply raised a brow in question.

"Paul owns Flat Mike's, the biker bar just outside town, and the mechanic shop next door to it. He and Poco are Cherry Bay's criminal element in its full glory."

The US Marshals had investigated them before we'd moved here, and they had no ties to any of the gangs in Chicago. No way for our presence here to get back to Aaron and his thugs. At least, it was what Deputy Marshal James had promised while also telling us to stay clear of Paul.

"He's hit on you before." It wasn't a question. It was a snarl of disapproval. When I didn't respond, Lincoln said, "He won't be happy about how tonight went down."

Outside, a crash of thunder and a streak of lightning was followed immediately by the pounding of hail on the windows. I hadn't looked at the weather before I'd set out this morning or even registered the scent of rain over the smell of the cherry blossoms.

But the sound of the storm jerked me back to my reality. Not only to the increasingly desperate need to get to work before all the pastries were late, but also to the fact that this man was unattainable for more reasons than just who his family was.

I squared my shoulders, set down my cup, and dug around in my bag for my umbrella. It was my mini one and wouldn't do much to keep me dry in this deluge, but it would have to do. I'd get through it. It was just water.

"I have to leave, or I'll be late for work," I said.

"It's not even three in the morning."

His shocked tone caused my lips to twitch. "Baker's hours. If I don't get into the kitchen soon, the scones will be late. I work at The Tea Spot, which is why I was surprised I hadn't seen you in there before."

He hesitated for a beat before asking, "Will you be there by yourself?"

"Until sixish."

He glanced out the bay window where a row of pots with brightly colored flowers were carefully lined up. Lincoln was full of surprises—and not just because he'd offered to help some random woman in the middle of the night. The brewing anger and darkness hovering around him were also unexpected, especially when the media portrayed him as some careless partier living off his trust fund and his father's fame. If I believed what the news said, I wouldn't have expected him to stick his nose out for anyone.

"You'll get drenched walking," he said. "I'll drive you."

He was back to being annoyed and put out at the inconvenience of it all, which only made me want to soothe him again, so I gave him a reassuring smile I reserved for the rare irate customer. "It's not that far, and I'm used to walking."

"You're not walking," he grumbled. "Not tonight. Not in the rain and not after…" He waved toward the window and the cemetery. "Let me grab my keys."

Before I could argue, he strode from the kitchen toward the front of the house. Maybe I should have been pissed at the high-handed command, but the truth was, I didn't want to walk in the rain. And I certainly didn't want to walk in the dark after the encounter with Poco. I could ignore the tempting but mixed signals simmering between us for a few minutes longer. Just like I could ignore the temptation to explore the rest of his house to see if it was as forcefully light as this space. As if he was cloaking himself in sunshine to ease away the dark.

So, I'd let him drive me to work, and I'd thank him and send him on his way. Then, I wouldn't see him again for days, or weeks even. And when I did, there would likely be a counter between us and people around, and whatever spark I thought I'd felt would be completely gone.

Which hurt more than any other thought I'd had since he'd rescued me.

The music shut off, and the house seemed unexpectedly empty and forlorn without it.

Or maybe that was just me.

To have a glimpse of desire and lust and the imagined chance at something, only to have it pulled away, seemed unfair. But then again, I shrugged to myself, life wasn't fair. It didn't mean I couldn't relish the tantalizing memories of this morning. I'd met Lincoln Matherton in person. I'd spent a few moments in this lovely kitchen, feeling emotions I'd always wanted to feel. I'd smiled and laughed and seen him do the same. Those were the memories I'd keep from today, and I'd let go of the rest.

Lincoln came striding down the hall, sliding his arms into a gray wool jacket and fisting a set of keys. I was struck all over again by how magnificent he was. Dark and dazzling with those eyes that could peel back all your layers. The intensity of his gaze rippled across the space on invisible waves. It was the same one that had stared out from *The Reporter's* cover a year or two ago when he'd been declared the most handsome man under thirty.

Simply taking in the beauty of him made it incredibly easy for my smile to return. He waved me out the back door, and I focused on the pure energy of life beating around us as we raced through the onslaught of ice and rain to a black Range Rover parked at the end of the drive. He got to the car before me, opening the passenger side in a manner that made my insides melt. The longing I had for a boyfriend, dates, and love threatened to rip through the joy of the moment before I pushed it all aside. Either I'd have those things someday, or I wouldn't. But right now, I had this—a handsome man making sure I got to work safely.

I slid inside the vehicle while he jogged around the front. We were both soaked by the time the doors shut. When I looked over at him to apologize for the rain dripping onto his expensive interior, the wide smile on his face planted itself in my chest.

Another happy memory to hold.

He shook his hair and water danced through the air, landing on the dash and the center console. A bead even landed on my hand. I fought the urge to lick the single drop, wondering if it would taste like he smelled. Like anise and clove and forbidden fruit

I returned his smile because I couldn't help it. Because he was gorgeous and kind and had taken a huge risk to come to my defense. I suddenly realized I hadn't even thanked him for it, and embarrassment flooded through me.

"I'm truly grateful for what you did. Thank you for stepping in to help me."

It wiped the pleasure from his face, stiffening his shoulders, and I wanted to kick myself for stealing the lightness from him.

"I'm glad I could be there," he grunted out as if there was a deeper meaning to that handful of words. A meaning I didn't have a key to decode.

After he'd backed out of the drive, I asked, "Are you always up at two in the morning?"

If at all possible, he went even more rigid, back so straight and tight I thought he might break at a mere touch.

"I've been unpacking. I don't like living out of boxes," he offered, but I knew it wasn't the entire truth.

His face was cast in blue shadows from the dash lights, but I thought back to him in the bright, sunny kitchen where darkness had still clung to him. Purple smudges had hung beneath his tired eyes, and there'd been an ashen sheen to his naturally bronzed skin.

I recognized that look—the aftereffects of weeks of sleepless nights.

I'd seen them in the mirror. Worse, I'd seen them eat my father alive, changing him completely. If Dad hadn't been murdered, the fatal familial insomnia would have gobbled him up and left only a vacant stare and angry, frightening words.

Worry for the man in the driver's seat tightened my stomach briefly before I remembered that the likelihood of Lincoln having the same disease was astronomical. Only sixty or so families in the entire world had FFI running through their DNA. It wasn't an actual sleeping disorder. It was a degenerative nerve disease, and it certainly would have been in the news if the president of the United States or his son had the mutated gene inside them.

Lincoln's tired eyes were likely because he'd been unpacking, just like he'd said. Of the two of us sitting in the SUV, it was only me who might have the gene. It was only me living with the unknown because I couldn't be tested while in witness protection. The risk of being identified as one of the rare people with the mutation would only increase the likelihood of the Viceroys finding me as they'd known my father had been diagnosed with it.

Not being sure if I carried the gene or not, on top of losing Dad, may have sent me into a tailspin for a few years, but now I just wanted to live as fully as possible within the bounds of witness protection protocols. It was an oxymoron of sorts, wanting to truly live while hiding at the same time. Just like it was an oxymoron to crave falling in love, knowing your own body might be the reason you can't keep it. Asking someone to take such a staggering leap into the unknown with me was like asking someone to skydive without a parachute. And so far, no one had wanted to step out of the plane.

But even if I never found someone willing to take the hurdle, I still had dozens of other joyous adventures to mark off. And I had love in all its different forms. Family. Friends. I had passion in my life, even if it was for a job and for my craft rather than from bodies twined. I wouldn't let what-ifs rule me any more than my early morning incident with a half-assed criminal.

# Chapter Five

## Lincoln



**THE AIR IN THE VEHICLE SMELLED** like Willow, like browned butter and sugar, but it had turned from enticing and warm to withdrawn and cold in a nanosecond after she'd asked about my sleepless nights. It wasn't just my reaction to her question but something else that had her mentally pushing away from me just as she'd physically pushed away from that man Poco.

It was for the better.

I didn't want this beautiful and brave woman poking at me, pushing past barriers.

Hell, in mere minutes I'd given her more information than I'd given most of the people in my life. I'd trusted someone outside the family with my truths, and it had completely backfired with Felicity's smear campaign.

This journey to Cherry Bay had to stay focused on recovering myself and burying the last of my ghosts. Maybe someday I'd be ready to let another woman into my life, but not now. Especially not someone my family would immediately see as a Sienna look-alike, even if Willow now seemed as different from Sienna as sunshine to moonlight.

If Willow left my car thinking I was an ass, it was better than her knowing just how attracted I was to her vibrant glow.

The way she'd bounced back from Poco, the way she'd been able to smile even after what had happened, had hit me like rays peeking through a dense canopy of leaves. I had a feeling it would be all too easy for her to slip past my barely rebuilt defenses.

So instead of breaking the uncomfortable air, I left it there to stew and become stale. The only sound in the car became Willow's light voice directing me to the alley behind the building The Tea Spot was in.

As I pulled up to the entrance, the tension in my shoulders rolled up another notch. Two large dumpsters cast shadows over the meek light put out from a single bulb hanging above the door. The headlights of the Rover could barely dispel them. The hail and rain that had forced me out of my home to drive Willow here had slowed but was still coming down fast enough to have my automated windshield wipers beat out a steady tune. Who knew what was hiding in the damp and darkness? Hardy, the former head of my Secret Service detail, would have completely objected to this setup.

"Poco know you're here at this hour by yourself?" I asked before I could stop myself.

She tugged at a necklace. It had been tucked beneath her jacket earlier when she'd done the same. It was some sort of round charm I barely caught a glimpse of before she'd palmed it. "Most people in town know I do the baking, and that it means early hours."

The wildly protective feelings I'd had all morning spiked once more. How many times had I wished I could go back in time and stop what had happened to the women in my life? But damn it, I didn't know her. Didn't owe her anything. She wasn't someone I had an obligation to. I ground my teeth together, fighting with myself for too long before asking, "You got an alarm system in there?"

She huffed out a breath, half exasperation and half humor. "Yes."

She opened the car door, and I instinctively reached out as if to draw her back. Instead, I settled my hand on her puffy jacket. It collapsed until I felt the thin arm beneath it like I had in the graveyard. It seemed so tiny. Fragile. A wing that could easily be broken. And now I couldn't get that image out of my head. Her broken.

Damn it.

"You need to be careful, Willow," I grunted out.

"I'll be fine. I honestly think Poco will want to forget this as much as I do." It sounded hopeful, wildly optimistic in a way that made me want to push at it.

"I wouldn't count on it." The man had looked too gleeful when he'd had her captured and all too pissed off when I'd intervened.

She slid out of the car, shifted a brightly colored patchwork bag onto her shoulder, and said, "Thank you again for helping me. Not many people would step up for others like you did."

Her words slammed all my past failures into me like a punch to the gut. I could barely breathe, which made my words sharp and harsh as I insisted, "You can repay me by staying safe."

Her lips curved upward as if she found my growliness humorous. My eyes lingered on those sweet lips shaped like a pretty bow, fuller on top and made for tasting. Licking. Enjoying.

Just not by me.

And certainly not now when she was mere minutes past having been attacked.

Without another word, she shut the car door and quickly made her way to the café. After unlocking the back door, she annoyed the hell out of me by leaving it wide open so anyone could follow her inside. The alarm I could hear beeping even through the Range Rover's tinted glass finally shut off, and she reappeared two seconds later in the darkened entrance. She gave me a small, almost bashful wave before finally closing the door.

I sat there, fighting a silent war. My body and mind were in deep debate. Go. Stay. Wash my hands of her. Demand she do anything but remain in that building alone.

A light appeared in a narrow window above the dumpster on the left.

Should I shut off the engine and wait until another employee showed up? Should I mind my own business and head home to the quiet of my house?

Neither felt like a choice I could live with.

My gallery was on the opposite side of the street from The Tea Spot, angled in such a way that if I was in my studio on the third floor, I might be able to see the front windows of the café.

Decision made, I backed out of the alley and drove along the wet cobblestones glistening in the beam of the lantern-like streetlights. The fog that had been in the cemetery was nonexistent here—just the dark damp of a nighttime storm and the quiet of a small-town Main Street in the wee hours.

I parked in front of the gallery, ducked my head, and made a run for the front door with its red-and-white striped awning over the glazed-glass windows. The colors and pattern were more appropriate for the bath shop that had been in the unit before I'd bought it than an upscale art studio. It was on my list of things to replace once I had an actual direction for the gallery in mind.

As I stepped inside, instead of the lavender I'd been smelling for days as a bath store leftover, browned butter and sugar flooded my senses. The sweet smell of Willow had followed me from the car and it irritated me all over again. I didn't want to be enticed by another woman, damn it, and certainly not one standing in harm's way, shielded by nothing but a pretty smile. All I wanted to do was find myself and my art again. Figure out who the hell Lincoln Matherton was without the baggage of ghosts and grief and remorse.

Even doing that seemed almost impossible at times.

I relocked the door and made my way through a handful of crates I'd brought with me from D.C., taking the wide stairs leading to the loft two at a time. They creaked and groaned with age but held with the sturdiness of hardwood and skilled craftsmanship.

The bath shop owner had, unimaginatively, used the loft as an office, even leaving an ugly metal desk behind. I envisioned it as the second floor of an elegant showroom. I'd keep the eighteenth-century architecture with its wooden beams crisscrossing the ceiling and add a chandelier dripping with crystals. The rich planks of the floor would be refinished, and the brass birdcage elevator would be buffed and polished until it glowed. When I was done, both floors of the gallery would scream of an old-world grace that matched the cobblestone streets and gingerbread facades of downtown.

At the back of the loft, another set of stairs, much narrower and darker, led to an attic room in the rafters. Instead of being gloomy and dim as it might have been, a pair of floor-to-ceiling, circular windows on either side of the room filled the space with natural light during the day. The skylights I planned to add would guarantee even more. In the middle of the wee hours, like now, I had to rely on oversized photography lights to chase the dark away.

With Willow on my mind, I made my way directly to the front window made of paneled, antique glass. As I'd expected, I had an angled view to the front doors of The Tea Spot. The windows were dark, and my chest tightened.

The battle continued to wage inside me, concern fighting with annoyance. I didn't know Willow. I didn't know Poco. She'd never even said what either of them was doing in the cemetery at this hour. It wasn't my place to look after her, to worry about her, and yet I couldn't seem to stop. At this distance, I would be no help if Poco showed up at the café while she was alone. And yet, sitting in my car in the alley wasn't an option either. It felt entirely too stalkerish. Too close to how I'd been hounded by Felicity.

My teeth ground together as chaotic emotions seesawed through me.

I turned my back on the window, eyeing the blank canvases and easels sitting along one wall and the dozen or so boxes with my supplies inside them.

When was the last time I'd actually used them?

When was the last time I'd been proud of something I'd created?

The answer spun quickly into my mind. A painting of a dark-haired rock star in a burnt-orange, organza dress with rows of bracelets jangling down her arm and bells dancing on hoops in her ears. I'd spent a multitude of nights with that image of Leya Singh playing on repeat in my head before I'd finally put it down on canvas.

I shrugged out of my jacket, letting it drop to the floor. I opened box after box until I found the charcoal pencils I was searching for and then eyed the different-sized, pre-hung canvases. I'd need a trio of tall, skinny ones to reveal the scene filling my head now.

A cemetery shrouded in fog.

The cliché I'd scoffed at the other night.

But it would be different. It would tell a different story.

It would be Willow. Complicated sunshine caught in the shadows.

I lined the canvases along the wall, charcoal already moving, casting a dark sooty stain upon the white surface. Colors would appear amongst the blacks and grays. Pastels that turned vibrant like the sky awakening. But first, the dark had to exist. Otherwise, the light would never truly be appreciated.

The pencil flew over the linen.

Line after line.

Stroke after stroke.

It wasn't until a streak of sunshine streamed across the canvas that I realized I'd been at it for hours. I could go days without raising my head from my work when something had me in its thrall like this. Felicity had hated it, Sienna had loved it, Lyrica understood it, and my family just rolled their eyes and shoved plates of food within my reach.

A glance at the decorative clock Katerina had given me, sitting on the floor, waiting to be hung, showed three hours had gone by. Shapes had turned into details. Details into shading. It needed finessing. It needed much more, but it felt both scary and exhilarating to be creating again.

Even after all these years, even after Sienna's ghost had stopped haunting me, I could still hear the words she'd often repeated to me about my painting, or lack of painting, or the crap I'd drawn after she'd died. *Your art will never be everything it's supposed to be if you keep holding on to guilt and regrets. Let go, Lincoln. Stop waiting for punishment that will never come. That you don't deserve.*

Right after Sienna had died, it *had* felt sinful to paint, to return to the one thing that had bound us together. And later, it seemed as if whenever I started to paint again, another tragedy struck my life, sending my creativity cartwheeling back into the abyss of my brain. A Pavlovian bell ringing, warning me that one went hand in hand with the other, as if I was reaching for something and being slapped back for even daring to capture it.

Lyrica hated the association I'd made, insisting one had nothing to do with the other. Just like she'd insisted it wasn't my fault I hadn't been there the day she'd been shot in the convenience store. I was the only one unable to forgive myself for abandoning her. If I hadn't been chasing after my ghost, she wouldn't have been alone. I could have stepped between her and the bullet—and would have without a single hesitation. Maybe, with the martial arts training I'd had, I could have prevented anyone from being hurt that day.

After the press had investigated and talked to our friends, they'd blamed me too. Just like they'd blamed me for Sienna's death and for Leya's kidnapping. Maybe they were right. Maybe there was some darkness in me that would always lead evil to the women in my life.

Only Felicity had escaped before harm had come to her.

Although, I doubted she'd consider herself scar free. But then again, Felicity had her own darkness surrounding her. In hindsight, I thought it was what had drawn me to her to begin with. Had I really imagined two darks could bring the light? Or had I just thought it might protect her from being shadowed by mine?

I stared at the black-and-white strokes on the canvas,

assessing the lines critically. My fingers itched to continue working, my mind already visualizing the changes. The feeling was as strong as the one that woke me in the middle of the night and begged me to get out of bed when the insomnia struck.

But even as the itch remained, crawling over me like ants, the woman who'd inspired the work called to me with an overpowering urge to check on her. Guilt for having stopped watching the window blended in with my need to continue drawing. I wasn't sure what to make of it, of Willow or these disquieting feelings of responsibility, or even the fact that I was creating again because of her.

I set down the charcoal and moved to the front window. The rain had stopped, but the clouds hadn't completely blown away. They floated dark and gray through skies just starting to come alive with soft colors, shifting over the slick cobblestones that mirrored the pastel shades of orange and pink above them. The wakening heavens were reflected in the dark windows of the shops along Main Street. All except The Tea Spot's, which glimmered with the warm lights from within. The neon *Open* sign glowed a vibrant shade of magenta—the same color as the patches on Willow's bright bag.

It was useless to think I'd get more done. The need to see if she was okay was too overpowering.

I grabbed my coat off the ground, jogged down the stairs, and let myself out of the gallery. Even as I locked up, I cursed the irrational need to see her, repeating to myself that what had happened this morning had nothing to do with me. And yet, my feet continued to move across the street.

The Tea Spot's front door pushed open just as I got there, almost smacking me in the face. A different blonde than the one I'd come to see shoved her way out with her head down. I knew her—not her name, but her face. She was the owner's daughter, and I'd seen her behind the register many times when I'd been in the café.

She was shouldering a loaded backpack while precariously carrying a to-go cup without a lid. It's steaming liquid sloshed haphazardly toward me before she jerked it back.

"I'm so sorry. My fault," she said. "I didn't expect anyone out here this early."

"No problem," I replied, catching the door above her head.

She stared at me with curious green eyes, and my chest tightened, waiting for her to recognize me. A man's booming voice from inside pulled her gaze away and back into the shop.

"Love you, Shay! Have a good day."

"Love you too, Dad!" she yelled back before shooting me another apologetic look and heading down the street toward the Bonnin campus.

When I stepped inside, the warmth hit me as strong and addictive as the caffeine they sold. For the first time since the streak of light had interrupted my drawing, I realized my hands were nearly frozen. I hadn't turned on the heat in the gallery, hadn't even realized it was cold.

I rubbed my fingers together and stepped through the tables to the partially filled display case. The entire shop smelled of a tantalizing chocolate and cinnamon that had nothing to do with the coffee brewing.

"First customer of the day! Means your order is free." The owner greeted me with a friendly grin. He looked nothing like his daughter, and it was obvious enough that it made me wonder what their story was before I shoved it away as more curiosities that weren't my business.

The café door swung open behind me, a brush of cool air accompanying it, and I heard a groan. I turned slightly to see a college kid striding in, weighed down by a backpack. "Damn. I missed the freebie again," the kid whined. "I got up even earlier today."

His dejection made my lips curl upward, and I stepped away from the counter, ushering him forward with my hands. "Please, be my guest."

His eyes brightened. "Really?" And when I nodded, he mumbled, "Thanks, man."

While the owner went about getting the kid's order, I watched the swinging door to the kitchen with its little round hole. It was asinine to try and catch a glimpse of Willow. It was the very last thing I should have been wanting or doing or thinking about, but there I was, craving a glance nonetheless.

It was only once the kid had his free purchase and had thanked me again as he scurried out that I realized he'd been staring at me the way I'd been staring at the door. My hand went instinctively to my head. No hat. No sunglasses. No disguise. Damn it. But it was too late to fix it. At least he hadn't taken a picture. Or maybe he had, and I'd been too caught up in the swinging door to notice.

It was just one more reason for me to leave.

I wasn't ready for the press to find me here any more than I was ready for the pull I felt toward Willow. It had been less than a year since I'd ended things with Felicity. Not even three months since she'd stopped harassing me. The woman I'd dropped off this morning certainly didn't need my shadows darkening her world.

The owner's booming voice drew me out of my thoughts and back to him. "That was good of you."

I shrugged.

"What can I get you?"

"I don't see the chocolate I'm smelling," I told him.

His eyes sparkled. "Mexican brownie scones. Recipe my *abuela* swore me to secrecy on and that Willow has somehow improved, which is surely causing *Abuelita* to turn over in her grave." He huffed out a laugh at himself. "They'll be out in just a few minutes. What can I get you to drink while you wait?"

"Large s'more tea, thanks," I told him.

He nodded and set about making it. When he placed it on the counter, I stuffed my hand into my pocket only to realize I'd left my wallet at home and my phone along with it. I winced, thinking of the messages I'd likely have from my family.

"I forgot my wallet. Just put it aside, if you don't mind. I'll run home and get it. I live right down the street. I'll be back in five."

Just as I said the last words and started to turn away, the

door from the kitchen opened, and Willow walked through carrying a large tray. It was my first time seeing her without her puffy coat, and the T-shirt she wore beneath a white apron showed off surprisingly strong arms. The muscles flexed as she shifted the tray from one shoulder to the other, easily contradicting my skin-and-bone theory from earlier this morning.

Her eyes met mine, darting around the room and then back as if looking to see if I'd been followed…by who I didn't know. Maybe my detail. Or Poco.

"Lincoln!" My name escaped her lips and went straight to my chest before settling in my groin. Her voice was airy and light. Breathless almost. And I suddenly wanted her breathless for an entirely different reason. I needed that sound to escape her lips while my hands and mouth drank in her sugary-scented skin. And damn if that didn't irritate me all over again. Wanting her. Wanting anyone.

My voice was thick and dark with need and irritation as I said, "I see you didn't have any more trouble."

"Trouble? What trouble?" Worry coasted over the owner's face. "Did someone bother you this morning, Willow?"

Her gracefully shaped pale brows pushed together, and she shot me a glare as she slid the tray into the case. She hadn't wanted this man to know she'd been accosted in the cemetery. I understood not wanting to worry the people you cared about, but I was almost certain Poco wasn't just going to slink away without exacting some kind of retribution. His sickly cheerful whistle as he'd left had said as much.

The people around her needed to be aware and involved so I could back the hell out of her life, which was why I coughed up the truth she obviously didn't want to give. "She had some trouble with a man named Poco early this morning."

Willow turned toward the owner and put her hands out as if to hold him back as he took a step toward the back door. "It was nothing, Hector. Seriously." She blocked his path, pushing against his chest. "Don't start something with Tall Paul."

The panic in her voice caused the first shot of doubt to hit me. I didn't know the players. I didn't know what had really gone on. So why was I pushing this? Why was I inserting my foot in when all it could do was bring trouble to my door that neither my family nor I could afford?

My therapist would have laughed at the inane question because the truth was glaringly simple. I'd never turn away from a woman in need, because I couldn't shoulder any more guilt if I did. It would bury me.

The irritated look Willow sent my way was nothing.

It was too damn bad if she was upset.

I'd do anything to make sure she didn't end up lying amongst the tombstones where I'd found her.

# Chapter Six

## Willow

**BREATHE**

Performed by Kenzie

*I BLEW OUT A BREATH AS* annoyance and worry sped through me in equal measure, taking the good mood I'd finally settled myself into as I'd baked this morning and sending it back into the ether. Hector did not need to get involved in this. Who knew what would happen if he started something with one of Paul's henchmen? A flash of a body riddled with bullets hitting the ground whipped through me before I could stop it.

"What happened?" Hector demanded. "Did he try to get into the shop? If he did, I'll have it on camera. We can give it to Dexter and his deputies, and they'll follow up on it."

I shook my head, putting a hand on Hector's arm, attempting to both reassure him and hold him back. "No. Nothing happened here. It's fine. A little misunderstanding. Lincoln interrupted us, but I'm sure I would have been able to work it out."

Lincoln grunted his disagreement, and I shot him another glare, hoping he'd take the hint.

"Where were you?" Hector demanded.

I hesitated for a beat too long, and it was clear to everyone I didn't want to say. It wasn't that I was embarrassed exactly about my visits to the cemetery, but I also understood it wasn't a normal hobby. After we'd buried my dad, I'd become fascinated, maybe even slightly obsessed, with the wording on the tombstones. That had turned into an interest in the artistry of them and then into a desire to make sure the people there were remembered in some way. That their life had meaning. The gravesites without flowers were the ones I gravitated to the most. Names I looked up on the internet. Lives I tried to imagine. A whisper in the dark that said, *"You weren't forgotten."*

"I was on my way to work," I finally said.

"He was on your street? Stalking you?" This hadn't calmed Hector down the way I'd thought it would. He twisted away from me, heading for the old-school landline hanging on the wall near the cappuccino maker. "That's it. I'm calling Dexter."

"Hector, please!" I begged, and maybe it was the unusual desperation in my voice that made him stop. "I can't talk to Detective Muloney. It needs to be forgotten."

Even though the Marshals pretty much left us on our own now that we weren't in active protection, if a police report was filed, it might flag in their system, and they might scurry back into our lives. They might make us move all over again. I didn't think Mom would make it through another recreation of our lives. The first one had taken almost everything she had. It wasn't just losing Dad. It was the fact she'd lost everything. Everything but me. And even though we'd had each other, neither of us had been the same for a really long time.

I couldn't do that to her again. And I was happy baking. If we were relocated, would they make me give up my career like they'd made Mom give up her nursing? Would I ever be able to bake professionally again without fear that it would tie back to this version of me who'd lived to bake? That thought nearly stole my breath. It was scarier than being caught in Poco's grip. A cold sweat broke out along my neck.

Still, I forced a smile, knowing from experience if I kept it long enough, I'd actually feel it, while I underplayed the events of this morning. "It was nothing, really. Lincoln didn't hear the entire conversation. Everything is fine."

Lincoln stepped up to the counter, and when I risked

looking at him, anger had returned to his eyes. The same anger I'd seen when he'd stepped up to defend me, but I couldn't help it. I shook my head at him, pleading with him in a different way than I was with Hector.

A timer went off in the kitchen—the second batch of the Mexican brownie scones ready.

Hector looked from my forced cheerfulness to Lincoln's glowering face, and his hand dropped away from the phone. "I don't want you alone with him ever again. If he comes into the shop, and you're at the counter by yourself, I want you to get me or Shay or whoever else is here."

"Deal," I said quietly.

"I'll get the timer," he said, tilting his head toward Lincoln. "You get him one of those scones he was waiting for. It's on the house. I won't take money from someone who defended you."

Then, he disappeared behind the swinging door, and I turned back to the display case with a mix of emotions flowing through me. Frustration that Lincoln had inserted himself into this. Panic at the thought of the Marshals getting involved. Warmth from Hector's protective love. And over the top of it all, that heated zing of attraction as Lincoln's eyes watched me putting a scone into a paper bag.

Had I really thought this spark would disappear if we met again simply because a counter was between us? Did this kind of lure ever go away? I wouldn't know because I hadn't had enough experience with it. But the attraction I felt didn't change the impossibility of chasing it. Didn't change my aggravation at Lincoln telling Hector about this morning. I hadn't even been sure I'd tell Mom, and I told her practically everything—I mean, as long as it didn't threaten her safety or send her back to those first awful days of depression.

I pushed the scone across the counter to Lincoln and met his penetrating gaze, surprised to find his face was now completely shuttered. The anger I'd seen moments before was put away behind a blank façade—a stunningly handsome one.

He was his own work of art.

Not only gorgeous, but kindhearted. Sure, he'd interfered,

but it had been out of consideration. Out of worry. So, when I finally spoke, it was with a gratefulness I hadn't felt just seconds before. "Thank you again for helping me this morning. But everything is fine."

I accompanied the words with a beam I hoped was reassuring. One he didn't return.

When he spoke, his tone had a surliness that tried to bite at me. "I obviously don't know you very well, but I didn't get the impression you were stupid."

I could have been offended by his taunt, but instead, I was overwhelmed with the same desire I'd had earlier to soothe away his ruffles until nothing was left but joy. The absurdity of my thoughts as much as the strangeness of the president of the United States' son sticking up for me had me letting out a huff of air, half chuckle and half annoyance.

His intense gaze narrowed on my mouth.

I had the distinct feeling this man could easily tear away my layers if I let him. I was uncomfortable at what he'd find, even while I longed for him to do it. To find the *me* buried deep inside. Not the cheerful baker Willow, nor the terrified teenager Wendy, but some amalgamation of them. Something more. Someone he'd find worth holding on to regardless of the risk that came from wanting her.

Too bad I couldn't even let him try.

The sooner I severed the bond tying us together since the cemetery the better.

"I know Poco isn't a nice guy," I told him with a shrug. "But I also know he won't do anything serious enough to draw police attention to Tall Paul's business. So, he'll drop it."

"You have a lot of experience with criminals that tells you this?" Lincoln asked, and I could hear the disbelief but also the disappointment in his tone.

It took a practiced effort to prevent a dizzying slew of ugly images from my last tangle with criminals from taking over, but I did it. I did it and increased my smile to full wattage. "No experience. I've just lived in Cherry Bay long enough to know what's what."

The tension in the air was much more than just that enticing pull of desire. Frustration brewed as we stared at each other in an unspoken dare. Who would back down first?

He dragged his hand through his hair, that wayward lock falling gently back over a brow, and I noticed his fingertips were black. Ink or chalk or something similar, and it reminded me he didn't just own an art gallery in D.C., but that he was an artist himself.

"You were drawing?" I asked.

My attempt to change the subject didn't go unnoticed, but he seemed to accept it. Relief and a strange giddiness washed over me as I realized I'd won the dare. I'd pushed, and he'd given in. I had a feeling it didn't happen often. I'd bet every last, limited dollar in my bank account that Lincoln Matherton wasn't used to people ignoring the commands he issued.

His voice dropped an octave as he responded. "I started something new for the first time in over a year. I guess I have you to thank for it." An eddy of dark emotions existed in those words, like a secret pond hidden in a shadowy forest. Emotions that might drown me, ripping away the light I'd fought for in my life, and yet I found myself stepping up to the waters anyway.

"Me or Poco?" I teased, wanting him to say it was me as much as I wanted to continue flirting just to test these new depths. I wanted to see if, instead of him dragging me toward the murky waters, I could fling the sash wide and let the sunshine burn through the gloom around him. Let it burn through both of us.

His blue eyes narrowed. "I saw you before. You were at the cemetery on Sunday also."

My stomach lurched at the question I heard there. The desire to know why I was spending time in the dark with the dead. But before I could even decide if I'd respond or not, the bell jingled over the door, and three college girls hurried inside, bringing the remainder of the damp and wind with them as they laughed and joked with each other.

It jolted me back to reality in the same way the hail on the roof had earlier.

For the first time in forever, having to get back to my baking felt like a burden instead of a gift. I wanted to stay right here, taunting Lincoln until he gave me that stunning, real smile I'd seen briefly in the car. But instead, I'd go back to work, holding on to another tantalizing memory where I'd flirted and bantered with a famous artist, and later, I'd add it to my list of beautiful experiences.

The sound of the door brought Hector from the kitchen. He glanced over at Lincoln and me again before wiping his hands on a towel and stepping up to the counter to help the trio.

"I have to get back," I said, pointing toward the swinging door. "Lemon poppyseed scones are calling me, but thank you again for stepping in and also for knowing when to leave things alone."

It was a preemptive thank you because he hadn't said he was letting it drop. But all I wanted to do was put the entire thing behind me.

I *had* to put it all behind me, including Lincoln.

Lincoln picked up the drink and scone before saying, "I'll see you around, Willow."

And in that handful of words, I heard a quiet promise that sliced right through my intention to be done with him. Because it was clear Lincoln wasn't done with me. He hadn't gotten the answers he wanted. I'd thought he'd backed down from the dare, but instead, he'd simply called a momentary halt to the war.

It thrilled me as much as it terrified me.

My body was glad, humming softly as if loaded up with sugar and cream. But my conscience was screaming at me to stop this before it went any further.

As I watched him stroll out of the café, one of the three teens followed him with her eyes before swirling back around to whisper to her friends as if she'd recognized him. And that right there was just another reason why spending any time at all with Lincoln was an impossibility.

The answers he wanted weren't going to happen.

♪ ♪ ♪

The kitchen was spotless as I tossed my apron into the hamper with a pile of towels. The café was hopping with noise I could hear through the swinging door. Ted and Shay were out front, but Hector was in his office when I went to grab my things from the lockers.

He pushed his glasses up on the top of his head and set aside his paperwork as I let my hair down and pulled a gauzy skirt on over my leggings.

"Want to tell me what really happened?" he asked.

I sighed. "Truly, it was nothing. You know how Poco is. Sort of creepy, pushing to see how far he can get. But he always walks away."

I wanted to believe if Lincoln hadn't shown up in the cemetery, I would have been able to convince Poco to let me go. I just hadn't had the chance to get that far.

"I can refuse to serve him," Hector said.

"It's not necessary, really."

Hector's kind eyes took me in. "Make sure your mom knows so she can keep an eye out."

I didn't really want to disrupt her good mood. But if Hector knew, it was just a matter of time until Mom did, especially if the plans Shay and I had been making to throw them together took shape.

I shouldered my bag and slung my coat over my arm. "I'll tell her. But you worry too much. Everything is fine. I'll see you tomorrow."

As I headed out, my feet halted in the hallway, thinking of the dark and shadowy places in the alley. After a brief internal debate, I headed for the front entrance instead, making my way through the throng of customers, relieved when Poco wasn't one of them. I hated that he'd returned to me the skittish feeling I'd finally shaken after the trial.

I'd lived four years waiting for the shoe to drop while the wheels of justice turned slowly in Chicago. I'd waited for the Viceroys to find us—for the worst to happen. The first year here, I'd rarely left the house. The second year, I'd signed up for classes at Bonnin and felt both relieved and terrified to leave the four walls of our cottage. But blending in, staying invisible, had still been the goal. Needing to lie about who I was had made me uncomfortable enough that I'd been afraid of making friends in case I let something slip I shouldn't. Something that would lead Aaron Vitale and his gang to our door.

I'd sort of gotten my feet underneath me by my second year at Bonnin and had even gone on a couple of dates with Chad. But he'd dropped me like a lead balloon once I'd hinted about the truth of my potential medical situation, and I'd stuck to the things that brought me the most pleasure. The Tea Spot. My friendship with Shay and the warm glow of Hector's praise as I puttered around with his recipes.

Spring of my junior year, the trial had finally taken place, and I'd found myself retreating to the darkness of that first year. The look of anger and hate Aaron had shot me once the guilty verdict had been read was hard to forget. Hard to shake. But knowing the two men responsible for Dad's death were in jail for the rest of their lives had allowed me to breathe easier. The risk that any of the Viceroys would come after me had decreased by leaps and bounds after I'd testified.

I'd come back to Cherry Bay determined not to waste my life. I'd made a list of things I wanted to experience while living within the bounds of witness protection, and culinary school had been at the top. I'd accomplished it along with many more tiny, daily pleasures.

I wouldn't let Poco take my good life away.

As I stepped out of the café, the wind snapped at me, sending a cloud of cherry blossoms whirling into the air much as it had the day before. I caught one in my hand, and the sweet color and smell sent a wave of ideas through me for the piece I was working on at home. For two seconds, everything around me disappeared as my mind filled with frosting and tarts and shades of pink.

Whistling brought me out of it. A sickly cheery tune that had goosebumps crawling over my arms. I jerked my head up from the petal, scanning the street.

Nothing.

No Poco. No lurking gang members.

A black Range Rover pulled up along the curb, and the passenger side's tinted window rolled down to reveal Lincoln leaning over from the driver's seat. "Get in. I'll drive you home."

Had he been waiting for me? That idea brought a wash of mixed emotions. Joy and hope that needed to be squashed. Irritation. Worry. It was all too dangerous. Too complicated.

I stepped over to the window. "I live literally five minutes away. It's the middle of the day. No rain. No Poco. I'm fine." But the echo of the whistle reverberated in my head, mocking me.

"If you don't get in, I'll get out and walk with you, but I'm running out of steam. So, do me a favor and climb in?" The firm set of his jaw told me he'd do just that.

As I opened the door, I told myself I was only getting in because of the shadows under his eyes that I didn't want on my conscience, but a little voice was laughing at me. I was tempting fate. Daring the universe. All because of the lure of attraction buzzing inside me.

The warmth inside the vehicle had me shivering after the chill left over from the storm. I buckled my belt, and when Lincoln didn't move from the curb, I looked over with a raised brow. "Home?"

Those strong and sensual lips quirked upward. "And where's home?"

I laughed softly, realizing he had no idea we were neighbors. "Mom and I live in the cottage across the street from you."

Surprise lit his eyes. "The house with the fairy-tale garden?"

I beamed up at him. "Yep. That would be us."

He looked over his shoulder and pulled out into the lunchtime traffic. It was heavier this time of year with Bonnin's semester in full swing and tourists flocking to the greater D.C. area for all the different cherry blossom festivals. Those first few years here, not knowing who was coming in and out of town, not knowing if one of them was looking for me, the volume of visitors had been disconcerting. Now, the ebb and flow of people was one more thing I loved about Cherry Bay.

Lincoln took a right at the stop sign, and the hustle of downtown turned into the quiet of houses tucked up against the meadowland bordering a forest of cypress trees. Neither of us spoke as he drove the short distance, the tension in the air causing me to tug at my necklace and fidget in my seat. I expected him to stop in front of our cottage, but instead, he pulled into his driveway. We got out in the same silence, meeting at the back of the SUV. I stopped there, ready to try and say goodbye one more time, but he simply strode across the street toward our gate.

"You don't have to walk me to my door," I called out to him.

He looked over his shoulder with one eyebrow raising. "You can't get out of answering my questions that easily. Plus, I want a closer look at your garden."

Bewilderment swam through me as he let himself into our yard. I really didn't understand why my safety had become so important to him or why he so desperately needed answers. Maybe it was simply because I hadn't been good at pushing him away. I'd sent mixed signals, teasing and smiling one moment and then trying to close the door the next. But the truth was, the pull I felt toward him was confusing. Heady and tantalizing, it was hard to find my way while juggling the new emotions. Juggling dreams with protocols.

By the time I caught up to him, Lincoln had stopped in the middle of our riverwalk path, spinning to take in the cherry tree at the back and the willow tree up front with its feather leaves in full bloom. In between was a chaotic mix of flowers and herbs and wild ground cover bursting with new buds. The yard had already been full of plants and color when we'd moved in, but Mom and I had added to it, making it into exactly the fairy-tale garden Lincoln had called it. One where imps and gnomes might come alive at night. Where the insects shared secrets and butterflies felt safe to rest their wings.

"It's a bit of magic," he said with a small grin that set my pulse flying. "How long have you lived here?"

"Almost six years."

"It's beautiful. Peaceful."

It was. Working on the garden had marked off a box in my journal. Life had bloomed and blossomed under my fingertips. Seeing Lincoln's pleasure, the awe and contentment on his face, was another beautiful moment. It was an image I'd keep and cherish, just like the life and magic pouring from the garden.

I continued down the path to the cottage. The solid oak door stood out against the gray stones, white-washed plaster, and gingerbread Tudor trim. The leaded-glass windows in the dormers reflected the clouds drifting by, and the steeply pitched roof, now a faux-thatch, made it easy to imagine the prince and princess from the mural at the café calling it home.

Lincoln followed me to the door, and I tried once again to end our time together by saying, "Thanks for the ride."

His eyes narrowed. "As I said, you're not blowing me off, Willow. Tell me what's really going on. Why were you in the cemetery, and why did you refuse to call the police on Poco?"

I wanted to roll my eyes. I was so tired of talking about it already. I wanted to just let it blow away like the storm. I turned up my smile and said, "Really, there's no need for you to be involved."

He was standing so close I could feel those sparks of attraction traveling over me again. I imagined myself grabbing hold of each tiny flame, holding on for a brief moment before letting them fly up into the sky as I sent Lincoln on his way.

"I'm afraid it's too late for that," Lincoln insisted. "Even more so now that I know you live across the street from me. If I still had my detail, they'd be knocking down your door and Poco's after it. I don't want to have to call them back. I like my privacy too much."

"So, in order for you to keep your privacy, I have to give up mine?"

My words seemed to hit home, because he looked uncomfortable for the first time since laying out his demand for me to get into his car. Brilliant blue eyes looked both sad and determined.

And suddenly, I was angry. At him for not letting go. At my life for making me shove this stunning man away. At all the things I couldn't have. I let the emotion sink into my veins for all of two seconds, but then I let it go, just like the sparks. I knew more than anyone what anger did. It destroyed. It tore through goodness and let evil win.

I wouldn't let it back in my life. I'd already had enough of it.

# Chapter Seven

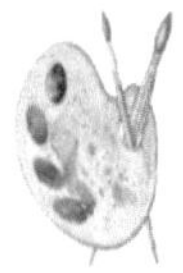

## Lincoln

**HOLD MY HAND**
Performed by The Fray

**SHE HAD PUT ME IN MY** place with her comment about her privacy. I *was* demanding she give it up—but only to me. Only so I could sleep at night, knowing she was safe. Not that I'd sleep for long, but she didn't need to know that. Just like she didn't need to know that if she didn't give me this, the insomnia would likely worsen until I was back on the sleeping pills I hated with a passion.

I watched as waves of emotions crossed her expressive face. Sorrow. Anger. Resignation. Sadness. It was the sadness after she'd seemed so light—even after Poco's assault—that hit me the hardest.

"I promise, I'm not going to shout your business to the world," I said, gentling my tone from the growly demand it had been. "I'm asking you to tell one person. To tell me so I rest easier."

Our gazes locked once more, debate warring between us. This morning, I'd backed down, only because I'd realized arguing with her at her work wasn't going to win her over. Instead, I'd gone back to the gallery, unpacked a few more things, and then set up the computer in the window along the street. I'd logged in to another round of messages from my family I hadn't had the energy to answer and deleted another from Felicity that had my jaw clamping tight.

It had been pure luck that when I'd left the gallery, Willow had been exiting the café. I'd tried not to put too much meaning into it as I'd pulled up beside her and demanded she get in. I'd been half surprised when she'd agreed. Just like I was half surprised when she relented now and turned without another word to unlock the cottage door.

I stepped in behind her as she disarmed the alarm system, taking in the low ceilings crisscrossed with exposed beams and the dormer that let in more natural light than the series of tiny windows along the front. The furnishings were very feminine. A creamy-yellow couch littered with a multitude of floral pillows, and a striped, mint-and-cream armchair that matched the sheer curtains.

It felt sweet and sunshiny.

It felt decidedly like Willow, even though she'd said she lived there with her mother.

She tossed her patchwork bag and coat over the arm of the couch before making her way toward the kitchen separated from the living area by an island of brick and granite. The cabinets were painted a modern white, proving the place had been renovated sometime in this century, even though the cottage felt like stepping back in time.

"Tea?" she asked.

"No, but thank you."

Silence settled between us. Not uneasy exactly but edgy. Both hers and mine. She didn't want to talk, and yet I couldn't let go of the idea that she needed protection. Even recognizing my need to shield her was a result of the baggage of my past, I couldn't walk away. I wouldn't let another woman be hurt, knowing I could have prevented it.

She fiddled with the edge of a towel covering a large rectangular pan on the island. Alongside it were jars of colorful pastes, paintbrushes, and stacks of culinary tools I'd only seen in professional kitchens. It was a weird mix of baking and art supplies.

Curious, I nodded toward the items. "What are you

making?"

She practically glowed at the question, a smile taking over her face that turned her into a dazzling display so bright it was hard to look straight at her. "Just playing around with an idea."

Willow tucked the towel closer to the pan, clearly unwilling to share more, which only piqued my curiosity. She was a series of contradictions—shiny vivacity and quiet mysteries—that would have intrigued me even if my body wasn't already craving her. And there was no denying that it did.

How had I gotten here? All but forcing my way into her house and requiring replies to questions she had no obligation to answer.

I tore my gaze away from her glow, and my eyes caught on a large picture hanging on the wall near the archway leading to the bedrooms. It was a photograph of Willow and an older blond-haired woman. They had their arms around each other, cheeks pressed together. The woman was a sturdier, slightly taller version of Willow with blue eyes instead of gray. A sadness dripped from her gaze defying the happy tilt of her lips.

"Your mom?" I asked, and she nodded. "Where is she?"

"She teaches science at the high school."

It was a brief answer, and it caused a wary look to slip over her face, which only increased my desire to unlock all her secrets. I wanted to find out everything there was to know about Willow. Not just the why of the cemetery or what had her scared enough to not call the police. I wanted to know where she'd grown up, and why they'd moved here, and where her father was. I wanted to know how she ended up baking scones at three in the morning when she looked like she should have been shouldering a backpack onto the Bonnin campus and sitting through boring lectures.

"You said you'd lived here for six years. What brought you to Cherry Bay?" I asked.

She curled a finger around the edge of the cloth and then said, "After my dad passed away, we needed a fresh start." Her eyes darted up and away as she spoke, as if what she said was only a partial truth, but it also gave me a glimpse of the pain that shot through her eyes at the mention of her father.

"Losing someone you love is hard," I said carefully. I wouldn't say sorry. I wouldn't offer some half-assed condolence, because nothing could curb the pain of real loss. The grief was always with you, some days burning like a flaming sword, other days a soft flicker of a sputtering candle.

Her head tilted sideways, taking me in, and I wondered if she was thinking of the old news articles on me. How I'd been close to death multiple times. How too many women I'd loved had violence impact their lives. Accidents. Gunshots. Stalkers chasing them.

"Is that why you were up at two in the morning?" she asked. "Your losses haunting you?"

It skimmed closer to the truth than I normally cared to acknowledge, and yet I was surprised by the urge to spew all *my* secrets to *her*. I clamped my lips together. I'd already given her more than I could afford. I felt oddly soothed by her presence. Comfortable in her space.

Comfortable and yearning for more. A taste of her sugary sweetness.

When was the last time I'd craved someone like this? Hungered for anything other than my art? Maybe not since Sienna and my wild teen infatuation. I certainly hadn't felt this way with Lyrica. That had simply been pleasure in finding someone who loved the same things you did. Dance. Art. Escape.

The T-shirt Willow wore clung to her slim frame. The muscles I'd seen earlier as she'd lifted the tray at The Tea Spot were more obvious now without the apron that had hidden her earlier. She had small breasts, lifted high, and full hips I wanted to explore. The layers of her chiffon skirt flowed down to her feet, giving me only shadowy glimpses of the toned legs I'd noticed earlier. I wanted to uncover all of her. See all of her. Splash her on canvas. Cut her from stone.

While I hadn't been prepared to let a woman into my life again, now that Willow had thundered in, temptation was knocking at the doors I'd sealed shut, tapping loudly and insisting I open up to the possibility of letting someone new inside my walls.

*Ask her out.* The voice in my head startled me, sounding decidedly Sienna-like. It had me glancing both ways for a translucent figure I hadn't seen in years. The back of my neck prickled before I assured myself it was only Katerina's voice. After all, my sister was the one badgering me to put Felicity behind me.

Willow shifted, drawing my eyes to her hand tugging at her necklace and her teeth biting her lower lip. I'd been staring at her for way too long. What had she said? Something about my losses haunting me?

"More like a new house keeping me up," I told her. "New sounds. Or rather a lack of sounds? I'm still getting used to the quiet."

It wasn't a full lie any more than I imagined her response about her dad had been. But I think she knew, just as I had, that neither of us had been completely honest.

"So, the cemetery?" I asked.

She played a shell game with the colorful jars on the counter, avoiding my eyes as she said, "It's peaceful there at night."

Another half-truth.

"And?" I pushed.

Her fingers stilled, and when she looked up, I got a glimpse of sadness again. "They deserve to be remembered."

Those words lodged deep in my soul. I'd spent over a decade ensuring that Sienna would never be forgotten.

"Who?" I breathed out.

"Any of them. All of them." She tugged on her chain again.

Confusion drew my brows together.

She chuckled softly. "I sound dark and broody, don't I?" She paused, as if debating saying more, and then shrugged. "My dad is buried…in our old town. I don't get to visit his grave. I guess I just hope someone will do for him what I'm doing here.

Seeing them. Thinking about them. Acknowledging they had a life. Saying their name aloud so they aren't lost."

It was beautiful and tragic. It made me want to add another layer to the charcoal drawing I'd started of her and the cemetery, blending names onto the gravestones so they faded away and yet still stood out.

"Is there a reason you have to do that at two in the morning?" I asked.

Her eyes sparkled with humor as she replied, "There's nothing gothic or dark about the timing. I don't go because it's the middle of the night. It's simply the time I get up. If I went to work at eight, I'd be there at seven."

"Maybe you should start visiting after work instead of before?" I suggested dryly.

"The real question is what was Poco doing there at two in the morning with a shovel?"

I frowned. I hadn't seen a shovel. "You've never seen him there before?"

She shook her head.

"Do you think he was stalking you? Watching your house?"

"No."

"I have cameras surrounding my house. I'll reposition some so they face the cottage," I offered.

"We have our system too. You don't have—" she stopped herself. "Thanks, that would be really kind of you."

It wasn't a good idea for me to drag my dark around her light. Given my track record with relationships, the likelihood of things ending well was almost nil if I pursued the longing for her growing exponentially by the minute. And yet, I knew it wasn't just my desire to protect her that had me saying, "I'd like to walk you to work for a while."

Her brows raised. "At two-thirty?" She shook her head again, moonlight strands swinging about her. "I don't think so."

"Just for a few days," I pressed. "I can guarantee I won't be asleep."

Even though she hadn't been moving, it still felt like her entire being froze before she slowly breathed out, "Because of me?"

The answer was complicated. But I kept the demons of my past to myself because I knew what happened when you let them out. "For many reasons, of which you'll be one."

"Lincoln, I'm fine. I don't know how to convince you that nothing is going to happen."

She couldn't guarantee it. But then again, neither could I. A change of tactics was required in order to get her to agree, so I tried a teasing taunt instead of a demand. "We'll start a club. We'll call it *Night Risers Unite*."

Her laugh was enticingly merry, a song I wanted to dance to, and it brought the beaming smile back to her face. The one so dazzling it flung aside the natural dimness of the cottage.

"It sounds like a vampire book," she snickered. "I'd be decidedly out of place." She glanced down at her pink-and-white outfit, and my gaze followed hers. The skirt she wore was graceful. Gauzy and dreamy. Angelic even.

"As a proverbial vampire, I can guarantee you are exactly what would attract one. It isn't the dark of their world that draws them. It's the light they hunger to absorb."

She blushed prettily. The pink skimmed her cheeks, blending with the freckles and amplifying the attraction humming through my veins. Desire seemed to wrap a string around us, knotting and tightening until it felt as if the counter was no longer between us. Until it felt as if our bodies were slammed together.

I stepped back. Afraid if I didn't leave, I might actually try to take a bite of her.

As I headed for the door, the knot that had drawn itself around me seemed to tighten further. Rather than snapping, the string grew tauter, tethering me to her with an unyielding bond.

It was uncomfortable. Troubling. But instead of breaking it, I did the opposite and drew it closer by saying, "Tell me what time to meet you in the morning."

As she joined me at the door, I sensed rather than saw her hesitation, and I just continued as if she'd already agreed. "I'd say text me when you're ready to leave the house, but I'm notorious for losing my phone. Just tell me what time to meet you."

"As I don't have your number, it would be impossible for me to text you anyway." She started to laugh before it turned into a garbled choke. "That wasn't me hinting at wanting it. I wasn't flirting…"

As her voice disappeared, the color on her cheeks deepened, enticing me all over again. It drew me to her sweetness as much as her light. I shoved my fists into my pockets so I wouldn't slide a finger along the fascinating bloom.

"Nothing wrong with flirting, Willow." I caressed her with my voice the way I longed to with my hands. "It's a delightful little dance, and I thoroughly enjoy dancing."

Her pale irises the color of clouds drifting across a shimmery sky expanded, and I wondered just how stormy they would get in the throes of passion.

We stood at the door, desire wafting between us. Her gaze slipped to my mouth, and it only increased my ache to taste hers. To savor every inch of her.

She was temptation and inspiration and damnation.

I cleared my throat. "What time?"

She sighed, palming her necklace again, and this time, I saw the charm was actually a class ring. Masculine and oversized. Jealousy flooded my veins. She belonged to someone? Where was he? Why wasn't he here defending her? I wanted to hunt him down and demand answers.

When she still hesitated, I growled, "What time, Willow?"

"If I don't go to the cemetery, I leave the house at two-thirty." She breathed it out, letting go of the ring. I barely resisted the urge to grab it and discover who it belonged to before it hit me that it might have belonged to her father. The man she'd lost.

The intensity of my own reaction to her, bouncing from

anger to jealousy to desire to laughter, made me feel like I was finally losing my sanity. As if I'd finally collapsed from sleeplessness into a dream world that would never again reach a solid shore.

And that, more than anything, had me giving her a curt nod and striding out the door, hoping to break the tenacious grip she'd sunk into me.

Except, as I walked down the path toward her gate, the string that had seemed to bind us only grew tauter, pushing at my Adam's apple until my breath was rocky and uneven. And I knew, with a painful certainty, it wouldn't release until I'd found myself at her side once more.

# Chapter Eight

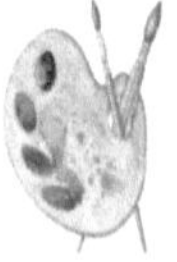

## Lincoln

**KEEP ON WANTING**
Performed by The Fray

**ONCE I'D LET MYSELF INTO MY** house, I headed straight for the study still battling the intensity of emotions flooding me. At the desk, I opened the security system software on my laptop that was linked to both my phone and computer. The cameras gave me a three-hundred-and-sixty-degree view of the outside of my property with no obstructed views.

I played with the angles of the ones out front until the gate and the front of Willow's cottage came into view. It wasn't good enough. What I really wanted was an unobstructed three-hundred-and-sixty-degree view of *her* property. But if I demanded cameras be added, she'd likely think I was a door with a missing hinge. I wasn't her friend, her boyfriend, or a relative.

I was a stranger who'd shown up at a bad time. My behavior was borderline obsessive at this point, especially considering how short of a time I'd known her.

I meant nothing to her. She meant nothing to me.

Except, the knot at my throat disagreed. The fact that it was there, tugging and tightening, was almost as troubling as the idea of Poco showing up in the middle of the night when I couldn't see him.

I closed the security app and opened my email to find a

flurry of messages from Mom. The subject line of the top one read, *If you don't answer your phone today, I'm sending Hardy.*

Shit.

I slammed the laptop shut and jogged up the stairs to my bedroom. The phone was right where I'd left it, charging on the nightstand. When I picked it up, I had twenty text notifications. It wasn't the worst I'd ever found, but it was enough to make me grimace.

Katerina's was at the top, begging me to answer Mom once again. I groaned as I realized I hadn't sent the message I'd intended to. I'd gotten sidetracked with cardboard and cemeteries and Willow. I shot off a note saying I was responding right now.

I debated texting before wondering if Mom knew what was eating at my sister. Talking would be easier.

"The lost boy awakes," Mom answered in a tease that barely covered the worry.

"Just because I'm not tied to my phone like it's a body part the way Katerina is, doesn't mean I've disappeared off the face of the planet." It was an old argument. Even with the enormous things that had happened to me, even when I'd lost myself to alcohol for weeks, or been in a haze of sleeping pills that made me forget, I'd never been suicidal. That would have been the easy way out.

I'd needed the pain of existing in order to earn my penance.

"It's a mother's prerogative to worry about *all* her children," she said.

"Like Katerina? What's the deal with her these days?"

Mom hesitated for a beat. "What do you mean? What's wrong with Katerina?"

Well, hell. Now, I'd just given her something else to worry about instead of easing her mind. I tried to cover up my mistake with Katerina's own words. "I suppose she's just working too hard."

"Hollywood is almost as bad as politics," Mom said with a sigh. "It can eat your soul if you're not careful. I'm seeing her soon, so I'll get to the bottom of it."

That meant I'd be getting an irritated message from my sister about siccing Mom on her.

"Where are you today?" I asked, hoping she'd forget all about our conversation.

"Arizona. In ten minutes, we're leaving for lunch with the governor."

"You're schlepping around in sweats, then," I teased, knowing she was done up elegantly in a perfectly fitted dress suit. Just like I knew her brown hair layered with highlights of cherry wine and gold would be coiled neatly at her nape. Her light-blue eyes framed by expertly sculpted brows would sparkle and charm whomever they were with, her lean, tall frame standing regally at Dad's side as if she'd inherited the posture from her English-royal ancestors. My twin sisters had inherited her looks, while I took after my father. Dad got his code name of Gibbs from his resemblance to the actor who played the *NCIS* character.

She huffed out a laugh and then asked, "How's Cherry Bay?"

Entrancing. Captivating. I'd felt that way about the town even before Willow had shown up and added another layer of interest to it all. Instead of saying any or all of that, I simply said, "I started painting."

"Lincoln...that's wonderful, darling." Her voice was full of emotions. The press had nicknamed Mom the *Ice Queen* decades ago when nothing they said ruffled her feathers. But she'd never once been that way at home. My sisters and I had always felt the full force of our parents' love. Even when their lives were chaotic and busy, they'd always made time for us. They showed up when it mattered. They were front seat at Katerina's plays and Juliette's academic decathlons and in attendance at as many gallery showings as they could manage. They'd been the first ones at the hospital the night Sienna had died.

"You know how it is. You'll likely hear less from me while

the painting works its way through my system," I told her.

"You're sleeping enough?" she asked.

"I'm getting used to the change in my environment," I said instead of lying. "You won't recognize the house when you see it again."

"After California, we'll be back in D.C. We'll get a trip down there on our schedule."

"It's a busy time for you right now. Save it for the gallery opening."

"Do you have a date?" She sounded surprised.

"No," I chuckled. "But it has to be soon. Otherwise, I'll be in the red before I even open the doors."

I was proud of the fact Sienna's gallery had been profitable after its first year, and I had no intention of the gallery here leaching into it. I was using the salary I'd paid myself to start up this one, and while I could lean into my trust fund, it was the last thing I wanted. I had every intention of passing my trust down to the next generation of Mathertons in better shape than I'd inherited it.

"Trish is waving me toward the door," Mom said with a sigh. "Try to respond to me once in a while so I don't have to worry quite as much."

"I'm good, Mom. Just concentrate on getting Dad through this last campaign."

"I can't believe it's almost over," she said quietly. In those words, I heard all the pride and relief my sisters and I felt, but I also heard sadness. For my parents, it was an era coming to an end. I couldn't really imagine their lives without politics. What would they do when every minute was no longer carefully choreographed and accounted for?

"It'll be done in five years, Mom. You'll both have done your time."

"You know we don't see it that way. It's been an honor to serve."

And wasn't that just the crux of it? I'd always seen Dad's career as a burden while they'd seen it as a gift. A duty they happily fulfilled. An attempt to protect a nation that didn't always deserve it.

Maybe protection was in our blood.

After hanging up with I love yous in the air, I returned to the office and the security system. It wasn't my responsibility to look after Willow, not even considering my past and the failures hanging over me, but it was a duty I would happily and willingly perform.

♫ ♫ ♫

After searching the internet for anything I could find on Poco and coming up empty—the man didn't even have a social media account—I turned to Willow and was surprised to find she didn't have any either. At least, there were no accounts with her real name. I tried a few different usernames like 'Cherry Bay baker' and such before giving up. In today's day and age, it was odd to have no accounts. No footprint at all. Didn't everyone leave some kind of trail?

I didn't know her mother's first name, but when I searched for a Cherry Bay teacher with the name Earhart, an article came up in the local paper. It was about a science decathlon Erica Earhart's students had recently won and how they were moving on to the state championships. What was odd was that there wasn't an image of her in the paper or on the high school's staff directory.

Something was off, but I couldn't put my finger on it.

My stomach growled loud enough to jerk me from my online search.

When was the last time I'd eaten? The scone this morning, but what had I had the day before?

Nothing. My refrigerator was empty except for a few condiment jars I'd brought with me from the D.C. condo. I needed to go grocery shopping, but I had no intention of doing so tonight.

I could order in, but escaping from the rabbit hole I'd journeyed down was the better option. I found my keys on the desk, grabbed the baseball cap from the coatrack by the door, and headed out into the fading sunshine.

Across the street, a well-used Pathfinder now sat along the curb in front of Willow's cottage. My stomach tightened uncomfortably, desire and concern mixing. Was it her mother's car? Some man's?

I shook my head, shoving the cap on my head and striding toward downtown. If I continued down this path, investigating her online and standing moodily outside her door, fixated on who was at her house, I'd cross over into the stalker category that Felicity had entered.

It wasn't until I'd broken up with her and refused to answer her calls that the Secret Service had found the cloning software on my phone placed there by a private investigator she'd hired to investigate me. She'd dug into my past as well as my present, trying to uncover all my secrets. She'd downloaded messages between me and my family and tried to use them to reel me back in. She'd cried large crocodile tears, saying she'd hired the PI because she had a stalker when we had proof that she'd asked the PI to follow me rather than any obsessed fan of hers.

When the Secret Service showed up at her door, she'd retaliated by releasing a twisted compilation of my private messages with my family to the media. She'd cut and spliced them with the secrets I'd given her, the truths about my ghosts and the guilty conscience I carried, hanging it out for all to see. She'd used her sad, baby-blue eyes, shiny auburn hair, and fragile air to convince them I was a heartless deranged sadist who'd tossed her aside after I'd promised her a lifetime.

The fury and disgust I felt every time I thought of her betrayals fueled my steps. It stayed with me until I hit Main Street where the sun setting on the cozy village sucked my breath away just as it had when I'd stayed there late last summer. The peaceful haven eased the boiling in my blood, shoulders relaxing. If anything good had come out of my time with Felicity, it was this—the fact that it had led me to Cherry Bay.

I scanned the buildings, eyeing the handful of restaurants tucked into the gingerbread façades. I'd eaten multiple times at the Italian restaurant while staying at a bed-and-breakfast down the street. Remi's had decent lasagna and a killer chicken parmesan, but I wasn't in the mood for red sauce laden with garlic. A wry grin hit my lips. Maybe I really was turning into a vampire.

I strode past the restaurant, and the bar next door tempted me. The stained-glass window showing a prince and a princess bursting into light added another layer of magic to the downtown. I stared at it for a moment, something wavering at the back of my mind—an idea for the gallery that wouldn't quite take hold.

I started toward the bar's door, but a loud burst of laughter traveled out and halted me. Even if I didn't take my hat off indoors like my mother had instilled in me, I might be recognized while eating a meal. I needed takeout.

I turned, intending to head toward the Chinese restaurant at the far end of the street and ran straight into a man standing directly behind me. He had dark hair and angry eyes behind thick-framed glasses. His face was so white it bordered on pasty. He wasn't as tall as me, but his frame was stocky, and his clothes hung off him in a disheveled sort of way. Not quite dirty and torn as someone living on the streets might wear, but more a look of being worn down by drugs or life.

"My apologies," I said, moving around him and away.

"You should be sorry."

The fury of his tone had me glancing over my shoulder. His fisted hands, clenched eyebrows, and scowl screamed an aggression that startled me. I'd barely bumped into him.

Attempting to ignore it, I strode down the street only to have him follow me. I groaned internally. I couldn't afford a confrontation. Not here. Not now. If he attacked, and I had to use my years of martial arts training to defend myself, it would make the news. I could see the headline: *Lincoln Matherton Attacks Man on Streets of Cherry Bay*. My parents would have to deal with the fallout. The town I'd escaped to would be flooded.

I crossed the street, and the man did the same. As I neared

the doors of the yoga studio, a group of twenty-somethings with rolled mats under their arms emerged, laughing and jostling each other.

The man was forced to step to the side to let them go by, and I ducked into the studio.

The man glared through the window at me but didn't venture in.

I approached the desk where a petite blond woman in yoga pants and a sports bra sat. Her stomach was round with pregnancy, and she had a hand resting on top of it. She turned a serene smile to me as she asked, "Can I help you?"

"Just looking for a schedule of your classes," I answered.

She stared at me for a long moment.

"Have you been in here before?"

My jaw tightened, hoping I could get out of the place before she recognized me. I tugged at the brim of the baseball cap before saying, "No. I'm new to town."

Her eyes narrowed as she tried to figure out where she knew me from. I held my breath, waiting for the aha moment. When it didn't come, she turned and pulled a brochure from a stand behind her, handing it to me. I thanked her and walked out.

I glanced both ways down the street, the tension in my back easing when I didn't see the angry man. The crisis had been averted. But for how long? How long would I be able to remain anonymous in this tiny town, especially after opening the gallery? And once word spread I was here, what would the locals think? What would the press do?

I adjusted the baseball cap again as I strode down the sidewalk, continuing to scan for the man just in case. An engine revved, and a beat-up Civic sedan sped by. I wasn't sure if it was the same man behind the wheel, but I had a distinct impression it was.

Unease crept over me, the entire exchange leaving a bad taste in my mouth. The Secret Service had instilled in me the importance of listening to my gut, but in this case, I had no idea what it was trying to tell me.

What I did know was that my appetite was gone. So instead of heading toward any of the restaurants dotting the street, I made my way to a tiny shop that was little more than a convenience store. The prices were high and the stock low, but I grabbed a basket and dropped in a few essentials and microwave meals that would tide me over for a day or two.

The sun had drifted even lower over the buildings, all but fading away by the time I'd paid and exited the store. Shadows blended in with the pink blossoms scattered across every available surface. I'd found peace here when I'd visited last August, and I'd hoped it would surround me permanently once I'd moved here. But now, within a matter of hours, my peace had been disturbed by a stranger and Poco. Even more so by Willow.

As I left the slow hum of downtown behind and ventured along the quiet of my street, I glanced one more time at Willow's cottage. A warm light leaped from the antique windows, pirouetting over the roses and shrubs in the delightful garden.

More painting ideas swept through me. The continued twirls of dark and light I'd already started but also images of her flitting along the canvas like a butterfly dancing through marigolds. Fragile and yet incredibly strong as long as the oils of humanity didn't touch her wings.

My fingers itched to capture the image, long strokes transitioning from black and white into color. The urge was so strong, so intense, I almost dropped my bags and headed straight for the studio. Instead, I finished carrying them home, knowing I'd be getting very little sleep again tonight.

# Chapter Nine

## Willow

**CRAZY DREAMS**
Performed by Carrie Underwood


**A**FTER **L**INCOLN LEFT, **MY** EMOTIONS *AND* thoughts were all over the place. Excitement at the idea of seeing him again. Regret knowing it was stupid to play with fire. Hope that I couldn't quite squash. With my mind whirling, it was impossible to nap, so I threw my restless energy into my dessert art. By the time Mom finally made it home well past dinnertime, it was finished.

Analyzing it critically, I could see where it fell short. The tarts needed more color to really stand out, and the miniature pies made the faces a blurry oval reminiscent of a George Seurat painting. I'd have to stick to impressionist art unless I found a way to add more detail to the pastries. Still, the dessert looked surprisingly like the mosaic on the wall at the cemetery.

Accomplishment zipped through me. I'd done it. Which meant I could do even more. Another thrill ran up my spine.

After setting her stuff down, Mom came into the kitchen, looked over my shoulder, and gasped in delight. Satisfaction zipped through me at her reaction, and my smile only grew as she said, "It's beautiful, kiddo."

I turned and hugged her.

She laughed quietly as I released her, tucking a soft strand of blond hair that had escaped her bun behind her ear. Her eyes were a bluish gray that landed somewhere between Lincoln's stunning sapphires and my mist-colored ones. I looked like her in a nesting-doll kind of way, the same but only two sizes smaller. I felt lucky to have any of her features because she was beautiful.

Dad used to tell Mom she was the belle of his ball. He'd whirl her into his arms, swing her around the kitchen, and kiss her softly. I'd never been grossed out by it. Instead, I'd thought it was sweet and been reassured by the love I felt drifting around them. It was the cornerstone of our family. I wanted Mom to experience it again. I hoped we'd both be able to seize love and joy with both hands.

At the moment, I didn't have anyone in my life who I'd ask to take the leap into the unknown with me. Lincoln certainly didn't count, but Mom had Hector just waiting to shower her with adoration.

"What are you going to do with this?" Mom asked.

I shrugged. "I haven't a clue. All I know is that I love it."

I'd left a few of the tarts, pies, and petit fours out, and I handed one of the butterscotch bites to her. She bit into it, eyes closing in pleasure, which only made me prouder. Happier.

"You just get better and better," she said. "You should bring this to Hector. He'll know what to do with it."

My stomach fluttered with nerves. Anticipation. Hope. "It doesn't exactly fit The Tea Spot's brand."

"Brands change," she said. "And you know Hector would adore showing you off."

He would. He'd be just like a parent putting a kid's stick-figure drawing on the refrigerator. But that was exactly why it made me nervous. Would I really know if it was good enough if it was just a parent bragging about a child's amateurish design?

Mom tugged at the braid I'd twisted my hair into while I'd been working.

"Show him. He won't blow steam up your ass."

"Mom!"

She laughed, finished the treat, and reached for another before taking it with her and sitting on a barstool. Her energy shifted, away from teasing and happy to serious. I'd gotten really good at reading her moods over the last six years. She'd never once taken any of her anger or loss out on me, but for a long time, her grief had felt like it was my fault. As if I could have done something to stop what had happened when I knew, logically, I couldn't have.

My throat bobbed.

I needed to tell her about what had happened with Poco. I wanted to, and yet I also wanted to protect the last vestiges of her good mood. I'd just worked up the courage to tell her, was just inhaling to let it all out, when she said, "Deputy Marshal James called today."

I bit back my words, waiting for her to finish with a dread much larger than Poco had caused when he'd grabbed me this morning.

"Roci Vitale died in prison last week."

My eyes widened, body tightening automatically at Roci's name on her lips. Roci had been the youngest of the Vitale brothers who'd attacked Dad. He was my age and had attended my high school, but we hadn't hung out in the same circles. I'd known to stay away from him even before that awful night. Everyone at school had known he was part of the Viceroys street gang.

"What happened?" I asked.

"He was shivved in the showers and bled out before they could save him."

Goosebumps sprinkled my skin, and panic tried to swallow me as the memory of hate-filled eyes flashed before me. Evil eyes. Not Roci's but his brother Aaron's. He'd been Roci and Danny's defense attorney, and when the jury had read out the guilty verdict, he'd sent me a look that would have left me dead if it had taken real form. It had been sharp. Brutal. Cold.

"What does that mean?" I choked out.

Mom shifted on the stool uncomfortably before saying, "Deputy Marshal James doesn't think it means anything. She insists they're watching Aaron and that he's still in Chicago. There's been no murmurs of him looking for us. She thinks his hands are full enough with the RICO case pending against him and his buddies that he doesn't have time to even think about you, let alone look for you."

The Racketeer Influenced and Corrupt Organizations case had developed from the evidence the police had collected after Dad's murder. My identification of Danny and Roci had led to search warrants uncovering other crimes. The RICO case was part of the reason Aaron had worked so hard to get my testimony, and the warrant granted because of it, tossed out. I'd been the linchpin, and if I'd been taken out of the picture, it would have unraveled all the government's cases. The Viceroys might have gotten away free and clear.

Mom read my fear just as I'd read her seriousness. She reached across the island and squeezed my hand. "There's nothing for us to worry about. They haven't come after us once since we left Chicago. And even if they tried, they can't find us. The Marshals haven't lost a single witness in their protection who were following their protocols. We've never deviated from them."

We let that settle between us. And it was comforting. If we did as we were told, if we stayed under the radar, the Viceroys couldn't find us.

"Maybe I should find someone else to go with the kids this weekend," Mom said.

"What? No!" I pushed aside my fear. "It's the state championships! The kids are counting on you. You've all worked hard for this. Like you said, there's nothing for us to worry about. Go. Have fun. Revel in all your coaching paying off."

She still hesitated. I walked around the counter and hugged her.

"We're okay. I'm okay. Really. If I get freaked, I can call Deputy Marshal James, and if I need anything else, I'll just call Hector. He'd do anything to make you happy."

Her lips turned upward, and her eyes sparkled at my words.

Her reaction made every tight muscle inside my body loosen.

"He'd do anything for *you*," she said, patting my cheek. "Now, go get some sleep. Otherwise, you'll be a zombie by the time your alarm goes off."

I squeezed her hand. "I love you, Mom."

"Love you too."

♫ ♫ ♫

After I'd changed into my pajamas, I climbed into bed and fought the urge to search for the news about Roci and the rest of the Viceroys on the internet. I pushed the worry and fear as far away as I could. I chanted the mantra, *We're safe and they can't find us*, over and over again until, like always, I almost believed it.

I picked up my journal and opened it to the dog-eared page with the list of joyous experiences I wanted to have before any signs of FFI exhibited themselves and ended my life. I ran a finger down the words I'd first scribbled on the flight home from Chicago after the trial, happy to see so many already marked off. They weren't huge things, like going on a baking competition show, because those large events could never happen within the bounds of witness protection, but they were small and doable and simple. Everyday kinds of joys.

An X sat next to *find a passion, go to culinary school*, and *sing karaoke with a stranger* along with a dozen others. My finger stalled on the line that read, *Ensure Mom finds love again*. I was so close to checking that box I could almost taste the sweetness of it.

The next line down had me trembling as I pulled the metallic-pink pen off the spiral and drew a heart in the box next to, *Flirt with someone who made my stomach whoosh*.

The day may have started with a scare, but it had also been full of tantalizingly beautiful moments with Lincoln. I relived the heart-stopping smile he'd given me in the car after we'd dashed through the rain, and the thrill that had coursed over me when he'd said flirting was a delightful dance with those intense blue eyes boring into me. I wished I had a photograph of every moment so I'd never lose any of them the way moments with Dad were fading. I wished I knew more about Lincoln and what had happened in his life that had shadows clinging to him.

It felt deeper than just whatever had hit the news recently about him and Felicity Bradshaw. Something about him proposing and then taking it back? Leaving her to foot a huge resort bill? I couldn't recall the details. I looked over at my phone, almost as tempted to search for him as I'd been to search the Viceroys.

But I didn't. Not only because simply thinking about Lincoln was dangerous but because I didn't want to see him through someone else's tainted eyes. I knew the truth from what I'd witnessed today. He was a brave, confident man who'd stood up to protect a random stranger. So what if he was a bit bossy and broody—who cared? And in truth, in some secret part of me, I'd liked the way he'd demanded I do as he said. I wasn't sure exactly what that said about me.

I slid my finger down to the very last line on the page: *Experience the love my parents had.*

I'd written that one with a shaky hand, barely able to admit that hope, that wish, to myself because there was so much standing in the way of it. Not only the inability to tell the person you loved about your past for fear that somehow, in a moment of anger, they'd out you, but also because I'd have to ask them to take a leap of faith with me.

Look at what had happened with Chad. Unable to use FFI as the real reason, I'd told him I had a brain tumor that might someday turn deadly, and he'd bowed out before we'd even begun. He'd said it was just too heavy for him. Too much for a college fling. That had hurt even more because I'd thought we were on the track to something more. True love. Forever after.

It wasn't his fault. How could he have known all the pieces of my past and future had me wishing for fairy-tale endings at twenty years old? It hadn't been fair to him.

The danger for me now was in thinking, for even one brief second, that the sparks and whoosh I'd felt today around

Lincoln could lead to marking off that last box.

Just the idea of the twenty-nine-year-old president of the United States' son wanting any kind of relationship with some twenty-three-year-old nobody was ridiculous. I wasn't completely naïve. I'd seen the heat in his eyes when he'd looked at me, and I'd heard the sensual tone that had felt like a caress as he'd flirted his way out my door. But even if, by some magical miracle, those feelings could have possibly turned into something more, my witness-protection situation made it impossible to pursue.

I had to remain invisible. A nobody. A baker in a café no one really registered. And Lincoln was very much in the public eye. In fact, I was surprised it hadn't been all over the media that he'd moved to Cherry Bay. Sooner or later, the paparazzi would track him down here. He'd be in the headlines again, especially with his dad's election heating up.

I let out a soft sigh, put the journal down, shut off the light, and sank down under the covers.

If Lincoln showed up at all in the morning, I'd let him walk me to work for a couple of mornings—for both our sakes. So he could sleep, and so I didn't jump at every shadow. There'd be no need for him to walk me home when it was daylight, when there were plenty of people to help me if Poco did show up, but also plenty of people who might see us together. I couldn't afford for someone to take a picture of the president's son with me at his side and having them blast it all over the internet. But no one would see us in the dead of the night. I rarely saw anyone on the street when I walked to work.

Seeing Poco had been a rare exception.

So we'd walk together for a few mornings, and I'd keep all my attraction and wishful thoughts wrapped up tight. And if everything was still quiet by Thursday, the end of my work week, we'd both be reassured. I could thank Lincoln and send him on his way, and my life would go back to the simplicity of before.

It was the only possible ending to this story where once upon a time a lowly baker met the prince of the kingdom.

# Chapter Ten

## Willow

**PLAY ON**

Performed by Carrie Underwood

**BY THE TIME I'D WALKED OUT** the door the next morning, clutching my bakery box, I'd almost convinced myself that yesterday had been one big overreaction by both Lincoln and me. I was certain Poco would leave me alone and that Lincoln would come to his senses and not show up in the early hours just to walk me to work. And I'd also convinced myself that going our separate ways now was for the best. We could just wave at each other occasionally without anyone, namely me, having gotten too attached.

So, when Lincoln stepped out of the darkness, I let out a yelp and jumped, almost losing my hold on the precious pink box.

"I didn't mean to startle you," he said, steadying the box in my hands.

As I tried to slow the hammering of my heart, I stared up at him. In the mix of shadows and light from the streetlamps and mist, he looked just like the vampire we'd joked about the day before. Defined muscles layered over a lean frame gave the impression of a speedy stealth. Add in those eyes that mesmerized, and it was easy to imagine him ensnaring a victim.

"I wasn't sure you'd be here," I said breathlessly.

When his lips quirked upward, it only added to the rapid

rhythm banging away at my veins, causing me to bobble the dessert again.

"I always keep my word," he said before swooping in to grab the box. "Let me carry that for you."

I rolled my eyes as he lifted it with ease. "What are we, in middle school? You don't need to carry my books to class."

As soon as the words were out, I tensed, biting my lip and wishing I could take them back. They sounded even worse than when I'd basically asked for his phone number yesterday because these words sounded like I thought we were dating. As if I thought this was something more than one neighbor going out of his way to help another.

When he let out a gloriously deep and sincere laugh, the warmth of it coasted over me like opening an oven door. The low pitch echoing in the dark was more addicting than the growl he'd sent my way multiple times.

"It's heavier than I expected. What's in here?" he asked.

Pride filtered through me. While I was pretty damn happy with this first attempt, I was also unsure what others would think of this weird combination of food and art. My mom and Hector were inclined to like it simply because I'd made it, but what would our customers think? What would someone like Lincoln, whose job was to showcase art, say about it?

"Dessert," I finally replied before setting off toward Main Street.

"I am all in favor of dessert for breakfast. What are we having?" His long legs easily kept pace with me as we made our way through the mist crawling up from the pavement. The storm from yesterday had disappeared, but it had left behind a bitter cold that whipped through me.

"It's a variety of miniature pastries."

"Why were you hiding it on your counter?" he asked, brows furrowing.

"It's something new and…" The words died in my throat as a quiet whistle broke through the air. Several notes of a cheery tune before it disappeared again. I spun around, looking into the darkness behind us. I'd just barely gotten my pulse under control, and now it spiked again.

I'd thought for sure Lincoln and I had overreacted. That Poco would be nowhere near me.

When I glanced up at Lincoln, anger flickered over his face in the glow of the streetlamps.

"Did you see anyone on your security system?" I gulped.

Lincoln stepped closer, our jackets brushing. "No. I went through the footage from yesterday, and there was nothing there, but I also didn't check the cameras this morning before I walked out. I won't make that mistake again."

I inhaled sharply and then forced my feet toward the safety of the café.

"You should really reconsider talking to the police," he said. This time there was none of the anger and irritation that had been there the day before when he'd asked about it. This was gentle. Soft. Almost pleading.

I hated that my excitement about my finished piece and, if I was honest, about seeing Lincoln again, had been ruined by Poco's ugliness. A shiver ran up my spine. How long would he continue to torment me?

But maybe he wasn't. Maybe he was back in the cemetery this morning, doing whatever it was he'd been doing the day before. Maybe this had nothing to do with me, and we'd just happened to hear him whistling. If I stayed away from him and the graveyard, maybe it would be the end of it.

As my mind whirled with all the possibilities, silence settled between us, and it was Lincoln who broke it. "I searched the internet for you yesterday."

When my heart skipped another beat, it had nothing to do with a whistled tune. This was all Lincoln and his being curious enough about me to look me up—not that he would have found anything, but he'd tried. I bit the inside of my cheek, unable to respond because of the flurry of hope and joy that brought me, even knowing I couldn't afford his curiosity.

"You have no social media accounts," he said, filling in

my silence. "There's no mention of you anywhere. Your mom is easily found as a faculty member at Cherry Bay High, but there's no picture of her in the online directory."

The unasked questions hung in the air, and I saw the danger signs flashing. I could only hope he stopped before he asked something I couldn't respond to but found myself wanting to anyway.

My hope was washed away when he just continued to prod, asking, "Are you hiding from someone? On the run? You said your dad was dead and that you needed a new start, but are you hiding from him? Was he abusive to you or your mom?"

"My dad was a beautiful man!" I replied instantly and defensively. "Warm and funny. The very best kind of father."

"But you're hiding?"

I was grateful we were almost at the café, because that desire to answer him was only growing. Instead, I hurried ahead of him, leading the way into the alleyway behind The Tea Spot. The bulb above the back door was out, casting the entire area into a darkness that felt foreboding. I turned on my phone's flashlight app so I could see to unlock the door. The alarm squealed as I flipped on the lights, and Lincoln followed me inside while I punched in the code.

When I turned back, he was standing at the door, looking down at the ground outside with a frown. I joined him, noticing the broken glass. The back of my neck prickled with unease. The light being out was one thing, but this was different. This was purposeful. A knot formed in my throat.

As I went to step outside and get a closer look, Lincoln put out an arm to block me, pushing me back. The bakery box tilted in his hold, and my gut dropped at the thought of it falling, but he easily caught it.

"Shut the door," he demanded. With a nervous glance out into the dark, I did just that, locking the deadbolt as well.

"He didn't expect me to be with you again." Lincoln's voice held a barely veiled fury. "He thought he'd catch you alone in the dark."

His words kicked up the panic in my veins. My palms

turned sweaty, and cold spiderlike fingers raced up and down my spine. Was this Poco? Or was this a sign of something far worse? Had the Viceroys come for me because of Roci's death? That thought had a fist tightening around my lungs, stealing my breath.

As quickly as it had come, I rejected the idea. It couldn't be them. It had to be Poco. It was the only thing that made sense when we'd done nothing to break the Marshals' protocols. The hold on my lungs eased ever so slightly. It was Poco. Of course it was, but I'd truly thought he'd let it go. Yes, he'd been pissed when I'd gotten away. I'd seen it clearly in his eyes. But I'd thought that once he'd calmed down, he'd realize it had been for the best. What would Paul have to say if Poco had taken it further, and I'd been forced to report it?

My mind flashed to the shovel he'd been carrying. What if I hadn't lived to report it? What if I'd ended up buried under dirt in a grave? My stomach revolted, and my head spun. I'd never once considered him ending my life. I'd thought it would all go away because I'd never taken Poco very seriously. The Cherry Bay criminal element seemed like boys playing cops and robbers rather than the true evil I'd witnessed up close and personal in Chicago.

Was it stupid to not have told anyone? The police? The Marshals? My mom?

God, I couldn't think clearly over the churning in my stomach and hammering of my heart.

So I did the only thing I could do, which was to grab the bakery box from Lincoln with hands that trembled and head farther into the kitchen. I set it down on one of the long steel counters and gripped the counter tightly to steady myself.

What would have happened if Poco had stepped out of the shadows this morning and confronted us? What would have happened to Lincoln when he tried to shield me as I knew with every fiber of my being he would have? Would he have been seriously hurt? Killed? Another wave of nausea hit me, and my eyes pricked. My dad had been murdered for his attempts to defend a stranger. It was only due to a moment of clarity and quick thinking on his part that I hadn't ended up dead too.

How would I ever recover if someone else died while I watched?

What if the person who died was Lincoln?

I squeezed my eyes shut, trying to get a hold on the fear running through me.

When I turned to face Lincoln, I was greeted with a gentle look that practically undid me. It promised things I couldn't afford. Friendship. Caring. More. The secret wishes I'd kept wound tight like a ball of cooking twine began to unravel. I longed to close the distance between us, put my cheek against his chest, and let his strong arms hold me.

But I couldn't take him up on the offer his eyes were making. I couldn't let the twine unroll. Not only because of what it might do to me but what it might do to him.

I cleared my throat, determination and resolve helping push back some of the fear and nausea. "I think it was a mistake to let you walk with me. I… This… It put you in danger."

His eyes widened as if shocked I was worried about him. "I've got years of martial arts training behind me. I'm not worried. I can take Poco if he comes at me."

The pure confidence of that statement was some reassurance, but what if it wasn't Poco? Or what if he had a gun or a knife and caught Lincoln off guard? I hated that I was letting the what-ifs spiral out of control. I didn't know what the right solution was. I was scared to walk alone. Afraid to call the Marshals and end our life here. Terrified Lincoln would be hurt.

And I absolutely despised that this was pushing me back to the state I'd been in that first year. When I hadn't even been able to walk out the door without having a panic attack.

Anger found its way past the fear. I might have to take Poco seriously, but I didn't have to let him and his stupid actions control me.

"Tell me why you don't want the cops involved," Lincoln demanded, crossing his arms over his broad chest, stance wide, and giving me a taste of why the world had named him the most handsome man under thirty. It wasn't just his chiseled good looks. It was that dark superhero vibe wavering around him—

broody millionaire and president's son by day, avenging angel by night.

"Please don't push me on this," was all I could offer him. I might have to get the authorities involved, but it would likely be the Marshals rather than the Cherry Bay police.

But if I could just get a handle on it. If I could just make sure Poco stopped, it would be fine. Everything would go back to the way it had been.

I slipped out of my coat and took it and my bag into the office, giving myself some space and time to collect myself. I breathed in deeply, slowing my pulse, steadying my hands, and then replaced my skirt with an apron. By the time I'd returned to the kitchen, I'd pushed some of the worst emotions behind me, grounding myself again.

Lincoln was right where I'd left him, face still shadowed with concern.

"Just tell me one thing," he said softly. "Before the incident with Poco yesterday, were you afraid?"

"No. I hadn't been afraid in a couple of years." I was glad I could say that with some truth. After Danny and Roci had been sentenced to life in prison, I hadn't been scared. It had felt like our nightmare had finally come to an end. Deputy Marshal James had told us we still had to be smart, stay off social media, and keep our pictures off the internet because there was always the chance the Viceroys would seek revenge if they stumbled upon us. But Mom and I had both believed if we lived a quiet life, we'd be fine.

Lincoln's intense eyes took in every breath, judging the sincerity of my words. I had no doubt he could see the truth or the lies I told, which only added to my unease. I held my breath, wondering if he'd truly let it drop, and was surprised when he did.

He turned to the counter and the pink box. "Do I get to see what's in the box I carried?"

A little thrill at the thought of what I'd made pushed the fear and doubts back another notch. I hurried over before he could open the box, setting my hand on the lid and saying, "We can't eat it. Not yet. I need Hector to see it first."

His lips quirked upward. "That just means I have a reason to come back later."

I rolled my eyes both at his tease and at the way my insides squished at the thought of seeing him again. What would Lincoln say if he knew just being with him could put me in as much danger as Poco's threats? One random photo was all it took.

And it wasn't just the danger of discovery that put me at risk. Every moment I spent with him, every smile he gave me, every kind word, every time he stepped in to protect me, risked my ridiculous heart. It made me wish for things that could never come true.

I swallowed hard, looking down at the box. I wanted to show him what I'd created. Artist to artist. I rubbed a finger along the opening, a wave of nervousness like I used to feel when I'd finished a project at culinary school and handed it over to be judged settled over me. What would Lincoln think of my attempt at recreating the beautiful mosaic out of nothing but flour and sugar and fruit?

I'd never know unless I risked showing him, and I'd promised myself I would take all the risks I could within the boundaries set by witness protection. Within the safety of the program. So, after taking a huge inhale, I held my breath and lifted the lid.

It took a moment for him to really register what it was, but there was admiration in his voice as he said, "Willow. This is…wow!"

I exhaled softly, his awed look spinning through me with the same exhilaration of spun sugar.

He tilted his head, assessing the layers from another angle. After a moment, he asked, "What is it supposed to be?"

My bubble popped. The idea that he didn't know what it was had doubts creeping into my words. "It's a mosaic. On a wall at the cemetery."

He reached out as if to touch one of the tarts, and I snapped the lid shut. It was as much from my mortification at failing to capture the art as it was to keep him from touching it. His eyes flew back to mine, gaze skimming the heat filling my face.

"Wait. You're embarrassed? Why would you be embarrassed?"

"It was just a ridiculous idea. It was fun, but it's not like I could actually capture the genius of the original piece."

He leaned against the counter, arms crossed again, eyes darkening. "Don't do that. Don't sell yourself short. If I hadn't known you'd made that out of food, if I'd just glanced at it, I would have thought it was a beautiful painting."

I snorted but was unable to meet his eyes.

"I'm serious. I know many chefs who consider the food they make art, but I never knew you could literally create a masterpiece with it. It's interesting and stunning. The smells of the fruit and the sugar combined with the visual colors and texture make it a different kind of genius, and believe me, I know genius when I see it. I've made my livelihood out of it."

My eyes leaped to his, and my breathing turned erratic as he locked me in a tantalizing stare.

"I was just playing around," I breathed out quietly. "It's far from perfect."

"Art isn't supposed to be perfect."

Those words spiraled through me, taking the attraction I felt for him and sending it to a whole new level. I felt raw from all the layers he'd pulled back in the mere hours I'd known him, revealing secret parts of me I'd kept hidden for so long.

After several long moments, I finally broke our gaze, and as I did so, my eyes landed on the clock. I was late. Again. I pushed away from the counter, reached for the scrunchie on my wrist, and tied my braid up in a knot before reaching for one of the plastic caps. Lincoln watched my every move, and my already furiously pounding heart twitched and twirled as if in anticipation of a favored treat.

"I have to start the scones," I said.

I hadn't heard him move, but he was suddenly there, grabbing my hand, tugging it into his, and placing it on his chest. Warmth crept through my fingertips, flashing down my wrist to my elbow before easing along my shoulder and lodging deep in my chest. The erratic rhythm inside me grew stronger. Louder. Faster.

He nudged my chin, forcing me to meet his gaze. His thumb gently stroked my jawline. Flames leaped inside me even as my natural preservation instincts screamed at the danger he posed.

My eyes fell to his mouth. Strongly shaped, gorgeous lips that I'd bet were strong and firm. Demanding like his words. Fierce. Lincoln would never be happy with someone simply accepting his touch. He'd want them to participate. To meet him equally. To actively engage in every single act and motion.

The handful of kisses I'd had over the years had been mere whispers of skin on skin. I'd witnessed them as if a third party, detached but curious. The men—no, the boys—I'd let that close had felt my lack of interest. They'd felt it and ran. For a brief moment with Chad, I'd thought it could be stoked into something more, but then he'd vanished at the first hurdle.

"Who hurt you, Willow?" Lincoln asked with so much tenderness it brought a sudden rush of tears to my eyes. I didn't cry. Not anymore. And yet, the gentleness of his words made it hard to fight them off as he continued, "Who left the wounds you so bravely hide?"

I blinked rapidly, desperate to hold back the onslaught. The speed at which he'd switched gears, going from talk of art and baked goods to things I couldn't discuss, unwound more of my strings. My world spun, and I barely caught my balance.

"Lincoln…" I shook my head, trying to remove his hand, but his fingers gripped my chin harder, refusing to let go.

"Don't. Don't tell me to leave or that I have no right to know. Just tell me the damn truth."

I closed my eyes so I wouldn't be forced to look at the intensity in his. I needed him to back down before he slid past my defenses and I spilled everything. I raised my hand to his wrist and tugged, trying to dislodge him once again, and when it didn't work, I looked up at him and answered with my own challenge. "Who left the scars on you? The ones that cling like a Grim Reaper to you?"

He dropped me like I'd burned him.

We stared at each other for another long moment, the air tense and heated with want and hope and fear. I shook my head, turned away, and washed my hands before breaking the silence. "We've known each other for twenty-four hours. You don't get to demand I tell you anything about my life, especially when you have no intention of sharing anything about yours. You may be used to getting your way. You may be used to thrusting around the power that comes with being the president's son, but that won't work with me. It's for the best if you just leave."

The words were true but also sharp and harsh. After grabbing a clean towel to dry my hands, I dared to look up, and I saw my words had hit home. It tore at me that I'd hurt him. The last thing I wanted to do was cause more pain to this beautifully protective man who carried his wounds like a penance he was paying. But I desperately needed him to back off before I crumbled and gave him everything. I swallowed the apology that automatically rose, knowing it was better to let the words stand as they were in order to grow the chasm between us rather than shrink it.

There was no other choice. It was just too risky to continue.

# Chapter Eleven

## Lincoln

**_CORNERS_**
Performed by The Fray


**_HER BARB LANDED HOME WITH A_** surprising bite that left a new mark on my soul already littered with them. I *was* used to people answering me, cowing to me, bending over backward to give me what I wanted. But what she couldn't know was that I'd never requested it and was often disgusted by it. The simple fact she wasn't willing to cave in to my demands drew me to her more.

As I watched her throat bob and her shoulders straighten in determination, I realized she wasn't all but begging me to leave because she didn't want me there, just like she wasn't declining to tell me her secrets because she didn't want to share them. In fact, when I looked into her eyes, when I touched her, I saw the opposite—the longing to unburden herself.

But something—someone—was stopping her.

Cold fury washed over me at the thought of not only Poco, but some other asshole who'd hurt her, jerking her around, causing her to live in fear, and living some half-life.

Unfortunately, I wasn't sure I could leave like she asked. It was more than just wanting to protect some random woman in danger. And it was more than me being intrigued by the complexities I saw—the cheerfulness layered over grief. It was that damn string that had knotted itself around me and all but choked me as I'd left her house yesterday. The string that was still there, tethering me to her. Binding me. I couldn't walk away and leave her to whatever fate Poco and her past had in store for her without it ripping new holes in me.

"If I was going to use my father's power," I told her, "I'd just ask the Secret Service to run a check on you. They'd know everything there was to know in less than a day."

She ignored me, going to a large refrigerator, pulling out ingredients, and setting them on a steel counter near an enormous electric mixer. She was excellent at keeping those pretty lips sealed tight when she wanted, at keeping her thoughts and feelings to herself. I hated that someone had forced her to be this way when it was obvious, regardless of how little time I'd spent with her, that her normal inclination was to open up to everyone who even brushed along the edges of her life.

"I don't want to learn about you from some report that gets emailed to me," I said quietly. The truth of those words hit me with a force that almost stunned me. Maybe I hadn't rid myself of my ghosts or completely shaken off the recent betrayals, and maybe I never would. But if I waited for all the wounds to disappear, I'd be dead. I'd miss the moment when a brave, interesting woman walked into my life, offering the possibility of something beautiful. If I left right now, like she'd asked, I'd miss out on the chance of having all her secrets and all her dreams belong to me.

And I wanted them more than I'd wanted anything in months…maybe years.

"Your safety is very important to me, Willow, but it isn't the only reason I showed up this morning."

She looked at me, exasperation and longing running side by side in those troubled gray eyes.

I longed to soothe her at the same time I longed to push until she broke open, but she wasn't ready for me to do so. And if I pushed now, if I told her just how much I yearned to discover all the nuances that made her Willow, she'd pull back even more. I could wait. I could be patient. But I wasn't going to just scuttle away either. In time, I'd convince her I was someone she could trust. Someone she *should* trust.

So, for now, I'd do what she needed me to do—I'd leave—but I'd also be back.

I made my way to the door, and the reminder of broken glass just outside had me saying, "Make sure Hector replaces the bulb. Didn't he say he had cameras? Have him check them and send what he finds to the police. I doubt Poco's face will show up, but if it did, it's vandalism. So this doesn't have to be about you, but it can still protect you. You get off at noon, right? I'll see you then."

She looked frustrated, on the verge of telling me once again that she didn't need me, that she thought this was a bad idea, and then she said, "I appreciate you walking with me at night for a few more days." I could have sworn she shivered before she pulled her shoulders back and added, "But I'll be okay during the day. You don't need to come by this afternoon. I'm perfectly safe with people around."

When I simply raised a brow in her direction, she looked away.

Regardless of whether I was the right person to protect her or not, I was dedicated to the cause. I'd be a wall standing between her and whatever came after her.

And until I knew more, until she opened up, I'd call Hardy and ask him to do his own digging. Not on Willow, but on Poco and this Tall Paul he worked for. Maybe my father's power and position could actually assist the town I was making my home by getting rid of a couple of its criminals.

As I opened the door, I looked back at her and was caught all over again by her bright glow. Even now, after a scare and holding back things that clearly upset her, there was a sweetness about her that lured me in.

"Come set the alarm."

She pulled off one of her plastic gloves and joined me, practically shoving the door closed in my face. Instead of being put off by it, as she probably hoped I would be, it just made me chuckle. I liked seeing her riled up as much as I liked her smiles.

I liked the passion it revealed underneath her lighthearted façade. I liked pretty much everything I'd seen about Willow Earhart.

Except those damn secrets.

Only, maybe I liked those too.

She'd kicked me out of the dark spot I'd been stuck in for months. I'd been unable to paint, unable to even look at art for the gallery. I'd had to let Lyrica completely take over in D.C. But now, it was as if I was waking from a deep sleep.

I made my way around the front of the building, crossed the street, and let myself into the gallery as images of Willow filled my mind. Smiling. Scared. Sarcastic. She'd given me multitudes of expressions in a handful of minutes.

The play of color against black and white seemed to surround her the moment she'd walked out of the house this morning. Her skirt with its parade of flowers and her pink coat had stood out against the dark sky just like her freshly scrubbed face, rosy from the cold air, had danced with the shadows from the streetlamps. Her platinum hair pulled back in one long braid falling almost to her waist had been a halo of sparkling diamonds. Just the sight of her had been enough to catch my breath and flame my imagination, and when I'd stepped closer and caught the scent of her…it had been pure addiction.

She was a multi-sensory work of art, just like the dessert she'd created. Could I even call it dessert? What did you call it? Art in edible form? I'd been surprised and stunned by what she'd shown me. Intricate miniature desserts that, when you took the time to examine each one, had structure and form and smells, but when you stepped back and let your mind register the whole, it was clearly a watercolor landscape brought to life.

I wanted my paintings to have the same visceral impact on your senses as she'd given me by both her own appearance and the art she'd created. Except, I wouldn't have the advantage of using all the senses the way she could. I'd have to trick the viewer's mind into believing it could taste and smell and touch what was portrayed.

It was a new challenge.

But first, I had something else to do. Something more important.

As soon as I stepped into the studio on the third floor, I whipped out my phone and placed a call I'd sworn I wouldn't make.

"Lincoln?" a groggy voice greeted me, but it took only a heartbeat for Hardy to become alert. "What's wrong?"

Suddenly aware that it was three in the morning, I dragged a hand through my hair. I should have waited until at least dawn before calling him. "I'm sorry. I forgot it was so early. I'll call later."

"I'm awake now. No reason to call back. Hold on a sec." I heard a murmur on the other end and felt even worse. I'd woken his wife as well. After a few seconds, Hardy returned. "Tell me what's going on."

"I need everything you can get on some local thug named Poco and his boss, Tall Paul."

"Poco is his nickname. He's Paul's muscle," he responded. "Let me bring up their file." There was some tapping on a keyboard before he continued. "Poco was born Pacheco Malta to Betty and Tomas Malta. They were a housekeeper and garbage man until they died in a car crash. Poco went into foster care at age fifteen, was arrested for larceny, and met Paul White in juvie. At twenty, Paul took over his dad's garage and expanded into sports betting. Bought the bar next to the garage and expanded some more. He's mostly known for his loan sharking and illegal gambling, but he dabbles in a bit of drugs. A local motorcycle club uses his place as their headquarters, although he doesn't appear to be a member. Nothing about Paul or Poco has caught anyone's eye enough to take them down. About eighteen months ago, a murder two towns over was attributed to Poco being too aggressive while collecting on a gambling debt, but there wasn't enough proof to even get a warrant. And as you can't squeeze money from a dead body, there's not normally a lot of real ugly associated with their business. You have a run-in with one of them?"

"Not me. My neighbor."

"The Bristols?" Hardy sounded surprised.

"I don't know the Bristols."

"Live on your west side." I shouldn't have been surprised he had this much detail about my life and the bad elements in Cherry Bay. I may have walked away from the Secret Service, but they still had to keep an eye out to ensure nothing about me came back to bite Dad in the butt.

"Not the Bristols." For some reason, I was reluctant to tell him about Willow. Maybe because I knew he'd dig up a file on her as well, and I didn't want him to tell me her secrets. As messed up as it was, I wanted her to give me her truths because she chose to. It was what had made me stop scouring the internet last night after the basic search. "Any sexual assault charges in that file on Poco or Paul?"

Hardy grew quiet before saying, "Nothing on paper. But with these kinds of small-time criminal elements, I wouldn't be surprised. Big fish, small pond, end up thinking they have rights they don't."

It was my turn to be quiet, and it raised alarm bells for Hardy. I was sorry I'd called him when he offered, without hesitation, "If you need me down there, I'll find a way to scramble a team. Even if it's off the books until we get the paperwork sorted."

He'd do it too. Because he was a good man. Because he'd seen me through some rough spots. Some of my own making, like letting Felicity into my life when I'd known deep inside it was wrong from the start, and some caused by the life I was forced to live, unable to go anywhere without the press following me. I'd kept to the shadows not so much to stay safe as to keep my life private. In many ways, I knew what Willow was going through, even if our circumstances were completely different. Half-lives were never going to fulfill us.

"No. I'm good. Information is king, right? I just needed to know who I was dealing with."

"You shouldn't be dealing with anyone, especially not with the election looming."

"I think it'll resolve itself. If it doesn't, I'll give you a shout." I could practically hear the frown I knew he was wearing. "Seriously, Hardy. I need you to keep a tight lid on this for now. If I need you, I won't be stupid about it."

Hardy sighed. "Do me a favor?"

"Yeah?"

"At least keep your goddamn phone with you."

I laughed as he'd intended, but I also got the message he was delivering. "I'm calling you on it, aren't I?"

"Well, slide it into a pocket right now, and keep it there. GPS locator is on, right?"

"Yep." I hardly ever had it off, as it was an easy way for me to find it when I'd misplaced it. "Sorry I woke you, Hardy. Give Libby my love."

"Keep your smooth words away from my wife, Picasso," Hardy grumbled, tossing the Secret Service's code name for me in my face.

I was smiling as I hung up and felt better than I had since hearing that creepy tune drifting through the fog while I'd walked Willow to work.

I slipped my phone into the back pocket of the jeans I'd pulled on at one in the morning. I'd gotten maybe three hours of sleep before my eyes had jolted open. But three hours was better than the zero I had some days.

I flicked on the photography lamps and took in the work I'd done the day before.

I hadn't completely filled in Willow yet. I'd just left a vague impression of her on the canvas. But I knew now that she wouldn't be in ghostly white. Her dress would be cotton-candy pink. The cemetery would have its dark shadows, but it would slowly blend into more vivid colors the nearer the objects got to her, as if she was changing it, bringing it to life. The second panel would show a mosaic on the mausoleum like the one she'd designed for her dessert. Except, this would be one of my own making.

Something about the broken-winged angel I could see from my bedroom window was still calling to me, but I didn't have it right yet. Maybe it would come alive. Maybe it would flutter like the butterfly I'd also imagined her to be, disappearing off the final canvas. I wasn't sure yet.

For now, I'd get to work on the finer details tucked into the gloom. The headstones and the names Willow wanted to be remembered. The twirling curves of the wrought-iron gates and stone pillars. The black and white and gray before the color emerged.

I tossed my jacket in a corner, grabbed my charcoal pencils, and started where I'd left off, clearer now than before on the details I wanted to surround Willow.

♫ ♫ ♫

I worked for hours while the sun shifted through the room, spreading a pastel color as sweet as Willow across my painting before disappearing into the bright white of late morning. I was almost done with the shadows and getting ready to drift into the color when my phone rang.

I was tempted to ignore it as usual, but it was Lyrica's ringtone. I'd left her to single-handedly run my business, so it would be stupid and cruel to ignore her.

"You're interrupting me mid-stroke," I said as way of a greeting.

"You're painting?" Surprise littered every syllable, proving again that it had been too long since I'd had pencils and brushes in hand.

"Just starting the sketch. But yes, I'm working on something. What do you need?"

"I had an artist pop by yesterday. Her work is all wrong for our vibe here, but it might work down there in that disgusting fairy-tale town you've hidden yourself in."

I chuckled, set aside my pencils, and made my way down to the loft's bathroom to wash my hands. "Tell me how you really feel about Cherry Bay."

"I have nothing new to add that you don't already know. Seriously, Lincoln, you need to see this woman's art."

"What is it?"

"I don't want to tell you. You'll say no before you even see it."

I stifled a groan. "I haven't found a vibe for this place yet."

"Even better. This might push you toward one."

Irritation wafted through me. I didn't want to be pushed. I wanted to find my way to it. But as I wasn't going in any direction right now except the fantastical of my own paintings, I wasn't sure I could argue. "Fine," I bit out. "Send me some shots."

"No."

"Lyrica—"

"You need to see it in real life. The images just don't do it justice. The way she bends light and brings things to life— Look, I don't want to say too much. I don't want you to have any of those preconceived notions of yours and dig your heels in."

"Me? Dig my heels in?"

"Stubbornest man I know. Look at how long you carried around undeserved guilt for what happened to me."

I still carried it around. I simply stopped showing it to her once she'd broken up with me. I wasn't sure if it was my hovering after the shooting that had forced her to call it quits, or if she'd realized what I had even before she'd been hurt— that we loved each other, but we weren't in love with each other.

When I didn't respond, she sighed. "Just call her and set up a meeting. You won't be sorry."

"Is this like the time you said I wouldn't be sorry and a guy showed up pedaling his caricatures as the newest wave of portraitures?"

Lyrica's snarl ripping through the phone made my lips tip upward. "One time. I got drunk, let amazing sex befuddle my brain one time, and you've never let me live it down."

I chuckled. "We've all had alcohol and sex goggles at one time or another."

"Yours was named Felicity Bradshaw."

That wiped away my laughter. I *had* been momentarily blinded by her. She'd played on my desire to protect the women in my life, using those world-class acting abilities to make me think she needed a strong pair of shoulders around while she avoided the media. For a while, I'd thought she really was America's sweetheart instead of a fame-seeking manipulator and slightly unhinged stalker.

"Whole different ball game, Lyrica."

"Too bad the tabloids believed her story."

"The tabloids always believe every side of the story but mine. That isn't anything new. Thankfully, they haven't found me here."

"Merci told me you showed up on a college kid's social media account. You were at some coffee shop. She had it taken down."

Well hell. The kid from the coffee shop must have gotten a shot of me the day before when I'd been hatless, and here I was again without any disguise. I'd barely remembered my phone and a jacket as I'd hurried out the door this morning with Willow on my mind.

"I guess I owe Merci a bottle of that wine she's addicted to."

Merci was my mom's communications director. She and Lyrica had been dancing around a relationship for at least a year now. They fit in ways Lyrica and I never had. Sure, we'd had things in common—art, dancing. But we'd never truly blended the way I had with Sienna and the way she seemed to with Merci.

"The press is going to find you eventually, you know," Lyrica said. "Especially after you open the gallery. Is that sleepy little 'burb ready for it?"

It twisted through my stomach sharply. When I'd done the market research on opening an upscale gallery in Cherry Bay, the numbers had more than supported it, and I'd even considered my unwanted celebrity status as something that would benefit it and the other businesses along Main Street. But would the locals really want the crowds and attention that came once my whereabouts were known and shared amongst the paparazzi? I hadn't even given them a choice.

Regret flew through me. A feeling I was all too familiar with.

But the thoughts, the scare with the picture, hit home about why Willow was reluctant to be around me. It was clear she was hiding, and I was a beacon for news and tabloids. I was an idiot for not seeing it sooner. I could leave her be. I could hire a bodyguard to walk her back and forth to work, but every fiber of my being hated that idea. I wanted to be at her side. I wanted to get to know her.

But how could I do that if just being next to her put her in danger?

I had to know what she was running from, and then I could make a more informed decision. What I'd told Hardy was right—information was king.

"Earth to Lincoln. Where'd you go?" Lyrica jerked me from my thoughts.

"I'm here. But I have to go."

"I'm sending you the artist's contact information. Do yourself a favor, and take a look at her work."

"Fine."

"Was it really that hard to agree?" she asked with a snark to her voice that had no real bite.

"Everything with you is hard work."

"You love me for it."

"Love. Hate. It's a toss-up."

She snorted and hung up on me. Two seconds later, the contact information came through. I was tempted to look the artist up and see what the big deal was, but I also respected Lyrica's opinion. If she said I had to see the paintings in person, then I would.

I moved to the front window, watching the doors of The Tea Spot as I dialed the artist's number and left a message.

Willow would be off soon. My pulse picked up at just the thought of seeing her again. A day ago, I hadn't wanted anything to do with relationships and women while I was settling in here and ridding myself of ghosts, but none of that seemed important anymore.

I craved more of that sweetness. Of her.

But what if my wanting more was the reason something ugly showed up at her door?

I'd never forgive myself. I'd been part of the reason the stalker had hunted Leya. And while I hadn't been the reason Lyrica had been shot in a convenience store holdup, I also hadn't been there when she needed me. I'd been off with Sienna's parents. While trying to satisfy one penance, I'd added another wrong I'd needed to right on top of it.

But maybe with the resources at my disposal, with the people I knew, I could help Willow. Maybe I could find out what and who she was afraid of and make it disappear just like I could keep Poco away by simply letting him know someone was standing at her side.

Maybe this time, I could actually stop something evil before it struck another person I cared about.

# Chapter Twelve

## Willow

**SO SMALL**

Performed by Carrie Underwood

*I WAS JUST FINISHING THE CLEANING* when Hector came into the kitchen and asked, "Can you make samples of the miniatures for us to hand out tomorrow?"

When I'd shown him the piece I'd created, he'd beamed at me. And when I'd given him samples of each treat and he'd savored them with eyes closed, happiness and pride had shimmered through me, radiating outward like rays of the sun bursting through the clouds and sending the panic and fear of the morning further away.

After tasting each one, Hector had hurried to the pastry case and rearranged everything so he could place the mosaic dead center. I'd felt just as I'd thought I would—like a kid whose parent had pinned their art to the refrigerator. But then customers had started oohing and ahhing over it, and asking him if he'd created it, and how they could sample the treats, and the tension had eased.

"I'll make as many as I can tonight." I smiled up at him, heart light once more. The thought of not just making Hector's family recipes but my own was a dream come true. It was another box to mark off in my journal. Maybe I really would give people something to remember. Something that fed their souls as well as their bellies.

"Once people try the samples, they're going to come in specifically for them, so you'll need to make even more tomorrow night."

My smile widened, pleasure growing, not only at Hector's faith in me but at the idea of people showing up for something I'd created. I itched to not only bake more of the treats I'd used in this piece but to get started on a whole new vision.

When I told him as much, his brows went up. "If we changed the display each week, we could feature whichever dessert was most prominent. We could call it the Edible Art of the Week or something. I'll have Shay help me with a catchy tagline."

I tossed my apron and towel in the hamper before spinning around to hug him. He seemed startled, not because I'd never done it before, but by the pure force of it. He returned my embrace with a squeeze that filled my eyes with triumphant tears. When I pulled back, his grin matched mine—large and bright.

"Thank you for believing in me," I said.

"The desserts are tiny pieces of heaven. My *abuelita* would've been very jealous. I knew you were talented from the day I hired you and you criticized my chocolate scones, telling me exactly what was missing."

I was embarrassed by how cheeky I'd been that day. I hadn't meant my comment as an insult. I'd truly just been talking aloud more than tearing apart his grandmother's recipe. But Hector had only laughed and then added the cardamom I'd suggested without even blinking.

"Keep track of the expenses," he said. "I'll either give you a cut of the profit, or we can figure out a way where I'm buying wholesale, whichever gives you the biggest percentage."

Ted banged into the kitchen with his dark hair sticking up at all angles. "A huge crowd just came in. One of my friends said his art teacher took a picture of your dessert thing and was using it in class as an example of the evolution of modern art or something like that. The professor said she'd give extra credit to anyone who came and took a picture with it to prove they'd seen it."

I shot another amazed smile at Hector, who winked at me before going out front with Ted.

Excited butterflies flitted around inside me as I went and grabbed my things from my locker. I'd just slid back into the kitchen while unwinding my braid when the swinging door opened to reveal Hector's twinkling eyes.

"There's actually a line out the door!" he exclaimed. "If you increase my profits by drawing people in, we'll have to consider a way for you to get a cut of those too."

I pushed at my cheeks and the smile I couldn't stop with cool fingertips. "Of course not! It's your shop."

Ted's panicked voice called out for Hector, and he chuckled. "We'll discuss it later."

"Want help out front?" I hollered after him.

"No. Go home. Bake me some mini desserts to sell."

It was habit and happy distraction that had me stepping into the alley without thought. I barely held back a yelp as a body stepped toward me before I realized it was Lincoln. He moved from the shadow of the building into the sun, and the rays turned his brown strands into a kaleidoscope of dark hues while those cobalt eyes all but leaped out at me.

I beamed up at him for a second before the reminder of why he was there hit home. I'd swept away the glass from the alley and replaced the bulb before Hector had shown up. I'd meant to tell him about it, but then we'd gotten caught up in my creation, and I'd truly forgotten. Lincoln would be irritated if he knew I hadn't said anything, but I'd already talked myself out of worrying about it. And I didn't have time to get into it with him right now.

I had to get home, get a few hours of sleep, and then borrow Mom's car to hit up the restaurant supply store for more ingredients. I had samples to make and even more for the following day if they took off. Plus, I had another display piece to create. My mind was already whirling with lists of ingredients, supplies, and ideas.

As I started out of the alley, Lincoln slipped into stride with me. "I startled you, didn't I? You can't just walk out blindly. What if I'd been Poco?"

I hadn't been paying attention, not only because it had been a long time since I'd had to watch my every step but because I'd been lost in the pleasure of my success.

"No one was supposed to be here this afternoon, not even you, remember?"

As we rounded the corner from the alley onto Main Street, a group of students hustled by, joining the queue bursting from the door of the café. My feet faltered, some of the buzz leaving me as I realized we were walking together in the middle of the day where anyone could see us. I shot my eyes both ways, looking not only for Poco but for anyone who seemed interested in Lincoln. When no one seemed to even be paying attention to us, I hurried as fast as I could down the remainder of the block, only breathing easy again once we'd reached the quiet of our street.

Lincoln easily kept up with my frantic pace.

"Do you really think daylight would stop Poco?" Lincoln asked.

"I think the broken light was a fluke and that he was whistling in the cemetery while continuing with whatever nefarious activity he'd been doing last night. I think you and I overreacted."

After Lincoln had left this morning, it was what I'd convinced myself was the truth. I couldn't lie and say I hadn't been triggered by the events of the last two days. It had allowed the trauma of my past, which wasn't that far behind me, to resurface. But that was all it had been. Circumstances bringing those nightmares out of the shadows. Talking about Roci and Aaron with Mom along with Poco's ugliness had brought it all back to life.

But the truth was, I was safe in Cherry Bay, and Poco didn't care enough about me to follow me around.

"If I wasn't here and Poco approached you, attacked you again, what would you do?" Lincoln demanded as we approached our gate.

When I looked up at him, his face was shadowed with the sun shining fiercely behind him. Instead of the tortured superhero I'd thought him this morning, the halo of light turned him into a dark angel. Azazel rather than Michael. Any of the ones who tempted humanity with their fierce and treacherous beauty.

"I've taken some self-defense classes," I told him.

"Yeah? So, if I was him, and I stepped into your space like this." His arms and hips brushed against mine as he eliminated the distance between us. "What would you do?"

My body ignited, and my head spun. Not from fear. I didn't think I could ever fear Lincoln. This was a heady rush of lust. Pure desire.

My hand shook as I slipped the cat-shaped, self-defense key chain hanging off my bag from its hook and slid my fingers through the hard-resin, brass-knuckle-like weapon. Then, with as much force as I dared, I shoved the weapon toward his face, stopping mere millimeters from his eyes.

He jerked his head back, yanking at my wrist and then staring at the key chain with a look of disbelief. "What are you going to do with that cat toy?"

I shoved my hand toward his face without any real force, but enough to make a point. "Don't dis the cats. They can cause some serious damage to your eyeballs."

Before I even realized what was happening, Lincoln had crisscrossed my arms across my body and spun me up against the stone wall along our property. His front was tucked up right against my back, and his mouth was bent close to my ear.

"You weigh, what? A buck ten? You're nearly half my size, Willow. You get close enough to stuff that plastic riff-raff in Poco's throat, and he's going to be able to do a lot more to you than this."

My entire being throbbed as adrenaline crashed through me, and yet it still wasn't in fear. This had everything to do with him pressed up against me and the warmth of his breath as it brushed the shell of my ear, sending goosebumps over my skin.

"I stopped before I hurt you," I said, voice shaking from the desire humming in my veins. "I would have taken him by surprise and then run like hell."

Lincoln's face dropped into my hair, and I swore he inhaled before whirling me around so I was facing him. My wrists were still caught in his hands, our bodies were still aligned, and I felt every hard and sinewy muscle of his touching mine. His eyes were dark and hooded, and those beautiful lips were set in a serious line I knew he meant to be disapproving, but all I could think about was what they'd feel like if I kissed him.

Which was ridiculous. And far more dangerous than Poco. Because this complicated man, who'd had me on a roller coaster from the moment we'd met, could easily ruin me…and Mom. He could destroy everything we'd built here with one careless, misplaced snapshot.

I pushed against the solid wall of his chest, and he let me go but stayed close enough that his arms still brushed mine. We stared at each other, breathing erratically, the air full of want and need and fear and sorrow.

I swallowed over the lump that had suddenly formed in my throat and said, "Thank you for worrying about me, but we've both made too much of the entire situation." When he started to protest, I interrupted. "I won't be walking to work tomorrow anyway. I'll have all the samples with me, so Mom will drive me." Debate warred over his face, and I did my best to reassure him one final time. "I promise I won't walk by myself."

He stepped farther away, and the loss of his heat allowed the cold wind to slice through me.

He called out a series of seemingly random numbers that I didn't quite understand, and my obvious confusion made him raise a brow and growl, "Take out your phone, Willow. Put my number in so if anything changes, you can call me. I'll come whenever you need."

My heart leapt wildly. It wasn't wise to add him to my phone. Too much of a temptation. And yet, when he repeated the numbers, I still did it with trembling fingers.

When I looked back up from saving the information, he'd disappeared.

♪ ♪ ♪

I'd intended to take a nap, but for the third day in a row, I couldn't. My mind raced with memories of everything that had happened. Not only the alarming moments but the heady, forbidden ones. My mind lingered excessively on Lincoln, taunting me with a low throbbing deep in my belly at the thought of the many ways he'd touched me.

The result was that by the time Mom got home from school, I'd prepped as much of the baking as I could without shopping and was waiting anxiously with my list in hand. While I could have borrowed the car and gone without her, I was also ready to get out of my head. Ready for the distraction of company that wasn't Lincoln's.

Even though Mom had to be dragging after a long day on her feet, she didn't even hesitate when I asked her to go to the restaurant supply store with me.

"I told you Hector would like your miniatures," she said proudly as we drove.

A fuzzy warmth settled inside me, allowing me to meet her happy look with one of my own.

Shay had sent me a picture of the line in the café that had continued all afternoon. Even if most of it was due to the extra credit the professor had offered, I hoped it meant they'd come back for actual samples tomorrow.

"What are you going to do if a reporter shows up?" Mom asked.

My mind immediately went to Lincoln and the press who would eventually find him here, so my voice shook a bit when I asked, "What do you mean?"

"Hector texted me and said kids were posting pictures on Bonnin's social media pages and that they'd flocked to the store to get a look at your piece. I bet someone from *The Cherry Bay Gazette* will pop by."

"You're texting with Hector?" My excitement over that single nugget of fact shoved all the other concerns aside.

Mom looked away sheepishly, and it made me want to raise my hands in the air in a fist-pounding moment. I wondered if Shay knew our work had paid off and that our parents were *finally* stepping in the right direction.

"He's proud of you. Just like I am," she said. Pleasure bloomed inside me again. Even when I was little, Mom had never held back her compliments or her love, just like Dad never had. She'd always supported me in whatever I'd wanted to do and hadn't even batted an eye when I'd dropped out of Bonnin to attend culinary school. She'd been proud of me for following my dreams, especially when we both knew how short life could be—specifically, *my* life.

We pulled into the parking lot of the supply store, and I reached for the door handle before her words stopped me. "Were you ever going to tell me about Poco?"

I swallowed over a lump that instantly formed in my throat with regret at holding something back from her. I wanted to be mad at Hector for telling her before I'd had the chance, but I was also too happy that they were texting for any real anger to take hold.

"It was nothing, Mom," I said because I'd convinced myself it was true.

"Some guy intervened?" she asked.

The lump grew. If she'd been worried about a reporter showing up over my desserts, how much more would she worry if she knew I was spending time with the president's son?

"Our new neighbor heard us arguing in the cemetery yesterday before work," I said quietly.

Mom's eyes widened. "You were at the cemetery in the dark? Alone?"

I fiddled with the seam of one of the patches on my bag as I collected all my thoughts and emotions. Finally, I looked up and said calmly, "We're safe here. You said so yourself. I don't need to worry about the Viceroys."

"This isn't about the Viceroys, kiddo. You're a beautiful woman, in a college town. Other things can happen. It's bad enough you walk to work in the dead of the night without lingering in dark places."

"I always text you that I've made it safe."

"But you weren't, and you didn't tell me. And worse, you went in alone again this morning."

I hated the sadness that returned to her eyes when I'd been seeing so much light in the last few weeks. And the truth was, I was sure I'd blown everything out of proportion, right along with Lincoln. My natural instincts to protect her, to make sure she didn't have one more thing to worry about, had me saying, "Lincoln walked with me this morning."

Her brow furrowed. "Who?"

"Our neighbor."

Her creased brow only grew. "Why would our new neighbor be up that early?"

"He wanted to make sure Poco didn't come back."

Suddenly, her expression cleared, and a small smile curved her lips. "Aw. I see. He likes you."

I bit my lip, looking away and tugging at my necklace.

Her eyes lit up. "You like him."

I did. I really did, but it couldn't go further than that.

Instead of answering, I got out of the car and grabbed a trolley from out front of the store, wheeling it inside. Mom followed along, and I turned my mind back to the list I'd made. How fast the samples went would give me a better idea of how many I needed to make for the following day, but I didn't want to make two trips to the store if I could help it. I'd buy extra, and whatever supplies I didn't use, I'd take to the café where they'd be put to good use.

As I headed for the dairy section, Mom said, "You know it's okay, right?"

I glanced over at her, stopping to load two cases of butter into the cart. "What?"

"It's okay to start a relationship. To find love and happiness."

"It is. I know it is," I told her. And it was. I wanted it for her as much as I wanted it for myself. It just couldn't be with someone like Lincoln. That hurt more than it should after knowing him barely a day.

"But?" she pressed.

I inhaled deeply and let it out. "It's hard to do when we're in…you know…and can't be honest with the people in our lives."

"We're not lying. A name isn't who we are. We can still give the people we care about the truth of ourselves." She wasn't wrong, but she also wasn't right.

When I didn't respond, she pulled me to a stop, forcing me to look at her. "Hiding from the Viceroys is different than hiding ourselves. If you keep yourself closed off and don't let anyone in, then you've allowed them to steal your life even though you're still breathing. I don't want that for you. They took so much from us already. They don't deserve the rest."

And then, she hugged me tight in the middle of the dairy aisle, and I hugged her back.

The last line item on my bucket list taunted me. I wanted what my parents had. I wanted to open myself up to love. But it wasn't just the cold fury in Aaron Vitale's eyes that held me back. It was an unknown mutated gene and the look of horror on Chad's face when I'd told him I might die.

I might be willing to take a leap into the unknown to find love, taking a chance the tarot fates might still hand me the death card, but what if no one else was willing to take it with me? And was it even fair to ask them to?

My mind filled with Lincoln's intense gaze and the warm hand on my chin as he demanded to know who'd hurt me. How would that look change if he knew I wasn't just running from some external force but a genetic bomb ready to explode? Would his expression turn to horror like Chad's had?

A piece of me wanted to spill all my worries to Mom just to have her reassure me that it would be okay. That someone would take the leap, and if they didn't, I'd be okay. But I also didn't want to make her sad now any more than I had when Chad had first ditched me. If I'd told her back then the reason we'd broken up, all it would have done was make her feel bad. Make her remember all the things she'd lost with Dad. And I'd promised myself I would do anything and everything to make her life easy and happy, not the other way around.

So, instead of sharing the burden like I ached to do, I stepped back from our hug and turned back to the items on my list.

I didn't need to worry about ever having to tell Lincoln about the FFI anyway. Because the president's son wasn't going to whisk me in his arms and declare his undying love. Sure, there was physical attraction dancing between us, but mostly he was around because he was a heroic kind of guy. He'd seen a woman in trouble and stepped in to help.

Nothing would ever come of the sparks we felt. Lincoln was off limits to me, even if love wasn't.

And if that last item on my joyous-experiences list never got crossed off, I'd still live a full and satisfied life by marking off plenty of others.

# Chapter Thirteen

## Lincoln

**SAME AS YOU**
Performed by The Fray

**INSTEAD OF GOING HOME TO THE** quiet of my house after dropping Willow at her door, I took my pent-up energy back to the studio. I couldn't get the smell of her and the way her curves had fit perfectly into mine out of my head. Her courage—her resilience—was as big of a turn-on as that scent.

But I was also frustrated she'd reduced the threat of Poco to a passing inconvenience. She'd convinced herself it was just random and had nothing to do with her, while every instinct in me was telling me it was more.

In the studio, instead of going back to work on the cemetery scene with Willow, I pulled out a new canvas and tossed every one of my dark thoughts onto the pure white linen. The demons inside men. The shadows that lurked.

Anger. Jealousy. Power. Greed. Control.

Stroke after stroke.

It was gloomy. It was ugly.

But it soothed my soul to splash it onto the canvas. Dark brutal sweeps in dark brutal colors.

*She's what you need.*

The voice had me whirling around the studio, brush in one hand, palette in the other, insides screaming objections.

She was sitting on a stool in her black lace prom dress. Pastels and florals had been in fashion that year, so she'd hunted her dress down at a secondhand store, refusing to be seen in "any Easter egg color." Her hair, so fair it was the color of moonlight, had streaks of dried blood in it from the head wound at the back she was careful not to show me.

"You're not supposed to be here, Sienna," I said.

I closed my eyes, rubbing them and hoping it was just the exhaustion and turmoil of the last few days that had my subconscious bringing her back.

*Then, don't make me show up by doing stupid shit,* she said, hopping off the stool and sauntering over to the trio of paintings of the cemetery. Her stride had always been powerful. Purposeful. She'd held a confidence that had been hugely out of proportion to her mere seventeen years. She'd been a bright light. One of the ones snuffed out too early. Taken from us when they'd been destined to give the world life-changing gifts.

Every time I saw her like this, a translucent mirage, all I could think was it should have been me.

Should have been me.

Should have been me.

The dark cavern at the back of her head loomed momentarily as she eyed the painting, sinking into my gut along with a pile of remorse before she shifted so I couldn't see it.

After I'd opened the D.C. gallery and she'd disappeared from my life, I'd been relieved, which, in turn, had only caused me to feel guiltier. But I'd also been glad I'd been able to bring her some peace.

So why was she here now? It screamed something about me and my mental health and the state of my life that I wasn't sure I wanted to acknowledge. Maybe it was because I'd uprooted myself and was full of indecisions. Or maybe my worry over Willow had my subconscious playing back all my failures.

*If you'd painted* me *amongst the gravestones, it would have been a cliché,* she said. *A Goth girl in a cemetery. Borrrrring. But her? It's perfect. Do you see how she's already made you better? She's your person, Lincoln. She needs you as much as you need her.*

Her words swung through me like a hammer on an anvil, sparking and inciting. I'd barely gotten used to the idea of wanting to explore something with Willow, and here Sienna was, tossing around a much deeper meaning, as if the flame I felt could be forged into something permanent.

It was completely ludicrous and yet also felt frighteningly right.

Sienna looked over her shoulder at me, blue eyes seeing beyond skin and bone to the truth. To the scars Willow had said clung to me like a Grim Reaper. To the grief and remorse I hadn't let heal, but also to the flicker of light Willow had fanned into existence the moment I'd rescued her in the cemetery.

*This is where you belong, Lincoln. It's time to let it all go. To be happy. To move on.* Her head tilted. *Oh, and you're going to want to get that... Lyrica is right about that one too.*

She faded away as my phone rang in my back pocket.

The fact that Sienna knew so many things about my life that had happened after she'd died was one of the reasons my therapist believed her ghost was simply a manifestation of my own thoughts. But she felt real. Wouldn't a ghost haunting me see the people around me? Wouldn't she know what was happening? If she was real, why had she returned? If she was only a hallucination, what was I trying to tell myself?

Maybe I just needed to get more than three hours sleep tonight. If I didn't get more soon, I'd be back on the sleeping pills, and those would only add to my delusions.

I pulled my phone out of my pocket and answered it without looking. "Hello."

"Um. Hi. Is this Lincoln?" a quiet but rough female voice whispered on the other end.

"Yes."

"Oh. Hi. This is Trinity Carerra. You left me a message." She sounded as if she was about to be sent to the hospital with pneumonia.

It took me several seconds to register she was the artist whose contact information Lyrica had given me. "Right. Lyrica sent me your name and told me I'd be an idiot not to look at your work."

Quiet settled over the line for several seconds before she said, "You liked my work?"

If possible, she sounded even more breathless and broken than before.

"I haven't seen any of it yet. Lyrica threatened much-needed body parts if I didn't see it in person. Do you think you could bring some pieces out to my new place in Cherry Bay? You can wait until you're feeling better."

"I'm not sick," she said, but her voice denied her words. "I actually live in Cherry Bay. I'll be working most of tomorrow at my catering job, but I can come by Friday morning. Will eight work? Otherwise, it would have to be in the afternoon. I have class in the morning at Bonnin. I guess I could just skip—"

"Eight is fine," I said. What were the odds she was local? Maybe Lyrica had seen it as another reason to send her my way. Or maybe Sienna, fate, or whatever existed on the other side of this life was just messing with me. "I'll text you the address."

"I know where it is. Lyrica told me. It's across and just down the street from The Tea Spot, right? In the old bath works shop?"

I didn't know how to feel about Lyrica giving away the information about the gallery here. I hadn't told anyone but those in my closest circle I was opening a second location. We'd kept the purchase of the storefront as quiet as possible, hiding it behind a new corporation I'd formed, just like we'd hidden the purchase of my house behind a generically named trust. I'd spent a lot of money to hide myself away, not only from the media, but also from Felicity.

In the end, I supposed it didn't really matter as I would have given Trinity the address anyway. "I'll see you on Friday, then."

"Lincoln?"

"Yes?"

"Thank you. Even if you decide my work isn't what you're looking for, I truly appreciate having the opportunity to show it to you."

And damn, did that take away the annoyance I'd felt at Lyrica's interference and make me like her. But I wouldn't sell anything I didn't think was quality, and I wouldn't show anything that didn't fit with the as-of-yet undecided vibe I wanted here.

"I'm going to be honest, Trinity. I haven't narrowed down a direction for the new gallery yet, so if I say no, it won't be personal, nor will it be because I don't believe your work is good enough. It simply might not be right for me at this moment."

"I understand."

"I'll see you Friday morning."

We hung up, and I turned back to the place Sienna had last been. It was right in front of the loose impression of Willow. A ghost-like apparition on the canvas waiting to be filled in, to be given back her soul. Over her right shoulder was a smudge I didn't remember making. It looked, from this distance, almost like a butterfly…or a fairy. A guardian angel.

Maybe I really was losing it. Maybe this was the final straw that would break the proverbial back of my mental health and leave me mumbling nonsensical words into my teacup.

I looked back at the dark, vile image I'd just created. Demon horns peeked through a fine tapestry being torn by sharp claws, giving a glimpse into a room shrouded in a poisonous cloud. Blood drenched the ripped bed linens and spread over the tips of broken furniture. An elegant, feminine foot stuck out from the bloody sheets. A television in the room was barely visible, and although it wasn't finished yet, I knew what would be on the screen—a very different version of the demon, the same creature but with a decidedly human face.

What was I doing?

As an artist, I'd always been more of a realist, painting landscapes and people with an almost photographic level of detail. I'd always steered away from uncanny dreamlike images of surrealism and the evocative, spiritual nature of expressionism, and yet, here I was, embracing both. The art still held the photorealistic details I'd always captured, but it was layered with emotions set in fantastical scenes. Statements about humanity poured out through light and dark magic.

Was it something about the events in the past six months that had added another veneer of darkness to the shadows of my mind? Or had the events with Willow really impacted me so severely in such a short span of time? Maybe it was simply Cherry Bay sinking its fairy-tale vibes into my subconscious as Lyrica had insisted. I wouldn't know until I'd finished the pieces. Until more of the art spiraling through my head ended up on canvas.

So I picked up my brush and went back to work.

♫ ♫ ♫

After staying way too late at the gallery, I'd come home and slept for only a couple of hours again before rising and heading to the home gym at the back of the house. The workout had burned through my lungs, proving I'd let it slip for too long.

By the time I'd showered and changed, the sun had just started to rise. When I stepped out of my house, a light mist was clinging to the grass in cobweb-like strands rather than the dense fog of the previous morning.

As I slid my baseball cap on my head, an engine revved, and my eyes were drawn to a gray sedan parked in the shadows of a large cypress tree outside the cemetery gates. I couldn't see who was inside it, but my mind flashed back to the altercation with the guy downtown the night before last and the Civic I'd thought he'd sped off in.

I hesitated, debating whether to stalk over and demand to know what he was doing or minding my own damn business. Hardy would definitely encourage the latter, but then again, if he and his team were here, they wouldn't have let anyone loiter around just yards from my house.

I glanced over at Willow's cottage as I made my way toward Main Street. The house was dark and quiet. At around two-thirty, wide awake and flooded with concern that Willow would walk to work even though she'd told me she wouldn't, I'd found my way down to the office and brought up the security cameras.

Feeling uncomfortably like the stalker Felicity had become, I'd watched as Willow and her mom had loaded bakery boxes into the back of a Pathfinder. Staring at the screen, I'd wondered if the sick, voyeur-like feeling I'd had was how my security detail, or any detail, felt while watching the people they were protecting. Had Felicity ever been disgusted with herself for stealing parts of my life like this without my knowledge?

I'd almost reached downtown when Katerina's ringtone sounded from my pocket.

"It's too early in LA for you to be calling," I said in lieu of a greeting.

"Love you too, Mr. Grouchypants," she said. "I'm at the studio. I have a long morning of work ahead before I meet up with Dad at his last fundraiser here in SoCal before they head up to Santa Clara tomorrow."

I ran a finger over a brow and then tucked my hand into my pocket. "I'm sorry I've left you to deal with the campaign on your own. I know you have a lot on your plate."

"I do," she said with that recent bite to her tone that wasn't usually there. Then, she sighed. "It's fine. I understand why you've ducked out of the public eye. That's why I'm calling."

"What's up?"

"Felicity cornered me at the fundraiser last night."

Anger and concern flooded me, feet stalling. "She did what? Where was your detail?"

"She begged me to ask you to issue a statement saying you didn't take out a restraining order against her. The gossip is all over town, and she's getting backlash for it."

Any backlash Felicity got would be nothing compared to what she'd sent spiraling toward me. She'd tried to ruin me completely going into Dad's reelection year, making it sound like my family had hidden drug abuse, serious mental disorders, and even blaming me for what had happened to Sienna and Lyrica.

She'd used every single one of my ghosts against me, while I hadn't used any of hers. I could have easily sent out a press release hinting that she was stalking me and used the months she'd spent in a mental health hospital as a teenager to add credence to it. She'd once used that trauma and her fear of the media finding out about her past to tug me closer to her. And it had worked until she'd flung it all into the wind after I hadn't shown up at the resort in St. Micah like she'd expected me to. Even still, I'd done my best to keep the restraining order quiet. I hadn't flashed it in the media.

Feeling eyes on me, a ripple of wariness went up my spine, and I turned back toward the parked sedan. It wasn't the private investigator she'd had tailing me until Hardy had sent him on his way. The PI had been a fleshy, doughy man with a bald spot and a mustache that belonged in the 1970s. The person in the car, even shadowed, didn't look wide enough to have been the same person.

"Is she getting backlash?" I asked. "Or is this just more manipulation?"

"She's definitely encountering walls. No one is sending her any scripts. But that isn't just because of the rumors of what went down with you. It's because she's a diva and has burned bridges while on set. And you're not the only one she's tried to manipulate. I wouldn't have mentioned her at all if she hadn't demanded you 'stick your head out of the little town you've tucked yourself into' long enough to help her."

Acid burned through me. "She knows where I'm at?"

"Or she was trying to get me to cough it up."

"Damn it. Thanks for letting me know. I'm sorry you had to deal with this."

Katerina sighed, and she sounded really tired as she said, "She manipulated me first, remember? Like you said, I *am* the one who introduced you."

"I was just teasing," I said gently.

"You were, but it's true."

"Don't take that on, Bumblebee," I said, instantly trying to comfort her by whipping out the rarely used nickname she'd earned with her nonstop energy as a kid.

Voices came over the line—deep male voices—and Katerina covered the phone, but I could still hear something in her voice that put me on edge. She was frustrated with whomever she was talking to. She came back on after only a brief exchange. "I gotta go. Just wanted you to have the latest intel, seeing as you said *adios* to Hardy and his team."

I barely got out a goodbye before she'd hung up. An unease for my sister settled through me. Something was up with her, and I needed to nail it down before it turned into something bigger.

I'd just put the key in the lock of the gallery door when the gray sedan buzzed by behind me. I held my breath, but when it continued down Main Street, heading out of town, I let it out again.

It was nothing. Not the strange man from the other day and certainly not Felicity, who was obviously in Los Angeles since she'd cornered my sister. I seriously doubted she'd hire another PI after the Secret Service had shown up at her door to hand-deliver the restraining order. Felicity was manipulative, and her emotions swung wildly, but she wasn't stupid. She wouldn't come after me again. She had no desire to end up in prison instead of on a movie set.

My gaze landed on The Tea Spot's bright sign welcoming its early morning customers. Through the windows, I could see a crowd had already gathered, and another group of college students hurried down the sidewalk toward the café. Were they all going to sample Willow's desserts?

A surprising flare of jealousy rose up inside me.

I wanted my own damn sample. Not just of the treats she'd made but of her. I wanted to inhale that buttery, sugary scent of her all over again. To see the flush I'd imagined while we'd messaged back and forth last night in person.

When my phone had vibrated with a text the night before, I almost hadn't answered it as my hands had been covered in paint, and my mind was busy pretending the ghost pacing in the corner hadn't returned. But when the phone had buzzed again, Sienna had stomped over to my easel and hissed not to be an idiot and to answer the damn thing.

I wasn't sure what had disturbed me the most—Sienna being there, all dark and moody, or the pure pleasure that had whipped through me when I'd seen the picture attached to Willow's text. It had been a pretty row of petit fours decorated with flowers lined up on her kitchen island. What she probably hadn't realized was that the photo had captured her as well. She'd appeared in the reflection of a mirror over their dining room table. When I'd zoomed in, I'd seen she had flour on her cheek and a smile that reached her eyes.

I'd ached to brush the flour off and let my touch linger over those raspberry-colored lips. Instead, I'd had to make do with the words she'd written instead.

> *WILLOW: Just so you can see you don't have to worry. There are way too many of these to carry. I really will be driving to work.*

I'd replied instantly.

> *ME: They look incredible. I can practically taste them from here. You should drive some over to me right now.*

And I'd wanted her to. I'd wanted her to show up at the gallery so I could get another hit of all that sweetness.

> *WILLOW: Can't leave. Too much still to do. Everything is at a critical spot.*

I'd sent her a photo of my hands covered in paint.

> *ME: I'd come retrieve them myself, but I'm also at a critical spot. For the first time in months, I've got multiple projects going all because of you.*

After several long minutes, she'd finally replied, downplaying her role as my current inspiration. Or maybe she really didn't have a clue just how much she'd impacted me in the mere hours we'd known each other. Somehow, Sienna's words about Willow being my person had encouraged the subconscious thoughts I'd already had, making me wonder just what possibilities existed for Willow and me. After all, if a ghost told you something, even if it was just your own wants and dreams talking, shouldn't you listen?

> *WILLOW: I'm sure it's Cherry Bay inspiring you. It has a very magical vibe.*

> *ME: It does. But that's not the reason I'm painting.*

My response had pushed her too far, and she hadn't responded.

Now, with the lights streaming from The Tea Spot beckoning to me, I could acknowledge that the vibe of the town had been what brought me to Cherry Bay. It had stirred the creative well inside me, but it was Willow who'd truly sunk into my skin.

I ached to walk into the café, see the joy on her face, and pull her to me. While I could tell myself it was to ensure she was safe, which was certainly true, it was also because of the uncontrollable craving I'd been besieged with the moment our paths had crossed.

The intensity of those emotions, as well as the fact she kept pushing me away, made me hesitate. Made me think it might be best if I gave us at least the morning to recover before thrusting myself into her presence again. Otherwise, she might begin to think it wasn't Poco, but me who was stalking her.

So, instead of storming into the café and demanding to see her, I locked myself in the gallery and threw myself into my art. The work seared through me just as my workout had that morning, proving I'd been away from both for far too long.

# Part Two

The bait I'd laid on the dark web finally paid off, information streaming in from a new source.

But as I scrolled through picture after picture of the cherry blossom-filled town, my fury spiked and grew until it was all I could feel and taste and see.

I'd burn it to the ground.

There'd be no fairy-tale ending. No happily ever after. No hero to save the day.

The Reaper would arrive instead, offering only punishment and penance.

Bringing Hell.

# Chapter Fourteen

## Willow



*I WAS STILL PRACTICALLY VIBRATING WITH* glee as I unwound my hair from its clip and pulled on another maxi skirt over my leggings. The Tea Spot had been busier than ever this morning, and all my samples had disappeared by ten o'clock. I'd have to make a triple-sized batch tonight, at least.

My phone buzzed, and I pulled it out to see a text from Lincoln.

My overly full heart almost burst out of my chest.

> *LINCOLN: I'm out front when you're ready to walk home. Hector tells me there are no more samples. Did you really not save me any?*

I hustled through the swinging doors, eyes searching the café for him and pulse spiking when I found his tall, broad-shouldered frame waiting off to the side of the door. Only the very tip of his nose and chin were visible under the baseball cap he wore as he glared down at his phone.

Why, when I knew just how impossible it all was, did I still long to wipe away his frowns and scowls and bad moods? Why did I yearn so badly for the one man I couldn't have? Why was it only the idea of *his* smiles and *his* brilliant cobalt-colored eyes lighting up at the sight of me that brought happy butterflies to my chest?

A long-sleeved, white Henley was spread tight across wide shoulders, his carefully sculpted muscles were easy to miss if you gave him just a cursory glance, but when you lingered on him, they stood out, screaming strength. His shirt was tucked in at his narrow waist where artfully worn jeans covered equally muscled thighs. He was stunning. And people noticed, eyes drifting toward him and away.

Even though the café was extremely crowded, there was a bubble of empty space around Lincoln. I wasn't sure if it was because of the leave-me-alone vibe he was putting off, that rigidly straight back screaming confidence, or the simple fact the regulars didn't know him.

As if he felt me staring, his head lifted, and his gaze locked on me from across the room.

The grin that wiped away his frown caught my breath. A little thrill tripped through me, knowing I'd been the reason for it.

Mom was right that I liked this man. Utterly and completely too much. And even though standing next to him in the daylight was stupid and risky, my feet still moved toward him as if his gaze had reeled me in.

"Hey," I said, wondering why it sounded so stupid. And then all thought disappeared, and heat bloomed along my skin as he slowly took me in from head to toe.

He brushed a loose strand of my hair back behind my ear, finger skimming my cheek, and my whole body lit up. I'd never understood that phrase in books, the idea of my body literally bursting into awareness seeming impossible, but now I knew. No matter what else happened from here, I had Lincoln to thank for giving me that experience.

He looked down at my hands, where I was clutching my phone so tightly I thought it might break. "I don't see a treat in those pretty fingers. I can't believe you didn't save me even one."

He raised a brow, and the intensity of his stare made my

insides flip-flop.

"I forgot to tell Hector the little box in the kitchen was for you. He handed it to the art teacher at Bonnin who started this madness." I waved my hand at the crowd.

Lincoln's eyes journeyed around the room and then back to me. The upward tilt of his lips disappeared into a new scowl. "Poco show up?"

I shook my head and then hurried toward the door. Lincoln's quick stride allowed him to pass me and open it before I got there. I slid by, arm brushing along his chest, causing fire to erupt inside me.

As we stepped outside into the sunshine that dappled the tree-lined sidewalk with diamonds of light, we almost ran into another group of students hurrying toward the café. As they passed us, one of them turned to stare at Lincoln before whirling back around and whispering to her friends who all shot looks our way.

And that sucked some of the pleasure from my morning away, replacing it with panic. And while none of the girls took out their phone and snapped a photo, what was to say the next person who recognized him wouldn't? Or what if some paparazzi I didn't even see was staked out, trying to catch a glimpse of the president's son?

After I'd spurred our pace to almost a jog, needing to get to the safety of our street before anyone else recognized him, I asked, "How do you do it?"

"Do what?"

"Ignore the looks and the whispering?" His chin jerked up, searching behind us for someone staring. When he turned back to me with a furrowed brow, I waved my hand back in the direction of the café. "They're gone now. They went inside."

The rigidness of his shoulders grew impossibly tighter. "Did they take a picture?"

I shook my head.

"We're trying to keep it on the down-low that I'm here in Cherry Bay—at least until I open the gallery."

My gaze widened. "Gallery?"

He chuckled and pointed past Remi's and The Prince Darian to what used to be a custom bath shop. The owner had retired to Florida to be with her grandkids last year, and it had been empty ever since.

"I'm surprised it wasn't in the papers," I said, shaking my head.

"I bought it incognito. It'll come out eventually, and it'll draw people into the showroom when it does, but I'm hoping my peace will last a little longer."

We walked in silence, and some of the strain left my shoulders as we reached the quiet of our street. Not a single soul was there, and it allowed me to forget everything else and just be in this moment with Lincoln. To savor it while it lasted.

The birds were twittering above us, and a colorful butterfly fluttered past, darting into the roses in a neighbor's yard. Music drifted out an open window, a bright and uplifting pop tune.

Before I could register what was happening, Lincoln had whirled me into his arms and was dancing with me right there in the middle of the street. Our bodies were pressed up against each other, one of his hands was at the small of my back, and the other was cupping my neck. With an incredible amount of skill, he slid us together, grinding our hips, and causing every last bit of oxygen to leave my lungs.

"Wh-what are you doing?" I gasped.

"Dancing," he said beaming down at me. "God, I've missed it."

He spun me out and around, and when my feet didn't quite catch up, when I might have fallen, he caught me and drew me impossibly closer.

I wasn't much of a dancer. I hadn't ever gone out clubbing or danced in public, but I wasn't really sure this was dancing either.

These moves felt completely sensual. Each shift its own act of foreplay.

I'd never experienced anything like it.

I ignored the screaming at the back of my head telling me we were making a spectacle of ourselves. I didn't care that we were out in public where anyone could see us. I didn't care about anything but the way my body molded to his. How it fit. How it burst into heat and flame and want and need.

The song ended, quiet descended, and I might have made a deal with the devil to have it turn back on. To once again move to that erotic beat with him.

The pure pleasure on his face as he looked into my eyes sent another spike of lust to my already overheated body.

But his words broke the spell. "We should go dancing. Is there a club close by?"

I couldn't go anywhere with Lincoln—certainly not to a club where dozens of people would see us, take pictures of him, and capture me at his side. Disappointment slid through me. A bitter taste of pure chocolate before it was combined with sugar to cut the edge.

I pulled away without answering him, and his smile disappeared. I hated I'd been the reason for it. Hated that I'd taken his joy and popped it like a water balloon, making it leak out on the street where it evaporated in the sunshine.

At my gate, I turned back, battling the need to do something—anything—to bring the smile back, warring with the desire to ask him inside. I wanted to offer him a cup of tea and ask a thousand questions about his gallery. I wanted to feel the warmth of his hands on me again, to feel the flare of attraction and lust and want, but I couldn't.

So I'd simply tuck away this beautiful moment where I'd danced with a stunning man in the sunshine and hope it would be enough to last me until the pain of knowing him and being unable to keep him left.

"You're staying in now? Making more of those desserts I've yet to sample?" he asked. And the way he looked at me, the way his eyes lingered on my mouth before journeying back up, sent all the fire and flames licking through me once more.

For a moment, I couldn't find my voice, and when I did, it was breathless. "Yep. Staying in. I'll make sure to save you some tom—"

"Do you know that car?" Lincoln demanded. Any ease he'd had left from our dance vanished as he shoved his chin in the direction of a gray sedan parked near the cemetery.

A cold disquiet crept over my spine at his tone and the question. I wasn't exactly sure of the model, but it wasn't any of our neighbors' regular cars. I knew those like the back of my hand. But sometimes people dropped by the graveyard to pay their respects or wander the tombstones, many of which were as old as Cherry Bay itself.

I narrowed my eyes, trying to make out who was in the vehicle. It was impossible to tell if the person was a man or woman from this distance. It wasn't Poco. Poco had a big beefy truck raised too high to be useful, and once in a while, I'd seen him drive up to the café on a motorcycle. He wouldn't be caught dead in this banged-up car with its rusted hubcaps.

"I don't know it," I finally replied, trying to keep tension from my voice.

"That's it. I've had enough," Lincoln growled and started toward the car.

He'd only taken a couple of steps before the engine revved, and the car sped down the street with the driver turning their face away from us as they went by. My palms turned sweaty, and my vision swam.

It wasn't Poco. And it wasn't the Viceroys.

*We're safe here. We're safe here. We're safe here*, I chanted to myself.

But it could have been someone taking pictures of Lincoln, couldn't it? A paparazzi searching for the money shot? That thought set my stomach roiling. He must have seen the near panic on my face when he got back to me, because one strong arm went around my shoulders.

"Do you think they took our p-picture?" I choked out.

He shook his head. "No. I didn't see a camera."

I could practically hear his questions in my head. The same ones from yesterday. Why was I terrified? Was I running?

Who'd hurt me?

"Willow, I can help. If you tell me what's wrong, I know I can." His voice was deep and full of promises I wished I could take him up on. I wanted to spill my guts, wanted to tell him everything, just so someone would actually know the truth of us…of me.

I dragged myself from him, stepping back. "I can't be seen with you, Lincoln."

His frown grew, and before I could help myself, I pushed at the little lines between his brows just like I did with Hector. I held my breath as our eyes locked. Then, I pulled my hand away, tucking it into a pocket so I wouldn't do it again.

"Who are you hiding from? What happened to you?" Lincoln persisted.

I shook my head, backing through the gate and shutting it so a physical barrier existed between us—one I desperately needed.

"Thank you for walking me home. I think we can say Poco isn't interested in me anymore, so we should be good from here." I kept my voice as firm as I could, given how shaky I felt.

"That car might have nothing to do with you, Willow. I had a run-in with some guy the other night. I think it was him."

That didn't help my anxiety at all. I couldn't afford to be the center of any kind of run-ins or controversy or attention. Not even positive. With people flocking into The Tea Spot, I'd already told Hector he'd have to say he'd made the treats and the display. I'd made it seem like I was just really embarrassed…shy…but Mom had been right. I couldn't risk some reporter, even our local one, putting my face out into the world. It was enough to know people were enjoying what I'd created. I didn't need more than that.

"Have you even told your mom about what happened?" he asked.

"Yes. She was grateful you walked with me, but we both knew it was just for a few days. Poco hasn't bothered me. We're in the clear," I repeated.

I wouldn't tell him Mom also thought we'd started some big romance. I'd have to tell her the truth about who Lincoln really was before she found out. And I would…after she got back from the decathlon with her students.

Lincoln searched my face with that soul-deep look that pulled back my layers.

I glanced away and then back, raising my chin. "I'm off until Sunday anyway. Mom will go with me in the morning to drop off the desserts at the café, and then, I'll be back here working on a new piece. I'm not going anywhere for the next couple of days."

One long finger ran along his brow before he dropped his hand to his side.

When he still didn't say anything, the air between us almost started to broil with all the mixed emotions we seemed so good at flinging at each other. I took a step backward and said, "Stop by The Tea Spot tomorrow. Hector will have a box for you."

He just watched me as I continued to move farther and farther away. The sadness on his face almost made me run back, grab his hand, and drag him into the house with me. But this wasn't my fairy tale. *He* couldn't be my fairy tale.

Before I could be tempted, I hurried the rest of the way to the cottage. I rushed inside and leaned up against the door, trying to calm my racing heart. Just as I got myself together enough to punch in the alarm code, my phone chimed.

Somehow, I already knew it would be from him.

> *LINCOLN: You don't know me well enough yet, Willow. But nothing will stop me from protecting the people I care about ever again. So, I'll see you Sunday morning at two-thirty, if not before.*

My stomach dipped and whooshed at the strength of his words. The quiet promise laid out in almost every syllable. It was so very wrong, and yet I couldn't help the thrill that traveled through me at the idea I was someone he cared about.

# Chapter Fifteen

# Lincoln



***JUST LIKE THE DAY BEFORE, AFTER*** dropping Willow off, I returned to the studio and the fantastical art I was knee-deep in creating. I started to fill in the image of Willow in the cemetery but stopped almost immediately because I couldn't quite see her expression yet. Maybe because I'd seen too many on her real face. Terror. Fear. Defiance. Courage. Joy.

Instead, I turned to a sketchbook, trying to capture even a handful of the other ideas that had swept through me during the day. A butterfly darting through the opening of a cave in a forest with a clawed hand reaching out to capture it. A woman blowing a kiss to a gnarled tree stump that morphed into a man. More images than I could keep up with.

When Sienna reappeared, and the floor-to-ceiling circular window behind her turned her translucent form into the fiery colors of the sunset, I started a drawing of her as well.

When she realized what I was sketching, she huffed at me, crossing her arms over her chest as she snarled, *This isn't about me, Lincoln. Go back to drawing her.*

"Stop haunting me, and I'll stop drawing you," I told her, but I put down the pad and pencil.

*Damn it!* She stomped, looking so real and alive it was hard to imagine her *not* actually being there. *What will it take for you to really let me go?*

How could I truly do so when I'd never paid the price the women in my life had? And yet, I was also tired of living in this shadowy in-between world. Alive and yet not. Moving forward and yet not. In a hopeful moment, I'd reached out to Felicity, the mirage of her beckoning to me before I'd seen the truth—she'd just been another tunnel to hell.

But Willow…she was a true light. Even with her secrets, even with whatever she was running from, she practically glowed with an inner goodness. I wanted to hold it, savor it, make it mine even if I wasn't sure I'd ever earn it.

I made my way down to the bathroom to wash my hands, and my stomach rumbled loudly. After eating a microwave breakfast sandwich this morning, I'd gone all day again without eating. Looking at my image in the wavy, antique glass above the pedestal sink, I saw the wear and tear on my face. The dark bruising under my eyes. The pallor of my skin. I was going down a path that never ended well and needed to be righted.

When I came out of the bathroom, Sienna was furiously pacing the loft. She twirled on me, looking decidedly ghostly as she shrieked, *There's nothing for you to earn! No price for you to pay! Stop feeling guilty for surviving!*

For the first time, she looked nothing like the girl I'd once loved more than my own life. She was much darker—Gothic and ghoulish almost—and her voice was shrill as she continued to yell. *I adored driving, you idiot! You know that. I loved putting my foot to the pedal and feeling the spin of the tires on the ground. The idea of going anywhere enticed me! Being in charge did even more. It felt like freedom to me. Like independence and power. So even if you didn't have the meds in you that night, I still would have taken the keys away. I still would have been in the driver's seat!*

My hand went to my brow. She'd said this before. It wasn't new, and deep in my core, I knew there was a truth to her words. From the moment we'd learned to drive, she'd wanted to be the one at the wheel. So why had I held on so tightly to the notion it should have been me who died?

*And the nonsense you feel over Lyrica? It makes me furious. She wanted you to be with my parents the night she was shot,* she snarled. *She knew it was important for you all to be together on the anniversary of my death. She didn't begrudge you that time with them.*

Before I could stop myself, I snapped back, "I'm the one who forgot the ice on my way out of town. She wouldn't have been in that damn convenience store if I'd done the one thing she'd asked me to do!"

*She doesn't blame you!*

I headed for the steps with my anger growing. At her. At myself. At fucking life.

I didn't want to be stuck in this cycle. I didn't want to have darkness always tugging me back into its haze any more than I wanted my insomnia to tug me awake. But sometimes you didn't get what you wanted. Sometimes you just did the best with the cards you were dealt.

*You let it go for a while,* Sienna said. *You let it go and had hope.*

After Leya had been kidnapped because some fanatic thought her brown skin didn't mix with my white, I'd had a moment where I'd realized I couldn't control the evil of the world. And the way Leya had found love and goodness while right smack dab in the middle of it all had given me hope that I, too, could find happiness, if I let myself.

Felicity had entered at exactly the right moment. But any peace I'd found had been gone in a flash. She hadn't dealt well with my insomnia, acting as if I had a choice about it and telling me to just take the damn sleeping pills. When I'd told her I couldn't, when I'd told her about the hallucinations and my fear Sienna would return to haunting me, she'd tossed that aside too. "Excuses," she'd said, giving me my first glimpse of the ugliness that existed behind her façade.

When I'd put the brakes on our relationship, she'd insisted on the trip to St. Micah to help us move past it even though she'd known I couldn't go. I'd finally convinced Leya into letting me show her art at the gallery, and the opening had been that week. But choosing Leya and her art over Felicity had simply tipped the scales more. She'd given me an ultimatum. Choose her, all in, a life together, or it was over.

How she'd expected me to show up on the island with an engagement ring in hand after that was beyond me. But it was what she'd leaked to the press—that I was proposing and that we might even elope. She'd made sure I'd seen the articles too, texting them to me with laughing emojis, thinking they'd pressure me into giving her a ring. Instead, it had strengthened my resolve to end it.

And when she came back from St. Micah, pleading for me to reconsider, I'd almost wavered until Hardy had told me what she'd been doing with my phone and my computers and the investigator.

*Don't let Felicity's ugliness hold you back, Lincoln. She was never worth it. But Willow, she can be the light guiding you home. She can burn away every dark spot until there are none left, if only you let yourself have it—if you can convince her she needs you as much as you need her.*

I whipped around to stare at what was left of the teen girl I'd once adored. The only girl whose finger I'd truly seen myself slipping an engagement ring on.

We glared at each other for a long moment, but I didn't respond.

Instead, I picked up the baseball cap from the window ledge where I'd left it and stepped out of the gallery, locking the door, and leaving Sienna behind.

The sun was gone, the twilight having taken over the town. Time for vampires and night creatures to creep from the shadows. I shook my head. No creatures here. No ghosts. Just my own damn conscience and too many days without food and rest.

Laughter and music spilled out on the street from the bar. Dancing with Willow earlier had lit me up from the inside out, made me crave losing myself in the movement of my feet and hips. But thoughts of entering that bar and dancing with a stranger didn't tempt me. It was only a moonlit-haired baker I wanted in my arms.

I turned the opposite direction, striding down the almost empty street toward the Chinese place and the takeout I'd never gotten the other night after the incident with the guy in the glasses.

My eyes scanned the cars parked nearby. No gray sedan with rusty hubcaps.

The car hadn't had a front license plate when it had zipped by Willow and me this afternoon, and the back plate had been covered in dirt. I had nothing to give Hardy. It had panicked Willow, but I'd told her I didn't believe it had anything to do with her or even with me being Lincoln Matherton. But it didn't mean it wasn't something that could become an issue.

More darkness drawn to me.

Would I forever be the demon in my painting, drawing someone like Willow into my lair, only to have her become the bloody leg sticking out of the bedsheets? Would I destroy her?

As I lifted a hand to open the restaurant door, a chill hit me. Eyes on me. And while I was accustomed to the feeling of being watched by my detail or the paparazzi or some everyday Joe staring at me with curiosity, this felt different. Heavier.

I did another scan of the street and saw nothing.

Maybe it was just Sienna's ghost glaring at me from the window of the gallery.

Fuck it all.

Let the eyes search and find.

Nothing to see here but a man ordering sweet and sour chicken.

If that seemed worthy of a photo, let them take it.

♫ ♫ ♫

My body woke, itching and scrambling for me to get out of bed when I'd barely been asleep for an hour. Lying there was useless and counterproductive. So, at barely eleven, I headed downstairs to the study. The first thing I did was check the security app I'd left open on the desktop. The front yard was cast deeply in shadows. The lantern-like streetlamps near the cemetery and farther past my neighbor's pushed dim, circular rays through the mist, but the light never quite reached my house.

The Pathfinder was parked out front of Willow's place. No sedan in sight.

I sat in the rolling office chair, hands on top of my head, looking out the multipaned window to the garden that had been shaped and molded by the landscaping company I'd hired. It was too neat. Too tidy. Willow's garden screamed of whimsical creatures dancing with tiny flutes and flitting wings. I wanted that. I wanted the magic of fairies and instead had brought the stiff formality of my family's home with me here.

Wasn't this move to Cherry Bay about finding something more? Something different?

Finding me.

I spun the chair around, taking in the bookshelves. Straight and neat. But the knickknacks peeking from the stacks of books hinted at the fantastic. Smiling Buddhas. A pewter dragon with its wings spread.

I rose, pulling down the art history books I'd kept from my college days and then some of the oversized coffee-table books filled with photography and art. I spread them out on all the available surfaces, flipping through them, stopping whenever an image somehow clicked inside me.

And when I stood back after hours of work and scanned across the open pages, I saw the beginnings of a theme. An extension of what I'd been drawing and painting for the last few days. Sienna's words about Willow's light burning away the dark were taunting me. But maybe we weren't supposed to exist without the dark. Maybe without it, we'd never see the light for what it was. We needed both in order to be whole. The yin and the yang. Just like it was possible that we needed a bit of make-believe, a little bit of magic, to exist alongside the reality so we could understand and appreciate both.

We needed to be reminded that heroism existed as well as

evil.

Maybe I was losing my hold.

It was just fanciful thinking to dwell on villains and heroes.

This wasn't a story or a dream. This was real life.

I inhaled sharply, taking a moment to catalog my physical and emotional state in an attempt to center myself. To pull myself back from the dark abyss that sleeplessness could send me spiraling into. The odd prickling sensation that always curved up my neck and scalp after days with little sleep mingled with a haze as real as the mist on the streets. Neither was ever a good sign for rational thinking. Add to it the anxiety that spiked every time I thought about seeing Sienna again and the incompetence I felt in protecting Willow, and the danger of paranoia stood just around the bend.

I'd be grasping for the brushes of reality before long.

And yet, when I looked back at the pages spread out around me, I still saw a fairy tale emerging. I sensed hope. New beginnings. Possibilities.

I forced myself away from the study, focused on the mundane aspects of fixing a tea concoction purported to soothe, and then returned to my bedroom. I took a shower and let the heat work its way into my bones as much as the tea. Only when weariness draped over me like a weighted blanket did I climb back into bed.

A pair of fairies with faces like Sienna and Willow danced into the midnight of my mind. Hair spun from the silk of moonbeams flew about them. Sky-colored eyes in different shades of blue and gray beckoned. One of them was all sassy, snapping, pounding feet, while the other was laughing, smiling, prancing leaps. Their own version of dark and light leading the way in different directions.

I didn't even realize my eyes had drooped, didn't even realize I'd actually slept, until my phone, singing out my sister's ringtone from the pocket of my jeans I'd dropped on the floor, woke me. I didn't have a clock on my bedside table, as it only added to the ants crawling through me when I woke in the middle of the night, but there was some light peeking through the blinds. A gray otherworldliness declaring the early morning.

I'd slept.

The music stopped and then started again, and I finally realized it wasn't Katerina's tone, but Juliette's. And because she rarely called, and especially not this early, I scrambled from bed to retrieve the phone.

"What's wrong?"

"Hey, good morning. Did I wake you?" Her question was soft and hid a hint of worry.

I'd never tell her she had when she hardly ever reached out.

"No," I lied, rubbing my jaw and feeling the hint of stubble I hadn't shaved in a few days. So unlike the neat-and-tidy Lincoln the world was used to seeing. "What's up?"

She hesitated, and that only increased my worry. "Nerdette, talk to me."

We went weeks, even months, without using any of our nicknames, and now I'd used both my sisters' in a matter of days. More things that screamed different since I'd moved. Since I'd let Cherry Bay and Willow slide under my defenses.

Juliette laughed, and it was as low and soft as her voice. She talked so quietly and moved with an almost uncanny stillness that had people missing her stubborn determination, especially when it was in contrast to Katerina's in-your-face energy. "Mom made me call. She says you've been dodging her."

I bit back my quick retort. "I haven't been ignoring her, or anyone else, any more than normal."

"How's the new house? The gallery?"

I frowned, picking up my jeans and heading for the closet.

"Since when are you the one to give me the third degree? Tell me why you really called."

"I do want to know how things are with you, but you're also right. I'm worried about Katerina."

I dropped the jeans in the hamper as the concern I'd felt

the last couple of times I'd talked to our sister hit me again.

"She has been acting weird," I said. "She insists she's just working too hard on this new film."

"I don't like the guy she's seeing."

"What? She has a boyfriend?"

Juliette let out an exasperated half-laugh. "I don't know that I'd call him a boyfriend. More like someone she's bang—"

"Stop. Stop right now. I don't want to know about either of your sex lives. I can't handle it. My little sisters will never have sex in my mind. End of story."

She laughed again, but then it died away. "He's creepy."

"Define creepy."

"I don't know how to explain it, Lincoln. That's just what I feel when he looks at me."

"When did you meet him?"

"When I flew out for the movie premiere in February."

"Who is he?"

"Some executive producer. A guy with power who knows he has it and likes to wield it," she said.

"That doesn't sound like someone Katerina would ever be interested in," I said honestly. Silence settled down between us. "Do you want me to have Hardy reach out to her detail? See what's going on?"

"No. She'd be pissed if we went around her like that."

She would. "Okay, then, we tag-team her. We schedule a time and call her together."

A door slammed in the background, and I could hear a voice telling Juliette she was needed. "We just had a three-car pile-up come in. I've gotta go. I'll text you later, and we can set up a time. Make sure you respond."

"I'll respond. I've been making a concerted effort to keep my phone with me." It was the truth, even if it was Willow's entrance into my life that had caused it and not the promises I'd made to my family.

After we hung up and I saw the time on the screen, I realized I'd gotten nearly five hours of sleep. For the first time in days, my body felt energized. Ready. Actually eating a full meal the night before had also helped.

I slid into a pair of basketball shorts and a T-shirt and headed for my home gym for the second day in a row. I'd work out, eat another breakfast sandwich, and then head to the gallery. I'd establish a new routine and shake the hallucinations that had taken hold. I'd throw off the dark trying to drag me down. If part of that routine just so happened to include walking a pale-eyed, moonlit-haired baker to work and back home, so be it.

Two hours later, I pulled up to the curb outside the gallery to find a large canvas wrapped in a tarp propped by the door and a dark-haired, fair-skinned woman pacing in front of it. As I slid out of the Range Rover, she looked over at me with brown eyes hooded by heavy brows.

"Trinity, I take it?"

She nodded. "Thanks again for seeing me."

I unlocked the door and punched in the alarm code while she drifted around, taking in the mostly empty gallery.

"It's a great space for art," she said in that same, oddly broken voice she'd had on the phone.

I nodded, lifting a chin to the painting she'd dragged in with her.

"If you don't mind…" She hesitated. "I'd like to set a couple of the pieces up before you see them."

"Sure. Take your time. I'll head upstairs to the studio. Just holler when you're ready."

"Thank you. Really."

"Don't thank me yet. I only promise to be honest." But I wouldn't be cruel. You didn't have to be cruel to deliver a critique. Some people didn't understand that, using harsh words that often destroyed a person's confidence more than not selling their work did. Although, both were still rejection, a kind of death to us creative types.

I made my way up to the third floor, leaving the door open so I'd hear Trinity when she called. After spending hours looking at the art books last night, I viewed my started pieces with a new, critical eye that could be both a hindrance and a blessing.

All the art I'd started still spoke to me. The play of darkness and lightness that existed in every corner of humanity was displayed on the canvas. The demon painting needed a partner piece. An angel. A hero. The duo would carry the same theme as the cemetery with the sharp shadows and Willow bringing the light. The yin and yang that had haunted my early morning frenzy in the office.

I itched to pick up my brush again but couldn't afford to get lost in it with Trinity downstairs.

When she called out a shaky, "I'm ready," I jogged down the stairs only to freeze once the art came into view. The center piece was larger than Trinity herself. I wasn't even sure how she'd gotten it into the room until I saw a kid with a backpack lingering outside.

All three pieces she'd arranged were…breathtaking.

Real and fantasy combined.

A castle was brushed along the middle canvas. The light from the breaking dawn was reflected in windows shimmering like jewels. The forest crept close. Briar vines and thorns dangled with flowers edging over the ground. The castle itself was stunning, the marble sparkling as if diamonds were embedded in the stones. But the brilliance of the castle wasn't the focus of the painting. Instead, it was the dragon curled around the top turret. I could almost see it breathing. Could almost smell the singed air as smoke drifted like fog from its nostrils. Could almost feel the slice of pain that would come from touching the cold scales gleaming with an iridescent light. It seemed real and yet completely magical at the same time.

The two canvases on either side showed the forest surrounding the castle. Dark trees and bright flowers. Cherry blossoms you could almost smell. And amongst the leaves and branches, peeking out, dancing and leaping toward the castle, was a menagerie of animals, fairies, and gnomes.

As if my thoughts in the middle of the night had made their way onto the canvas.

If Lyrica had told me what the subject of the paintings was when we'd talked, I would have laughed and told her no way. If I'd seen it on a website, I wouldn't have been much more inclined to reach out to the artist. In person, Trinity's art seemed real. As if I could literally step into the forest or reach out and touch the diamond-studded stones of the castle as the dragon roared above me, wings shifting the air as he lifted off, crumbling granite and wood beneath mighty claws.

Except, that didn't fit either because the dragon didn't look as if it was ready to destroy the castle. Instead, it looked like it was protecting it. A lover shielding their partner.

And that was when I saw it—a woman with dark hair and dark eyes and a look of ecstasy on her face reaching from one of the turret windows to stroke scaly skin.

It was exactly what I'd imagined last night.

Reality and magic.

Fantasy and truth.

Humanity. Imagination. Hope.

Love.

Lyrica was right, and so was Sienna.

Trinity was waiting for my reaction, chewing on her nails and pacing off to the side.

"It's perfect," I said with a grin.

Her eyes widened, her fingers dropped from her mouth, and she froze. "What?"

"First, the artistry is incredible. I don't even know how you did it, but the dragon's scales change colors as I move, and I swear I can smell the sulfur of his breath. And, Jesus, the castle itself. It's literally glowing."

"The first time I saw the castle, the painting popped into my head."

"Wait. This is a real castle? Where?"

Trinity laughed, and with her beat-up voice, it sounded weirdly off-kilter. "It's actually just down the road a bit. It's called River Briar, and I work for the catering company the owners use for all their events, so I'm there quite often."

"There's a fairy-tale castle here in Virginia?" I repeated, shock turning me stupid.

"Yep. Some recluse built it, and no one even knew it was there for a long time. But after his daughter inherited it, they started using it for weddings and charity events, that sort of thing."

"Do all your pieces have the castle in them?"

"No." She shook her head and tugged on her turtleneck. It was then that I saw the scars. Long streaks down her throat. She'd been hurt. Somehow. Someway. Another woman with wounds. I almost let out a dark laugh. Leave it to Sienna and Lyrica to bring me another person who'd suffered and needed looking after. Needed good in their lives.

It only made me think of Willow and whatever it was she was hiding from—whomever she was hiding from. My eyes darted out the window, but I couldn't see the café from this angle. She wasn't supposed to be there today. She was supposed to be tucked away in the cottage with her own bit of fairy-tale magic out front.

Trinity bent to a backpack that she'd left by the door and brought out a tablet. "It's not the same. I swear they look better in person, but…"

She handed me the device. It was open to a seascape with a mermaid peering over a modern-day sailor's shoulder as he drank from a mug that read, *Life is more than coffee, but coffee is life*. I swiped to the next image and saw a frog chasing after a little girl as if caught in a game of tag. The girl wore jeans and a Watery Reflection band T-shirt. Modern and yet a fairy tale. Another painting had a person with a backpack and sneakers walking along the forest floor while, in the treetops above, little lights waved, and I swore I could hear wee-folk pipes playing.

They weren't the same on the screen as they would be in real life, but if the paintings in front of me were anything to go by, the light would shimmer from all of them. The scents and sounds would almost twirl through the air. Trinity captured and used life and light in such a vivid way it was tantalizing.

It firmed up the ideas that had started to form last night. Her paintings were real life and fantasy twined together. Just like my own. Fairy tales in our modern world. Good and bad. The best and the worst. And in the end, the magic winning out.

"I definitely want to do a show," I told her.

Her eyes lit up, a brightness seeping through the dark clothes and the shadows that clung to her. "Really?"

"Really."

She squealed and jumped and spun around. She came at me, wrapping her arms around me and hugging me tight before dropping back and looking at me with startled eyes. "I'm so sorry. I don't know why—"

I waved her off. "Don't worry about it." I pointed down at the screen, which appeared to be just a normal beach. Water and sand and early morning dawn. "What's this one?"

She stepped closer, and we were head to head when I caught movement out of the side of my eye. When I lifted my gaze, I saw Willow framed in the doorway. Happiness instantly wove through me, and a sudden rush of air filled my lungs as if I'd been holding it ever since I'd last seen her.

I stepped toward her just as her eyes darted between Trinity and me. A look of surprise, and resignation, and maybe even sadness drifted over her, as if she thought there might be something between Trinity and me that didn't exist. The hug I'd shared with Trinity had been a connection born purely of art, whereas the strings binding me to Willow felt like a permanent part of my soul. And in that moment, I knew Sienna had been right. Willow was the light guiding me home. She'd be the beam that ensured I was never lost in the dark again.

# Chapter Sixteen

# Willow

**HAPPINESS**
Performed by The Fray

**MY MORNING HAD STARTED WITH A** joyfulness that had been contagious.

After Mom had taken me and the trays of miniature desserts to the café on her way out of town for the decathlon, Hector had walked her out to the car. Shay and I had given each other a high five. And when Hector had come back, beaming and doing a little two-step as he said he was practicing for his date with Mom, we'd hugged each other and did our own dance.

"What made you finally ask her out?" Shay had demanded.

"Did you see how beautiful she looked? How could I not?" His grin had slipped as his eyes met mine. "I should have asked you first."

I'd shaken my head. "Of course you shouldn't have! And I'm thrilled. Honestly. Shay and I have been plotting ways to force your hand for weeks."

He'd brushed a hand over his hair in an awkward and endearing way, but a customer asking him about the new desserts had let him escape without having to respond. The smile on his face had remained, leaving happiness in its wake.

Shay had given me another one-sided hug, done the same with her dad, and then left for school. Even though I technically wasn't working, I'd spent a few more minutes futzing with the desserts and listening to Hector's conversation about them while pleasure danced through me.

As I'd stood up from the case, I'd come eye to eye with Poco in a black jacket with a black beanie pulled low on his brow. The look on his face had been all smug satisfaction that had slithered along my spine.

"You lied to me, Willow," he'd said with a hint of anger mixing in with a sneer.

"And what exactly did I lie to you about?"

"You said you weren't dating, and yet it seems you've got a man trailing your every move."

"Other than you?"

That icky grin had grown, and he'd replied, "Always surprising what you find when you start pulling back someone's layers."

My breath had caught as my mind whirled with questions. *Had he found something out? About me? About my past?*

"I thought I'd get a glimpse of the wild in you once you were off your leash." His tone had been full of the same dirty innuendos it had held in the graveyard. His gaze had dropped to my mouth and lower to my breasts. When his look had made it back to my face, he'd licked his lips, and I hadn't been able to help the shudder that had gone through me. "Maybe I'll get to see you beg instead. People do all sorts of things when they're pushed up against a wall."

My body had frozen, feet melding with the tile floor, and blood had pounded in my ears.

*What does he know?*

But then, the truth had settled over me. He knew nothing. He couldn't. The Marshals had never lost a witness following protocol. Not once. And while we were no longer in active protection because the trial was over and done with, we were still following all their rules.

Poco had just been tossing out taunts because he was pissed Lincoln had saved me and had been there every time he'd whistled his stupid tune, attempting to frighten me. That knowledge had finally loosened the panic that had sealed my tongue and allowed me to respond, "You don't know me, but I can promise you'll never see me beg."

His laugh had been a dark one, scathing and harsh. Then, he'd narrowed his eyes and said, "Maybe, or maybe not. Either way, I'll get something more out of you yet."

He'd tapped his fingers on the counter and then sauntered out the door, leaving a trail of foreboding tripping along my veins.

And instead of running for home, instead of going to the place that had been safe for me for six years, I'd run here…to Lincoln. I'd seen his Range Rover parked outside the gallery when Mom had driven me to the café, and I'd reacted on instinct once Poco had left. My feet had led me straight to the gallery's door, looking for the comfort I'd felt every time Lincoln had been at my side since he'd rescued me in the cemetery.

But those notions of safety and comfort were as ridiculous as the jealousy that spiked through me the moment I stepped up to the gallery door and saw Lincoln hugging a woman. He had that wide grin on his face I'd stupidly thought he'd only sent in my direction. The one I'd thought I'd been responsible for bringing to his face.

But I had no right to the jealousy. No claim on him. The opposite was true. I needed to let him slide from my life entirely. I shouldn't have even been standing at his door.

I hesitated there for a moment too long, wavering between proceeding and retreating, while gripping the pink bakery box with the treats I'd promised him just a hair too tight. I should have left them at the café where I'd told him they'd be. I should have stuck to the decision I'd made not to see him again after our enchanting dance in the street had dissolved into a scare with the car zooming by us.

When Lincoln looked over at the door and saw me standing there, the smile on his face grew impossibly wider. It turned from something stunning into something out of this world. Magic and beauty twined. And I realized he hadn't given her *my* smile after all, hadn't even come close to giving it to her, because the one beaming from his face at that moment was the one I'd claimed.

His gaze shifted, taking me in, and I automatically felt that connection again, that pull, that zing of attraction and want and hope that traveled through me each time I was in his presence. I shouldn't have come, not because of my idiotic jealousy or because he'd been hugging a woman after flirting and dancing with me, but because I couldn't have him for all the reasons I'd already told myself.

Panic welled. A different kind than Poco had brought. This alarm was because I didn't trust myself anymore to give him up in order to protect my family.

"Just dropping off some desserts so you won't harass me anymore about not getting any." My words sounded stilted and tight, just like my body felt.

Lincoln took a step toward me, but I knew if he closed the distance completely—worse, if he touched me—I wouldn't walk away. I'd stay just to see if I could get another tantalizing dance. If I could get a hug. A kiss. Anything. Something. Simply more.

So, before he reached me, I set the box on the windowsill and backed out of the gallery. "I'll just get out of your hair. I hope you like them."

I spun around, heading down the sidewalk at a frantic pace.

"Willow, wait!" Lincoln called from behind me.

But I didn't. I couldn't. If I did, who knew what might happen.

Mom was finally happy again. I was happy again. I couldn't ruin that.

I'd thought it had been Poco who'd ruined the joy of our morning, but I could ruin it even more.

I was already near the corner of our street before the memory of the look Poco had given me made my feet slow to a more reasonable pace. I made myself take a deep breath in and out and look around. I couldn't be running headfirst anywhere right now. I had to keep my wits about me, especially with

Poco's half-assed threats hanging over me.

I'd made it to our street when the sound of a meaty engine made my pulse leap, and with a hand jumping to my cat-eared key chain, I turned to see Lincoln's Range Rover whip toward me. My feet stalled as he pulled up to the curb. He swung the door open, stepped out, and thundered, "You're by yourself. You said you wouldn't be alone today!"

The accusation wound through the air, but it was full of a concern that had my insides fluttering for all those same wrong reasons. "I told you Mom was driving me to the café, and she did."

"She's not here now," he growled.

I blew out a frustrated breath—at myself and at him. "It's the middle of the day. I'm walking a couple of blocks. I'm fine. Go back to the gallery and whatever you were doing there."

He stared at me for a moment, brows burrowing together. "Whatever I was doing there. Wait. Were you jealous?"

I had been. For a brief moment. But it wasn't why I'd left. "No."

He closed the distance between us, hand going to my chin and forcing me to meet his gaze.

"Little liar." The tone was soft, sensual, daring me to deny it again. The simple touch of his fingers had those flames licking through me again. Heat pooling deep in my belly.

I wanted to kiss him. Yearned for it with every nerve ending in my body in a way I'd never yearned to kiss anyone. Not like this. Not with an overpowering need that had me forgetting everything else. Had me forgetting Mom, and her safety, and the promises I'd made in the dead of night that she'd only be happy from now on.

"Try again." His voice was all sexy command, the syllables sliding over me like a soft caress.

I couldn't talk. Not when his touch was lighting me up like sparklers that had sat on a shelf too long and were now in danger of exploding.

When I didn't say anything, he filled the void, a tiredness

entering his voice that instantly made me want to fix it. "I'm used to the media making assumptions about me, Sweetness. But my friends, the people I care about…they know to ask before they assume."

My hand went to his wrist, intending to push him away, but the smooth caress of his thumb along my jaw had me stilling. Aching. Wanting him and all the beauty that could come with it.

I closed my eyes as pain ratcheted through me.

I couldn't have it.

None of it.

The banging of my heart was so strong, so loud, I wondered if he could hear it…feel it. His gentle caress continued for several long swipes, and then he was cupping my face with both hands. Tender strokes of skin against skin. I'd never known it could feel like this when two people touched. Like they were slowly blending together, fusing like a flambé melting sugar into something new. Something smoky and rich and vibrant.

That thought brought reality crashing in.

I really was ridiculous if I was equating his touch to flambé.

I stepped back, and I thought I saw disappointment course over his face before it disappeared. Or maybe it was me who was disappointed. In myself. In him for letting me go.

I spun around, heading for our gate, full of conflicting emotions as Lincoln followed me.

Every single one of those tantalizing and confusing feelings disappeared when I reached our front step. Shock and fear took its place as I stared at the piece of butcher paper taped to our door. Dark-red paint dripped down from the words scrawled over it.

*You don't deserve a fairy-tale ending.*

Just as my knees buckled, warm arms surrounded me, stopping me from hitting the ground. Every emotion from the last few days collided together, the roller coaster of desire and regret and panic and terror finally allowing the tears I'd refused for so long to surface.

Was this Poco? His little threat from this morning delivered with more force?

Or had the Viceroys finally found me?

We were supposed to be safe! God. Mom! I had to call Mom.

We'd have to call Deputy Marshal James.

Her date with Hector would be a thing of the past.

A sob ripped out of me.

I didn't want us to lose everything we'd built, but even more, I didn't want evil to find me again. I knew what it did. I'd seen it firsthand.

Without thought, I turned into the warmth and comfort of Lincoln's embrace. I pressed my face into his chest. The rich anise and clove scent of him and the soft cotton of his sweater was the balm my soul needed. He squeezed me to him, chin resting on the top of my head, murmuring words I couldn't hear because of the blood pounding in my ears.

I wasn't sure how long we stood like that, with him soothing and me trying hard not to throw up. But finally, the sounds of the birds and the buzz of the bees filtered in past the blinding alarm.

And with the fading fear came anger. I was so tired of suffering because of other people's messed-up souls and whatever darkness drove them. Tired of being forced to hide. Tired of not being able to have who I wanted and do what I desired without wondering if it would let some asshole win.

I jerked out of Lincoln's embrace and ripped the paper from the door. I stuffed my key in the lock, twisted it open, and slammed my way inside.

Lincoln caught my arm. "You shouldn't have touched it. There could be prints. And you need someone to clear your house before you go in farther."

The alarm beeped incessantly. I flung off his arm, stalked over to the box, and jammed in my code.

I brushed at the tears that had defied my attempt to stem them. "No one is here."

I crumpled the paper and tossed it on a side table. Lincoln shut the door behind us as I threw my bag on the couch.

"Call the police, Willow."

Not the police. The Marshals. I knew I needed to, but every part of me was still revolting at the idea. Those stupid, silent tears leaked from my eyes once more, chasing each other down my face and dripping off my chin. I sank onto the couch while Lincoln watched. His silence was a wall of indecision, frustration, and sadness that I could practically feel touching me.

Finally, he moved to sit next to me, pulling me up against him. I let him, easing myself into the warmth of him and tilting my head onto his shoulder. I'd known the man mere days, and yet he felt like…safety. Like home.

Until I remembered who he was.

Until I remembered the ugliness peeking at the shadows of our life wasn't something that should darken the door of the president's son.

Until I remembered that one photograph with him could lead the Viceroys to us.

Is that what had happened? Had someone taken a picture while we'd danced on the street? The person in the car? Some college student who'd seen us together at the café?

And still, I didn't move away from him. I let his warmth and kindness hold me up for a few more seconds.

"Tell me what's going on. Believe it or not, I really do know people who can help." He said it in a self-deprecating way that broke through my anger and fear enough to make my lips quiver upward momentarily.

God, I wished it was that simple.

I pushed away from him, hoping the space would help me remember all the reasons telling him the truth was a bad idea.

"Just tell me."

It was the raw plea in his voice that did me in.

"We're not supposed to tell anyone. Not anyone. Not even boyfriends or future husbands or kids. Because if any of those relationships go sour, they could 'out' us in spite. But I don't know that it matters now. Whether this was Poco or if they've found us, the Marshals will still want us to move. We'll have to start over again."

The words burst from me fast and furious before trailing away at the end. I watched as his eyes widened in shock. Then, he said, "You're in witness protection?"

I nodded. "If we move, I won't be able to bake professionally, as it would tie me to who I am now. Mom will lose the second career she's worked hard to build. She just agreed to a date with Hector after years of being on her own…"

My voice cracked, and Lincoln reached for my arm, pulling me into him once more.

"That's why you wouldn't tell the police about Poco. You were afraid the Marshals would catch wind and want to relocate you."

"If it was just Poco being overly aggressive, I could handle it, but if it's…"

Lincoln rubbed my back, a soothing gesture.

I took in a deep breath and said, "Poco came into the coffee shop this morning. He thought…" It was embarrassment that had my words fading away this time. Saying out loud what Poco thought made it seem like I thought it too.

"He thought what?"

"He thought I'd lied about not wanting to date anyone. He was angry because he thought you and I were together, and he said…he said he'd make me beg…and that he'd get something else out of me."

Goosebumps broke out simply remembering his words and the look that had accompanied them. Lincoln's eyes darkened, fury radiating from him. He shoved up from the couch to pace in front of me. His warmth slowly bled away, leaving me trembling from head to toe. Not quite as bad as I had been that awful night in Chicago. My entire body had hurt from shaking that night. This time, when those dark memories threatened to overtake me, it was almost impossible to keep them at bay.

"Let's check both our security systems. We might catch Poco at work. If it's him, I have a few friends who can stop him from coming at you again without telling the Marshals."

"Isn't that, like…misuse of federal resources or something?" I said, giving him a watery smile.

"First, you're a citizen needing protection, so I don't believe so, but I wasn't talking about the government. I have friends who can hook us up with private security." He stopped his furious pacing in front of me. "You have the alarm app on your phone?"

I nodded, digging through my bag until I found it buried at the bottom. Lincoln squatted in front of me, watching as I found and opened the app and ran backward through the morning. Only minutes after Mom and I had pulled out of the driveway, a person in a ski mask showed up. Flat chested, muscled arms, a square body. Every inch of him was covered in black from the mask on his head to the boots on his feet. Even his gloves were black. As if aware of the cameras, he kept his face turned down and away.

It could have been anyone at that door.

It could have been Poco, as he'd been wearing black this morning, and the person at the door was shorter than Lincoln, but nothing on the video really revealed who the person was. Neither the police nor the Marshals would be able to do much with this.

I had to call Mom. I had to make sure she hadn't been followed. I had to make sure she was safe. And she needed to hear this from me before she saw it on the app. She'd leave the decathlon, and that made me sad for her and the kids who'd worked so hard for an entire school year, earning their spot at the state competition. She'd have to wait for another adult to get there, but she would leave. If push came to shove, she might even leave them alone in order to get to me.

But what if this was really just Poco? He'd just given me those weird, vague threats. It seemed much more likely to be him than the Viceroys. As the first wild edge of panic left and reason started to take over, I knew it couldn't be the Viceroys. It couldn't. The Marshals would know if Aaron Vitale had left Chicago. They'd know if he'd sent any of his men after me. Wouldn't they?

I'd just call Deputy Marshal James to check. I'd call Mom to make sure she was okay and that she hadn't been followed. Once they confirmed what I already knew, I could decide what to do about Poco trying to frighten me.

I hesitated for two seconds, saved the video to my phone, and then deleted it from the security app. I wasn't stupid enough to erase it without backing it up. I knew we might need it, but this way I could tell Mom in my own way and on my own time table.

"I don't think you should stay here. Let's go across the street and have a look at my cameras. Then, we can decide who to call," Lincoln suggested.

I met his concerned gaze with a much calmer one. "What's the point of looking at your cameras? No one is going to be able to tell who this is. And since they wore gloves, there isn't going to be any prints either."

"First, whoever this is may not realize I had cameras directed at your house, and they could have taken the ski mask off as soon as they left your yard so as not to draw attention to themselves on the street. Second, they may have worn gloves while sticking the note to your door, but they may not have worn them while writing it. So there may be prints. And if there isn't, just the paper and ink might be able to tell us something."

He waited for me at the door, and my old fear about leaving the house hit me in the stomach. It had taken me weeks before I'd been able to leave the hotel we'd been moved to while the Marshals disbanded our lives in Chicago. Once I'd gotten to Cherry Bay, staying at the cottage while I'd finished high school online hadn't been a problem. Leaving had been. Mom had encouraged me step by step, first with work on the garden and then with shopping for ingredients to make some of the recipes from the food shows and videos I'd been watching. Short trips blended into longer trips until I'd been able to enroll in classes at Bonnin and leave for hours at a time.

Lincoln held out his hand. "I've got you."

The statement was sure and strong, just like him. But still, doubts plagued me. Could he really keep me safe? Could anyone? Didn't I know personally just how easy it was to break into a house? A single gunshot could dismantle a lock. A second gunshot could disable you before you had time to move. Would that happen again? To me? To Lincoln?

My throat seemed to close.

"Willow. I promise. No one is going to hurt you while we cross the street, and I'm not leaving you here alone."

It was the absolute resolve in his tone as much as the words themselves that allowed me to breathe again. That had me reaching out a trembling hand to take his. His grip was firm. Sure. Warm. His eyes were full of compassion. As we went by, I grabbed my keys from where they'd landed next to the balled-up paper on the side table. I shuddered just looking at it, but Lincoln picked it up with two fingers.

I armed the system and locked the door all while Lincoln held my hand. His thumb rubbed along my skin. Reassuring and also terrifying in its own way. That soul-stealing attraction humming even now with evil tapping on my shoulder once again.

Across the street and through his door, he repeated the process in reverse, disarming his system in a grand entryway full of shimmering, incandescent surfaces. I barely had time to take it in before he led me into a bright office done in beautiful shades of blue and white and silver. He flicked a light switch, and an antique chandelier sparkled to life, leaving patches of rainbow confetti along the surface.

As Lincoln left me and walked over to his desk, the cold pushed at me. It let in the darkness and memories that tried to pull me into the shadows.

I concentrated on the room instead. The walls were lined with antique white shelves, and while all of them had books and knickknacks on them, it wasn't crowded, leaving room for new additions. The office was calm and soothing just like Lincoln himself. It fit him. When I'd seen the bright-yellow kitchen, I'd wondered if the rest of the house would be as forcibly cheerful as that singular room, pushing at the shadows Lincoln had clinging to him, but I didn't see that forced brightness here. Only serenity.

Lincoln opened his laptop, clicked through some screens, and then shook his head, face grim with frustration. "He must have hopped a wall before he got to your gate, because there's nothing here."

Dread filled my stomach.

If we'd had video proof it was Poco, it would have been so much simpler. Even though I still believed it had to be him, I'd make the calls I needed to make. Once I confirmed with the Marshals that the Viceroys couldn't be here, and once I'd confirmed with Mom that she was okay, I'd tell her about the note and our suspicions about Poco. I'd reassure her I was okay and tell her I was with our neighbor.

Maybe just that would ease her concerns. She'd be happy I was with someone, wouldn't she? She'd told me she wanted me to have someone in my life, just like I wanted her to have Hector. She'd be thrilled as long as she didn't know who Lincoln *really* was. How just his name could shred our safety even more. But maybe if I could keep her at the decathlon and I had time to figure this out before she came home, I wouldn't have to rip her life away all over again.

# Chapter Seventeen

## Lincoln

**COLLIDE**
Performed by Howie Day

*I WAS TRYING HARD TO CONTAIN* my rage, not only at whoever had left the note on Willow's door in blood red but at her being in witness protection to begin with. The fear in her voice when she'd talked about "them" finding her had sent waves of fury through me. The loss I'd heard in her voice at the idea of having to give up everything in her life to relocate again felt like a physical stab to my heart.

While I didn't normally consider myself a violent man, I'd felt this same way before. First, for the truck driver who'd killed Sienna, then the kid who'd shot Lyrica, and finally, at the woman who'd kidnapped Leya. Every time those horrible tragedies had occurred in my life, I'd felt this same helpless rage. This same desire to do damage to the person who'd hurt the ones I'd cared about.

Maybe a man could only take so much of living with those emotions before they burst free. I wanted to drive down to Flat Mike's bar, put my hands around Poco's throat, and squeeze until no breath was left in his body. But I'd promised Hardy I wouldn't do something stupid, and there wasn't anything stupider than thinking I'd get that close to Poco in a bar full of bikers and criminals. He may have been nothing more than a local thug, but that didn't mean he wouldn't have a gun. That all his pals and his boss wouldn't have a dozen between them.

What did I have? A pocket knife from my grandfather and a childhood spent learning martial arts. While I could defend myself in a physical fight, I wouldn't be able to ward off bullets. I wouldn't be able to stop an entire biker gang.

But I had something else that might help. I had people I could send to talk to Poco if Willow would let me. If not official Secret Service agents, I could ask Leya's husband to give me the name of the security team Leya's band used.

When I glanced up from my laptop, I noticed how pale Willow was, her naturally creamy skin taking on the same hue as the apparition who'd returned to haunting me. She kept tugging at her necklace as if it was a life preserver. She was terrified and trying to hold it together. The tears had stopped, but I could feel her uncertainty and sadness from across the room. My body practically vibrated with the intensity of the rage I felt for whoever had done this to her.

I relived our moments together over the last two days. She'd been courageous. Optimistic. She hadn't cried after Poco had tried to haul her away that night. And yet, she'd almost fallen apart on seeing that damn note pinned to her door.

The letter. It needed to be examined. I had to get it to someone—Hardy, the police, anyone with a lab at their disposal. Would she let me?

I reached her in two strides, pulling her close once more, trying to let the touch calm us both. Her fear. My fury. The complete and utter frustration I felt at being, once again, too late to stop something already heading toward another woman in my life.

But I swore it wouldn't reach her.

Whatever evil this was…Poco, whoever "they" were…they would *not* reach her.

I would stop this.

"We need a plan," I told her softly. "Let me make you a cup of tea, and we'll decide on a course of action."

I tucked her hand into mine, the fragility of those fine bones landing home, especially given what I'd learned about her. And yet, at the same time, they felt strong as her fingers squeezed me back. It was a dichotomy I'd sensed in Willow from the moment I'd sped across the cemetery and heard her demanding Poco let her go. Brave and delicate at the same time.

We made our way into the kitchen, and when I let go of her to fill the electric tea kettle, I felt the loss in every part of me. I gathered the mugs and went about pouring loose leaf into the strainers as I had the first time she'd been in my kitchen.

Sienna had said Willow was my person. The light guiding me home. I could easily believe it when she practically glowed. But Sienna had also said that while we needed each other, I'd have to convince Willow she needed me as much as the other way around.

How did I do that? How did I convince someone I'd known for mere days that I could be what they needed? That these intense feelings I had were much more than attraction? If Sienna was right, and my soul was whispering something I needed to pay attention to, then I needed to get my act together now before Willow slipped through my grasp—before some damn agency hid her away from me.

Reality hit me with the force of a dagger to my chest.

She was in witness protection. It was so much worse than just her hiding from some guy who'd been abusive. The skittishness about being seen together was more than justified. The idea of exploring these intense feelings and desires and connection was asinine. Because what would happen when she was photographed at my side? It was a foregone conclusion she would be if we continued to see each other.

A heaviness settled over my chest, sliding down into my gut.

While we waited for the kettle, I asked, "Can you tell me what happened? Why you're in the protection program?"

She ran a finger along the smooth granite island, rotating the barstool side to side as she swung her body back and forth. I tried not to take it personally when she didn't immediately launch into the story. She had to be fighting years of being told *not* to speak the truth. I knew what it felt like to hold back secrets. I'd spent a lifetime keeping mine.

Maybe she simply needed proof I had as much to lose as her. Proof that I'd share my secrets as she shared hers.

After I poured the water over the strainers into the cups, I brought them to the island and sat next to her. "I was diagnosed with idiopathic insomnia when I was eight."

She looked up from her tea, surprise in her eyes.

"No one really knows that except my immediate family," and Felicity, but I didn't let that thought derail me. "They thought I had ADHD or some other disorder because I couldn't sleep. I went through a bunch of doctors and therapists before they realized it was child-onset insomnia. I was in my teens before they decided to try drugs."

"Why are you…?" she started and then settled her gaze on me. "Thank you for trusting me."

I ached to pull her to me again and made do with brushing a hand over her cheek before retreating and continuing my story. "Because of the drugs the doctors had me on, I wasn't allowed to drive. So, it was my girlfriend, Sienna, who was in the driver's seat on prom night. We'd left the limo and our friends behind at a party and headed to her grandparents' cabin. On our way, a night shift road worker crossed the double yellow and wiped out the driver's side of the car. My car. That she was driving because I was on too many drugs to get behind the wheel."

"Lincoln..." The empathy, the pure sadness in Willow's voice, didn't make me cringe as it normally did when talking about that night.

As if talking about her had beckoned her from the beyond, Sienna appeared on the far side of the kitchen with a raised brow. I heard her voice in my head all over again, telling me how she'd wanted to drive, how it wouldn't have mattered if I'd had the drugs in me or not.

I turned back to Willow, continuing the story I rarely discussed with anyone. "By that time, my dad had already made his fair share of enemies on the Hill, people who wanted to discredit him so he wouldn't get reelected as senator and definitely wouldn't make a run at the presidency, which everyone knew was his ultimate goal. So, someone dropped it to the press that I was drinking and driving and that my family was lying when they said I wasn't at the wheel. Even though every single police report showed I couldn't have survived if I'd been in the driver's seat. But it was where I should have been." I choked on the last couple of words. I shook my head, took a sip of tea, and tried to loosen the tightness in my shoulders that came whenever I talked about it.

I ignored Sienna as she shot me an annoyed glare.

Normally, the depth of the guilt eating at me when I thought or discussed that night would leave the taste of metal and blood in my mouth. But today, the scent of Willow, her sugary essence, was pushing it back. The load I carried seemed lighter, as if in unburdening it now so Willow would feel safe to share her own heavy weight made it less about me and more about the *us* I could almost visualize shimmering in our tomorrows.

I put my mug down, drew her hands into mine, and held tight. I met those gray eyes with honesty. "My point is, I know about secrets and keeping things hidden. I've lived my life as the son of a politician. We don't share our dirty laundry no matter how angry or ugly things get with someone. You can talk to me. I need you to talk to me so I can figure out a way to help you. And, for what it's worth, I think you need to talk about it. I think you need to give that secret to someone you can trust."

Her eyes scoured my face in silence, assessing and debating, but I never looked away, not even when I saw Sienna fading away out of the corner of my eye. I let Willow see whatever she needed to in my gaze. My honesty. My desperate hope she'd open up and share her story.

"It's not logical, but I do trust you," she finally whispered.

My lips curved upward just enough to be considered a grin. "Yeah?"

She leaned in, brushing at the damn lock of hair forever falling into my face. While I normally cussed out that wayward strand, her fingertips coasting along my forehead had me suddenly grateful for it, relishing the way her skin skimmed over mine. I ached to have her. Not just physically—although that need was coursing through me with such power it was almost embarrassing. I ached to have her soul tucked up against mine. All her secrets. All her dreams. All her laughter and delight. No one had made me *want* this badly. Not even Sienna.

Willow pulled back, and I snagged her hands again. She stared at our tangled fingers for a moment before finally giving me a piece of her story. "I recognized the insomnia in you. My dad…he had fatal familial insomnia. Do you know what it is?"

That was the last thing I'd expected her to start with. I nodded, knowing what it was from the tests done on me as a child. My mouth went dry, and the tightness in my chest grew. Did that mean Willow had it as well?

As if reading my thoughts, she said, "We don't know if I have it. My dad had barely been diagnosed with it, maybe eight months, before he was killed, and the only labs that can do the testing are in California. It was too expensive at first, and then, after everything went down, the Marshals said I couldn't be tested because the defense knew my dad had it. So, if I was positive for the mutated gene, they'd be able to find me just by searching for people being treated for it."

Dozens of questions popped into my mind about her, about FFI, and about her family, but the one I got out was the one that had the threat showing up on her doorstep. "You're in witness protection because of something that happened to your dad?"

She nodded, pulling away, grabbing the mug, and sipping. "The disease had progressed far enough that he'd lost his job at the 9-1-1 center. He kept forgetting things mid-call, and he'd lost his cool a few times with callers. He was becoming angrier every day, but he was also terrified he might have passed the FFI to me. When the nights got too long, and the emotions heavy, he'd go for a walk.

"Mom worked nights as a neonatal nurse at the hospital. So, often, it was just Dad and me at home in the evenings. With the speed at which he was losing his memory, I was uncomfortable letting him go out alone, but Mom said to leave him be. It was one thing he still had a choice about when so many of his choices had been taken away. We always made sure he took his phone, and he had a cane we'd had our address engraved into, so if he couldn't find his way on his own, someone could help him.

"One night, while out, he passed an alley where a woman was being attacked. Two men, both in ski masks…"

Willow swallowed, fear trembling through her as she looked in the direction of her house. I imagined her mind had gone right to where mine had when she'd mentioned the masks—to the man at her door in the video.

Damn.

"They had her on the ground… They'd…you know." She blew out a breath. "From what we could tell, they didn't hear Dad coming. Didn't even know he was there until he'd smacked one of them on the head with his cane. Even with all he was going through, my dad was a big, strong guy, so the first one went down. But the second one pulled his gun before my dad could get close enough. First, he shot the woman…Mary. Her name was Mary."

I squeezed her knee while she got ahold of herself.

"Dad ran. We don't know if he forgot he had his phone or just didn't remember he could call 9-1-1. The only thing we know for certain is that he ran home. He must have thought he'd lost them when he got to our street and they weren't behind him. But he'd also dropped the cane back in the alley with our address carved right into it."

Willow shook her head, pressed her hand to her chest, and then got up. She put her cup in the sink and stared out at the cemetery. I wasn't sure what to do. Go to her. Stay. Let her finish. Make her stop.

"The sad thing is," she said as she turned, leaning on the counter with a look of true grief in her eyes, "if they'd waited a few days, Dad likely wouldn't have remembered what had happened. And he could never have testified. The defense would have made mincemeat out of his disease and his bad memory."

Tears flooded her eyes, and I couldn't stop myself any longer. I went to her, pulling her into me, trying to give whatever comfort I could.

"He came into the house, screaming for me. I was in bed, but I was awake because it was hard for me to sleep until he got home. When I hit the hallway, he was frantic, eyes wild. I could barely understand what he was saying. Babbling about the attack and them chasing him, screaming at me to hide. At first, I thought it was just him losing it a bit more. There'd been a couple of incidents when he'd been violent without understanding it. So, when he shoved me into the coat closet near the door, my first instincts were to calm him down and call Mom. I'd just started to push the closet door open to try and talk him down when the first bullet hit. They shot out the lock and then slammed into the house."

She took a deep breath, arms reaching around me, fisting my sweater at the back. Her forehead rested against my chest.

"Danny Vitale emptied a clip in him. Through the crack in the closet door, I saw every single one of the bullets hit him. Saw…"

She didn't sob. She didn't cry, but I could feel the tension in her body as she relived it. I understood and wished I could take away the pain. But it was impossible. The moment I'd come to after the crash and seen the gaping hole in the back of Sienna's head had never gone away. It would never go away.

Willow trembled but kept going with the story. "They must have thought Dad was alone, because they weren't wearing their masks anymore, and when Danny turned to talk to his brother, I saw his face—the scar on his cheek and the terrifying satisfaction in his brown eyes. He was high on drugs for sure, but I think he was higher on what he'd done… I was petrified he'd see me peeking out. I didn't breathe. I didn't move."

She paused to collect herself, but I felt the tremor that went through her as she held on.

"I thought for sure I'd be next. Then, as if he'd heard or seen something, he took a step toward the closet just as his brother stepped farther into the room where I could see him too. I knew Roci from high school. He was in my PE class."

She squeezed me tighter again and then looked up. "My

phone started vibrating in my pocket. I didn't know it, but Dad had called Mom as he'd run home, and she was trying to get ahold of one of us. The noise…" She shook her head. "They both turned toward me just as the first sirens could be heard. I dropped to the ground seconds before Roci emptied his clip into the closet door. The only thing that saved my life was this set of old speakers my dad had been meaning to take to the recycling center."

Absolute fury rolled through me, mixing with her fear. It bled from her to me until I could almost imagine being there, huddled on the floor of a closet as bullets rained around me. *Fuck.* "As the sirens got closer, they ran, jumping into their truck and roaring off. As soon as they were gone, I flew out of the closet and tried to save Dad." Willow let go of me and looked down at her hands as if they were covered with his blood. "But I couldn't save him. There were too many holes."

I brushed a long strand of moonlight behind her ear, and she looked up at me with eyes that were seeing the past rather than my sunny kitchen. I wanted her here, in the present, where nothing could touch her, but instead, I let her finish. I let her purge it from her soul so it wouldn't continue to fester.

"The first day I went back to school, I was beat up by one of the Viceroys' girlfriends. I was told if I testified, I'd be as dead as my dad. We got death threats every day. In the mail. On our computers. Even text messages on our phones after we changed our numbers. They seemed to find us everywhere we stayed, even when we were at our friends' and coworkers' houses. They even found us when we stayed in hotels. That was when the Marshals got involved. For the first year or so, the Viceroys didn't give up, trying everything they could to find me. The Marshals kept us abreast of each effort. The Viceroys hurt people we knew, people Mom worked with.

"They were only kids, seventeen and nineteen years old, but the Viceroys have serious clout amongst the gangs in Chicago. They'd moved up the criminal food chain, bordering on mafia status, while not a single charge had stuck to any member of the group before then. Their brother, Aaron, was a criminal defense attorney, so everyone assumed they had police officers, administrators, and judges in their pockets. But because of me, because I saw them, the authorities got a warrant that allowed them not only to bring Danny and Roci in but also gave them access to locations the police had never entered before. They collected evidence on a host of other illegal activities that they used to make even more arrests and put additional Viceroys in jail.

"Everything hinged on Dad's case. If the prosecution couldn't get the murder charges to stick, or if the original warrant was thrown out, everything they'd found when they'd taken Danny and Roci into custody would be inadmissible. I became the cornerstone of not just the murder case but all those other cases."

My stomach bottomed out.

"When did this all happen?" I asked. "You said you were in high school?"

"Six years ago. I'd just turned seventeen."

"They're behind bars now, right? It's over?" I asked.

She nodded. "It took four years to bring them to trial."

"Four years!" Disgust wound through me. "You've got to be kidding!"

"Chicago has the worst arrest-to-trial rate in the United States, and Aaron made appeal after appeal, trying to get my statement, the warrant, and any evidence thrown out. The prosecutor told us they suspected Aaron was actually the head of the Viceroys, but no one could prove it. His role in the case and the people he bribed were how they got so much information about me. About us.

"For the first two years, I was terrified I'd walk out the door to find a gun in my face. But slowly, after we were here a while and nothing came for us, I started to breathe easier. The Marshals have never lost anyone in active protection. Not a single person in their custody who followed the protocols has been hurt, and that helped. Still helps. When I finally got to testify, when the jury came back with the guilty verdict, the relief I felt..." She paused, head tilted, brows burrowed. "I thought maybe it was over. But Aaron turned and looked at me that day, and there was so much hatred in his eyes. I knew he still wanted me dead."

"You're afraid this is him? Out for revenge?" I asked, acid burning through my insides at the mere idea. Willow moved restlessly through my kitchen, touching things, righting things, running a finger over the ivy I'd painted along the cabinets.

"No... Maybe. We got news this week that Roci was stabbed in prison. He died. So maybe Aaron blames me for that too. But I keep reminding myself that we've done nothing to blow our cover. The Marshals won't let the Vitales find us. That's why the note has to have been from Poco. No one else can find me."

She was trying to convince herself as much as me that it was true. The protective instincts that had flared to life from the moment I'd met her raged even stronger until they were a burning inferno.

My dad had plenty of hate groups who'd like to see him dead, but I'd never had one personally hunting me down. Who'd be happy to see my blood splattered. I just knew what it was like to want to switch places with the ones who'd died.

The fact Willow had built a life for herself here, the fact she could smile and create food and art and laugh and joke, was nothing short of a miracle. It made her courageous in ways I couldn't begin to name.

It made me want to give her a host of new memories so they would bury the dark, ugly ones under an avalanche of beautiful, happy ones.

# Chapter Eighteen

## Willow

**_LOVE WINS_**

Performed by Carrie Underwood


**_AFTER YEARS OF SAYING NOTHING, TALKING_** about that night and what had happened afterward broke open a scab that had barely healed. I saw Dad's bloody, mangled body again. I saw the evil pouring from Danny's and Roci's eyes. It made it feel like that evil could find me simply because I'd spoken the words aloud.

After being on the witness stand, I thought I'd never talk about what had happened ever again. I couldn't even tell a therapist about it. But now, having told Lincoln, it was as if one weight had been lifted while another had been added. I'd shared my burden, but now he was tied up in it too. I'd put him at risk in order to lighten my own load.

My jaw clenched tight as I saw the worry creasing his brows. I'd wanted so badly to turn his scowls into smiles, and now I'd done the opposite. Brought more grief.

I inhaled deeply, trying to push back the ugly memories enough to offer some reassurance. "I believe it's Poco rather than the Viceroys because Aaron isn't the kind to give a warning shot. He'd just send his men in, guns blazing to end me and whoever was with me. My mom…you…"

His eyebrows raised. "You're worried about me? After all that?" Then realization seemed to hit him. "The other day, when you said you were worried I'd get hurt, it had nothing to do with Poco or even really who I am. It's because you're afraid they'll come after me too."

It wasn't a question because he knew it was true. The risk was just too great for all of us.

I wanted him so much it was its own kind of torture. It wasn't just about looking for love and happiness, or marking off a few more experiences in my journal, or finding someone who would love me enough to not care about the risk of my having a fatal health condition. This was about Lincoln. About wanting to add joy and comfort to his life. To help him shove off some of the burdens clinging to him. But I'd never put someone I cared about in physical danger.

I couldn't be with him, or anyone, if I was going to lead the Viceroys to their door.

I'd convinced myself it was behind me.

But the truth was as harsh as the red ink on the letter that had been left at my door. I swallowed over the large lump that had formed in my throat and whispered, "You shouldn't be anywhere near me."

He closed the distance, tucking a stray strand of hair behind my ear, fingers lingering on my skin, and his voice dropped to a sensual hum. "It's too late, Sweetness. I'm here. I'm in your life. Fate took it out of both our hands."

Frustration welled at the beauty and ridiculousness of his words, and I welcomed that feeling as it helped shove back the fear and sorrow. "Fate isn't a real thing," I huffed out. Because if it was, I had some serious bones to pick with it.

"Fate is just one of the many unexplainable things I believe are real. I have it on good authority that you've come into my life for a reason." He said it with a conviction hard to discount.

"So, what? You've talked with God?"

Apprehension clouded his eyes as they darted to the side of the kitchen just like I'd seen him do while he'd shared his secrets with me, as if he was seeing something or someone. But then, he looked at me, and his mouth broke into that stunning, glowing, full smile that made me feel special every time I experienced it. The one that was mine, and mine alone, and made me forget every reason for not being with him.

"Maybe an angel or two," he said as he wrapped an arm around my waist and drew me closer. I threw my head back to look up at him, confusion warring with the frustration even as desire burst through me as our bodies collided. I didn't just feel him everywhere we touched. It went so much deeper. Like souls touching souls.

When my eyes locked with his, the fire I found there took my breath and sent it sailing.

Our heartbeats pounded together.

He scoured my face, and I wasn't sure what he was searching for. All I knew was this—the feeling I had tucked up against him was something good and beautiful. Feelings I could let push away the ugly that had crossed my path. Bright shimmers of hope I yearned to have. It wasn't just a connection with some random person I craved. I wanted it with *this* brave, gorgeous man. I wanted all my joyous experiences to be with Lincoln.

It was too much. Too fast. Too ridiculous.

But as his gaze slipped down to my mouth and back, my breath evaporated once more, my blood boiled, and my limbs grew roots.

"I'm going to kiss you," he said huskily. "Because if I don't, I'll never sleep again. I'll spend every single minute of every night wondering if you taste as sweet as you smell."

When I didn't pull away, when I didn't even shift a millimeter, his head descended, mouth inching closer. He stopped with his lips so close to mine an exhale would have them touching as he whispered, "Last chance to slap me and send me on my way."

My response was to push up on my toes and smash our mouths together.

The world exploded into a kaleidoscope of colors and smells and emotions right before everything in the room disappeared, leaving only the bright light of me and Lincoln and our skin touching. Like walking through the gates of heaven.

He'd spoken of angels, and I'd seen him as one. An archangel, a godlike apparition lassoing me to him with a golden rope that would be impossible to remove once it wrapped around me. And I didn't care if it tethered me to him for an eternity. Because the touch of his lips—the brilliance and heat of it—was a paradise I welcomed. It was a moment that moved beyond simple existence to a place where love was created. Beauty was crafted. Where memories would linger until time stopped.

The pressure of his lips increased, causing tingles to spread from the balls of my feet to the tip of my head. A sigh of pleasure escaped me, and Lincoln licked into me, tongue lapping inside smoothly, swiftly, assuredly. Sipping, tasting, discovering.

He fisted my hair, angling our mouths so he could discover every corner and savor every drop. He dragged me closer until we became one. No longer two beings. No longer two souls. Just one heartbeat. One gasping breath. One hot, fiery touch.

It was like standing in the middle of a flame and watching the world burn around you, knowing there'd be nothing left when it was over and not caring. Rejoicing in it instead.

Never in my wildest dreams had I considered a kiss could be like this.

A beginning and an end.

He shifted our bodies, lifting me onto his counter, fingers digging into my hips, and then soothing the pain. All the while, his lips and tongue did things to me, to my soul, that I could only describe as magic.

Pure enchantment.

He groaned, whispering throatily, "I knew it. I knew you'd taste just like you smell. Toasted butter and sugar. Cotton candy. Addiction." And then he devoured me all over again. As if he'd never get enough. As if he was afraid I'd disappear.

I answered each move with my own desperate ones, needing this to continue forever. Needing to live in this moment permanently so I'd never have to step outside of the heaven we were creating. My hands slid under his sweater, smooth skin hitting my palms and radiating a heat that made me shiver. The very best kind of tremors. Nothing scary. Nothing dreadful. Glory. Pure splendor.

The hand he had fisted in my hair dragged my head backward, exposing my neck. His blue eyes were midnight skies as they drank me in from my flushed cheeks to my wet, bruised mouth. His breathing was as ragged as mine, warm air escaping those divine lips. I needed them back on me. I needed to keep the gates of heaven sealed around us so I wouldn't think. Wouldn't doubt. Wouldn't fear. My legs circled his waist, drawing him in. Rubbing our centers together. Molten lava spread through me at the motion, at the pure rawness of it.

"Kiss me again, Lincoln. Kiss me and make me believe in your fate and your angels."

And he did, lips searing into me. Tongue branding me. The moan that escaped me was needy and full of pleasure. His groan echoed it. His mouth slid over my jaw, onto my neck, sucking at the pulse point. It thudded wildly, as if my veins wanted to feel his kisses as much as my skin did. As if they were jealous to be inside my body instead of out.

His hands tugged at the hem of my T-shirt, and it was gone, flung from my body before I could even register we'd broken apart. Then, his hands and mouth were on me once more, showering needy kisses along my collarbone, my shoulder, and the swell of my breast.

My legs flexed. My core clenched.

No wonder people ended up pregnant. Because this enormous passion, this enormous, painful longing, demanded to be quenched. Needed an outlet. It commanded my body to find release. No other rational thought existed. Just the hunger and need.

He unsnapped my bra, and the sound registered in the haze just before his hands and those glorious demanding lips covered my breasts, sending all thought spiraling away again. My palms landed on the cool granite as my body arched into him, into the feel of burning…of being consumed.

"More," I heard myself murmur, not even sure I knew what

I meant. Not even sure I knew how to make it happen. I moved my hips, rubbing against the hard length of him covered in denim.

Aching longing filled me.

He squeezed one tip as his tongue and teeth dragged on the other.

My entire being convulsed. Soul. Body. Mind. Pleasure ripped through me in ways I'd never experienced with my own hands and certainly never allowed a man close enough to cause.

The air filled with a sound I thought vaguely was me chanting his name as my body shook from the release.

"God, you're gorgeous," he said, throaty and deep.

His lips returned to mine, and the hunger was still there, but I sensed immediately that he was slowing us down. He turned the desperate plunder into lazy sips and sucks while all I wanted was to continue to live in the wild, white cloud of passion.

His mouth left mine completely, arms banding around me tightly, securing me to him even as I felt him letting go. My brain finally registered what we must look like. My naked chest pushed into his sweater, my skirt hiked up with my legs around his waist, and my breath coming in pants.

Embarrassment crept in amongst the lust.

He'd kissed me, and I'd gone at him like a person deprived.

It was exactly what I'd been for so many years. Deprived of human connection. The Viceroys had taken this from me, not only because of the fear I lived with but because I wasn't able to get tested for the FFI. If none of that had happened, and I'd had access to a genetic test, and Lincoln was standing before me, I'd dive in with full steam and never look back.

But that wasn't the case.

So, I'd take this moment—this wonderful, amazing, skin-tingling moment—and add it to my list of joyous experiences.

I pushed against his chest and the steel band of his arms, but his forehead landed in the crook of my neck.

His voice was raspy, hoarse and sexy as he said, "Don't.

Just stop moving for a second."

My body flamed at the tone—and what it meant.

"God… Lincoln… I'm so—" His head whipped up, finger landing on my mouth.

"Don't you dare apologize. For what? For giving in to this thing that's been pulling at us since we met? For feeling? For accepting a few seconds of pleasure? Don't. Don't you dare. It was beautiful to see you unravel. *You're* beautiful."

A weight lifted, and I beamed up at him, his words marking me as much as his body had.

"It was just supposed to be a kiss." My lips twisted upward. "And then…"

"And then every damn cell ignited," he said, and I nodded, glad he'd felt it too. This was what life was supposed to be about. Not the ugly note pinned to a door, but this—passion and touch and pure humanity that burst through you without control.

I pushed back the lock of hair that always fell onto his forehead, meeting his gaze with a hungry one.

His throat bobbed. "It was beautiful. You're beautiful. But you need to stop touching me before the hunger I feel has me hauling you onto the floor and making love to you right here. I don't want our first time together to be fast and furious. I want to take my time with you. So, I'm not going to take our kiss and turn it into something you'll regret later because I lost control."

The simple idea of it, that he was about to lose control because of me, thrilled me. And I almost pushed. I looked down at his lips and felt myself leaning into him more. He caught my chin, saw the look in my eyes, and chuckled softly before stepping completely away.

The loss of his heat was almost as painful as the loss of his kiss had been. He leaned down and picked up both my T-shirt and bra. He tugged the shirt over my head with a gentleness that had me shaking from head to toe again. With want. With need. With a desire to rip it back off and do the same with his clothes. To take him up on the offer to make love on the stone tile of his kitchen floor.

The experience would be worth it, wouldn't it? With him? A happy memory I'd have until I departed this earth. It didn't have to be more.

I slid off the counter, and it caused our bodies to collide. The air vibrated with the unsatisfied craving humming through us. At least I knew he'd wanted this too. He'd started it, and yet, he'd also ended it.

He'd said it was beautiful. That I was beautiful.

But what did I know about any of it?

Nothing. On purpose, I knew nothing.

Whereas he'd likely had many women since that girl he'd spoken of dying in his car.

God…we'd both been talking about people we'd loved and lost.

Our emotions were incredibly high.

It was as if sharing our secrets, our burdens, had heightened what we'd already felt, taking the want already sifting between us and turning it into something more.

Except, he was right to have stopped us, because nothing we did here, nothing I allowed, would change the facts of my life—or the facts of his.

He'd said fate or angels had brought us together, but that couldn't be true because if it were, then God was having a great big laugh. The possibility of our lives blending for more than a few days was nil. And I wasn't sure I could survive the loss. Wasn't sure I could inflict that kind of damage on him if he ended up feeling as bound to me as I felt to him and then I was forced to walk away. I didn't want to be that cruel to either of us.

# Chapter Nineteen

## Lincoln

**TURN ME ON**
Performed by The Fray

**WHEN SHE SLID OFF THE COUNTER**, pushing our bodies back together, I was overwhelmed all over again with the scent and feel of her, aching for more of the sweetness I'd been able to savor. The sounds of her coming apart with just my mouth and a few slams of our hips hadn't been nearly enough. I needed to know what she'd look like, sound like, feel like as she quivered around me when I was buried deep inside her, riding out the waves.

I was harder than I'd ever been in my life.

But damn if I'd take her on a cold tile floor after we'd just spilled our guts about some of the worst nights of our lives. No. I wanted the moment we came together to be just like this kitchen. Full of light and warm memories. Not an escape from the dark.

Maybe it was an impossible thing to want. Maybe there would never be that kind of a moment for me in my life or Willow in hers, but I believed what I'd told her. Fate had given us to each other. Sienna had insisted Willow was my person, and I believed her, even if it was only me believing my own dark wishes.

So, I stepped back even farther away from her, allowing the cold air to shift between us.

We needed to think. We needed to take some sort of action so she didn't have to hide in fear.

"We need a plan. If you call the Marshals and tell them about the note, and it ends up being just Poco, they may still insist on moving you. If we tell the local police about it, we still risk the Marshals finding out. But I can ask Hardy to come and get the note and have him run some tests on it. I'd already asked him to do some digging on Poco, so he won't be surprised if I ask him to find out where he was when the note was left."

She frowned at me, the dazed passion in her eyes slowly dissolving. "Who's Hardy?"

Right. I had to remember she didn't know everything about my life. Just like I knew so very little about hers—just the worst parts.

"Hardy is Secret Service. Former head of my detail, but he's also a friend. He'll keep this quiet."

She hesitated. "I still need to call Deputy Marshal James, even if it's just to make sure Aaron is still in Chicago and hasn't found out where we are. I need to make sure my mom is protected."

"Can you just say you've been worried since you found out about Roci?" Her brows pushed together, doubts running through her mind. I pushed at them, trying to shove them away, trying to hold on to more time with her until I could find a way to cross the chasm between us. "If we have even one inkling this is something more than Poco, we can explain everything to them. I want—" My breath caught. "I need you to be safe. Nothing will stop me from making sure you are."

Could I sacrifice being with her if I knew it would ensure her safety? Abso-fucking-lutely. But I wouldn't sacrifice her, us, if I didn't need to. My conscience wiggled with thoughts of paparazzi. With thoughts of the many photos leaked in my lifetime where I hadn't even known someone had taken them. We'd deal with that too. Somehow. But first, we had this to handle—an ugly note and a threat from a local thug.

"What would you tell Hardy?" she asked. "About me?"

"He might already know everything there is to know about

you. He ran my neighbors." I waved to the house on the opposite side of mine. "I guess the people next door are the Bristols."

"He won't know I'm in witness protection. The Marshals don't share that information with any other law enforcement group."

I wasn't exactly sure it was true when it came to the president's family. I wasn't sure any secrets were kept, but maybe some were. She was right when she'd said the Marshals hadn't lost a single person under active protection, so maybe they did keep secrets from even the president.

She pulled on the chain at her neck and the class ring there. After what I'd heard, I was even more convinced it was her dad's. A way to keep him close. To remember him. What had she said about the people in the cemetery? About wanting someone to think of them so they weren't forgotten? She couldn't go visit her dad, so she visited others like she hoped someone was doing for him. It sliced through me, making me want to find a way for her to visit him, making me want to end both the Viceroys and Poco.

"If there's a way to keep Mom safe and to keep us from having to give up our life here, I want that," she said with a quiet determination. "If it's Poco who did this, and we can just end it before it gets further out of hand, then that's what I'd like to see happen."

Her strength awed me. The way she'd crumbled and then yanked herself back to stable ground was stunning. After Sienna and after Lyrica, I'd wallowed in self-pity, and remorse, and what-ifs. Maybe she had too, but what I saw before me now was a woman who didn't let the knocks that came at her keep her down.

"Let me call Hardy while you call the Marshals and your mom."

I reached for my phone and stepped toward the kitchen table. While I talked with my former Secret Service agent, she stepped out of the kitchen with her phone to her ear.

Hardy wasn't thrilled things had escalated or that it was

happening across the street with me tagging along for the ride, but he said he'd send a rookie to get the note this afternoon. He asked for the videos from Willow's alarm system, and I told him I'd have Willow send them as soon as we hung up.

I was just shoving my phone in my pocket and heading to find her when she came back in, still talking. "I just want to make sure you are taking extra precautions. I just got off the phone with Deputy Marshal James and confirmed Aaron is still in Chicago." She paused, listening to her mom. "I just… I don't know, Mom. I didn't tell her about the note because I'm pretty sure this is Poco, and I didn't want her to overreact. He came into the café today and said some nasty things." Another pause. "Hector didn't know, or he would have kicked him out. Don't say anything to him. I don't want him getting into it with Tall Paul." The quiet made me wish I could hear her mother's side of the conversation. "No, I'm okay. I'm with Lincoln." After a beat, her eyes went wide, and she put a hand to her forehead as she lied. "No. He didn't hear me talk about the Marshals. He doesn't know anything. He was in the other room. What? I don't think—" She grimaced. "Hold on. Let me go get him." She waited for a second, as if she'd really had to come find me, and then offered me her phone with a hand that shook. "She wants to talk to you."

I reached for it without hesitation. "Hello?"

"Lincoln?"

"Yes."

"My name is Erica, and we haven't met, so pardon my directness, but who the hell are you, and why are you doing this?"

Even though I knew she was right to demand answers to those questions, it still irritated me. My voice was sharp as I replied, "You're right, we haven't met, and you don't know me. So, let me put it simply. I'd never stand by while someone was accosted or hurt, but it's much more than that now. As I've gotten to know your daughter over the last few days, I've been amazed by her strength and courage. I can easily say I'd do just about anything to make sure she remains unharmed."

Willow inhaled sharply, but silence hummed over the line between her mom and me for a moment before Erica finally spoke again. "Willow has been through a lot in her short life. A lot. Things we can't and won't discuss. If you're not okay with any of that, you need to step back right now."

"I won't push her to do or say anything she's uncomfortable with," I growled out.

A little huff of something close to laughter drifted over the line. "I see. You like my daughter quite a bit."

"Like is putting it mildly." Every word was spoken with a vehement truth.

Willow's eyes grew wider, and the remnants of the desire we'd flamed sparked between us.

"Hmm. I'm quite happy with this development. What I'm not happy with is some local yokel thinking he can scare my daughter. I'm out of town for the weekend—not far, just in Richmond—and I can come home if I need to, but I think me changing my plans and leaving my students would upset her almost as much as Poco has."

She was right. Willow would hate it. "There's no need for you to come home. I don't plan on letting her out of my sight while you're gone."

And maybe that would have raised some parents' hackles, but I swore I heard a smile in Erica's voice as she said, "Good. When I get home, I expect to have dinner together."

If she thought to scare me off, it didn't work. The idea of embedding myself further into both their lives was exactly what I wanted. "I'd like that."

"Well. Okay, then," she said before clearing her throat. "Lincoln?"

"Yes?"

"Thank you." Her voice went soft, tucked full of emotions. "Not just for taking care of her when Poco confronted her at the cemetery or even when he's obviously upset her today. Thank you for seeing her for the smart, courageous, brave woman she is and giving her some beautiful memories. You are going to do that, right?"

For the first time since I'd picked up the phone, a spike of panic welled. It wasn't because of her words or because of what was blooming between Willow and me. It was much more because my world could easily shatter theirs.

Still, I kept my voice steady and sure when I responded, "I'm hoping to give her more than just a few."

Erica laughed again. It was light and lyrical, just like her daughter's. I handed the phone back to Willow, and they said goodbye with warm I love yous that reminded me of my family. Living through trauma either bonded people together with a cement-like glue, or it tore them apart. My family had only grown closer. Not just because of the traumatic events of my life, but because of Dad's career choice and the hate that got tossed our way.

Willow bit her lip and wouldn't meet my gaze. "I'm sorry…she just—"

"Loves you. Wants you safe and happy."

She ran a hand up and down her arm before tugging on the ring at her neck. She cleared her throat. "I don't know what to do now."

I had plenty of ideas of what I wanted to do with her, starting with taking off every article of clothing and exploring every sweet-smelling inch of her. But I wouldn't. Not yet. I'd spoken the truth when I said I wouldn't take our first kiss and turn it into something she wished she'd stopped.

I could take her to the gallery with me, but if I did, I'd get lost in my paintings like I always did, and I couldn't guarantee I'd know if something or someone showed up at my door when I was lost in my art. But thoughts of the gallery reminded me of the way I'd all but shoved Trinity out of the shop with barely a word while I'd chased after Willow.

"Crap. Hold on. I need to text Trinity—the artist at the gallery. I left her in a bit of a hurry."

Willow grimaced again, as if she was upset that she'd messed with my day.

I jotted off a text to Trinity.

*ME: I'm sorry I had to rush out like I did. Your work is truly incredible, and it will be an honor to show it, if you're still interested.*

*TRINITY: You've got to be kidding, right? I'd be a moron not to be interested. Besides, I knew you'd get back to me. You have three of my pieces sitting in your gallery.*

I couldn't help the smile that curled my lips. I *had* basically stolen her work, but at least she wasn't upset about it.

*ME: I don't have a date for the opening yet. Send me pictures of everything you have completed and are willing to part with as well as what you're working on. We can decide where to go from there.*

*TRINITY: Thank you. Thank you so much. I'll send you everything once I get home from class.*

When I put my phone back in my pocket and raised my eyes, Willow's were hooded, taking in my grin. She was jealous, just like she'd been when she'd seen Trinity and me at the gallery. It shouldn't have, but it made me happy to know she was. That somehow, what we already felt for each other was enough for her to not want to share me.

Lord knew I didn't want to share her.

"What were your plans for the day?" I asked.

Her gaze flicked to my lips and away, and once again, I had to fight off the urge to pick her up, take her upstairs, and finish what we'd started.

"I was going to work on ideas for a new dessert piece, and you?"

"I need groceries. I've been putting it off for too long. I'd planned on shopping after I met with Trinity." The silence that settled wasn't awkward so much as expectant. "Come with me?”

She shifted, looking away, and I had a moment to wonder if it was smart, leaving the house in the daylight with her. But before I could take it back, she responded, “Okay.”

I patted my pockets. I needed my wallet and keys. Where had I put them? “I think my keys are in the study.”

Her lips twitched. “Think?”

I grunted. “I’m good at losing keys, phones, and wallets.”

“Your detail must not have liked that,” she said as I led the way out of the kitchen.

“When you have a security detail, you rarely need anything with you. I blame them for adding to my problem rather than helping it.”

The keys were sitting on the desk next to my laptop. I opened the drawers and sighed with relief when I found my wallet sitting there, which only meant I’d driven to the gallery this morning without it. Shopping would have been a short trip if I hadn’t remembered to come back for it.

As we stepped out of the house, I felt the tension that had left Willow for a few moments return as her body stiffened. She scanned the street, and I did the same. No gray sedan. No Poco. No random people raising their phones to take a shot. And yet, just like when I’d left the gallery the other night, I felt eyes on me. On us.

After I locked up, I tugged her closer and kissed the top of her head.

“It’s going to be okay.” It was a statement I hoped I could make true somehow.

“Do you need anything?” I asked with a chin nod in the direction of her house.

A shudder went through her as she stared at the gate. She shook her head. “I’m not ready to go back in yet.”

I put a hand on the small of her back, directing her to my Range Rover I’d left parked at the curb down the street. I opened the passenger door, and as she slid in, I caught the scent of her once more. It made me hungry, deep-in-the-soul hungry, and made me wonder why the hell we were leaving instead of retreating to my bedroom.

I jogged around the car and got in before I hauled her back into my lair.

I looked over at her and asked, "Where's the grocery store?"

Her eyes widened, and then she giggled. "You live here and don't even know where the grocery store is? What have you been eating?"

My lips twitched. "I've been subsisting on takeout and tea."

It was only partially true. I hadn't been eating much at all because I'd been lost in unpacking, insomnia, and painting. But I was suddenly ravenous. For more than just Willow. For actual food rather than microwaved junk. For a drink and a meal I'd be able to share with her.

"But how can you have moved here not knowing where the store is?"

"I know about the convenience store on Main Street, but I don't want to do my bulk shopping there. I'll use it for the day-to-day stuff. Where's the nearest chain store?"

She waved at my console. "I think your fancy GPS can tell you." But she still gave me directions, and I headed out. "Do you really shop at regular stores?"

"Sure. Why wouldn't I?"

She shook her head, the blond waves shimmering in the sunlight that glinted in her window. Even in the golden rays, it still looked like moonlight. "It just seems so...normal."

I chuckled. "Hate to break it to you, but being the son of the president doesn't get you out of shopping for your own groceries. Now, if I lived with my parents at the White House, it would be different. But my siblings and I are only there for a few days at a time, usually for the holidays or for special events."

"Where do your sisters live?" she asked.

"Juliette is in her final year of residency at Boston General.

Katerina is working for a studio in Hollywood. I take it you don't have siblings?"

Willow shook her head. "No. Mom had a hard time carrying me. I was born premature and spent a couple of months in the neonatal ward. Which was why Mom ended up working there. She wanted to pay it forward."

"Did you ever wish you had a brother or sister?"

"Sometimes, when I was little. But after everything went down, I was glad we didn't have to drag another person through all of it with us."

The shadows returned to her eyes, and I didn't want them there, so I kept talking, sharing things about myself I normally kept private. "Sienna was an only child too. When we first became friends in elementary school, her parents sort of adopted me as their second child."

"You were together since elementary school?" she asked, eyes curious but hesitant.

"Well, we were obviously just friends for a long time, until puberty hit, and then—bang—all of a sudden, there were all these feelings and emotions we hadn't expected." I'd felt the bang with Willow too. Different...but stronger, more demanding.

"Do you still see her parents?" she asked gently.

I nodded. "They're usually with us for the holidays, and they spoil me and my sisters like we're their favorite nieces and nephew. They're also the reason I have the gallery in D.C."

"They are?"

"They had a trust set aside for Sienna for college and weddings and stuff, and they handed it over to me so I could open the gallery she'd always dreamed about. I was actually with them, talking about the plans, when Lyrica was shot."

Willow inhaled sharply. "Wh-who's Lyrica? Did you lose another friend?" The pain and sorrow in her voice made me want to kick myself.

I pushed the hair back from my forehead with one hand. I kept forgetting Willow didn't know every single fact of my life like most people I met.

"Lyrica is the manager of my gallery in D.C. These days, we're just really good friends, but at the time she was shot, we were dating." I glanced over to see how this news landed, and Willow's eyes widened.

"What happened?"

"It was the anniversary of my accident with Sienna, and every year on that day, I spent time with her parents. Lyrica knew and was happy for me to go, but I still felt bad about leaving her, because her sorority was throwing this huge, end-of-the-year bash that she'd been responsible for organizing. She couldn't just leave to go with me any more than I could not go see Henrik and Shannon. We didn't argue about it, but she did give me crap for feeling guilty. She told me if I felt so damn bad that I wasn't sticking around to help, then I could go pick up the ice for her on my way out of town." My voice faded away before I cleared my throat and kept going, trying to keep it nonchalant. Just the facts. "But I forgot to do it. I was so focused on getting to Delaware, so in my head reliving that awful day, that I didn't even realize I'd forgotten until I got the call. Lyrica had gone into a convenience store to buy ice and got caught in the crossfire of a robbery gone bad."

Silence settled down into the car.

"Oh, Lincoln… I'm so sorry."

Damn. Why had I told her all that when I was trying so hard to push aside the dark of the truths we'd already shared?

"Mumbles were already hitting the streets about Dad running for president by that time, so anything they could get on our family was food for the machine. The press talked to her sorority sisters," I said with an inward sigh. "The way the media twisted their words made it seem like I'd abandoned Lyrica right outside the store. Like I'd sent her in there on her own and hadn't shown up when the bullets started flying. If you look me up on the internet, it's still one of the top search results. The gallery's success is always buried under the tragedies tied to me—Sienna, Lyrica, Leya's kidnapping, and even Felicity's bullshit."

Quiet settled down, and then, to my surprise, Willow started laughing. I looked over at her, confused. "What? What did I say?"

She put her hand over her mouth, horror in her eyes, but she didn't stop laughing. Eventually, she stuttered out her thoughts while still trying to control the chuckles. "I'm sorry. That's awful. I'm just… You've had so much happen to you. Here I am, like, 'Woe is me, my dad was shot,' and you're like, 'Every woman I thought I loved has experienced death and tragedy, the press has repeatedly used me for fodder, and I've been made into a villain by America's sweetheart.' You've just had so much happen…" The laughter drifted away, and she reached over to squeeze my hand resting on the console. "It isn't funny. Not at all. But it made me feel ridiculous. It put things in perspective. I'm just incredibly sorry you had to go through all of it."

We pulled into the parking lot of the grocery store, and I cut the engine before turning in my seat to look at her. "Not that it's a competition, Sweetness, but I've never once had shots fired at me and a street gang threatening to murder me and my family. Let's not minimize what you've gone through by narrowing it down to a 'Woe is me.'"

That sucked the laughter away. I reached over, skimming her jawline with my knuckles. Her breath caught while mine disappeared completely for several seconds. She was so beautiful. Stunningly gorgeous. Unforgettable.

"None of it was your fault," she said with deadly seriousness. I knew it. My therapist, my family, Sienna, Lyrica, and even Leya had all said the same thing. But for the first time, the words carved a place deep in my soul and stayed there. Every single person who'd ever said it to me had been right, but it was Willow saying it that finally found a lasting home. None of it had been my fault or really about me. I couldn't change the past, but I damn well could influence the present, and I would. I'd keep Willow safe and build a life that meant something.

# Chapter Twenty

## Willow

**TWISTED**

Performed by Carrie Underwood

*I UNDERSTOOD SO MUCH MORE ABOUT* Lincoln from that handful of sentences he'd offered up. He'd said them as if they were simple facts, but I knew, both from instinct and from how he'd been acting ever since we'd met in the cemetery, that he carried remorse for all those tragedies. It hung on him like a badge he couldn't throw away. He felt responsible for those women. For all of them.

Which was why he hadn't been able to walk away from me.

Why he'd followed me down the street at two thirty in the morning.

Why he'd shown back up and demanded I not go anywhere alone.

I understood guilt. What if I hadn't let my dad walk alone that night? What if I hadn't seen their faces? What if Mom hadn't had to tear apart her life in order to give me one?

While neither of us could take responsibility for the tragedies that had woven their way into our past, I could understand his determination to not allow something else to happen on his watch. Just like I was determined to not let Mom lose everything all over again if I could help it.

When I'd spoken to Deputy Marshal James, she'd assured

me Aaron was tucked away in Chicago, and there was no chatter about him searching for me. He was busy with the RICO case set to go to trial this summer.

Mom was safe, miles away with her students. The ugly note on the door had to have been Poco, and Lincoln had someone running that down. Everything was going to be okay. We weren't sliding back into the nightmare of those first years. I was grateful I had not only the Marshals but Lincoln to keep me safe.

Except, just being photographed with him could slice through our protective wool hiding us from the Viceroys. Coming here, to the grocery store, in the middle of the day wasn't smart.

I tore my gaze from his, watching the automatic doors swooshing back and forth as dozens of people walked in and out. "Aren't you afraid of being recognized?"

Maybe he heard the tremor in my voice, because he tried to ease it by grinning and saying, "I have a disguise." I raised my brows, and he winked, leaning into the back seat and coming back with a baseball cap. After putting it on with a snap, he opened the center console, grabbed a pair of sunglasses, and slid them on with a flourish of hands. "Voilá, I'm no longer Lincoln Matherton."

I couldn't help the giggle that escaped, because there was no way it was a true disguise. Sure, the bright-blue eyes the world adored were hidden as well as his lush, dark waves, but every ounce of his nose, jaw, and broad shoulders still screamed the truth of him.

"You can't be serious. The girl at the café recognized you with that hat."

"But I didn't have my sunglasses. That's the ultimate shield."

I shook my head, but all my doubts disintegrated with the force of his wide smile that stopped my lungs from filling completely.

He got out of the car, and I opened my door and stepped out just as he came around and shut it behind me.

"Watch and learn, little Padawan. The Force is with me dressed and acting like this."

He hunched his shoulders, grabbed my hand, and headed for the row of carts with a shuffle that was anything but confident. It was the first time I'd seen him without the rigidly straight back and assured air I'd come to equate with him.

In some ways, he was right. He didn't look like Lincoln Matherton, world-famous artist and president's son. He looked…normal. Everyday. But also stunningly gorgeous enough people would look. So I still expected someone to recognize him, to shift their eyes and phones toward us, but not a single person glanced in our direction, even when he kept the sunglasses on inside the store.

While I continued to look around nervously, Lincoln led us to the produce section where he started tossing items in the cart that felt utterly random. This was a ridiculous risk. Stupid in just the way the Marshals had taught us not to be. But I hadn't wanted to go home when he'd asked me to come. I'd wanted to stay in the one place where I felt safest—with him.

My palms turned sweaty, and I shot a nervous look in the direction of a man staring at the bagged salad display.

Lincoln put a bunch of bananas in the cart and then pulled me closer. "You're going to ruin everything and get us spotted if you keep looking around like that."

"Me?" I asked. "You're the one who was on the cover of *The Reporter*."

He shifted me so I was caught between the handle of the cart and him. My hips pressed against his, and a fire flew through my veins that felt like a heavy pull of alcohol.

"You're supposed to be part of the disguise, not shaking it. No one expects to see me here in Cherry Bay with a blonde they can't name."

One glance over his shoulder proved we had caught the eye of an elderly woman. Her pursed lips and narrowed eyes screamed her disapproval of this display of…whatever it was.

"I should be offended that you consider me no one, but I'm not," I said. "I need that anonymity. It's kept me safe."

His face softened, and he leaned in and gave me a soft, quick kiss. "You're not no one, Sweetness. You're the bravest, strongest woman I've met."

My heart and soul flipped at those words said with a surety that allowed for no argument. I pushed against his chest. "You're the one making a scene. That woman is about to call security." I flicked my eyes in the older woman's direction, only to have her glance away with disgust.

He looked over his shoulder, caught the woman's eyes, and gave a little wave.

The woman turned beet red, turned on her heel, and rounded the next corner.

I couldn't help the giggle that escaped me once more. "Nice way to *not* call attention to yourself."

I shoved against his chest once more, and this time, he released me. As he pushed the cart down the aisle with those uncharacteristically slumped shoulders, I walked by his side, scanning the fruits and vegetables. When my eyes landed on baskets of perfectly ripe strawberries, I wished I'd at least brought some money with me. I picked the berries up, sniffed them, touched their firm skin, and then set them down with a sigh, moving past them as I followed Lincoln.

"You make it really hard not to touch you," he said.

"I'm not doing anything," I huffed out.

"You practically made love to the strawberries."

I beamed up at him. "They're perfect. It's hard to find perfect strawberries this early in the season, especially at a regular market."

"And yet you left them behind."

"I don't have my purse."

He stopped, stared at me over the top of the sunglasses for a moment, and then turned the cart around, going back to pick up the basket I'd held, along with three more.

"What are you doing?" I asked.

"Willow, the one thing I have in spades is money. Get whatever you want."

"We're supposed to be here shopping for you," I said.

"We're here together. If you see something you need or want—or hell, just decide to try—I expect you to put it in the cart." It was a grouchy command that somehow wound its way through my heart more than a soft request would have.

"I'm not mooching off you, regardless of how much money you have to throw around."

Pleasure filled his face, lifting his lips once more. "You realize that only makes me like you more, right? How about we make a trade?"

And the way he looked down my body set my nerve endings on fire, but I frowned at him. "I don't trade like that."

He laughed gently. "Neither do I. You can make me something fabulous for dessert while I make dinner."

"We haven't even had lunch."

"I'll make lunch *and* dinner, and you can make dessert."

"Do you like to cook?" I asked. We'd moved away from the berries, but I grabbed a variety of citrus as we went by.

"No. I can't stand it. I have exactly two dishes I can make well. You'll see both of them today."

More laughter erupted from me, and it drew another pair of eyes as we went down the next aisle. "Not to brag or anything, but I did graduate from culinary school. How about I make you dinner and dessert and leave you to lunch?"

"I happily accept," he said.

♫ ♫ ♫

Even though I'd offered, Lincoln refused to let me help make lunch, so instead, I started on the dessert I was making with the strawberries. Finding things in his kitchen was like a scavenger hunt, and some of the items were in all the wrong places for their use, but it wasn't my kitchen to reorganize. When I didn't find a zester and had to ask, he lifted a brow.

"I'm pretty sure I don't own one of those."

I huffed, thinking of the three in different sizes I owned at the cottage.

But I was still reluctant to go back, not only because it had been violated with an ugly note but because I'd be alone there and I'd have to leave Lincoln to do so. Right now, the trip to the store with him had shoved aside all my fears and sadness and replaced them with a lightheartedness I wanted to hold on to as long as possible.

As if reading my thoughts and also wanting to stay away from anything that could send us back to the darkness, Lincoln asked, "Where'd your mom go this weekend?"

"State Science Decathlon. She and her students have worked hard to get this far, so I didn't want her to miss it. Thank you for reassuring her I'd be okay."

I was still uncomfortable I hadn't told her the truth about who Lincoln really was. But she'd agreed with me the note was much more likely to be from Poco than the Viceroys, and I had to believe Poco wouldn't do anything if Lincoln was with me. He was too much of a coward. Up until now, he'd only approached me when he thought I was alone and defenseless.

Regardless of what Lincoln had told Mom about not letting me out of his sight, I'd have to go home at some point. But for now, I'd enjoy these moments with him. I'd savor the company, and the connection, and the thrill of having him at my side while we were tucked away where no one could see us.

Lincoln plated two basic grilled cheese sandwiches and brought them to the beautiful oak table in his kitchen with a bag of potato chips. He turned back to the fridge, "Water? Tea? Lemonade?"

"Water. Store-bought lemonade is way too acidic."

"Because the culinary chef makes her own?" he asked, lips twitching.

I shrugged. I could make my own, but drinks weren't my expertise.

Instead of sitting across from me, he had us sitting side by side, and every time I moved my right arm, it brushed against him, sending secret little thrills through me. I was enjoying this way too much. Liking it way too much. It already hurt just thinking about losing him, but I'd allow myself to play with the fire just a bit longer. I'd revel in the bliss of every second at his side until the crash of reality came.

"So, if I'd let you make me dinner, would it have been mac and cheese?" I asked, biting my lip to keep from smiling.

He elbowed my arm playfully. "Nothing wrong with mac and cheese. The White House chef makes one that melts in your mouth. But no. I'd planned on spaghetti."

"With that garlic-laden jarred sauce you picked up that is nothing like authentic marinara?"

He snickered before saying, "This is very unexpected."

"What?" I wiped my face with a napkin, wondering if I had something on it.

"You're a food snob. I would never have expected you to be snobbish about anything, and yet, there it is."

His smile was so contagious I couldn't help but return it. "Garlic is overrated. There's a time and place for it, but the way most American's slather it around, all it does is hide the real flavors."

"Did you earn that snobbery degree in culinary school?"

I wasn't the least bit offended because there was no real jab in his words. It was all delightful tease. "My dad was a pretty decent chef for having no formal experience. He liked playing with food, and I learned a lot from him before…" I shrugged. "When we moved, Mom's time was absorbed with working and studying for her teaching credential, and the Marshals had decided I should finish high school online, which was fine by me, so I was pretty much in the cottage twenty-four seven. I started watching all these food shows, especially the competitions, and then I began experimenting with different recipes, and it helped get me through. When I started at Bonnin, I got a job with Hector and learned more."

"You went to Bonnin?" he asked.

"I dropped out in the spring semester of my junior year."

"How'd your mom take it?"

I played with a potato chip, crumbling it. "Honestly, Mom

understood. That semester was Danny and Roci's trial, and I had to go back and testify. I wasn't sleeping well and couldn't concentrate on my classes. We were both terrified it was the fatal familial insomnia rather than just nerves and terror."

Lincoln pushed his plate away and turned in his seat so his knees banged into my thigh. Heat and desire burst through me in a sudden, fiery crescendo.

"I can't imagine. That must have been terrifying to face them in court. I didn't have the pleasure of seeing the man who shot Lyrica declared guilty, because he copped a plea."

"What about the truck driver who killed Sienna?"

"He died in the wreck too. Hard to take your anger out on a dead guy."

My heart bled for him. For me. For the things we couldn't change. "On the plane ride back from Chicago, I had this moment of clarity about living as much as I could regardless of being in witness protection and having the unknown of the FFI hanging on me. I took out the pamphlet Hector had given me for the culinary institute and talked it over with Mom. She agreed that life was too short to piddle around with things that didn't make me feel alive. If college wasn't for me, she was okay with that."

"She's a good mom," he said softly.

"The very, very best. I just want her to be happy, you know? To get back some of the joy I always saw in her eyes when she was with my dad. She just accepted a date with Hector today. They're adorable together…" That damn lump came back, and I refused to let it grow, so I changed the subject back to him. "Did your parents support you and your art? Is that what you studied in college?"

He laughed, leaned in, and kissed me on the tip of my nose in a way that made my breath disappear. "It's so cute that you don't actually know anything about me."

I huffed. "Sorry I didn't major in Lincoln Matherton at school."

His lips quirked upward more. "I got a master's in Art History and played around with getting my doctorate, but opening the gallery took precedence." The smile he'd had disappeared. "It was important, not just to me but to Sienna and her family."

His eyes traveled across the room and stayed there, as if watching something—someone—in the same way he had earlier. A chill went up my back that I couldn't explain. But the simple fact his light had faded made me tease instead of offering more condolences.

"Overachiever." I pushed at his arm just like he had mine. He chuckled.

I wanted to kiss him. I wanted that deep laugh to turn into the passionate groan he'd let out while we'd devoured each other. Instead, I got up from the table, taking our plates with me to the sink.

He sat, watching me while I cleaned up, before I turned back to the flour I'd spread on the counter and the covered pastry dough waiting for me. He rose and came to stand across the island, watching me as I worked.

When I looked up, his expression was soft and gentle, swimming with an emotion I couldn't possibly name.

"What?" I asked.

"You look really good here. In my house. In my kitchen." The words were deep and guttural. The intensity of his eyes was almost too much. I looked down at the dough I was kneading way too hard. The pastry would be tough. "It's like I designed it for you. The sunshiny mood fits you way better than it ever fit me."

Butterflies danced in my chest, and it took me a moment to respond. "If we put together all the time we've spent together, it hasn't even been twenty-four hours. I don't think you really know what fits me. Just like I don't know what fits you."

"You truly are a little liar," he said softly, and it drew my eyes back to his. The lit flame that danced between us sparked once more, settling down low in my stomach.

"I get it, though. This…" He waved a hand between us. "It hit fast and furious in the middle of an intense situation. It's hard to know what's real." He moved around the island, stopping just short of coming into my space. Even still, the connection binding me to him dragged itself through my veins. "But that, Sweetness…that feeling you just got that changed the pale-gray clouds in your eyes into thunderstorms…that's real. That's rare. That's us. We don't need to know much else."

I couldn't respond if I wanted to. As absurd as the declaration was, it also rang with the truth. Whatever this was between us *was* real and rare. It should make me happy. It fit nicely into the last line item in my journal. I wanted that beauty and joy and love more than he could imagine.

But it seemed impossible to think there was a way to surmount the hurdle of his fame and my need for anonymity.

He hadn't been scared off by my potential FFI and what it could do to me, and that made my soul dance a little jig. I'd wanted someone who wouldn't care. Who could take the leap into the unknown even if it meant a fall. What had he said? Fate had already brought us together. He'd accepted it.

I was the one holding back. Afraid to fall.

Afraid what it could mean for not just me but my mom.

"I know what I want, Willow," he insisted. He wanted everything. All of me. "But I'm also not enough of an ass to push it, because I see your hesitation. It's part of why I stopped earlier instead of stripping you bare, laying you on the floor, and feasting on you."

My core clenched at his words.

I let out an exasperated breath. "How would that even work, Lincoln? Your life plays out across the pages of magazines and TV screens."

"I'm not sure yet," he said honestly. "So we'll wait until we figure it out."

The surety of his words, the sweet temptation of them, had me hearing popular fairy-tale songs in my head. If he'd reached out and touched me right then, I would have crumbled, just as I'd known I would when I'd seen him walking toward me in the gallery this morning. I'd tried to grasp the ledge and hold myself back, but my fingers were slipping. Pretty soon, I wouldn't care about the risk to me or Mom, and that truly terrified me more than the note on the door had.

Instead of closing the distance between us, Lincoln stepped back, crossing his arms over his chest, tucking his hands under his armpits.

"I can be patient. But not for too long. Because your mom is right. Life is too damn short to turn away from something that makes you feel alive." He walked away, calling back over his shoulder, "I have some work to do in the study. Let me know if you need anything."

I stared after him for at least a minute. Maybe two. Trying to right the tumult and chaos that twirled inside me. Trying to steady my pulse. Trying to call back my heart that seemed to have followed him out of the room.

When I looked down at the pastry, I sighed. I'd have to start over or make something different. Something new. I wanted to give Lincoln something more than a regular tart for dessert. I wanted light and airy, melt-in-your-mouth goodness. I tossed the ruined dough. It would have been a fine dessert, but fine wasn't always enough.

I wanted big and beautiful. I wanted more.

# Chapter Twenty-one

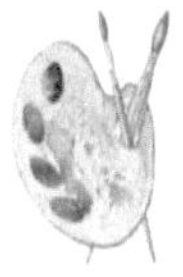

## Lincoln

**ELECTRIC TOUCH**
Performed by Taylor Swift

**IN MY OFFICE, THE PAPER BAG** I'd placed the crumpled note in greeted me like a warning sign, reminding me of the ugly that had lined up in my life once more. I'd be happier when the note was gone, when Hardy and the Secret Service were tearing it apart and finding out who'd left it there.

But even with all that had happened, even with everything Willow and I had shared about the tragedies in our lives, my soul felt lighter than it had in…years. Maybe a decade. And that had everything to do with the woman making me dessert in my kitchen.

Her hesitancy made me want to push. To break it down. To make her see what I saw—what Sienna had seen. But Willow was also right. This thing between us had grown like a flash mob out of nowhere. And it could disappear just as quickly if we didn't stop to acknowledge what we felt. If we didn't stop to build a foundation that wouldn't melt away.

It surprised me just how much I wanted that foundation with her.

With Willow.

But how? How to do that when my life, the publicity of it, was a threat to her?

I didn't know the answer. I also knew I didn't need to find

it while we were tucked away in my home with no press, no cameras, nobody but us. We were safe here.

Sure, the grocery store had been a risk, but I'd been careful, hadn't I? Even the unhappy old woman who'd stared at us hadn't whipped out her phone and taken a snap. No one knew where I was. Mom and her team had squashed any photos that had tried to leak.

I had a few days to figure it out. A few quiet days with Willow that I absolutely wanted.

Maybe it was selfish. Maybe it was another thing I'd regret. But bringing her joy, touching her and listening to her gasp and moan… Damn, did I want that. And I could have it in the quiet of these four walls.

To stop my mind from whirling in a repeated circle of self-flagellation and hope and back, I turned from thoughts of her to the work I'd been putting off for days—bills, expenses, and new inventory for the D.C. gallery. It kept me occupied for a couple of hours until my phone rang, jingling in my pocket. I was almost surprised I actually had it on me still, and I picked it up without looking. "Yeah?"

"Who's the woman?" For half a beat I thought the husky, sensual voice was Felicity, and panic reared, but then Lyrica cleared her throat and added on, "Is she the reason you moved to Cherry Bay?"

My tension released once I realized who it was.

There'd been a few times last year when I'd been photographed with someone, an artist I was courting for the gallery or a random person at one of Dad's fundraisers, and Felicity had instantly called and demanded to know who the woman was that I was with. It had happened even before the breakup and restraining order. I hadn't understood how quickly she'd seen me with people until we found out she'd been having me followed.

Still, unease crept over my spine at the idea of anyone knowing about Willow, especially after I'd just convinced myself we were safe within these four walls.

"Exactly how did you find out about her?" I demanded.

"When I didn't hear from you after the meeting with Trinity this morning, I sent her a text. She said you ran out of the studio, chasing some blond apparition."

I swiped a hand over my face as thoughts of Sienna's ghost lingered in the room.

When I didn't respond, Lyrica apologized. "I'm sorry. That was a bad choice of words. You know I don't believe you see ghosts, right?"

I closed my eyes. All my secrets had come out because of fucking Felicity. For so many years, I'd thought it was just a shame-filled hallucination. But now, with Sienna back, demanding new things of me, I didn't know what it meant. Maybe the truth was much simpler. Maybe she was real—a ghost coming and going in my life.

I cleared my throat, ignored her question, and said, "You were right about Trinity's work. It's incredible. And, oddly enough, it's exactly what I was starting to envision for this gallery."

"You're changing the subject, but I'll allow it for now. Just know the conversation isn't over."

"You sound like Katerina."

Lyrica laughed. "I'll take that as a compliment. Now, tell me this vision you have."

I told her about the blend of photorealism and surrealism I was considering, the hint of fairy tale that this town seemed to bring to life. She listened, dropping a question or two here or there. "It's what I'm painting," I told her honestly. "Nothing I've ever done before. Might be crap. You'll have to be the judge of it, but regardless of whether I display my art or not, it's the vibe I want here."

"I can't imagine anything you created being crap, Lincoln, but I also know you sensitive-artist types need to have your egos stroked. I'll come down next week." She said the last part as if she was being forced into hell. "Now, tell me who the woman is."

My eyes went to the doorway and the sounds of the stand mixer I'd never thought I'd use but bought with the vision of family holidays in mind. The whirring noise was strangely and pleasantly calming.

"I'm not ready to share Willow with anyone yet."

There was silence over the line for a beat before Lyrica said, "Well, fuck. That means it's actually serious. Why didn't you tell me?"

I was caught between a rock and a hard place. If I told her I'd known Willow for mere days, I'd never hear the end of it. But if I let her think it had been longer, she'd be hurt I hadn't told her before now.

"I didn't know her before I moved here," I finally said. I'd lived here for over a week, hadn't I? Wasn't that enough time to find someone and date them?

She huffed out a laugh. "Now, that's my Lincoln. Always feeling too much, too quickly. I hadn't even recognized that you'd whirled me into a relationship until the rest of the world proclaimed it."

"This is different," I snapped.

"It's not a negative trait," Lyrica said softly. "You stick your heart on your sleeve, and it's beautiful to watch. It worked its spell on me until I realized I loved you but wasn't in love with you. You've been hurt a lot, by me and others. I just don't want to see you get trampled again."

My jaw ticked. "You were the only one who got hurt."

She sighed. "How many times have I told you—"

"It's not my fault. Believe it or not, I'm getting there."

Surprise drifted over the line. "Really?"

"Maybe."

"If this is because of her, I like her already," Lyrica added.

The doorbell rang at the same time as I got a notification on my phone app. When I swiped it open, I saw a man in a black suit and sunglasses that all but screamed special agent.

"Gotta go. Someone's at the door," I said. "I'll talk to you later."

I barely heard her goodbye before I hung up and headed

toward the entryway. When I looked toward the kitchen, Willow was in the archway with a frown on her face.

"It's the Secret Service," I told her and saw her shoulders relax.

I opened the door slightly and was barely able to get out a hello before the man in front of me was whipping out his badge. "Hardy sent me. Special Agent Johnson. You have something for me to pick up?"

The guy was irritated, likely figuring whatever job he'd been doing in D.C. was more important than this. But it wasn't on me that Hardy had sent him.

"Come on in," I said, swinging the door open. He barely glanced around before following me into the study where I picked up the bag I'd put the note in. As I turned to hand it to him, Willow came in, wiping her hands on a towel, nervously glancing between me and the agent.

The look on the agent's face as he glanced over her was enough to make a feral growl lodge in my chest. He took her in slowly and appreciatively from the top of the long moonlit hair she'd secured in some messy contraption on top of her head, over the slender curves and her fuller hips, to the hint of long leg that showed through another diaphanous skirt. His gaze lingered on those curves on the way back up before landing on her face once more.

I wanted to punch him. I wanted to shove the note in his hands and slam him out of the house.

And yet, I also couldn't blame him because Willow was stunningly beautiful even with a swipe of flour on her face and a berry stain on her shirt.

I crossed the room and handed him the note before clenching my hands at my sides. "Thanks for making the drive out."

"Hardy said it was important," Special Agent Johnson said, but the doubt rang through his words. As almost every agent I'd encountered had been excellent at keeping their emotions from their voice, it made this guy's rookie status clear. "Has me going over to some place called Flat Mike's to follow up on a guy named Pacheco Malta."

Willow snorted, and both our eyes snapped to her. She bit her lip, tugged at her necklace, and then said, "Sorry, but if you show up at Flat Mike's looking like that, you'll be lucky if you *just* get tossed. They don't approve of law enforcement there."

Johnson looked down at his suit, tugging at the lapel with a snap, ears turning red. "I have a change of clothes in the car."

Instead of allowing this conversation and his clear interest in Willow to continue, I directed him toward the front door. "Tell Hardy I said thanks for looking into it for me."

I basically shut the door in the guy's face before whipping around to Willow.

"That was rude," she said.

I stalked over to her, brushing at the flour on her cheek. "He was ogling you."

She laughed, batting my hand away and using the back of hers to rub at her face. "Ogling? Is that even a word we use in the twenty-first century?"

I shrugged, eyes narrowing in on the bits of dust still clinging to her and wondering what she was creating. "What are you making?"

"Dinner and dessert, just like I promised. I hope you don't mind, but I borrowed a sketchpad you had on the buffet."

I tried to remember when I'd left one there and couldn't. "Was it empty?" I asked.

"Had a bunch of sketches of the angel from the O'Bannon mausoleum," she said, eyes darting away. "I'm sorry, I probably should have asked… And I definitely shouldn't have looked if you didn't give me permission."

I remembered drawing the broken-winged angel over and over after I'd first seen Willow in the cemetery and thought she was Sienna. I hadn't been able to get it out of my head, and it still wasn't right, even now, as part of the scene I'd spread across three canvases at the gallery. But I hadn't just sketched the angel in that book. I'd also drawn Willow before I'd seen her up close and personal, before I'd been able to give life to the vision, and before I'd figured out why something was off as I'd tried to force Sienna into the scene.

"You're welcome to anything in my house," I told her honestly.

Her eyes drifted back to mine, wide and surprised. "You really shouldn't offer that sort of thing to people who are practically strangers. They could steal from you."

"I didn't make that offer to anyone. I made it to you. Are you going to steal from me, Willow?"

"Of course not!" she blustered.

The timer went off, and she rushed down the hall to the kitchen. I followed, drawn by the sweet scents coming from the oven as much as her.

I almost laughed when I walked in. Almost every available surface in the kitchen was being used. It wasn't messy as much as organized chaos.

I approached the sketchbook on the corner of the island. Sitting just above it was her phone, open to an image of a Gustav Klimt landscape. On the sketchpad, she'd drawn a rather crude recreation of the masterpiece and then dissected it with circles, writing the names of different sweets inside them.

"You're going to make a Klimt?"

She pulled something that smelled like warm brownies mixed with the scent of a berry field from the oven.

When she turned, her face was flushed, and it wasn't just from the heat coming from the open door.

"It's probably ridiculous. But I don't have the skill for faces yet, and I love the gold leaf he added to many of his pieces. I'm probably trying too hard, but I can't get it out of my head, so I know it's what I should be working on."

I understood that more than she'd ever realize, an idea taking hold and not letting go. But the only thing I couldn't get out of my head right now was Willow. I itched to be back at the studio, painting her. Brushing her over canvas. Portraying her as I saw her now with the light pouring in from the window, turning those moonlight strands into sparkling crystals.

Beautiful pink staining her cheeks. Brilliance surrounding her like a halo.

The angel I needed to match the demon I'd painted.

I did what I always did when an image consumed me. I headed for the door and my studio. I fished around in my pockets, trying to remember where I'd placed my keys. "I have to go. Stay here. Don't leave. I'll set the alarm."

She followed me. "You're leaving?"

The hint of panic in her voice stalled me just as I picked up the keys from the side table I'd tossed them on earlier. I turned around to see alarm flit across her face that she tried to hide.

The artist in me was clamoring to pour her onto paper. The need was so great I could almost feel the strokes. The squish of the tube. Smell the turpentine and oil paints.

But then, the image of my kitchen and the carefully constructed chaos hit me. She'd stayed here all day after visibly shuddering at the idea of going home to the cottage. She didn't want to be reminded of what had happened, but more, she didn't want to be alone. She'd bounced back from the note, from the flicker of fear that it might have been the Viceroys coming after her, but that terror still lurked under the surface, ready to burst out again at any moment.

She'd lived with that nightmare for six years. I hated it. It made me want to find and destroy Aaron and whoever else was tied to his organization with my bare hands.

So, for the first time in maybe my entire life, I denied myself the thing I'd always allowed to consume me. Instead, I tossed the keys back where I'd found them.

"No. I'm not leaving." I shook my head.

Her shoulders went back, and that resilient smile I now saw as forced returned. "It's okay. Seriously, go do what you need to do. I'll clean up and try to get out of your hair."

She was halfway back to the kitchen before I caught her, banding my arm around her and drawing her to me. With a hand to her chin, I forced her to look at me. "You're not in my hair, and I don't want you to leave. I've told you that already, and I absolutely meant it."

She pushed her forced beam up to full wattage. "I'm being ridiculous."

"Even if you hadn't had a huge fright today, I'd ask you to stay. I'd want you here. But knowing you'd be at your house alone, that someone else might know that too…" I shook my head, acid burning my throat at the mere idea. I brushed my thumb over her lower lip, and her breathy exhale coasted over my skin, setting me ablaze. "Stay. Stay here. Stay tonight. Stay tomorrow. Stay for as long as you like."

Her eyelids fluttered closed. The long pale lashes another image I wanted to capture.

"I'm off today and tomorrow. Mom will be back on Sunday by the time I'm done at The Tea Spot. If you don't mind, I'd like to not be alone until then."

I wanted her to stay because of me. Because she couldn't get enough of me. Not because of the fear about being by herself. But I'd take whatever I could get. I'd take what I could of Willow whenever and however she was willing to give it.

# Chapter Twenty-two

# Willow

***THAT'S WHERE IT IS***

Performed by Carrie Underwood

***THE RELIEF THAT FLEW THROUGH ME*** when Lincoln didn't leave was just another ridiculous emotion in the sea of them I'd had since the minute he'd walked into the cemetery. His house was hardly a good hiding spot if it was Poco who'd left the note. He'd assumed we were dating. He'd seen Lincoln and me together several times now, and he'd likely know to look here if he couldn't find me at the cottage. But as irrational as it might be, I felt hidden here. Not only hidden but safe and cared for. As if he was just a regular guy, and I was just a regular girl, and we could let these tantalizing emotions run free.

Maybe Lincoln had cast a spell on me with the seductive rub of his thumb along my mouth, or maybe it was just years of aching for this type of connection and affection, but I wanted the spell to last for at least a few hours more. I wanted to suspend time while we were secreted away from the world.

So, instead of objecting, instead of insisting he go do whatever he'd been about to do, I simply breathed out, "Thank you."

He leaned down, lips brushing a feathery kiss along my forehead that had my eyes fluttering shut and my entire being convulsing as his scent, his kindness, his brave humanity filled my soul. It was all too much and not enough.

He released me, stepping back, and I opened my eyes to see his smile had returned. What would it be like to see him like this all the time? Happy. Content. I ached for him to have that possibility—for us both to have it.

"Do I get to have dessert before dinner?" he asked. "Because that smell is taunting me."

I shook my head. "No. Absolutely not. It's not even ready yet. That's just the base. Plus, I've got the meal completely planned out, and I refuse to let you ruin it by starting with sweets."

"The culinary snob in you is coming out again. Tell me, Sweetness, have you ever had cake for breakfast?"

I rolled my eyes. "I mean, loaf cakes and scones might as well be cake."

"No. I mean a full-on, layered cake with buttercream icing and all."

"And I suppose you have?" I asked, but there was doubt in my voice.

"It was practically a requirement in our house after any celebration. We always had too much cake left, and my sisters and I made it a thing. Cake for breakfast. Sometimes…" His voice lowered as if telling me a sensual secret. "Sometimes, we even put it in a bowl, poured milk over it, and ate it like cereal.

I gasped, and he snickered.

"The absolute horror on your face is worth the risk that came from telling you that secret. If it ever appears in some news article someday—*the Matherton siblings ate cake for breakfast*—our parents would take the heat for our unhealthy lifestyle, the press would make some Marie Antoinette reference about us needing to be beheaded, and yet it would still be worth it."

Multiple emotions ran through me. Pleasure that he trusted me. Frustration that he'd had to live with those kinds of thoughts most of his life, doubting all the people around him, having to hold back his secrets from those who only saw him as the president's son—someone to use, someone to gain something from. Even once I'd figured out who Lincoln was,

I'd never really seen him in that light. And now, knowing him more, all I saw was a passionate, talented, caring human. A man living with buckets of grief and yet able to see through it enough to reach out to others.

The dark superhero and archangel mixed, hiding in plain sight.

I knew what it was like to always be keeping part of yourself from those you were with.

I wanted his playfulness to remain, the teasing taunts rather than the dark shadows that could crawl over him as easily as they crawled over me, so I kept the horrified look on my face before responding. "It's blasphemy. That's utter blasphemy. Not only because milk would ruin the texture and flavor of the cake as it was designed to be eaten by the chef who made it, but because that is not breakfast."

"Please. And donuts or pancakes or fancy crepes are any better?"

I shook my head. "Different textures. Different combinations of flavors and purpose."

He stepped around me, heading back toward the kitchen. "I'm going to turn you from a food snob yet. Where's the dessert?"

I chased after him as he searched the kitchen, eyes landing on the chocolate layer I'd pulled from the oven. He slid open a drawer and grabbed a fork. I barely reached him in time to stop him from plunging it into the center of the brownie-like combination.

"Don't you dare ruin my dessert!" My laugh spoiled the command. I brought his hand with the fork to my chest, snaking the utensil away with my free hand and flinging it toward the sink.

"What are you offering instead? You know, to keep me from diving into this treat that is just sitting here in my house, waiting for me?" he asked, gaze falling to my lips and then down to my chest, which was rising and falling quickly with each wild beat of my heart.

When his eyes returned to mine, they were molten. Warm

blueberry syrup melting my reserves as if they were butter, making me want to throw every caution to the wind and take, take, take. Gorge myself on the passion he was presenting me with. That all-consuming want sucked me right in because before I knew it, I was rising on my toes and placing a soft but almost chaste kiss on his lips.

When I went to step back, one of his hands gripped my hip while the other went to the back of my head, and he pressed our mouths together with a fierceness that surprised me. Every vein that had been dancing along the edge of the fire burst open. Twined in deep with the longing was a feeling of utter acceptance. For some reason, this man saw me. All of me. And liked it. Wanted more of it.

Joy. This was joy. All the other times I'd thought I'd experienced pure happiness, I'd been wrong. Locked to him, bodies and souls melting together…this was what happiness was. It was the absolute definition of it.

God, I wanted to keep him. Keep every moment.

When I finally came up for air, when I finally broke away, my voice was breathless. "Dinner will be ready in an hour if you get out of the kitchen and let me finish rather than distracting me."

His eyes lit up. "I've been blamed on numerous occasions by my family for forgoing food in lieu of a good distraction."

"Not on my watch!"

"Food snob *and* food police."

I laughed and turned back to the pancetta I'd been in the middle of chopping when the doorbell had rung. Lincoln stepped away, sitting on the barstool at the island, and pulling his sketchpad to him along with the pencil I'd snagged. He flipped past my design to a fresh page and started drawing while I worked.

I hadn't meant to look at the drawings when I'd been searching for a blank page. But it wasn't just the angel statue that had snagged my eye. It had been the pictures of someone who looked like me but not quite. A blurred version of me, without the freckles and a more pointed chin. He'd said he'd seen me in the cemetery before that night with Poco, and from a distance, he wouldn't have known I had the marks running along my nose and cheeks. It had been odd to see myself, or some strangely fuzzy rendering of me, on the page.

But I didn't let it go to my head. He hadn't known me. He'd been caught by the idea of someone in the cemetery in the middle of the night.

As I finished the meal, he sketched and asked a million questions. Innocuous, getting-to-know-you kind of questions about favorite books and shows and music. Places in Cherry Bay I liked, and did I know there was a fairy-tale castle just down the road, hidden away?

"River Briar, right? The theater department at Bonnin uses it once a year for their annual fundraiser. The woman who owns it graduated from the university. I heard she didn't even know her dad before she inherited the place, but her husband makes movie sets there now."

"Can anyone visit it?" he asked.

"It's not open to the public, to my knowledge, but they hold private weddings in addition to the charity events there, so they must let prospective clients on site. I'd bet they'd be happy to show *you* around."

He grinned. "Me? You think?"

I tossed a piece of bell pepper at him. He caught it and munched on it.

"If I can get someone to find out about it, do you want to go with me?" he asked.

My breath faltered, lungs spasming. It would mean being seen in public with him again, risking someone who actually knew who he was taking a picture and posting it. But that was a worry for another day, so I told him the simple truth. "I'd love to see it."

He pulled out his phone, fingers flashing over the screen before pocketing it again.

"So, you just text someone and magically get what you want?" I asked.

His brows bunched together in thought. "Not quite. The artist you saw at the gallery this morning…she's painted the castle. She said she works for the caterer who does their events, so I thought she might know someone who could get us a tour."

He went back to drawing, and the silence settled down between us for so long this time I started to worry I'd said something that had offended him. Had it been the tease about him magically getting whatever he wanted?

When we sat down to the first course, and he was still lost in thought, I missed the easy laughter and the playful back-and-forth we'd had.

"I'm sorry if I offended you."

He looked up at me, brows lifting. "What?"

"Ever since I made the dig about you getting whatever you wanted, you've been quiet. If I hit a nerve, I'm sorry. I don't really think it's true. I was just teasing. You aren't spoiled or entitled. If I didn't know who your dad is, I'd never assume you'd led a privileged life. You're way too… I don't know what the right word is. Down to earth? Empathetic?"

"I'm the one who should apologize," he said. I'd tried putting our plates on opposite sides of the table, but he'd moved them side by side again like he had at lunch, so when he put his fork down and turned to face me, our knees collided. "You didn't offend me at all. My brain got caught up in an idea for this series of paintings I'm working on. It's what I was drawing." His head tilted toward the sketchbook on the island. "I get lost in my art all the time. My sisters call it my Mr. Grouchypants state because if and when I'm pulled out of it, I usually howl like a beast. But the truth is, most of the time, a gorilla in a tutu could dance in front of me, and I wouldn't see it. The worst sort of tunnel vision."

The tension released from my back. "A gorilla in a tutu?"

He chuckled.

As we finished the rest of the meal, he returned to the more talkative, inquisitive man I'd seen earlier. His gaze, full and intense, was on me once more, and I felt ridiculous all over again. Needy. Silly. I didn't know how to do casual friendships any more than relationships. Other than Shay, I hadn't had any real friends since the ones I'd grown up with in Chicago. At first, I'd kept to myself for fear of slipping up, and then later because it had become a habit.

I hadn't felt lonely.

I hadn't been unhappy.

But now, having this simple, ordinary conversation with Lincoln proved I'd forgotten what life was like when you weren't alone. After the trial, I'd told myself I'd do everything I could to experience life and find joy in every day, but I'd still been holding myself back. Mom had been right when she'd told me the same thing in the store. I was letting the Viceroys win.

As Lincoln pushed his plate away after the main course, he said, "That was incredible, Willow."

Happiness coasted through me. Not since receiving praise from my instructors at culinary school had a compliment hit me so hard. Not even Hector's expounding on the piece I'd brought to The Tea Spot.

"Have you ever thought about opening your own restaurant?" he asked.

I shook my head. "No. Absolutely not. I don't want to run a business. I want to create not manage a restaurant or deal with finances and taxes and the health department. I like making meals for people I care about, but I don't love it the way I love making pastries."

I deftly sliced the tall layers of strawberry chiffon and chocolate torte and brought him a piece.

He closed his eyes while taking a bite, pleasure coating his face in a way that made my belly go soft once again. When he opened his eyes, the heat there only melted me more.

"Delicious. Sweet but not too sweet. Vibrant. Complex but light," he said, sticking his finger into the whipped cream frosting and licking it off.

I could only watch. Fascinated. Full of that hunger and yearning I'd been having since the moment he descended into my world.

"It's just like you." The words hummed out of him.

I jumped up from the table. I recognized it as running and knew it made me a chicken, but he was terrifying in the way he kept breaking through all my boundaries. Every moment I sat with him, I wanted more of the impossible. I'd wanted someone who would take the leap, take a risk on me, but I hadn't really thought about the reverse. What would I risk for them?

Would I risk Mom? Her safety? Mine?

I started cleaning the mess I'd made in the kitchen while he finished his dessert, watching me the entire time. The quiet now wasn't a vacuum. Instead, it was loaded with the passion that moved between us.

When I'd finally righted the counters as much as I could, he came over and put his plate in the dishwasher. "What would you like to watch?"

It was the last thing I expected him to ask. I frowned. "What?"

He raised a brow, lips twitching. "Dinner. Dessert. Movie. I figure it's as close to a first date as we'll get at the moment."

My throat tightened at the thought of us dating. Of being on a date. More impossibilities. I shouldn't stay, but I also didn't want to go home. I was a mess. A movie would be a good distraction, wouldn't it? Still, I couldn't help but ask, "What would you be doing if I wasn't here?"

"Obsessing over the gallery, heading to the studio to paint, or reading."

"Do you read a lot?"

He nodded. "It occupies my brain. Allows me to fall asleep sometimes."

"What are you reading now?"

"*The Night Circus*. Do you read?"

"Not very much. I'd rather be baking."

He grabbed my hand and tugged me out of the kitchen, flicking off lights as he went and guiding me toward the stairs. My brain kicked into overdrive, longing and nervousness mingling and making my palms sweat.

"Where are we going?" I asked, voice breathless and airy.

"I don't have a television in the living room yet. The only one hooked up is in my bedroom."

My feet turned to cement blocks, dragging my fingers from his grip.

He turned back, lips twitching. "I promise to be the perfect gentleman. No nefarious reasons for inviting you into my room. I have a little sitting area there and the love seat is actually really far away from the bed—at least a good three feet."

It was a dare. I recognized one when I saw one. But the truth was, my curiosity was stronger than my nervousness. What would his room look like? Would it be forcefully sunny like the kitchen or a calm blue sea like his study?

I urged my feet to move again, and his grin grew. I followed him to the last room on the second floor and entered the dark side of his house. The place the tortured superhero resided. The mesmerizing vampire. The room was elegant and moody with woods stained almost black and burgundy brocades layered with the barest hints of purples and silvers. Angled several feet away from the king-sized bed with its intricately carved footboard was a low-backed love seat in a plush wine-colored fabric piled with accent pillows. A stack of paintings was propped up against a dresser partially hiding a wide-screened television.

Lincoln began moving the canvases into the hall. I went to help, and my hands stalled on a painting of a woman who looked a lot like me. Except, like in the sketchbook downstairs, she had no freckles, her chin was narrower, and her eyes were a soft, robin's-egg blue. A glance at the lower corner showed Lincoln's name scrawled with a date from over a decade ago. Long before he'd ever met me.

He came back into the room, stopping next to me and looking down at the painting.

"That poorly executed piece was my early attempt at capturing Sienna. I didn't know what the hell I was doing."

A million doubts flooded into me. I'd thought he was as attracted to me as I was to him. I'd thought he saw me…the real me. But what if, instead, he was simply capturing a fleeting reflection of the woman he'd loved and lost?

Why did that hurt so damn bad? Why did it make me want to slam the canvas down on something sharp and tear at the face that looked up at me? Why was I filled with the same jealousy that had coursed through me when I'd seen his head bent close to the artist at the gallery?

I swallowed over the lump in my throat. "I look like her."

When I risked meeting his eyes, I saw a flicker of something there I couldn't name. Loss. Compassion. Devotion. But was it for her, or was it for me?

He took the painting from my hand, saying, "That first night I saw you in the cemetery, I thought she'd returned to haunting me." He set the painting so it was lying sideways, propped up against the wall with her face turned away from us. I didn't have time to process the words about her haunting him before he'd captured my hand and was running his thumb along the palm. "We both know I'd be lying if I said there isn't a resemblance between you."

"Resemblance? We could be twins."

His gaze bored into mine. "Yes. But do you know what I've learned from actually living with twins most of my life?"

I shook my head, unable to speak.

"No matter how much they have in common physically, they're not anything alike. They're individual people. Individual souls. Their wants and needs and desires are different. Katerina may share Juliette's chin and eyes and hair, but my sisters are nothing alike. One is fire and sass and attitude, and the other is peace and calm and nurture. Anyone who met one and then expected the other to be the same would be quickly enlightened. You may look like Sienna, Willow, but you aren't her. There's nothing about you that's the same."

"I'm a flawed version of her perfection."

"Believe me, Sienna had her own flaws. That painting was done by a sixteen-year-old who idolized her and glossed over the nuances that actually made her interesting. She had a scar"—he ran his finger along my chin—"from falling out of a treehouse we tried to build in the backyard. And wild eyebrows that were never smooth." His finger skimmed my brows.

My body loved every touch. Longed for more. But my heart was still twisted and hurting from the seed of doubt that wouldn't be easily shaken after seeing the portrait. It had stolen some of my peace. Some of my blissfulness.

"Do you know what Sienna said when she saw that painting?" he asked, and as I obviously couldn't know, he kept going. "She told me I hadn't captured anything but a fake shell. It was missing her soul. And she was right. She's always been right when it comes to me."

His hand landed on the curve of my neck, thumb at my pulse point. The beat thudded fast and furious against the soft pressure of his fingers, revealing my anxiety to him.

"I miss her. I'll always miss her. But she wasn't perfect. Besides, it's neither her nor perfection I crave these days. The only thing I hunger for is you." His voice was so low and deep it vibrated through me. And I wasn't sure why those words stabbed even more when they were meant to soothe.

"I should go," I said softly. I should. For so many reasons, of which finding out I looked like his long-lost love was only one.

I was surprised when his hands picked me up and practically tossed me onto the love seat where I landed with a surprised huff.

"I'm not letting you turn this into something it's not," he said, glowering down at me. "My interest in you has nothing to do with her."

"Every time you look at me, you have to see her."

"I see Willow. That's who I see when I look at you. Just like I don't look at Juliette and see some imitation of Katerina."

I spun my dad's class ring in my fingers. So many reasons for me not to stay. But I also heard the determination in his voice. The raw truth. I believed him. He didn't see me as her. And he wanted me to stay. He hungered for me. When would I ever hear a man say that to me again? Would there ever be someone else who did?

The thought of walking out his door brought more pain than the idea of staying, because I hungered too. For the euphoria of his touch. For the connection. But also for the idea that I could mean something to this caring, protective man.

It was wrong because it could hurt Mom and me.

It was wrong because he'd already lost a woman he loved and seen others he cared about hurt, and I could lead more of that anguish to his door.

"Lincoln, I—" I started but then shook my head, cutting myself off. He simply watched me battle with myself. Patient. Waiting.

Hadn't I said I wanted more of him? This was more. This was him openly sharing his past with me. The grumpy man who'd saved me from the cemetery had peeled back that tough outer layer and shown me the gentleness beneath it.

I'd promised myself I'd take what I could get out of life, even when I was bound by so many restrictions. The rules governing me might be the reason I was forced to give him up before I was ready, so did I really want to walk away when I had the chance to stay, simply because his old girlfriend looked like me?

We had much bigger hurdles to jump than that. Impossible ones.

So, I'd take these few hours I had with him this weekend, and I'd savor the feeling of falling head over heels for someone before it was ripped away.

I released the tension that had remained in my shoulders and curled my feet under me on the love seat.

"So, what are we going to watch?"

The relief coasting over his face reinforced that I'd made the right decision. He'd done so much for me already. If my being here brought him some sort of comfort, any sort of pleasure, I could and would give him it. I'd give it to us both.

# Chapter Twenty-three

## Lincoln



*AS I TURNED BACK TO THE* television and started searching in drawers for the remote, I was able to breathe again. For a moment, I'd been certain she was going to walk out, certain she was going to leave when all I wanted was for her to stay…stay and stay and stay. Having her here felt like a soothing balm. It felt right.

When she'd looked up from Sienna's painting, the hurt in her eyes had sliced through me like a box cutter through tape. I'd meant every word I'd said. Other than those first two nights when I'd thought Sienna had returned to haunt me, I hadn't once thought of Willow as her. If anything, the yin and yang of them stood out more, twining around each other because of their physical similarities but standing out due to the strength of their opposing forces.

Sienna stomping and storming through my gallery and kitchen had only emphasized it more.

In some ways, I wanted Willow for every way her light opposed those gothic images. For the light that promised to always guide me home.

After I finally found the TV remote in a drawer with a pile of cords, I joined her on the sofa. Flicking the television on, I swiped through the movie choices on the streaming service.

"What do you want to watch?" I asked.

"You've been here over a week, right?"

I nodded and kept sliding through the movie options.

"You haven't watched your TV at all?" she asked with a head tilt toward the paintings that had been piled in front of it.

I turned to find her gaze locked on me. "No, I've been unpacking or painting." She raised a brow, and I kept going, "Truth is, reading or listening to music is better than television when I can't sleep, but sometimes watching reruns helps too. While I can't actually stay in bed if I'm awake, it's good to stay close if my eyes do get heavy." I waved at the stereo system, the shelf of books, and a little makeshift tea center on a corner table. "So I make sure I have everything I need close at hand."

She frowned. "What do you mean you can't actually stay in bed? Isn't that where you'd want to be if you hope to fall asleep again?"

Normally, when anyone probed about my insomnia and my routines, I'd close off, afraid they'd use some or all of it against me like Felicity had. But with Willow, I found myself wanting to tell her all of it so she'd maybe understand in a way that no one else could.

"Staying in bed is almost impossible because it's like ants crawling through me. The feeling eases once I move. Plus, it helps keep my brain wired right." She frowned, and I explained, "I've been through a shit ton of therapy. If you can name it, I've probably tried it. What works best for me is a combination of several but is closest to stimulus control therapy, which basically has your mind associating your bed with only the necessary activities. You use it just for sleep and sex."

At my mention of sex, her eyes darted to the bed behind us and back, and that delightful pink tinge hit her cheeks.

For the first time, I really considered her age—twenty-three. Life had already beaten experience into her no one should have had—but especially not at sixteen or twenty or twenty-three. But now, I thought about that delightful blush and the sweetness that followed her and wondered just what kind of sexual encounters she'd had.

Was there someone she'd made love to? Someone she'd cared about? Just thinking about it returned that feral jealousy to me I'd felt when the Secret Service agent had been here. But the idea of her not having had anyone in her life left me feeling almost as ferocious. If she hadn't had those experiences yet, it was another thing the gang in Chicago had taken from her.

Both times we'd kissed, she'd seemed just as greedy and hungry as me, but now, I was even more relieved I hadn't taken her to the kitchen floor this morning. If it was her first time, she deserved more than cold, hard tile. I couldn't make any assumptions, but I'd let her decide how far we took things, and I'd be even more careful about how we proceeded.

I turned back to the screen. "What do you think of *A Knight's Tale*?"

She frowned. "I don't think I've seen it."

My eyebrows raised. "That's settled, then. You're in for quite the ride."

And when the color on her cheeks grew at my words, my body reacted to it, tempting me to go back on the promises I just made to myself and show her just what a beautiful ride we could take together.

I cleared my throat and asked, "Would you like to change into something more comfortable? A pair of sweats?"

She looked down at the berry stains on her T-shirt with a wince, fingering her flowy skirt. "That would be great."

I went into my closet and brought out a pair of gray sweats and an old Penn State shirt for her, pointing to the door on the opposite wall. "Bathroom is through that door."

She thanked me and went inside.

I tossed aside my jeans for my own pair of sweats and then went to the linen cupboard in the hall, pulling out a blanket. When I came back in, she was on the love seat again. My sweats swam around her legs with the shirt covering her hips, and some animalistic part of me liked her that way. In my things. As if I was marking her with my scent like some ancient Homo sapien throwback.

I switched off the light and joined her on the sofa. As I started the movie, I swooped an arm around her waist and tucked her up against me before covering us with the blanket. She hesitated, resisting ever so slightly before she allowed herself to sink into me.

Within minutes of starting the movie, her eyes were already glued to the screen and Heath Ledger. The guy was dead, and I was still jealous of the way she was watching him so avidly. What had she called herself earlier? Ridiculous. I was equally ridiculous. The entire situation between us was, but I wouldn't change a moment of it.

Sitting there, with her in my clothes, sharing a blanket in the dark of my bedroom, it was intimate and personal. While my body practically vibrated in every place we were joined, a hopeful serenity also swept through me. As if everything in my life had somehow righted itself simply because she was at my side. As if this was what was always supposed to happen when I decided to move to Cherry Bay. I thought of Sienna's words once again.

*She's your person.*

I believed it. Not just because a ghost had told me, but because my soul felt such absolute tranquility with Willow there.

♫ ♫ ♫

The credits rolled, and I hit the off button, pitching the room into darkness.

Willow was asleep. She'd barely made it halfway through the movie before passing out, even though it was only nine o'clock. Her body was deep in slumber while mine was wide awake. While this was nothing new, I was more furious at the itching sensation growing inside me than I had been in years. I didn't want to leave the peace of our embrace. I was enjoying the full weight of her leaning into me, reveling in her sugary scent and the gentle warmth of her breath as it feathered along the arm I had around her.

Even with her eyes closed and her thoughts tucked away

in dreamland, my mind reeled with new ways to paint her. Ophelia. No…not the tragedy of Ophelia. Sleeping Beauty, then. Hunted by evil because of her parents, but kind and generous and gentle. With a bed of flowers and moonlight streaming around her as her inner light pushed at the shadows of the forest.

My fingers twitched. The desperate need to get up that always found me pricked at my insides. My brain was unable to stop flipping from scene to scene like an old slideshow reel. I spiraled from one idea to the next before slipping back to that first Sleeping Beauty image of her and how I would show the shadow and light.

My soul was happy here, tucked up beside her, but my mind wouldn't shut the fuck up. My restless body was even now threatening to wake her, twitching restlessly beneath her.

I closed my eyes, sighed, and then slowly and reluctantly moved. I held her up gently while I slid out from under her and piled several throw pillows in my place. When I eased her down, her lids fluttered, and I thought maybe she'd wake, but then she squeezed one of the pillows to her, and her breathing evened out again. I stared at her, the longing to wake her with a kiss almost impossible to ignore. I reached out, brushing her cheek that glowed even in the darkness of the room that was broken only by the starlight slipping in the window.

More kaleidoscope images reeled through me.

I spun on a heel and headed for the hallway, picking up a blank canvas from the stack I'd moved out of my room, wishing I hadn't taken the majority of my supplies to the studio. I needed more of my things at home so I wouldn't have to go downtown in the middle of the night. Although, it could hardly be called the middle of the night, even for people without insomnia. Maybe if you were a five- or six-year-old, you'd be tucked into bed by now.

But as Willow worked baker's hours, I figured it might just be her normal pattern. Maybe she was able to train her body to sleep in ways I'd never been able to teach mine.

In the kitchen, I propped the canvas up on the counter at

an angle against the upper cabinets. It wasn't an easel, but it would suffice. I turned on all the lights, made myself a cup of tea, and then stared at the blank linen for several minutes before finally starting a long curve that would be the slope of her lying in the grass. I let the Sleeping Beauty image guide me.

How long had it been since I'd had multiple projects going at once? I couldn't remember. Maybe before Lyrica had been shot. Before Dad was elected President. Before my life had been put on display more than ever before.

As I worked, I wished for music. The blaring of a symphony. But I couldn't put it through the house speakers and wake Willow. I could listen with my earbuds, but who the hell knew where I'd left them? I barely remembered my phone these days. Where was it now? In the pocket of my jeans? I could pause what I was doing to search for it and play the music softly in the kitchen, but my fingers were already moving. Black across the page.

Maybe I wouldn't do this one in oils. Maybe I'd do pencil and ink. Maybe I'd do watercolors.

The strawberry-and-chocolate dessert Willow had made sat nearby, adding an aroma to the visual, and suddenly, prickly berry vines grew around the edges of the drawing. Sweet and dangerous.

I wanted the smells embedded into the painting to give it the full sensory experience Willow's food art had provided. How would that even work? Oil scents near the display? A card below the image that people could scratch? But how would we keep the smells from blending in the gallery? Maybe only a few select pieces would have the scent. I'd think about it. Lyrica might have some ideas.

Somehow, I'd bring it together.

I had time.

Weeks, if not months, before anything of mine would be ready.

A loud crack drifted through the house from the front, ripping my eyes from the bouquet I was shading. Sienna's shimmering ghost appeared in the archway as another loud snap followed the first.

*Lincoln, go! Go quickly!* Worry bunched her brows together.

I dropped my charcoal pencil and headed for the front door.

One of the antique panes in the door was broken. A long, jagged slice skittered along the surface like a splintered windshield. My pulse raced, my gut twisted, and I fought the instinct to throw open the locks and chase after whoever had done this.

But I'd promised Hardy I wouldn't be stupid. Running, unarmed and barefoot, into the street while someone was taking shots at my house, with rocks or worse, would be entirely stupid.

Instead, I turned, intending to rush to the study, my laptop, and the cameras, when I caught sight of a figure coming down the stairs. For a single, panicked breath, I thought it was Sienna again until Willow's sleepy eyes, blinking awake in my clothes, registered.

"What was that noise?" she asked, confusion blending with a hint of fear.

"Get back!" I roared.

A third crash had the pane shattering completely. The glass tumbled to the doormat.

Willow cried out and instinctively crouched at the base of the stairs. I hurried over, grabbed her hand, and dragged her toward the study at the back of the house.

Once we were inside, she started to stand back up, and I pushed her toward the floor.

"Stay down!"

I stormed to the windows and drew the blinds before grabbing my laptop and joining her by the door. The cameras showed a masked man in all black dropping something on my front stoop. Even with the mask, he kept his face turned away just as he had when leaving the note at Willow's.

As we watched, he turned and headed down the street.

Outside my window, I swore I heard whistling. That serial-killer tune Poco was fond of, but it could easily have been all in my head.

My body shook with fury at the utter calmness of the man, the hubris to just assume he could do this and walk away.

Screw Hardy.

I flung the laptop and ran for the front door as Willow called my name in alarm.

I was out and down the sidewalk before I'd really considered what I was going to do.

"Come back and take a shot at me personally!" I snarled into the dark.

No one was there. No sounds.

No bodies.

"You won't get away with this!" I hollered.

"Lincoln!" Willow's voice was terrified, and I whirled around to see her haloed in the doorway. An easy target.

"Get back inside!" I thundered, heading her way.

As I went to step inside, I saw the note he'd left on the mat. The paper was old and torn. The ink spread through it like blood through veins.

I barely registered the words, *Next time it won't be rocks,* before I was forcing her inside and slamming the door behind us. I locked it, even though it felt useless with the missing pane, and shifted to take her in. Her eyes were wide and terrified, but anger had begun to make an appearance as well. Good. It would keep her from crumbling.

Suddenly, she shoved me in the shoulder with a strength that had me stumbling back into the wood frame.

"What were you thinking?!" she cried. "You could have been hurt. Shot. Oh my God. Oh my God." She was shaking, her entire being trembling. She sank onto the bottom step, dropping her face into her hands. "What was *I* thinking? Bringing you into this?"

I closed the distance, squatting before her and running my

palm over her silken strands. "Shh. It wasn't a gun, Sweetness. Just rocks. Just a coward taking a potshot."

Her head jerked up, sadness and fury there. "You didn't know that, Lincoln! You could have been hurt. I saw what happened to my dad… I saw his body jerk with every single bullet…" Her entire body trembled.

I wrapped my arms around her, pulling her into my chest. She buried her face in my neck as her body shuddered. "Shh. Shh. It's okay."

After the shaking slowed, I grabbed her hand and dragged her up the stairs, saying, "I need to call Hardy."

She was with me physically, but I could also feel her pulling away from me emotionally, erecting barriers she'd believe were for my own damn good. So she wouldn't be responsible for something happening to me. I understood that desire. It was the reason there was no way I'd let her walk out that door alone with someone after her.

I'd just found my jeans and recovered my phone from the pocket when she gasped, "You're bleeding!"

I looked down in surprise, searching for some unseen wound before finding the cut on my foot that had left a trail behind us. "The glass. I must have cut it on the glass. It's nothing."

I hit Hardy's number while Willow stared down at the blood for a long time before her eyes landed on the note I still had grasped in my free hand. She closed the distance, yanked it from me, and read. Her face paled impossibly more.

Just as she said, "I made you a target," Hardy's deep voice picked up, grunting out, "Lincoln?"

I didn't give a shit that it was the middle of the night, his time, as I said, "He took a potshot at us."

"What happened?" He was instantly awake as I explained the situation.

Willow turned, collected her clothes from the pile she'd made earlier, and pulled her phone from the table by the sofa.

If she thought she was leaving, she had another thing

coming.

I crossed over to the door, blocking it before she got anywhere near it, while I listened to Hardy's lecture about allowing a Secret Service detail back into my life. I was almost in agreement because, damn it, I needed someone with actual training to ensure Willow was safe. And yet, doing that—inviting them in—would end everything.

The Secret Service would dig around into her past, which would only flag the Marshals, and they'd come running. And everyone would agree our being together was an impossibility. Danger on both sides that the agencies would find unacceptable.

"I can't discuss this right now," I said to Hardy. "This is Poco. Find him."

I hung up and barred her exit as she tried to brush past me. When she refused to meet my gaze, panic worse than I'd felt while chasing an unknown assailant flooded me.

"Where do you think you're going?" I demanded.

"Home. If they're going to come, I won't let them bring you down with me. Let me by."

"No."

She stomped a bare foot. It was a soundless action, and yet it vibrated through me in a way that would have had me smirking if things weren't so desperate.

"If you go home, I'm coming with you," I told her with a deadly resolve.

"This isn't your fight!" she insisted, eyes flashing a warning I didn't heed.

"No?" I demanded. I'd prove to her just exactly why it was my goddamn battle.

I yanked her to me, pushing my lips against hers. All my anger and fear and frustration came out as I plundered her mouth. She held herself rigid for all of two seconds before I felt her drop her clothes and lean into me.

The taste of her overwhelmed my senses, instantly softening my kiss. I felt a tremor run up her spine that had nothing to do with fear. I slowed my frenzied pace, licking along her seam, seeking the inner recesses, touching, soothing, marking. Focusing on the beauty of our connection until I felt the edge of fear and darkness slip away from both of us. When I pulled back, her eyes were hazy with the same desire that tore through me.

"That feeling, Willow…that hunger we feel for each other…it proves this is very much my fight. Hell will have to rise up and swallow me whole before I let another woman I care about face tragedy on her own. I refuse. You go home, you lock me out, and I can guarantee I'll be sleeping on your front step. You kick me off your property, and I'll be lying along the sidewalk at your gate."

She shook her head, closed her eyes, and a single tear escaped, slowly traveling down her cheek as if connecting the soft dots of her freckles. I swiped at it with a thumb.

"It's not right, Lincoln," she whispered.

And because I was desperate, because I knew it was the last thing she wanted, I asked, "You want to call the Marshals, then? Have them come? Because there's no way I'm letting you face any of this alone."

She gritted her teeth and pushed out of my embrace. She crossed her arms over her chest, but I could tell my words had landed home. She was debating now just as fiercely as she'd debated leaving after she'd seen the painting of Sienna. We'd get through this just like we'd gotten through that. She'd see the truth. She had to.

"While you think about that, let me clean this foot up," I said. Because I didn't quite trust her not to leave, I grabbed her hand and pulled her with me into the bathroom.

I dug around for the first aid kit, soaked a cotton ball with antiseptic, and leaned against the cabinet, trying to locate the cut on the ball of my foot. She let out a huff, grabbed the cotton from me, and knelt at my feet, dabbing at the wound.

"I don't think there's any glass," she said quietly.

Taking a Band-Aid from the case, she placed it over the wound before surrounding the ball of my foot in medical adhesive to keep the bandage in place.

When she rose and placed the roll back into the first aid kit, her hands were shaking. I captured them in mine.

"It's going to be okay. This is just Poco. We're going to stop him."

"What if we're wrong? What if it isn't?"

"From what you told me, we'd both already be dead."

It was the wrong thing to say. Her eyes turned into huge wells of sorrow and indecision, a black hole of ugliness that shouldn't ever surround her eating her up from the inside. I brought her hand to my mouth and kissed the knuckles, trying to reassure her with my touch.

She watched the movement, and her breath caught.

I wanted to wipe away everything that had happened tonight. Yesterday. This week. I wanted to see only smiles on her face. Hear her laughter. Hear the soft breathy moan she'd let out when I'd kissed her in the kitchen. Feel her tremble from passion and pleasure instead of fear.

I swore I was going to make it happen. She'd be free of this nightmare if I had to use every single resource at my disposal…or my father's disposal. The goddamn military my dad commanded could figure this out. I'd do something to make sure Willow was never again in this situation.

# Chapter Twenty-four

## Willow

### *GUILTY AS SIN*
Performed by Taylor Swift

**WHEN I WAS THIS CLOSE TO** Lincoln, it was as if his pheromones rewired my brain, because the fear subsided, the self-reproach and terror receded to the far corners, and desire washed over me. A desire not just to have his body tucked up against mine, but a wild need to have this man in my life every day. Every moment.

He'd run down the street, chasing after Poco like some barefoot knight.

I snorted to myself. Falling asleep to Heath Ledger jousting had filled my brain with nonsense. But the truth was, Lincoln was more beautiful than any make-believe hero could ever be.

He was real. Alive.

His vibrancy was addicting.

While my conscience was screaming at me to go, to leave before he became collateral damage, before more darkness caught him in its grasp, my feet refused to obey. Indecision warred. Calling the Marshals was the smart move. Calling Mom.

But God, I didn't want to.

Instead, I wanted this. The tingling sensation that covered

me from head to toe simply because he was touching me.

It was selfish and risky, but all I wanted to do was exactly what he'd demanded. I wanted to stay. I wanted him. I wanted to stretch out every powerful second of these heart-stopping moments. To feel only the delight of his touch and the fire igniting deep inside. To celebrate the life streaming from us. Because living was all that mattered, wasn't it? Grasping with both hands at the good when it presented itself?

To steal joy instead of fear.

It should be so simple. But it wasn't. Everything with Lincoln was a dizzying twist of right and wrong. Everything was confusing.

Except one thing.

The yearning I felt for him wasn't confusing at all. It was clear cut, and it insisted on relief, required me to answer its call. It was louder than my conscience. Louder than my fears. So, instead of stepping away, instead of putting more space and an entire street between us, I stepped closer, eliminating any gap.

Our thighs touched, arms and chests colliding, and that flickering flame burst through my body. This. This was what I really wanted. Him. Me. The tantalizing touch.

Our gazes locked, his cobalt eyes darkening as he watched me rise on my toes and thread my hands behind his neck, tangling my fingers in those dark locks. It brought our mouths closer together, our breaths mingling so it was impossible to tell whose was whose. I wanted our bodies to do the same.

The blood pounding through my veins seemed to thicken. Goosebumps traveled over every inch of me, and still, we continued to stare. One heartbeat, two, a dozen went by until the desire in the room was so large it was almost its own entity.

I wasn't sure which of us made the final move, but suddenly, no air separated us, and our mouths were joined. He'd been furious when he'd kissed me in the doorway, insisting he had every right to make demands. But none of that fury remained. It had been replaced by a wild longing that edged toward madness as soft silk glided against silk.

He tasted of honey and tea.

He tasted of belonging and acceptance and courage.

I wanted it to be mine. All mine.

He deepened the kiss, parting my mouth with an expert flick of his tongue. The swift movement, the control and command, sent another wild throb through me, warmth settling deep in my stomach and seeping into my core. I pressed into him more, my soft curves colliding with the hard length of him.

He lifted me onto the counter, stepping between my legs, and all the while, his mouth did things to mine that felt illegal. That felt like sin had been given free rein. Or maybe the reverse. As if heaven was granting us a gift, and angels were singing.

My thighs tightened around his hips, and his eyes clouded with lust. Warm hands slid under the soft shirt I'd borrowed, lifting it and sending it sailing. And then, those clever lips dropped to my neck, sucking at my throbbing pulse before dipping down, down, down to taunt a pebbled tip with tongue and teeth.

I whispered his name like a song, and I felt him smile against my skin.

My body felt languid, drunk, and yet dizzily alive as he caressed and tormented and soothed.

He traced a wet line along my rib cage.

"Beautiful. This dusting on your body," he groaned as he tugged at the waistband of the sweats so his fingers could follow the smattering of freckles that pirouetted below. He pulled the sweats off, leaving me in a pair of basic white cotton underwear on his bathroom counter.

I didn't have time to think or be embarrassed as he moved on to worshipping my body. Warm hands slid over my legs, gently caressing an ankle, a calf, a thigh. He placed a hungry kiss on my belly button, tongue teasing the stud I'd gotten while at culinary school—an act of rebellion that seemed ludicrous now because no one ever saw it but me.

It wasn't like I ever had a chance to wear a bikini when I never left the confines of Cherry Bay. Never went beyond any of the boundaries I'd set for myself, including the cage that had nothing to do with location and everything to do with this…with emotion and lust and longing that I'd said I craved and yet had done everything to keep at bay.

Lincoln looked up, eyes darkening into pools of desire I wanted to dive into. Wanted to get lost in. I cupped his cheeks, drawing that wicked mouth up to mine, before devouring him as he'd been me, with want and wildness leading the way. Pure instinct rather than experience showing me how to plunder and demand.

Another breathy, desperate moan left me as I pressed my body closer. Needing more. Needing him.

He lifted me easily, moving us out of the bathroom. The cool air of the bedroom hit my naked flesh, causing a shiver to trail over me. He laid me down on the dark brocade before settling between my legs, our mouths already seeking each other again.

Strong hands glided down my arms, the gentle caresses turning me on one nerve ending at a time. Then he was stroking my sides, my waist, my hips, until his fingers slipped beneath the only item of clothing I had left and found a new home.

I broke our kiss as a gasp of pleasure ripped through me. My hips slammed against his palm. When I dared open my eyes, it was the look of awe on Lincoln's face that nearly sent me soaring.

"You're exquisite. So damn stunning," he said and took my lips with his again.

His fingers spun, turning, curving, sliding, cavorting.

A dam built inside me, stroke by stroke, threatening to break at any moment.

Until the intensity was almost too much to bear.

His mouth slid down my neck, teeth nipping at the soft juncture by my ear just as he plunged inside me again, and my body shook and let go.

I'd never felt more real. More human. More alive.

He slowly removed his fingers as my body trembled to a stop. His kisses turned softer and less demanding. I opened my eyes again as he rested his elbows on either side of my head, pushing up and away, taking that delicious mouth and keeping it just out of reach.

I knew what he was doing. I saw the look on his face as he tried to stop the train we'd started, but I didn't want it stopped. I wanted to finish this with him buried deep inside me. To feel that pleasure he'd just given me all over again. Stronger. Fuller. Deeper.

I tugged at his T-shirt, pulling it over his head as he huffed and laughed. His eyes were alight with humor when they found mine, but I wanted the dark pools of desire. So, I leaned up and nipped at his lower lip, sucking it into my mouth as my hands traveled over the tense muscles of his back. They were defined. Smooth as silk and yet hard as stone. A dichotomy that fit Lincoln completely.

When I squeezed his butt cheeks, his hips landed against mine with a grunt. "Sweetness—"

I cut him off with another kiss. It was hard and fierce, just like the one he'd given me by the door.

"Shut up, Lincoln. Shut up and finish what you started."

He laughed, and the deep joy of it rang through me, making my body quiver again, almost as if his fingers were inside me all over again.

"I think you're the one who started this in the bathroom," he said.

"Oh, believe me," I responded, "you started it from the moment you showed up in the cemetery."

He stared at me for a long moment, hand skimming my cheek.

I thrust my hips into his.

"Please. Please don't stop," I said, and I didn't even care that it sounded like a beg. All I knew was I needed this. I needed to feel and think of nothing but the way the weight of him felt on me. The way his kisses lit me up. The way my body seemed to notch perfectly to his.

He cursed and slammed his mouth against mine once more.

The gentle tango became a desperate crescendo. Bodies pushing. Hands seeking. Mouths soothing. Exploring each other with tongue and teeth and fingers. His deep moan sent a delightful thrill along my veins.

When I pushed at his sweats, he rolled away to stand by the bed, slipping them down his thighs, and I finally caught sight of all of him. He was beautifully carved. Every muscle held the same hungry look that existed in his eyes. I fought my natural instinct to cover myself. Instead, I placed a hand on my belly, playing with the diamond stud, and his nostrils flared.

He knelt on the bed, the mattress sinking, sending me sliding toward him as he reached for my underwear and all but tore them from my body before covering my core with his mouth. All it took was a few flicks of his tongue and those masterful fingers to send me over the edge all over again, my entire body crying out with pleasure and release.

It was too much and still not enough.

I wasn't sure I'd ever have enough when it came to him.

"Are you done yet, Sweetness?" It was a growl, daring me to say no, and when I responded with, "Not even close," those beautiful eyes turned to midnight.

He remained frozen, staring at me for a long time, as if trying to assess if I truly believed my own words. I pushed the dare, curling my hand around the length of him, palming the tip, sliding down the base. His eyes fluttered closed in the most delightful way.

He leaned across my body, reaching for a drawer and coming back with a condom wrapper he tore open with his teeth and slid on with an expertise that had one little beat of truth hitting me. This may be my first time, but Lincoln had done this many, many times.

It didn't really matter. All that mattered was right now. These seconds beating between us. My arms welcomed his return as he settled back between my legs, mouth finding mine as if we'd been apart months rather than seconds.

His tip was at my entrance when his hand tipped my chin upward.

"Are you sure?"

The deep, throaty question had me answering with a simple thrust of my hips that nearly embedded him.

"I don't want to hurt you," he said softly, eyes boring into me.

My soul seemed to expand at those simple words. I hadn't told him it was my first time, but he seemed to have figured it out anyway.

"The only thing that will hurt is if you stop."

He groaned, head resting on my chest. When he looked back up, he pushed slowly inside me, stretching me as my heart swelled. My body quivered. My lungs forgot to breathe.

"You feel so good. So goddamn good." Worry coasted his brow. "You're sure I'm not hurting you?"

It had pinched. There'd been a stab of pain mixed in with the pleasure, but it was already fading. I shook my head and shoved my hips at him again.

"Hold on, then," he said, and he drove deeper inside me. My entire being sighed in approval. In want.

We shifted into a slow, erotic dance that had every part of me melting into him until there was no end of him and no beginning of me. Just one being moving together. One kiss. One thrust. Singular touches and licks and gasps.

My legs curled up, locking behind him, the angle intensifying every stroke.

It was the singular most magnificent moment of my life.

Our movements went from soft and slow to hungry, searching for the mountain top, the edge we needed to dive off. And when the summit was reached, when the inexplicable gateway to heaven opened, pleasure slashed through me like nothing I'd ever thought possible.

And as my body trembled and shook, he let out a quiet roar and dove over after me.

We kept moving, gentle rocks, until every last ripple of pleasure had been felt.

When we finally came to a stop, I hated that we'd reverted to two people instead of one.

I wanted to go back to that place where nothing but the singular "us" existed.

He rolled to the side, taking me with him, arm banding around me with a force that felt both possessive and protective.

He pushed a strand of my hair back, tucking it behind my ear. His eyes glittered, and pleasure curved his lips. Happiness filled every crack and crevice of my soul until there was no more room. Until pure bliss threatened to explode from my body like confetti.

"You stun me, Sweetness. With your beauty. Your strength. Your passion. Thank you for giving me this time with you."

My hands slid over the dark stubble on his jaw. Rough and edgy. Sexy.

The reality hit me like a hammer.

I'd had sex with Lincoln. It was one thing to sleep with the determined man who'd come to my rescue. It was a completely different thing to have slept with Lincoln Matherton.

I swallowed hard as a wave of some emotion I couldn't quite define hit me.

I didn't regret what we'd done. I felt remorseful because I'd known if I took this step with him, I'd want to keep him. I'd want him to be mine forever, and my forever had the potential to be too damn short. Too damn hurtful.

This was absolutely the most selfish thing I'd ever done.

The risk to Mom's life and to Lincoln's life was just not worth any joy I might have received.

I'd taken the pleasure, these moments with him, even though I'd known I couldn't return anything more than these fleeting hours.

There was no forever. Not for us.

The love he'd experienced before had been accompanied by so much loss and remorse. How could I possibly have thought I could add one more to his list? He'd said he wouldn't stand by while another woman he cared about went through tragedy, and even if the Viceroys never found me, even if I could stop hiding or somehow stay hidden amongst his very visible life, nothing would stop me from dying if I'd inherited a mutated gene.

My eyelids closed as waves of grief and remorse flooded over the pleasure, stealing my joy.

He placed quick, gentle kisses along my cheeks, my nose, and my forehead. "You're making me worry here, Sweetness. Tell me you're okay."

When I opened my eyes again, only concern and kindness existed in the depths of his, and it made me feel impossibly worse. He'd given me so much in such a short span of time. Marked so many things off my list. Added so much happiness.

I'd wanted to banish his shadows from the moment we'd met, but all I could really do was bring him more.

I swallowed over the lump in my throat, knowing I couldn't tell him any of that, knowing he'd object and insist there was a way for us to be together. I stroked his face gently and gave him the truth so he'd feel it as much as I did. "It was beautiful, Lincoln."

When his face broke into an enormous smile, it took my breath away all over again. The exquisiteness of it had me leaning in to kiss him softly before burying my face in the crook of his neck.

I wouldn't ruin this moment for him. I'd already acted selfish enough. I'd give him this.

I'd give us both this, and then I'd have to find a way to untangle us. Find a way to sever the ties before I wounded him in some irrevocable way.

It was too late for me. I was already marked and maimed and branded. But the pleasure of this brief encounter would have to last me a lifetime because I'd learned something through it. I'd never let someone leap into the void of the unknown with me again. If you truly cared about someone, you wouldn't willingly accept their love and then turn around and put it in a blender. You did whatever you could to protect them.

To keep them whole in body, spirit, and mind.

I didn't need to worry about potential FFI symptoms kicking in and ruining things for us, because we'd never survive past these stolen hours. I couldn't choose my happiness over his or my mom's. I wouldn't risk either of them losing more than they already had.

So, in the morning, I'd go home. I'd do something to ensure he stayed away. Say whatever it took. Push him back to his corner before it was too late.

But for now, I wrapped my arms around him tighter and listened to the rhythm of his heart. Soothing. Calming.

He relaxed completely, his breath turning easy and soft, his shoulders letting go, and his arms loosening. And finally, he slept. Even though I desperately wanted to see his face while he dreamed, I didn't move for fear of waking him. If an insomniac slept, you let them. You did nothing to disturb them. You let them get those few minutes. Those few precious hours.

I'd keep him close for a handful more poignant and beautiful moments, and then I'd let him go.

# Part Three

This was going to be more fun than I'd expected.

I'd stormed into town with death on my mind.

But seeing what was already at play gave me other ideas.

Toying with them, taunting them, would increase their fear.

And when it had spiked to an all-time high, I'd go in for the kill.

It would never make up for what had been stolen from me.

But it would take a tiny bite out of the anguish, and that would have to be enough.

# Chapter Twenty-five

## Lincoln

**NEVER SAY NEVER**
Performed by The Fray

*I WOKE TO A GRAY HAZE* enveloping the room and a warm body tucked up against mine. For a moment, I thought maybe I'd died. Heaven couldn't be better than this. Soft lights and gentle touches. Sugary scents and delightful peace rippled through me.

How long had it been since I'd slept this long?

A lifetime ago.

Willow and I hadn't moved from where we'd landed together.

And my body responded to the feel of her naked curves pushed into mine. She must have been awake already, because she felt all the parts of me that stiffened and laughed quietly, tipping her head back to meet my gaze with tired ones.

"Good morning," I said and kissed her tenderly.

She put a hand between our mouths. "I stink."

I chuckled. "If this is what you smell like when you stink, I might pass out from delight when you don't."

I let my fingers glide over her bare shoulders and her arms, and then back up. Fire danced through my veins. I wanted her again. I wanted her maybe more than I had before last night. I'd thought her an addiction before I'd embedded myself in her, and now she was simply a necessity. The unbreakable string that had knotted into me was no longer unwelcome. Instead, it felt like comfort.

I'd come to Cherry Bay to find myself and found *us* instead.

I nipped playfully at the fingers covering her mouth. "I demand access to those pretty lips."

Her eyes flickered with a feeling I knew well. Remorse.

She pushed against me, breaking our connection, and I felt cold rush over me. Not just the air but the distance she'd somehow shoved between us while I'd slept.

She slipped out of bed, darting into the bathroom without another word.

I rose, pulling on the sweats I'd discarded before making love to her.

As I headed for the door, movement in the corner of my eye had my head swiveling to the side. Sienna stood by the television with a wry, knowing grin on her face as she scanned my shirtless torso. It disappeared into a serious frown as she said, *She's wrong. She won't die. This isn't the end of her story.*

I wanted to demand she tell me what she meant. To stop speaking in riddles. But she faded as the toilet flushed.

I pushed my hair back from my face.

Why the hell was Sienna back at all? I'd slept all night. I hadn't taken the drugs that could cause hallucinations. I'd given her what she wanted most—the gallery. It hit me like it had the day before that she must actually be real. Ghosts were real. Not just a twisted manifestation of my brain.

I didn't have time to analyze it further.

Instead, I headed for the bathroom, focused completely on the distance Willow was trying to push between us. She'd pulled on the T-shirt I'd given her last night and wouldn't even glance my way.

"I'm assuming you don't have an extra toothbrush," she said. "So, I'm just going to go home and clean up."

I blocked the door, reaching out to tip her chin up so I

could see the torment I felt drifting through the room. Damn. I'd never sleep again if it meant her retreat. I didn't need sleep. I'd proven it for the almost twenty-nine years of my life.

"What happened while I was passed out?" I demanded. "Why do you suddenly regret it? Regret me?"

She swallowed hard, shaking her head. "I don't. Not the way you mean. What we did... Like I said last night, it was beautiful..." She tugged at the necklace with her dad's ring. "It was more than beautiful. A memory I'll never forget."

"It *was* beautiful. And we can make more of those memories. Tonight. Tomorrow. Next year."

She pushed my hand away, stepping back and pressing the heels of her hands to her eyes as if fighting tears.

"Don't you see? That's exactly what we can't do." It was barely a whisper.

My heart spasmed. I wasn't stupid. I knew what she meant. I knew the chasm that laid between us, but I was determined to fight. Determined to find a way to bury the divide under a mountain of rock and stone. "Is it really that easy for you to give up before we even try?"

"Try what? To get you killed right along with me? Get my mom killed? Don't you see? It was so selfish of me, Lincoln. I've been playing make-believe, pretending I could live in this moment. Pretending that if someone was only willing to take the risk, then I could have this"—she swiped through the air between us—"for however many seconds it lasted. And hell, it had to be okay because, like everyone insists, life is short, right?" Derision crept into every syllable. Self-incrimination. "But I can't, Lincoln. I can't. I won't. I won't do this to you."

What had Sienna said*? She's wrong. She isn't going to die.* It hit me all at once. This wasn't just about Poco, or the Chicago gang, or even the damn press that loved to hate me. This was about her. About the fatal familial insomnia.

Easing closer, I took her hand in mine. She didn't pull it away, but she did step back and shift her eyes down, keeping the space between us. I wanted to laugh. To tell her not even the air could sever the bonds we'd forged long before we'd consummated them in my bed. "Why don't you explain what it is you think you're doing to me."

She looked up at me with defiance in her eyes, as if trying to deny what was wafting in the very air. "Look, even if it wasn't risking your life and my mom's for us to be together, the truth is, we'd still be an impossibility."

"Again, I'll ask, why?"

"Lincoln, I might die before I even hit forty!" The words burst out of her like a shotgun blast—frustration and remorse and anger that were all self-directed.

She twisted her father's ring again, and I realized the damn memento did more than remind her of someone she'd loved and lost. It reminded her of what he might have handed down. Irritation coursed through me. At her dad for maybe giving her the disease. At the Marshals and the Viceroys for ensuring she hadn't been tested. And even at Willow herself for not allowing love and human connection into her life.

It took me a moment to leash that frustration, and even when I thought I had, my words still came out as a guttural howl. "So what?"

Her eyes whipped up, wide and shocked. "Excuse me?"

I stepped completely into her space, backing her up against the counter and putting my arms on either side of her. "Don't get me wrong. I have no intention of just standing by and letting you die an early death, whether that's because some asshole comes after you or because some mutated gene thinks it can get the better of you."

She huffed out a breath but looked down in that way she did when she was afraid to meet my gaze. "Not even you or your dad or an entire army of scientists can change my DNA."

Something deep inside me denied Willow had the gene. Denied that this magnificent bright light could be snuffed out before she'd even had a chance to really live. I couldn't accept it when I'd already had one light squashed too early in my life. But the truth was, I wasn't sure there was anything to accept. Sienna had insisted Willow wasn't going to die. And if she wasn't just some figment of my imagination, then she was tied to whatever was on the other side. Sienna knew things us mortals didn't. But I had no way of explaining that to Willow. I couldn't tell her a ghost from the great beyond had assured me she wasn't sick. If anything, that would make her want to run even more.

So instead, I changed tactics. "Let me ask you something. Do you think I regret even one minute of the time I had with Sienna?"

She stared at me but didn't respond.

"The things I regret in my life have nothing to do with the time I spent with someone. I'm ashamed of the choices I made that meant Sienna was in the driver's seat that night, and I hate the fact that choosing to wallow in my past meant I wasn't standing with Lyrica the day she was shot. But even knowing what I know now, even knowing I'd lose Sienna, if I had the chance to do it all over again, I would. I'd take every second I got with her. Every damn second."

My body vibrated with the force of my words. My conviction. I wished I could *make* Willow feel it too.

Her chest was heaving. I reached out to cup her neck, my thumb landing on the wild pulse fluttering there. It made me ache. Made me want to feel it beating at that wild pace because we were skin on skin making love and not because she was fighting her fears.

"I haven't felt alive in a really long time," I told her. "I've been going through life more vampire than human. More lost than found. But as soon as I pulled you into me in the cemetery, a switch flipped. You're everything I need. Everything I want. The light forcing back the shadows. I have to believe, no matter what fate hands us, that spending this time, any amount of time, in light with you is worth it."

Tears flew down her face, and she brushed at them as if she despised them, shaking her head. "You're wrong. I'm not the light. I'm every shadow that still lingers. I'm everything that could destroy you, and I refuse to be the reason you suffer another great loss. It's easier, Lincoln, if you just let me walk out the door. It's easier to stop now before anyone falls too hard.

Before we completely shatter."

"I hate to break it to you, but I've already fallen. You walk out right now, and I'll already break."

"Don't say that. Please don't."

"I won't ever lie to you, and the simple truth is…my heart is already yours."

She inhaled sharply, mouth parting, pulse racing even faster. "You can't mean that."

Lyrica was right when she'd said I fell fast and hard, but what she hadn't realized was it hadn't happened nearly as often as anyone thought. Not even as much as I'd thought. I'd fallen for Sienna as we'd argued over a cupcake in second grade, and I loved her all through our childhood and teen years. And I'd loved Lyrica, but just like she'd insisted when she'd broken up with me, we hadn't been "in" love. We'd had affection and an easy friendship. We'd never been soulmates clicking together. And Felicity…that had been all wrong from the moment it had started. None of those times, none of those women, had tied permanent knots around me the way Willow had.

What I felt now, what we had, it was already an unbreakable bond.

Yes, it was too fast. Too furious. Too overwhelming. Especially for someone like Willow, who'd closed herself off for so long, who only saw all the risks because she had been forced to see them. But it didn't make it wrong.

She wasn't leaving. I wouldn't let her hand me back my heart and walk out without it.

But what she needed right now was time to see how deadly serious I was.

And time I could give her. I'd lighten the mood while ensuring she stayed. Until we could find a way across the cavern she saw swelling larger and larger between us.

I leaned in, kissed her temple, and then locked her gaze with mine as I felt around in a drawer. When I found what I was looking for, my lips curved upward in triumph.

"You're wrong, Sweetness. About all of it, but especially

about this." I showed her the plastic-wrapped item. "I absolutely do have an extra toothbrush."

She looked down at it and huffed out a little laugh that made every nerve ending in my body sing and my dick twitch. She grabbed the package from me, searching my face, indecision still warring in hers. "My house is mere yards away from your door. It would be easier to shower there, get a change of clothes."

*Go back to my old life.* I heard the unspoken rest of that sentence, even though she didn't say it aloud.

If I let her walk out, she'd take those mere yards and turn them into a brick wall I'd be unable to surmount. The only chance I had of making this stick, of finding a solution to all our problems, was if I ensured she stayed.

"I have several boxes of Katerina's clothes. Our things were in storage together, and the moving company accidentally delivered hers along with mine. I can't promise the clothes will be anything trendy, but you're about the same size."

"That's ridiculous. There's no reason for me to wear your sister's things."

"There's that word again. You like to throw it out when things aren't going the way you think they should. Not only are you a food snob but you're also a control addict. But fine, don't wear her things. Wear mine. I like seeing you in mine better."

I let my hands drift under the T-shirt she'd thrown back on and was thrilled to find her bare. I skimmed her thighs, fingers lightly dancing along her curls, and her breath evaporated, snowy eyes turning the color of a dark storm.

Every taste of her last night had been a sugary treat.

I wanted to dive in again. Wanted to live all day in that sensuous haze.

She was trembling as I brushed barely there touches along her skin, upward to the curve of her breasts. Small and firm and delicious. Golden apples. Snowy pears. I slid back down, thumbing the belly button piercing I'd been so surprised to find, before continuing to her inner thighs and finally palming her heat.

She trembled, and I kissed her neck, nibbled her ear, and muttered, "I've changed my mind. You can't have Katerina's clothes or mine."

"No?" she asked, a breathy gasp escaping as my fingers found home.

"No clothes. We don't need clothes. We should never wear clothes again."

Her enchanting, lilting laugh filled the air, and my shoulders finally relaxed. "Unfortunately, the world disagrees with you. Clothes are completely necessary."

"Let me prove to you why the world is wrong."

And I did, by showing her once again just how our bodies notched together. First, by exploring and tasting and teasing her with my hands and mouth until she was chanting my name as she soared over the abyss. And then, by spending a far longer time planted deep inside her, driving her up and over again. Driving me over the same ledge and knowing I'd never recover from the leap I'd made.

# Chapter Twenty-six

# Willow

### *ONLY US*

Performed by Carrie Underwood with Dan + Shay

***IT WAS HOURS BEFORE WE EMERGED*** from his bedroom with wet hair and clean sweats clinging to our bodies. Mine were his sister's that he'd grumbled about even as he'd given them to me. His were a navy-blue pair he'd partnered with a white Henley that fit him like a glove, showing off corded biceps, broad shoulders, and a rippling six-pack. A sight that had my insides clamoring for him all over again, even though we'd spent an entire morning lost in each other.

But the rumbling of our stomachs had finally drawn us from his bedroom.

As we headed downstairs, fingers twined, I knew it was wrong, that staying would make me hate myself. But he'd lured me once again with his lovely words and even lovelier kisses. He'd said it was already too late to stop the pain if I backed away now, and I knew it was true for me too. I could already feel the open wound that would sear through me when I walked out his door. I was branded by our time together.

But I also knew it would only get worse for both of us the longer I stayed.

We were playing with fire. The first time my face appeared next to his on some online site, it would burn my world to ash—and my mom's along with it.

And yet, surrounded by the flames Lincoln stoked just by looking at me, I couldn't force myself away. I'd never thought of myself as weak or stupid. I'd been a liar because I'd had to be. But I'd never been selfish and spineless. I was both of those things now because I didn't want to lose the feelings that swarmed through me when Lincoln touched me, when he looked at me as if I was something miraculous.

So, as we walked into his kitchen, I bargained with the fate Lincoln believed in, trading the happiness of these handful of hours we had left in today for a lifetime of missing it. I'd brand us both when I left, but the mark would fade. It had to. Like a very old tattoo that had lost its vibrancy, the heartache would become something less.

When I offered to make breakfast, he shook his head, told me to sit, and then brought the leftover strawberry chiffon over to the table with two forks and no plates.

"Dessert for breakfast," I laughed, running my hand through his dark hair, pushing back the lock that forever fell forward.

"The breakfast of the very best champions."

While we ate straight from the dish, my eyes kept going to the canvas he had propped up on the counter. It was me more than Sienna. And yet, it wasn't fully me either.

The woman was lying in a meadow surrounded by thorny vines and blossoming flowers. Butterflies flitted through the air. You could almost smell the heady scent of the grass and hear the buzz of the insects. But the woman's eyes remained firmly closed. She didn't budge. She was locked away in a deep slumber cast by some spell. I wasn't sure how I knew she was cursed rather than just sleeping. But I did. She was stuck there like Rip Van Winkle…no…

"Sleeping Beauty?" I asked.

He looked over at the drawing and back. "I was inspired while you slept through the last half of *A Knight's Tale*."

"It's weird."

"What?"

"Seeing me…but not me…" I waved toward the drawing pad I'd borrowed the day before as well.

"I can't seem to stop. Every time I look at you, an entire kaleidoscope of images hits me. So many that I'm considering naming the gallery *An Homage to Willow*." His lips quirked, and I smacked him in the chest with a hand.

"Don't be ridiculous."

"There's that word again. Maybe I should require you to pay a penalty each time you use it." His eyes flared, and my body responded. Even sore in the very best kind of way, I still ached for him.

If I only had this singular day, I'd make the most of it. I smiled coyly at him from under my lashes, and said, "You could try to charge a penalty, but there'd be little you could do to enforce it."

His voice was gritty and dark when he responded, "You wanna make a bet?"

I shouldn't like it. I shouldn't want to dance along the sensual edge those words promised, but I did. I shrugged as if I doubted him, allowing Katerina's oversized sweatshirt to bare a shoulder.

"I can make you beg to pay the penalty, Sweetness."

I scooped up some of the dessert, licked the fork while he watched with heated eyes, and then leaned in so close our lips brushed. "Ridiculous," I taunted.

I was flat on my back on the table before I could take another breath. The sweatshirt was gone, and one taut tip was covered with strawberry cream. Then, he was feasting on me. Nips and laps and feathery touches that had me writhing, had me aching and crying out…and finally…begging.

♫ ♫ ♫

We spent the day like we'd begun it—alternating between sleep, making love, and devouring food. I'd wake to him drawing me. He'd wake to me skimming through art on my phone, trying to find the perfect next dessert piece. And once we were both awake, we'd start the whole process over again with hands and mouths and bodies joined.

By the time the doorbell rang with a delivery from Remi's Italian Restaurant, my body had finally called *give*, and the bubble had started to pop once more. I wasn't sure when Lincoln had cleaned up the broken glass, but the missing pane he'd boarded over reminded me of what had happened the night before. We hadn't heard back from Hardy either, and I still hadn't told my mom about the latest threat.

Worse, it reminded me of what could happen if I stayed.

The smell of the pasta and garlic bread turned in my stomach as guilt landed home, starting the timer counting down on our time together.

I'd savor these last few moments.

But I had to let him go. I had to be strong enough to do it.

As I plated the food, Lincoln came up behind me, hands running over my bare skin beneath the sweatshirt, and my sore, tired body ignited. I pushed them away, laughing as I said, "You're impossible."

"Another word I might have to enact penalties for." His eyes twinkled, and heat flooded my face. He slid a finger down along my cheeks, as if tracing the color. "I love your blush."

My body froze at the L word falling from his lips before I rolled my eyes at myself. He hadn't said he loved *me*. As if realizing I was two seconds from freaking out again, he shifted the mood by lowering his voice and saying, "I love it even more when your flush and hot because I'm inside you."

His words spiked the desire all over again, scoring me with its spark. I swallowed hard and shoved a plate at him. "My body has screamed *give*, remember?"

"I remember. And I also remember every moment that led to your body screaming."

We'd just sat down at the table when his phone rang. He pulled it out of his pocket and greeted whomever it was with a barked hello that reminded me of the first time I'd been in his kitchen. A grumpy man who completely contradicted the smiling man from two seconds before. A man who was no more the real Lincoln than the one I'd seen on magazine covers.

I loved that I knew the real him even if I couldn't keep him.

The L word that had slipped into my thoughts as easily as it had slipped from his lips made my head spin dizzily.

"So, you're saying it couldn't have been Poco last night." Lincoln's words had my fork clanging to the plate. He turned to me with a frown before saying, "Hold on, I'm putting you on speaker." He put the phone down, hit the button, and then said, "Okay, go ahead."

"Special Agent Johnson reported in early this morning," the voice on the other end said, and I assumed it was his Secret Service contact, Hardy. "Poco was at Flat Mike's in a back room when the rocks were thrown, and from there, he went to a woman's apartment a town over, staying holed up there until early this morning."

Acid crept up my throat. If it wasn't Poco…that left Aaron and the Viceroys.

Lincoln reached for my hand, squeezed it. "So where does that leave us?"

"He still could have paid someone to throw the rocks and leave the note," Hardy said. "I'll have Johnson swing by and pick it up before he heads back to D.C. But at the moment, I'm not sure I can do more. My hands are pretty much tied unless you let the Secret Service protect you again. My boss isn't going to just let me keep sending our agents down rabbit holes—not when we all have actual assignments."

I could tell Lincoln was thinking about it. That he was willing to sacrifice the privacy he'd come to Cherry Bay seeking just for me. I shook my head vehemently. The frown between his brows grew, and he turned back to the phone. "I'll think about it and get back to you."

Hardy sighed. "Be safe, Picasso."

I heard the legitimate concern and caring in the man's voice. I may never have met him, but I still liked him because I could tell Lincoln was much more than just an assignment to him. They were friends.

Silence settled down between us. The food on my plate just made the bile in my throat grow, and I pushed it away, rising from my chair. Lincoln stopped me before I got too far with a soft hand on my wrist.

"Hey," Lincoln said softly. "You heard him. This could still be Poco."

"I have to call Deputy Marshal James. I need to call my mom. I shouldn't have waited this long. I shouldn't have—" He pulled me into his lap, arms surrounding me. Comfort. Safety. Belonging.

Oh, how I ached to keep it. Keep him.

His phone buzzed again, a text tone rather than a ring. Whatever he saw made him growl once more. "What the hell?"

"What's wrong?" I asked, and I leaned in, only to freeze.

The person texting had sent an image of Lincoln and me. We had our hands twined together just as we had when we'd left his house to go to the store yesterday.

Everything slowed. My vision turned spotty, and my lungs forgot to breathe.

The painful cramp in my stomach finally broke my trance, and I made a mad dash for the hall bathroom. I barely made it to the toilet in time.

I'd done it. I'd burned my life down and Mom's along with it.

We'd be relocated. Our life here would be wiped away.

I banged a fist on the wall next to me in fury and frustration. All self-directed.

The only tiny blessing in this was that at least Lincoln would be safe because it would force us apart.

He'd followed me into the bathroom. I could feel his presence, feel the wall of emotions he was experiencing tipping into my own bucket already full of them.

"Willow… Damnit. I'm sorry. But this hasn't hit the news cycle yet. That picture was from my parents. We still have time to stop it before it comes out."

I sat back, leaning against the wall, looking up at him as he clutched the top of the doorframe so tightly his fingers turned white. Debate waged war in his eyes.

"I've cost my mom everything. I've been so damn selfish," I whispered.

"You haven't done anything. My mom's press secretary, Merci, is working on it. She already put a kibosh on another image of me at The Tea Spot."

"With me?" I asked, gut churning nastily again.

He shook his head. "No, it was just me."

He closed the distance, hands going to my elbows, lifting me off the ground and wrapping me in a tight embrace. I buried my face in his chest and let his warmth seep into me.

If only we could stay like this.

If only we could get the bubble back.

If only I hadn't been so stupid and selfish, reaching for what I knew wasn't mine, reaching for the open flame, all while knowing the consequences.

His phone went off again, and a rumble of objections vibrated through him.

He stepped back, pulled his phone from his pocket, and swore under his breath before tugging me down the hall into the study. He'd shut the shutters the night before when the rocks had been thrown, so the room was dark, but the calm I'd first felt when I'd entered this room, the calm I'd thought had felt like him, was missing entirely now.

How could so much have changed in so little time? As if each moment had been years.

The only other time I'd felt this way was the day Dad had been shot. Those long seconds of watching him die. The hours that had felt like months with the police asking question after question after question on repeat. That had felt like a nightmare. This time with Lincoln had been the opposite. A heavenly dream.

Both had ended in my life changing. Mom's life being crushed.

I looked at the brass clock sitting next to a golden Buddha on a shelf. Mom would be at dinner with her students. She'd texted me earlier, saying the kids had won, and they were going out to celebrate. They weren't scheduled to leave Richmond until sometime tomorrow morning.

But she'd never stay. She'd come running.

How was I going to tell her I'd tossed our lives away for a few moments of pleasure?

# Chapter Twenty-seven

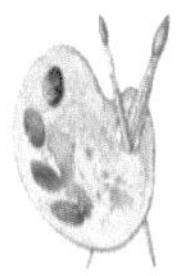

## Lincoln



***I GLANCED OVER AT WILLOW AS*** my phone buzzed yet again with my mom's ringtone. The night before, I'd been concerned Willow would leave thinking I'd used her as a replacement for what I'd lost. This morning, I'd been afraid her fears about her mortality would send her running. And now, I was terrified she'd disappear because my life had just dumped itself in her lap. The Marshals were going to lose their minds if that image of us went public.

My insides tightened, and fury rolled through me. I'd just wanted a few months of peace and solitude. Of anonymity. Was that so much to ask? No one had a right to every second of my life just because my father had chosen to devote himself to this country. I hadn't agreed to give myself to them.

Had the man in the gray sedan taken the picture? I hadn't seen him since the day we'd danced in the street, but I had felt eyes on me—had felt them and not done a damn thing about it. I'd been so caught up in Willow, her story, her emotions, as well as my own desire, that I hadn't protected her like I'd promised.

My fury turned inward as my phone rang a third time.

"Has Merci stopped it?" I asked in lieu of a greeting.

"We're trying. Merci's contact at *The Exhibitor* told her

someone sold them a handful of similar images," she said calmly. "We're seeing if they'll accept a counter-offer in order to not publish them."

A cold fear washed over me. "There's more than one?"

My phone vibrated with more photos. In addition to the one of us leaving the house, there was one of us walking side by side out of The Tea Spot and one of her trapped between me and the handlebar of the cart at the grocery store. I was disguised in two of them with my stupid hat and glasses, but Willow shined in every single damn one of them.

If these got out, the press would never let it go until they'd figured out who she was and why I was with her. Even if her witness protection cover story held, her picture would be right there for Aaron and the Viceroys to find. I didn't believe the notes were from them. I believed, like Willow had, a brutal street gang wasn't the kind to leave notes. They'd have taken a goddamn shot from the shadows. But even if it hadn't been them leaving the notes, they'd easily be able to find her now.

"I'll never understand why the hell they care about me! What does it matter who I date and for how long? There's no juicy story here, Mom."

She sighed, and I could almost imagine her running a single, elegant finger over an equally elegant brow. I'd picked the habit up from her, or maybe it was in our DNA.

"You know why, Lincoln. Americans crave their own royals to love and bash. You and your father are charming, attractive men. They want the gossip about you. You haven't made a single statement after Felicity's restraining order leaked. You simply disappeared from sight, and it left a vacuum they're desperate to fill. They've tossed around suicide attempts and rehab rumors. Merci read me a completely absurd one the other day where Felicity had you locked in her basement like that woman from the Stephen King book."

My chest grew tighter. Had I encouraged this? The mad search for Lincoln Matherton? Had I put Willow at risk even more than I'd realized because they were desperate to find me?

The guilt I'd recently thought I might be able to shed over

Sienna and Lyrica, that Willow herself had handed me, came rushing back. I wouldn't let anything happen to Willow because of my choices. Screw that.

"Who is the Sienna look-alike?" Mom asked, sounding suddenly more weary and tired than she had in years, as tired as she'd been after she'd dragged me away from Lyrica's bedside after she'd been shot.

I realized she was just concerned, but irritation still flew through me, knowing all she saw when she looked at Willow was Sienna. They were nothing alike. Nothing. Sienna was all bluster and storm. Willow was quiet strength. Not any weaker, maybe even stronger because she was required to live her life without being seen.

I knew if I denied the physical similarity between them, if I went on the defensive, it would only make Mom think it was why I was with her. Just like Willow herself had thought it last night until I'd convinced her otherwise. So, instead of addressing who Willow was and why I was with her, I focused on the problem.

"Mom, I need to know who sold all of those photos."

Willow's head jerked toward me, her face incredibly pale as fear drifted over her like a veil.

"You know it's impossible. They'll never reveal their source, even if we convince them not to run them."

Willow twisted my phone, and on seeing the additional photos Mom had sent, she went even paler. "Oh my God…"

"Lincoln?" Mom's voice demanded my attention, and I lifted the phone back to my ear.

"Get Dad's people on it, Mom. The Secret Service, his communication people. I need to know who did this. Where they are. I'll pay to stop them from taking more." I heard the wild frenzy in my voice, knew she'd snag onto it too, but it was the truth.

"Before, I was just concerned because you hadn't told us you were seeing anyone and because she looks so much like Sienna. Now, I'm really worried. What's wrong?"

"I can't talk about it. But we need to stop whoever this is. Right now. Tonight."

"I need an explanation, but for now, let me place some more calls." She hung up without another word.

I turned to Willow. "I'm so sorry. I'm… Damnit, I didn't think they'd find me so soon. Not like this. I thought we had time. I never would have risked going out to the store with you if I had. Mom is stopping it. She thinks she can. And we'll find out who it is. We'll keep them from taking any more."

I wouldn't just rely on my mom, and I couldn't bring Hardy in again, but I could hire someone else. My own damn security. An investigator.

"With the notes…and now this…" her voice cracked. "God… Mom…"

I pulled her into me, and she went rigid before finally resting her forehead on my chest. I surrounded her the best I could, trying to provide some kind of comfort. Some sort of peace.

"It doesn't matter if it was Poco now or if it was just his thugs last night," she said as her whole body trembled. I hated that it was because someone had made money off my life once again and sold me out to the press. "As soon as it breaks, the Marshals will move us."

"We still have time to stop it. All of it." Holding Willow with one arm, I flicked through the contacts on my phone until I found Leya.

Within seconds of explaining what I needed, she'd handed me off to her husband. Before he'd fallen madly in love with her, Holden had once been the lead agent on Leya's Secret Service detail. He'd walked away from his career to be at her side and was now heading up her band's security.

"I need a security team that can be here tonight."

"Hardy will come back if you ask," Holden said.

"That will take paperwork and time I don't have. Plus, he'll be governed by rules I have no intention of following."

He hesitated. "Do you think this is Felicity again?"

"No." But then I hesitated. Had Felicity hired the guy in the sedan? The guy on the street who'd looked at me with such unabashed anger? I'd thought he'd been angry over politics or just was naturally pissed off at life. But then I remembered what Felicity had said to Katerina about the small town I was in, and my fear grew. Maybe this was someone else she'd hired to hunt me down. "I don't think so, but that's an avenue whoever comes to work for me will have to consider. Do you know anyone who can get here tonight?"

"Reinard doesn't have anyone near you, but our partner company, Garner Security, is based out of D.C. Let me call Wayne and Axel and have one of them contact you. Is this the number you want me to give them?" Holden asked.

"That would be great," I said, inhaling sharply. "And thanks. I appreciate it."

We hung up, and I held on to Willow, wishing I could go back and redo those few moments when we'd been out in the open and I hadn't taken enough precautions. I'd been living a fairy tale, hoping the magic of the town could keep me hidden. But I should have known better. Shouldn't have expected the quiet to last. And now my slipup could cost me Willow. Even worse, it could cost her the entire world she and her mom had built for themselves out of the rubble of their old one.

♫ ♫ ♫

It took almost three hours before a black Escalade with tinted windows showed up at the curb. During that time, I'd fielded several calls from Mom and Dad. Between Merci and Dad's team, they'd gotten the article nixed, but they couldn't get anyone to cough up the source. I ignored several texts from both my sisters and repeated ones from Lyrica. Damn Merci had told her about the pictures. Maybe even shot her off a few to prove a point. If I couldn't keep my own damn family from sharing them, how would we stop the wolflike media from going in for the kill?

I'd prevented Willow from retreating to the cottage only by causing her more fear. By telling her whoever had taken the pictures might see her. That I needed the team I'd hired to clear the area. She hadn't called the Marshals, but she'd left a message on her mom's phone for her to call back. I could practically feel her self-reproach weighing her down as much as it dragged at me.

Now, I watched on my security app as four men slipped into the darkness surrounding the house just like the Secret Service used to. The fact I was letting them back in my life bit at me. The lack of privacy and knowing everything I did was going to be watched all over again made my neck crawl. But I'd do it. I'd give up every ounce of my privacy if it ensured Willow's safety.

The last man to get out of the SUV walked up to the front door, eyed the broken pane, and then rang the bell, staring directly into the camera. I let him in and showed him into the kitchen where Willow and I had retreated with the blinds all shut and cups of tea in hand.

The man stood well over six feet, even a few inches over me, and was built like a cage fighter with hair darker than mine that showed off golden eyes. His nose had clearly been broken without being reset, and his jawline screamed an arrogant, confident swagger I'd seen mostly from soldiers in special forces.

"Can I get you anything to drink?" I asked him.

"No. Thank you." He took in Willow, and unlike the Secret Service agent who'd shown up yesterday, the assessing gaze didn't curl through me. He was eyeing her like I eyed an art piece I was considering for the gallery. Like a job. He stuck his hand out to her. "Axel Garner. I'm sorry you've been having trouble. I'm here to ensure it stops."

"Whether the guy leaving us notes is also the person who took the pictures or not, we need to stop both from happening again. It's imperative we keep Willow's pictures out of the press," I told him.

While we'd waited for the team to show up, Willow and I had argued about how much to tell them. I'd wanted to tell them the whole story. The Chicago gang, the notes, Poco, everything.

If we didn't, they wouldn't know what to look out for and might be caught by surprise, but Willow had been adamant that telling them she was in witness protection had to be left off the table.

Axel took the decision away from us. His gold eyes landed on me before they went back to Willow. "Because you're in WITSEC."

It wasn't a question. It was a statement, and Willow's eyes turned wide. "Who told you that?"

"Your history did. I've had a team digging into both of you from the moment Mr. Matherton called."

"It's Lincoln. And I didn't ask you to do that." My irritation grew, wondering if this was just another colossal mistake. We could have waited for Hardy, or I could have let her call the Marshals. But if she did, I'd never see her again.

Damn it, maybe that was the only right answer. Maybe the only way for me to ensure she was safe was to push her as far away from me as possible. Even as the thought landed, Sienna materialized behind Willow, shaking her head violently, and I heard her voice in my head, *Don't be daft. She's the one, Lincoln. She needs you. You need her. Stick it out.*

When my gaze moved back to the live people in the room, they were both watching me stare at the air.

Axel's eyes narrowed in on me. "I don't take on a job without fully understanding what I'm getting my team into any more now than I did in my Army Ranger days."

"If you figured it out, does that mean others might have as well?" Willow asked shakily.

"Highly unlikely, but not impossible. I worked several cases with the Marshals in my past life. I know how they work. Your backstop is almost perfect. Maybe a bit too perfect, actually. We can fix that easily enough. Who are you hiding from?"

Willow's hands tightened on the teacup, and she looked to me and away before swallowing and giving him the highlights of her dad's murder and the trouble with the Viceroys. I was hit all over again with how brave she was. How brave she'd been at sixteen in a closet or at twenty testifying at the trial. Her strength was more than admirable. Even still, I could see it upset her, talking about it again. I wanted to hold her, but she'd pulled back emotionally and physically from me while waiting for Garner's men to show up. And maybe that was what we both needed. Time to calm down. Time to figure out how to keep her safe without the heady throb of desire overwhelming our senses.

"It should be over," she added softly after finishing the story. "But a few days ago, the Marshals told us Roci Vitale had been killed in prison, and then, I started getting the notes."

She showed him photos of the notes Special Agent Johnson had picked up.

"Why haven't the Marshals moved you?" Axel asked with a frown. After Willow and I exchanged another look, he added, "You haven't told them."

Willow set the cup down and told him about Poco and how we'd hoped that it had to do with him rather than anything from Chicago. I added on what Hardy had found out about Poco's whereabouts and how he could have used one of his men to throw the rocks.

Axel tapped his fingers along the table almost as if he was typing on a keyboard. "I'll have my people reach out to Hardy and follow up on Poco. We don't have anyone on the ground in Chicago, especially not inside the local street gangs, but I'll see what we can do."

Willow's shoulders slumped, and the way her naturally smiling lips were curved down ate at me. I slid my hand into hers, squeezing it reassuringly before turning to Axel and asking, "What else do you need from us?"

"You're both familiar with detail coverage. We'll need your schedule for the next twenty-four to forty-eight hours at a minimum. If you're going out of town, I'll need longer notice to ensure we have those locations secure. We'll also need a list of people you want to allow access to you and your homes. I'll add a few more men to the roster to make sure the house across the street is covered as well as this one." Like every security person I'd worked with, he was calm, emotionless, exuding confidence.

I hated it. I hated having it back in my life when I'd finally walked away from it. But then, I felt Willow's shoulders relax, and the hatred disappeared. If this was what it took to ensure she was safe, it was an easy sacrifice. I'd sell my own soul, my dirty laundry, all my secrets, to make sure nothing ever hurt her again.

# Chapter Twenty-eight

## Willow

**_LOOK AT ME_**

Performed by Carrie Underwood


**AS LINCOLN AND AXEL WENT TO** review his security system and the camera setup, I made my way to the cupboards and started pulling together the ingredients for a cake I was going to use as the base below the individual miniature desserts for my new piece. I wasn't really in a mindset to create, but making the cake would keep me busy so the doubts and worries didn't settle in.

Lincoln's family may have stopped the pictures from being released, but they were still out there. They didn't know who'd taken them. And Axel may be able to find out who it was, but would it be before more emerged?

After panic and worry had caused me to throw up, a weird numbness had descended on me. Lincoln had tried to push past it several times. Our argument about whether or not to disclose I was in witness protection had tried to slash into it, but then it had settled back over me.

It was too late to take back my selfish mistakes.

Too late to be strong.

I'd already hurt Lincoln and Mom.

That thought caused pain to twist like a knife again, threatening to push aside the numbness.

But I pulled the cold detachment back over me and concentrated on the recipe I could almost make in my sleep. I was just getting ready to pour the batter into the waiting pan when my phone rang, and Mom's face appeared on the screen.

I almost cried just at the sight of it—from relief but also sadness and dread.

"You sounded scared on your voicemail, Willow. Did Poco bother you again?" Her voice was full of worry. Fear. I hated that I was responsible for it this time.

"I messed up," I choked out, dropping the bowl on the counter, tugging at my dad's ring.

She inhaled sharply, holding her breath before breathing out softly and saying, "We all make mistakes, kiddo. Even nearly perfect humans like you sometimes do. Want to tell me about it?"

"Lincoln…" I choked again, losing my breath. Losing my way. I'd been lured by hope and connection and the beauty of a man I couldn't have. And now I had to tell her I'd tossed our lives away for a few moments of pleasure.

"Did he hurt you?" The ferocity of her tone made me realize the direction I'd sent her in.

"No. God no. He's kind and generous." Tears threatened, but I shoved them back with the heels of my hands. Tears did nothing. They were a release valve, but they couldn't change anything.

"Okay," she said, the relief in her voice clear. "So what's wrong?"

"He's Lincoln Matherton."

It took her a minute to catch up. To put the name together with the actual person. "Willow… Shit."

"It all happened so fast, Mom. It wasn't anything… He was just helping me with Poco, and then…" I trailed off.

She gave a little huff somewhere between humor and frustration. "And then you started dating the president's son."

It was so much more than dating. In some strange way, we'd gone from nothing to everything in a heartbeat.

"We had a scare tonight… Some photographs of us were taken, and his family stopped them from coming out. Lincoln has hired someone to try to figure out who took them. And before you start, I know I have to stop seeing him. I know that. And I will—"

"Now that's enough to make *me* want to cry," Mom said, breaking me out of my spiral.

"What?" I croaked.

"How did you feel when Hector told you he asked me out?"

"Joy," I said instantly. I didn't want her to doubt even for a second that I wasn't happy about things progressing for them. "So much joy, Mom."

"And don't you think I want that for my child? Love. Happiness. Someone adoring you. Because that was what I heard when I talked to him yesterday. I heard it in his voice. A fierce protectiveness that comes from caring deeply for someone. If I hadn't, I would have gotten in the car and come home just to make sure you were safe."

I almost wished for the numbness back. With dread, I said, "There's more."

"More than you dating the president's son?"

She was trying to make light of it, trying to make me feel better, but it only increased the burden I was carrying. "Someone threw rocks at Lincoln's house and left another note." I caught her up to speed on everything and then sighed. "I'm still sure it's Poco, Mom. I don't want to freak the Marshals out, but I do want to be kept abreast of Aaron's location."

"Leaving notes isn't the Viceroys' style. They don't knock and ask to come in." She took a breath and kept going. "I won't lie. I'm upset you didn't tell me right away—about Poco or Lincoln or any of it. And yet, I also understand why you didn't. You've been trying so hard ever since your dad died to keep me safe too. But it isn't your job, honey. I'm the parent. Not you. You couldn't have saved him that night. Nothing you could have done, even if you were the best surgeon in the world, would have stopped him from dying. I'm not going to disappear on you. I'm here. I'm here and happy."

Her words tore through the shield I'd placed between me and those awful memories. The blood. The lifeless look in my dad's eyes. It hurt so much more than I expected after all this time, but she was also right. I was trying to ensure she was safe because of what had happened, and she was also right that she was here and alive and happy, which was why I said quietly, "This is exactly why I can't see Lincoln anymore. Just imagine what it would do to both of us if the photos got out."

"What I imagine is that you must care for him deeply."

"Wh-what?"

"You'd never risk me or our life here for a random fling."

I swallowed hard. She knew me too well for me to lie. What I'd felt for Lincoln from that very first moment had been impossibly large. It wasn't just me trying to mark off some item in my journal or revel in a minute of happiness. Something between us screamed forever, but it was a forever I couldn't have. Not with him. "It doesn't matter how I feel. It's not worth it. Not if I cost us this life only to bring heartache and loss to his by dying in a few years."

"You're wrong." And when I started to protest, she rode over me. "No. Listen to me. Even if I'd known about your father's FFI, I still would have married him. I still would have built our life together. Because every moment with him was worth it. We had years of happiness and love. Not everyone gets that. You can't toss it aside just because there might be sorrow in some unknown future. Even knowing how everything ended, even though you and I had to give up our life and start over, I'd still spend every second I could with him."

Her words were so close to Lincoln's about Sienna that they weren't easy to ignore. They'd both loved with every piece of their soul and lost, and they both said they'd do it all over again. "But he's already lost a woman he loved, Mom. Nearly lost another who was shot. How could I possibly start this with him, knowing I'd only bring him more grief? More of the same?"

She was silent for a moment. "That's pretty awful for someone so young to have gone through. But it also sounds like he's someone who could truly understand your own loss. The real question, though, is what does he say about it? What does he want? Are you just some interesting diversion, or does he want more? Does he really want *you* with all the ups and downs that come with you?"

I could still feel the imprint of him on me. His hands and his mouth. The weight of him as he was inside me. But even more, I felt the imprint he was leaving on my soul, the connections bonding us together in some complicated, messy way sure to hurt one or both of us. I thought of the fierceness in his eyes as he told me I was everything he wanted and needed, how I was the light forcing back his shadows, and how any amount of time he spent in that light was worth it.

"He wants me," I said and meant it.

"Then, that's all that matters. That's all that's important. Live, kiddo. Live hard. Love fully. Otherwise, you might as well have died that day with your father." Her voice cracked, and I knew just how hard it was for her to have said something like that. To even think it.

"Maybe it would be that simple, Mom, if we weren't talking about Lincoln Matherton. We're not talking about me falling in love with some random college student. This scare with the photos…that's going to happen again. His life is large and visible. Can you imagine what Deputy Marshal James would have to say about this? She'd want to relocate us. We'd have to give up everything all over again. My baking. Your teaching. If this all comes tumbling out, we'll have to choose between moving and leaving their protection altogether."

"They might ask us to move, and if they do, we might have to consider leaving the program."

"Mom!"

"I'm not saying leave ourselves out in the open, unprotected. You said Lincoln declined Secret Service, but he's hired a team, right?"

"Yes."

"So, *if* photos emerge with you and Lincoln, and *if* the Marshals put us on the spot, we can decide then whether to relocate or leave their protection and hire our own." With every word she spoke, she was trying to remind me of the promises I'd made to myself on the plane ride home from the trial—my determination to not live with what-ifs and if-onlys holding me back. But these what-ifs were impossibly large and dangerous.

"Mom, be serious. We wouldn't be able to afford our own security." We weren't quite living paycheck to paycheck, but we were far from wealthy.

"We don't have to make a decision tonight. Or even tomorrow. It sounds like Lincoln is working really hard to help fix the situation as it stands now, both with the photos and with Poco. I'll be home tomorrow around the time you get off work. We can discuss our next steps..." She paused and then attempted to lighten our talk by adding on, "And then you can help me pick out something to wear for my date with Hector."

Some of the weight that had started to lift the longer we talked returned because I wanted her to be able to have many dates with Hector. Not just one. In choosing to stay and explore whatever this was with Lincoln, in choosing to risk another photograph, it felt like I was choosing my life over hers. And I didn't want to be that selfish. I'd already taken too much I couldn't give back. Both of hers and Lincoln's.

But if I said any of that to her, we'd be right back to the start of this conversation. And Mom was right. We could talk about it more when she was home. So, I did the same thing she had done—I lightened the conversation.

"You made Hector really happy when you said yes. He was all doe-eyed and goofy."

Mom laughed softly. "He is all doe-eyed. And I'm enjoying it. I'm enjoying him."

"Okay, we might have to draw some lines in the sand regarding our conversations. He's my boss and like a favorite uncle. I don't want to know how you two are enjoying each other."

She chuckled again. "I, on the other hand, want to make

sure you're actually figuring out how to enjoy someone."

I made a garbled noise. "Gross, Mom."

"If it's gross, Lincoln is doing it wrong."

It was my turn to laugh. "Oh no. There's nothing wrong with what he does. I'm just not sharing it with my mother."

"That right there. Your laugh. The way your voice changed so it's now full of delighted pleasure. I want to kiss him myself for giving it to you." Her voice got soft and tender again.

"I'm hanging up now because I'm not sure I can survive the embarrassment if we keep talking," I said, my lips curving upward even more.

"I love you, kiddo."

"Love you too, Mom."

When I hung up and turned to go back to the cake pans, my gaze landed on Lincoln lounging up against the archway to the hall. His hands were tucked in his pockets, and his hair was ruffled as if he'd been running his fingers through it. My body lit up. My heart soared. He was so damn beautiful, and somehow, he'd become mine.

Mom and Lincoln had both lost so much, and yet they were both ready to try again. To reach for love and happiness. My trying to protect them wasn't the answer. I was only bringing myself, and them, hurt and sorrow by doing so.

If this ended, it would hurt more for every second we spent together, but Mom was right. I had to let both her and Lincoln make their own decisions about how they lived and the risks they took. It was only completely selfish if I wasn't upfront with them about all the possible outcomes. If I laid all the cards on the table, and they still chose to stay, to gamble with me, then it was okay. Wasn't it?

I doubted I'd ever completely convince myself that it was.

It wasn't the only thing Mom had been right about. She'd said I'd spent too many years trying to protect the one parent I had left, the only family I had, and it was exactly what I'd done. In doing so, I'd allowed the Viceroys to have even more power over me because I'd still been letting fear drive me even if I hadn't known it. Living fully, regardless of what had happened or what might come ahead, allowed me to take back the power. It could be my own revenge for what they'd stolen. Maybe it was time I let Lincoln do for me what he'd said I'd done for him—let him lead me out of the shadows and into the light.

♫ ♫ ♫

After falling asleep tucked up tight against Lincoln, I woke disoriented just a few minutes before my alarm was set to go off. The space beside me was empty. When I sat up, I found Lincoln sitting on the love seat, his phone lighting up his face as he swiped at the screen. He looked up as I moved.

"Did I wake you?" he asked.

I shook my head. "No, it was my body clock. Did you sleep at all?"

He put his phone down and made his way over as I slid out of the bed. "I got about four hours. That's pretty good for me."

He leaned in and kissed me sweetly, and my body instantly lit up. Achy and sore as it was, I still wanted him. Wanted to experience the sparks we felt every time we were twined together. Wanted the light I'd tried to convince myself was worth the risk after hanging up with Mom. All the deep emotions from the last two days turned the tender kiss into something frantic and wild. It took every effort I could summon up to pull my lips away from his.

"Even if my body hadn't screamed *no more*, I'd still have to stop us from getting lost in each other again. I need to go home, shower, get ready for work."

His gaze dropped to my mouth, and I felt the intense longing in them, the desire to stay just like this. Even though our bubble had popped, we were still hidden away here momentarily. Still keeping the world at bay a tiny bit longer.

"Maybe you should quit. Start your own business out of my kitchen."

I laughed until I saw he was partially serious. "I love working for Hector."

"I love having you in my house." Our eyes locked. It wasn't quite a proclamation of love, but it was close. We'd danced around it several times yesterday, but it seemed way too fast and too soon to say it.

Instead of responding, I untangled myself from him, gathered my things, and headed for the door. I wasn't at all surprised when Lincoln tagged along with me as two men escorted me to my house where I got ready for work and then into the black SUV with tinted windows that drove me to The Tea Spot.

They told us to stay in the car while two of the bodyguards entered and cleared the café, using my key and alarm code. When one of the men came back out, it was with a grim expression on his face. "No one is in there."

The 'but' hung in the air.

"What is it?" I asked, dread spiking through me.

"There's some graffiti."

"Graffiti?" I was out of the sedan and rushing inside before Lincoln or the bodyguard could stop me. Nothing seemed amiss in the steel and granite kitchen. Everything was as spotless and shiny as Hector and I always left it. Nothing was wrong with his office as I flung my bag down and headed for the café itself. As soon as I saw it, my stomach bottomed out.

The beautiful mural on the wall was destroyed. Something had been tossed at it, bleach or acid, I didn't know what, but splashes of the liquid had eaten away the paint. The girl dancing in the meadow, the animals congregating around her, and even the prince riding in on his white steed had all been hit so they were now a macabre image.

"No, no, no, no, no!" I cried, moving toward it. Written in red paint across the remaining pieces of the once beautiful scene were the words, *Your life will never be a fairy tale.*

Lincoln grabbed my hand, pulling me back away from the wall. "It's fixable, Sweetness. It's just paint. We can fix it."

"You don't understand," I said, whirling to meet his concerned eyes. "Hector's wife…his wife that died of cancer…she did all the murals. The ceiling. The painting on the shelves. He can't just replace it…" My stomach cramped up so tight it made me hunch over.

He tried to pull me into him like he had repeatedly over the last few days, but this time, I was angry rather than frightened. I whirled around, looking at the men who'd accompanied us inside. "I want this person found. I want them found and held responsible. I need them to pay for this."

One of them was already talking through his headset, and I heard him say Axel's name.

I pulled my phone out, hitting Hector's number with a shaky hand. He answered on the second ring. "Willow. What's wrong?"

"Hector… God… The café." I swallowed.

"Have we been robbed? I'm on my way," he said and hung up before I could correct him.

Lincoln walked up to the mural, running a hand over the waves of bleached-out paint, sniffing his fingers.

"Turpentine," he said, turning to me and repeating, "I can fix it, Willow. It won't be the same because he'll know what she did was marred, but I can fix it."

"Axel is calling the local police, and he's on his way," the man said.

Not even fifteen minutes later, Hector raced into the café with Shay on his heels. They looked like they'd thrown on whatever clothes they'd touched first. I'd never seen Shay in anything but a perfectly pressed, coordinating outfit. Now she wore magenta leggings and a yellow sweatshirt that clashed.

Hector came to a stop in the middle of the tables, and his hand went to his chest, rubbing and pressing. He didn't say anything. His lips were drawn tight, jaw clenched. It was Shay's startled sob that expressed the pain I saw in her father's eyes. "Mom's mural!"

As she made to run to it, Hector caught her, drawing her into his side. "Don't touch it, Shay."

"The police are on their way as well as my boss," the man who'd spoken to Axel said.

"And who exactly are you?" Hector demanded, eyes bouncing from me to the oversized security team, to Lincoln, and back to me.

"These men work for a company Lincoln hired," I explained.

"What the hell is going on, Willow?" Hector's voice was sharp, pained, and angry.

I swallowed hard. We weren't sure this was Poco. I needed to believe it was, but there were too many unknowns. My tongue seemed stuck to the roof of my mouth as I batted around the truth, half-truths, and full-on lies. Lincoln came to my rescue, as he had for almost a week now, saying, "Willow has been receiving some threats."

"Poco! This is that little shit, Poco?" Hector snarled.

"I'm…I'm not sure," I finally was able to choke out.

"I'll kill him. I'll kill him with my own hands." Hector whirled, heading for the front door. Shay chased after him, catching his arm and tugging at him.

"Dad. Stop. Let the police handle it."

"He destroyed what she made, Shay. Completely destroyed it!"

"I know. I know. But confronting him, risking yourself… Dad… I can't lose you too."

The pain in her voice pricked at all my own thoughts and worries and fears about my mom and losing the only parent you had left. Regardless of who was leaving the notes, the blame for this landed squarely with me.

"I'm so sorry, Hector and Shay. I'm so sorry," my voice cracked.

Hector looked at me, and the grimness on his face softened. "Poco being an asshole isn't on you, Willow. You didn't ask him to do this."

The debate warred in me again. How much to tell? How much to hold back? If he and Mom hadn't set up a date, if I didn't know they were trying to start a relationship, I might have spilled my guts about everything, regardless of the Marshals' warning. But what had happened with Dad, how much Mom wanted to tell him, was hers to share and not mine. For now, I'd let him think it was Poco, like we were hoping it was.

Lincoln stepped forward, fingers twining with mine, and Hector's eyes landed on our joined hands. He glanced from my face to Lincoln's and then back.

"I know who you are," he said to Lincoln. "I also realized you didn't want people to know. But this"—he waved at the security and then the wall— "is this because of you?"

I was instantly shaking my head, but I felt Lincoln hesitate for a brief second, and when I looked up, his brows were creased.

"Have you at least told your mom about it?" Hector asked when neither of us responded.

"She knows. I've told her everything," I said.

"That's good. Secrets have a way of destroying things," Hector said, and my stomach plummeted again. What would he think of the secrets Mom and I had kept from him for years? It had been for our safety, but would he understand that? After everything he'd done for me, and the little dance he and Mom had begun, would he ever be able to forgive us?

I could only hope he would.

Could only hope he'd see not the secrets but the truths we'd tried to live by.

# Chapter Twenty-nine

## Lincoln

**_SINGING LOW_**
Performed by The Fray

**_I FELT WILLOW'S CONFLICT VIBRATING THROUGH_** her. She wanted to come clean with Hector about everything but was fighting the instinct to lie that had kept her safe for years. She cared for this man. Cared for him enough to want to see her mom with him. I couldn't imagine having to keep the truth of who you really were from everyone you loved. But then again, lying about a name and a past didn't change who you were. Your actions, how you treated others, how you lived was the truth of you.

Before Willow needed to lie even more, Axel showed up, and right behind him was the Cherry Bay police. A uniformed officer was accompanied by a man who introduced himself as Detective Muloney. He was in his fifties and was mostly bald but made up for the lack of hair on his head with an abundance of it on his face. Fit and trim in jeans, a button-down, and a wool blazer that seemed almost too much for barely three in the morning.

The detective took in the mural with angry eyes before saying, "Fuck, Hector. I'm damn sorry. Sophia's paintings…my sister was so proud of them. So proud of you and the shop." A stunned silence settled down in the room, and even Willow seemed taken aback by Hector's dead wife being Muloney's sister.

Jaw working overtime, the detective tugged on his beard, whipped out a notepad from a back pocket, and said, "Walk me through what's happened."

As Hector and Willow explained everything that had occurred leading up to the destroyed mural and why they thought Poco might be involved, Axel gave me a head nod, indicating he wanted to talk to me outside.

I squeezed Willow's hand, kissed her temple, and said, "I'll be right back."

She looked up with sad eyes that almost undid me. I wanted her joy, her infectious lightness, not the heaviness that had attempted to drag her down over and over the last few days. No matter how resilient she was, no matter how determined she was to focus on the good, even Willow had limits. The simple fact she wasn't smiling now made me yearn to destroy lives.

I followed Axel out the front door and onto the street. The old-fashioned streetlamps cast small circles along the cobblestones and sidewalks. The air smelled of cherry blossoms, and the fallen petals decorated the ground in a mosaic of pink and white shades.

"Is there a possibility this has nothing to do with Ms. Earhart?" he asked.

"If it's me they're after, I don't understand why they'd target Willow and Hector. I haven't known her for more than a week. The night things went down at the cemetery was the first time we'd ever spoken."

"But the note on the door arrived after you'd started spending time together? Is it possible this is the hate group who came after your father and the vice president and kidnapped Leya Singh?"

I hadn't even considered them being involved. "Willow wouldn't be their target. She's not a person of color. She's blond and white. They'd probably congratulate her on landing me." The bitter sarcasm in my voice wasn't missed by Axel.

"And you're sure the issues with Felicity Bradshaw are

behind you?”

What did it say that Holden had asked the same question? That my mind kept journeying back to the man in the gray sedan? And yet I hadn’t mentioned it to Axel last night. I’d wanted to believe Felicity was in my past, but she *had* reached out to me this week, and I’d ignored her. She’d tried to get information on me from my sister.

The angry grip on my lungs tightened even more. My finger found a brow, rubbing it before I pocketed my hand as dread wound through me. What if this was all because of me? Not just the photos that threatened to out Willow but the sick notes causing her fear as well?

The words written on the wall and the first note at Willow’s picked at a memory. Hadn’t Felicity said something similar to me once? After she’d finally realized she wasn’t getting me back? I tried to remember the actual words she’d used. Something about not deserving the fairy-tale ending she’d had in mind for us.

Acid burned in my throat as I told Axel about her recent attempts to contact me, the things we knew for a fact she’d been responsible for, and about the man in the gray sedan.

“Does she know about your move to Cherry Bay?” Axel asked.

I told him about Katerina’s conversation with her at the fundraiser. “Last fall, we removed all the malware from my devices. Nothing here is in my name, so it’s more likely she was just fishing for information. I know for a fact she was in LA earlier this week, but it could be she hired someone new.”

“The person who did this”—Axel looked at the destroyed mural through the windows—“knew how to get by the locks and the alarm system without leaving a trace behind. That’s a professional. From what I’ve gathered of Poco Malta, he’s some C-list criminal. I’m not sure he’d have the skills, but we’ll poke around more. If this is Felicity having hired someone, how far do you think she’d go?”

My voice was grim as I responded. “I’d say Felicity would go pretty damn far. She made up an entire history with a stalker to try and get me to stay after we discovered she'd been messing with me. She had some mental health issues growing up the press never found out about." I paused before adding, "Chase it down. I hope it isn't her, but I need to know."

If it was her, if my choices and my mistakes had come back to haunt me, I'd find a way to fix it before anyone got seriously hurt, before more trauma clamped its ugly claws around another woman I loved.

*That I loved.*

Those words landed like their own arrow deep inside me.

*I loved Willow.*

I hardly knew her, and yet I couldn't deny the truth of those words. I'd agreed with Sienna that Willow was my person, which in and of itself had an implied permanency, an implied sense of love, but I hadn't put the actual words to it. But it was love.

Fast and furiously, I'd gone over the deep end once again, and it would be stupid to try to deny it. I loved her, which was why I was more determined than ever to keep her safe, to ensure her light continued to shine as brightly as possible.

I looked inside The Tea Spot and saw Willow pacing in front of the display case while Shay and Hector held on to each other. She was alone. Again. How many times since her father was murdered had she been forced to be alone? She had her mom, who I could tell from our single conversation loved Willow and would do anything to protect her, but she wasn't here. I'd seen Willow do more to try to guard her mom and their life here than the other way around.

She was trying to protect everyone around her, including me, in the way she hadn't been able to protect her father.

I bit my cheek, thinking of how our pasts were bleeding into our present.

This morning, I'd basically told Willow I wanted her to quit her job and work out of my house. And yes, it was because of my feelings for her, but wasn't it also a reaction to what I'd lost? I wanted to wrap her up and keep her hidden so she wouldn't get hurt. How did I move past that?

I'd declined Secret Service protection because I'd wanted my privacy. And yet, now I'd hired a company to do the opposite with Willow, to shadow her every move.

It was messed up. I was messed up.

I didn't know the right steps to take from here.

I turned my gaze to Axel's. The man had been staring at me while I went through revelation after revelation. His all-seeing eyes were not only assessing but judging me as well.

"Do you think you can end this?" I asked.

"We'll find out who's behind it. Whether it's the same person who took the photos who's also leaving the notes or more than one." The confidence in his voice should have been reassuring, but I'd lived my entire life observing my father's opponents act equally confident while lying through their teeth.

"I need it over and behind us. She'll never be able to move on with any of it hanging over her. I'm not just talking about the photos and whoever the hell destroyed that mural," I said, waving a hand toward the shop and the ruined painting. "I'm talking about the Viceroys and their lawyer brother. I want to know she doesn't have to live with that shadow. How do we do that?"

"We're not a hit squad." Axel's voice was dark and forbidding.

"I'm not suggesting you kill anyone. I want to know what I can do. I *have* to do *something*." When he didn't respond immediately, I added on, "I recognize that money isn't always the answer, but I have a trust fund I haven't touched. I'd be willing to give it up entirely if it means she doesn't have to live in fear for even a second of one more day."

None of my family was the type to throw money at our problems. We worked through them and respected what had been passed down to us. But if I needed the money to keep her safe, I'd use every last dime of it, regardless of my original intention to hand it off to the next generation.

"You start handing out cash, and that will just ensure whoever this is comes back for more," Axel said curtly.

"I agree, but I also need to leave it on the table as an option. Give me an alternative. Give me something I can do to end this nightmare for her."

I didn't wait for another response. Instead, I strode with renewed determination back into The Tea Spot to the woman I'd fallen head over heels in love with. I wasn't asking to end this just for Willow. It was for me as well. If some asshole took her from me…if life or fate or whatever higher power that existed in the universe allowed that to happen…I'd never be able to open myself up to love again. Strike three, you're out.

So, I'd do everything in my power, use every resource possible, to make sure that didn't happen.

♫ ♫ ♫

I hadn't wanted to leave Willow at the café, not even knowing she was surrounded by Axel's team. But after the police left, she and Hector had hustled into the kitchen and scrambled to catch up on the baking, and I was left with nothing to do but stare at the ruined mural. I had nothing to keep my mind from spiraling with doubts about whether it was both my past and my family's choices that were responsible for destroying Willow's world.

If this was on us, I'd fix it, damn it. I had to.

So, I headed to the gallery, intent on doing two things. I'd gather the tools needed to repaint the mural, and I'd interrogate Katerina about Felicity. While I didn't doubt Axel could do his job and would follow any trails leading to my ex, my sister would know what was being whispered about behind the scenes in Hollywood.

I'd just walked in the studio door and pulled my phone from my pocket when it rang with my mom's number scrolling across the screen.

"Hey."

"So, we called in a few more favors and found out that the photos of you and the Sienna look-alike were sold to *The Exhibitor* by Poco Malta."

Even as relief rolled through me, knowing the photos weren't from the man in the sedan, a sea of other emotions roared into its place. Fury directed at Poco and irritation at my mother for the repeat *Sienna look-alike* dig. "First, she's not Sienna." The snarl in my voice should have warned her to step back, but she didn't.

"I'll have to make that decision for myself, won't I?"

"If you come into town hanging on to that assumption and treat her like she's nothing more than an imitation I've gravitated to, we'll have a serious problem."

I heard her inhale, but it was quiet over the line for several long seconds before she finally let it out and spoke. "You care for her. Deeply."

"I'm in love with her. Wildly and furiously. And I don't care that it's too fast, or that I can't possibly know her, or that some stupid-ass person is going to think she looks like Sienna—"

"Are you calling me stupid?"

"What I'm saying is, she's the one. She fits into all my grooves and notches, and no, I'm not talking about sex. I'm talking about how, when I'm with her, there's peace and calm even while things are blowing up around us. I don't know how that can be, but it's true."

"Lincoln…" Mom's voice was full and thick with emotions. "I'm… I'm happy for you and terrified at the same time."

"I've hired a security team. For her and me. I had Hardy looking into some things, but my team will take it over. And the local police are also involved."

"I wasn't talking about your physical safety, but why don't you tell me why you had to do all of these things?"

So, I did. I told her about Willow's dad, witness protection, the notes, Poco, and the destroyed mural.

"They'll relocate her, or she'll have to opt out," Mom said quietly.

My entire being ached at the thought of Willow having to

disappear. "I know. It's why I'm determined we end all of it for her—so they don't have to make that choice." I inhaled. "There's more."

"My God, Lincoln. More?" Mom laughed sardonically.

"Her dad would have died of fatal familial insomnia even if he hadn't been shot." I didn't have to explain the condition. Growing up with my insomnia, we'd been through all the possible causes for it. My parents knew all about FFI and just how rare it was. "The Marshals wouldn't let her get tested, so she has the possibility of it hanging over her."

"Finally, you give me a problem I can solve."

"What do you mean?"

"I'll put my people on how to get her tested if she ends up opting out of witness protection. If she stays in, I can understand why they wouldn't want her results in any database. She'd be too easy to find if someone offered up the right kind of money."

"It doesn't matter to me if she has FFI or not," I said, knowing immediately how Willow would react if she found out she had the mutated gene. She'd try to push me away again, to protect me from losing her.

"Mattering and knowing what's coming are two entirely different things," Mom said.

We let that sit for a minute before I returned to the original statement Mom had made. "What can we do about the photos Poco sold?"

I barely resisted the urge to slam my way out of the gallery, storm into Tall Paul's bar, and strangle the man. I wanted to ensure he handed over every photo he'd taken and erase every trace, one way or another.

"Merci and her team are making calls to as many of the papers and scandal sheets as they can. Even with that, I can't guarantee they won't show up on some independent blog because *The Exhibitor* didn't buy exclusive rights. If his main intention in selling them wasn't just about the money, if he wanted to expose her or you or both, he'll keep going until someone shows them. Or he'll just start sharing them on his own social media accounts."

"He's a petty criminal, pissed because he didn't get what he wanted. When he told Willow he'd get something else out of her, he must have meant the money. If he gives the photos away for free by posting them on his own accounts, that defeats the purpose," I said.

My relief at knowing where the photographs had come from was short-lived because it also meant it was unlikely he'd been the one leaving the notes and destroying the mural. He wouldn't want to scare Willow into hiding if he was hoping to take more and sell those too. Besides, Hardy's guy had said Poco had been at Tall Paul's when the rocks had been thrown. That left Felicity or the Viceroys who could be leaving the notes. As much as my stomach turned at both possibilities, I honestly would rather it be Felicity. She was less dangerous in the long run. Wasn't she?

"Even if this set of photos isn't leaked, Lincoln, you know someone is going to take one. You can't just disappear forever. If you don't show up at the inauguration or at any of Katerina's premieres, it's only going to fuel the media's speculation about you. The press will dig even harder." I could hear the worry in her tone. "If you really love her, if she loves you back, something is going to have to give."

"I'm working on it."

Silence settled for a beat. "We're attending our last event on the West Coast tonight. Your father is meeting with the British prime minister tomorrow afternoon, so we'll be back in D.C. Your father and I would like to meet Willow, but his schedule is impossible right now."

"We'll figure out something soon," I told her.

I wasn't sure I was ready for them to meet Willow. Not sure I could trust them not to upset her with their Sienna jabs and expectations, but as I had no intention of letting her go, it would happen eventually.

I wasn't letting her be whisked away by the Marshals or walk away to protect me. I wouldn't let her go without a fight. I'd battle the world, and even Willow herself, to prove that what we'd started could be forged into something stronger. We weren't an easy-to-burst bubble. We were something lasting. Nothing turpentine could wash away. We'd be granite. They could chip at us, but the base would still be there. Solid and unyielding.

# Chapter Thirty

## Willow

***I DARE YOU***
Performed by Kelly Clarkson

**A**S **H**ECTOR AND **I** WORKED SHOULDER to shoulder in silence, getting the scones and loaves started, my mind spiraled. Every painful and beautiful moment from the time Poco stepped into the cemetery last week whirled through me on repeat.

I was desperately trying to hold on to the delightful memories, the touch of hands, the look in Lincoln's eyes saying he'd battle the world for me. But the harsh realities of what was facing me and him and Mom were too much for the joy, and I could feel it withering. I could feel myself slipping back into the Willow of that first year who'd been afraid to leave the house.

I felt responsible for all of it, even though I wasn't the one who'd marred Hector's beautiful mural, or thrown rocks at Lincoln's window, or followed us around taking pictures from the shadows. Whether it was all the same person or multiple people, I was furious they'd broken the bubble I'd flung myself into with Lincoln and seeped away at the happiness I'd tried to let run my life since the trial.

The fury I felt only stole more of the joy. And I hated that too.

As if sensing my emotions, Hector let me pound and knead and slam my way through the list of baked goods we needed without asking questions. We were seriously behind this morning. The display case would be emptier than normal, and it would cost him business, which only added to my list of regrets.

It wasn't until hours later, when I was cleaning the stack of dishes and pans we'd feverishly whipped through, that Hector finally broke the silence. He joined me, taking items as I rinsed them and loading them into the industrial-sized dishwasher.

"Want to talk about it now?" he asked. When I shook my head, he said, "This isn't your fault."

I couldn't meet his look because even though I wasn't the one who'd defaced his dead wife's painting, it could be my fault. If I'd led the Viceroys here, it was definitely on me. If this was Poco being an asshole because I'd turned him down, then it was square on my shoulders even when I wasn't responsible for the actions either of those men took.

The back door opened, and one of the security team poked his head in. Voices behind him were slightly raised. "Mrs. Earhart is here and some woman with a US Marshal's badge. Shall I let them in?"

The world around me spun at the mention of Deputy Marshal James. The only reason she would show up was if the worst had happened. My throat nearly closed, and I had to press a hand to my chest in order to ease the pressure building.

Hector's eyes narrowed, glancing from the security guard to me. When all I could do was nod, Hector responded for me. "Send them in."

Mom rushed forward. Her blond hair normally so neat and tidy was askew. She drew me to her even though I had water dripping from the gloves I'd slid on to do the dishes. She held me tight, and I wrapped my arms around her, squeezing back. "I don't know if I'm frustrated that even more has happened while I was gone, or if I'm relieved that you have people standing at the door looking over you."

She let me go, cupping my face with her hands, eyeballing me in a way that said she was trying to read the truths I often tried to hold back to keep her safe and happy. "Love would look good on you if we didn't have all this nonsense hanging over us."

I couldn't help the color that bloomed over my face.

Behind her, a woman cleared her throat. We both turned to take in Deputy Marshal Rebecca James. She wore a dark jacket that curved over the straight lines of her muscular frame. With her square build, dark-brown hair closely shorn, and long, narrow eyes, she resembled a bull terrier. She'd protected us with a determined fierceness I'd been able to appreciate even when I'd first met her at sixteen.

"What exactly has been going on, Willow?" the woman demanded, her voice as brisk and tough as her appearance. "And why the hell didn't you tell me when you called the other day?"

My eyes darted from the Marshal to Mom to Hector. He ran a hand over his head, brows furrowed. "What's all this?"

Mom looked at me with surprise. "You didn't tell him?"

I shook my head as I peeled my gloves off and dried my hands. "I wanted you to be able to do it in your own way."

Mom leaned in and kissed my temple, and then she slid her arm through mine, grasping my hand as she turned us to face Hector. My palms grew sweaty as I searched his face, hoping the kindness and generosity I'd always seen wouldn't disappear just because we'd had to lie to him.

Mom took a breath and said, "Deputy Marshal James is our handler."

Hector's eyebrows almost hit his hairline as James cursed under her breath.

"You're in witness protection?" Hector asked, stunned. He was more surprised than Lincoln had been. If anything, I suspected Lincoln had come close to figuring it out on his own.

Mom nodded as James made another sound of protest.

A deep sorrow flooded me. It was over. Everything we'd built here would be gone. I already knew what James would say. I knew what the Marshals would want to do. Our lives here had blown up, so it was time to move on.

As if confirming it, Deputy Marshal James said, "We're taking you to the cottage until plans can be made for your withdrawal."

Like a toddler dragging their feet at bedtime, I said, "I'm not quite finished here." I didn't just mean the cleanup and the dishes and everyone knew it.

James's jaw ticked, and Hector took the towel from my hand.

"Go," he said. "Do what you need to do."

I heard the hurt in his voice and saw the confusion in his eyes as he glanced at Mom. She looked as sad as I felt, but her shoulders were back and her voice strong as she told him, "I'd like to call you later and try to explain, if you'll let me."

"That's not a good idea," James intervened.

Mom ignored her, letting me go. She stepped closer to Hector and took his hand in hers. "Please. It's important to me. You're important to me."

How much more could my heart take? How much before I broke like I had after Dad had first been killed? When I could barely move and was terrified to open a window. I didn't want to go back to that. I wanted my peace back, damn it. Even more, I wanted to keep Lincoln *and* what Mom and I had built here.

Hector stared at Mom for a moment before squeezing her back and saying, "I'll be anxiously awaiting your call."

The pressure eased off my chest just a hair. I retreated to the office to get my things, and Hector followed me. After I'd gotten my things from the locker, he pulled me to him in a hug. It was hard and tight and brought tears to my eyes.

"I don't know what's going on, but I have to believe, with all these people looking out for you, that you're going to be okay." I swallowed hard and met his concerned gaze. "You're weighed down, as if whatever is happening is something you're responsible for, but I know you didn't do that to the mural Sophia made. I know you wouldn't hurt your mom or me or the café. So whatever is happening, whatever you have to discuss with that Marshal, I know that, in here"—he tapped my head and then my chest—"and in here, you are bright and beautiful and good, and that will always win out over the bad."

I blinked furiously to keep the tears in. I was terrified this would be the last time I saw him. I hugged him just like he'd hugged me—fiercely. With all of me.

"Willow, we need to move," Deputy Marshal James said, stepping into the hallway outside the office.

I stepped away from Hector and felt him watching me as we walked through the kitchen and out the door, but I didn't look back. If I did, I'd lose it completely.

As soon as we were in the Marshal's vehicle with Axel's men following us, I demanded, "Why are you here? What's happened?"

Her two-way squawked, and she spent the time it took to get to the cottage discussing Axel Garner with someone back at headquarters. By the time we stepped out of the vehicle, whatever she'd learned had satisfied her enough to allow his men to help her and two other Marshals clear the house and secure the perimeter.

Once she joined Mom and me in the kitchen, I snapped out at her again, "What's going on?"

"Besides you telling the president of the United States' son everything about you?" she barked. I flushed and looked away before turning my eyes back to her. She swiped at her face, running a hand over her shorn hair, and then said, "We can't find Aaron Vitale."

The shock of the words reverberated through me, chills running instantly up my spine. Bile burned in my throat. God, I'd been so certain this entire mess could be laid at Poco's feet.

"What do you mean you can't find him?" Mom demanded. "We just talked to you and reconfirmed his whereabouts."

"When Willow's backstory was poked at yesterday, I traced it to that damn security company. At first, before I knew Matherton had hired them, I assumed Aaron had found you. We sent in a team in Chicago to have a conversation with him, and that's when we realized they haven't had eyes on the real Aaron in several days."

Blood stampeded through my veins, and I swallowed over the lump in my throat, asking, "What do you mean? The real Aaron?"

James's mouth tightened. "Someone who looks a hell of a lot like him has been moving back and forth between his home and work. It wasn't until we went into his office that we realized it wasn't actually Aaron."

I sank down on the barstool, and Mom stepped up to wrap an arm around me. "It's going to be okay."

But was it? Was it really? We had to leave. We had to run. We were losing everything. All of it. Lincoln. Hector. Our beautiful lives. Fury and disappointment and overwhelming sadness rushed through me, battling to see which emotion could do the most damage.

"Tell me what the hell has really been going on, and why the hell Matherton has hired a security detail for you," James insisted.

In a voice that felt wooden and numb, I explained for what felt like the thousandth time what had been happening since Poco and Lincoln had shown up in the graveyard. James took notes and asked some pointed questions about Lincoln and me that had me fidgeting and pulling on my dad's ring before glancing away at nothing.

After a moment, I took a shaky inhale and said, "I truly didn't think any of it involved the Viceroys. They'd just shoot me, wouldn't they? And even if they did decide to send a message, all I can see Aaron writing is, *I'm coming for you, bitch*, when these notes are almost…flowery."

"I don't disagree. The wording on the notes is strange," James said. "And we have no indication that Aaron has found you. It was Lincoln's security team who poked at your backstory and no one else. For all we know, Aaron has simply taken off to some non-extradition country because of the RICO case. But I won't be comfortable until we set eyes on him again."

The what-ifs and if-onlys tried to eat me alive from the

inside out.

"Either way, the situation here in Cherry Bay is no longer sustainable. The safest bet is to relocate you."

Bone-searing grief wielded through me. I tugged at Dad's ring. It was my only real, physical connection to him anymore. What would I be able to take with me from this life? What physical items would remind me of Hector and Shay and my time at The Tea Spot? What would remind me of Lincoln and a glorious weekend I'd spent in the arms of a man I'd cared deeply for…had been halfway in love with after mere days together.

"No." My mom's voice swung through the air like a gunshot, drawing our eyes to her.

She'd been quiet for most of the conversation between the Marshal and me, but her face was set now. I knew that look. That quiet determination.

Our handler shook her head and said, "You can't deny relocation. If you do—"

"I know," Mom interrupted. "We'd have to opt out if we say no to moving."

"Mom," I said, panic filling me. "We should talk about this before we decide anything."

She shook her head. "No. We've both got lives here we love. People we care about. A future. We're not running. We're not hiding. We've got the security team Lincoln hired. I'll hire more. We'll figure it out."

"A private security company isn't the answer, Erica. They'll bleed you dry if you try to keep them for the rest of your lives," Deputy James insisted.

"I can't do it," Mom said, hands shaking as she pushed a loose strand of hair behind her ear. "I can't start over again. Give up another career. Ask Willow to give up the career she was born to do. The art she's creating. She just fell in love for the first time, and I won't tear her from any of it."

"She's in love with the president's son!" James hissed.

I wanted to protest that I wasn't sure it was love yet, if only to ease Mom's conscience about moving, but the words turned to ash in my mouth. I wasn't halfway in love with Lincoln, I was fully, over-the-top, completely and absolutely in love with him. It had happened from the moment he'd swooped in and rescued me, and every single tingling sensation, every single beautiful moment after it had just strengthened the connection that bound us together. It was ridiculous, but true.

I desperately wanted more time with him. Whatever time my body gave me. Whatever time fate and the Viceroys would leave me with. But I also didn't want to put him or my mom in danger because of my need to mark off that last joyous experience on my list.

When neither Mom nor I said anything else, Deputy James said, disgustedly, "The little taste of his life you got with just the idea of a photograph leaking…that's nothing compared to what you'll get if you actually show up on his arm. Even if these notes have nothing to do with the Viceroys, you think Aaron Vitale is just going to sit back and watch as you live some huge-ass life with the president's son while his baby brother is pushing up daisies?"

Nausea returned, flipping my stomach in a nasty way. Mom grabbed my hand, squeezing it tight, comfort and solidarity. We were in this together. Somehow, I'd forgotten that even though it's what she'd insisted last night. That it was her choice. She had as much to lose—and gain—as I did. She was pale, and I could feel her shaking even as her words were confident when she spoke. "Then, I guess we'll have to trust the authorities to find a way to put him out of commission for good if he comes calling. We're not relocating."

James paced, shoved up the sleeves on her jacket, paced some more, and then came to a stop by the island. "I've never lost anyone under my protection. Not because they were killed or because they chose to walk away from protection. Please don't be the first. It'll haunt me for the rest of my life if something happens to either of you."

"It'll haunt *me* for the rest of *my* life if I let Willow walk away from the beautiful future she deserves. That she's earned! We've had enough tragedy and darkness, Rebecca. Enough is enough!" She pounded the counter to emphasize it, and emotions clogged my throat.

"Mom—"

"No, Willow. We're not leaving."

While the thought of giving up everything and everyone here tore at my soul, I wasn't sure I could live with the alternative either—because someone I loved could die again.

Deputy Marshal James stared at both of us for a second that felt like forever before sighing and saying, "I can give you forty-eight hours to think about it while we start arrangements for a move." When Mom started to respond, she waved it away. "Calm down and really consider what you're doing. When logic prevails, give me a call." She headed toward the door. "We'll have two deputies assigned to you until then. I'll have them coordinate with this Garner security company, but the Marshal Service is in charge, not them. What we say goes."

I didn't think Lincoln or Axel would agree with that statement, and just the thought of either of their reactions lightened the heaviness weighing on me just a bit. I wished it could wipe it away completely. Wished I could go back a handful of days to when I'd been smiling at the cherry blossoms and feeling like my life was all goodness and hope and rainbows.

But if I went back, I wouldn't have Lincoln, and that hurt more than anything had in a really long time.

James left, shutting the front door with enough force it made the windows rattle.

"What are we doing?" I asked, shaking my head.

"Living," Mom said quietly, sitting on the stool next to me.

"But what if someone else gets hurt… I'm not just talking about me or you, Mom. What if it's Hector or Shay or Lincoln…" My heart just about broke even thinking about it.

She patted my hand. "You gave Lincoln a choice and he's made it. He's stuck by you. I can only do the same for Hector. If we tell everyone the truth, and they choose to stay, then they've decided the risk is worth it. That's pretty beautiful, don't you think?"

It was similar to what she'd said and I'd thought last night. And while she was right, she was also glossing over it some. If something happened to Hector because of us, she'd be filled with guilt. Remorse would cling to both of us, following us wherever we went. That haunting she and Deputy James had talked about would be relentless. Goosebumps went up my arms and over my neck. We were tempting fate. Tempting the Viceroys. Tempting whoever this was leaving notes about the fairy-tale life I didn't deserve.

She nudged me with an elbow. "When do I get to meet Lincoln in person? I have some thanking to do."

We'd both gotten so good at brushing aside the hard topics and even harder feelings in order to force some peace and happiness into our lives that it was second nature now. But was it healthy? I didn't know the answer. But if it was what she needed right then, I'd give it to her. I nudged her back and said, "Don't embarrass me."

"Have I ever embarrassed you?"

She hadn't. Never. Not even when I was a tween and she'd dropped me off at school with hugs and kisses and love. I hadn't cared. I'd always felt lucky to have my parents. To be loved in ways some of my classmates weren't.

"I have a feeling he'll be knocking on our door soon." Just the thought of it was enough to curve my lips upward.

He'd basically asked me to move in, give up my job and work out of his kitchen. He'd been partially teasing, but there'd been a layer of truth beneath it, even if some of it had stemmed from the trauma of his past and his need to keep me safe. I understood those feelings better than maybe anyone who hadn't experienced losses like ours ever could.

So, right or wrong, ridiculous or not, I knew he'd be showing up at our door when his day was done. The thrill of that knowledge helped push away more of the doubts and fears and worries. Made it easier to smile at Mom.

"I need to talk to Hector," Mom said, standing up. "Thank you for letting me be the one to tell him."

"I would have hated it if Lincoln had heard about it from someone else." I reached over and hugged her to me, head on her chest like I'd done so many times as a child. "What if… What if Hector decides we're too much of a risk? What if he doesn't want to date you…and he doesn't want me to work for him anymore? We could lose everything anyway."

"What happened to my sunshine girl who refused to live by what-ifs anymore?" She pulled back to look at me, lips twisted upward with the tease. When I didn't return it, she asked, "Do you really believe Hector would do that?"

"He has Shay to protect. His livelihood."

"He considers you a second daughter, kiddo. He told me that himself. He's not walking away from you. That's part of the reason I waited so long to accept a date. I didn't want to start something that ended and could ruin what you have with him. I didn't want you to lose another father…" She choked on a wave of emotion, then she cleared her throat. "I have to believe what I said to Deputy Marshal James. We've had enough bad in our lives. Fate isn't going to hand us more."

"Hector was hurt. And the mural, Mom…you didn't see it…" I shook my head.

"Being hurt and being angry enough to walk away are completely different things."

She was right. Of course she was right, but it still didn't ease my worries. He'd basically acted as if we were saying goodbye forever as we'd left the café.

I felt like a boat on turbulent waves, heading for a rocky shore with no way to stop. I couldn't find my footing. No solid ground appeared at my feet. All I could do was let the tide ride up and over us and see what was left when it finally subsided.

# Part Four

Trouble had broken into their perfect world.

The fairy tale was tarnished.

The pleasure I got out of playing with them was surprising.

The quick death I'd first envisioned when plotting their demise would have been satisfying but fleeting.

The terror and tears I'd watched from the shadows were extending the gratification.

I just needed to give another nudge.

Pull another string.

Then, they'd finally get the full anguish and pain they deserved.

And I'd be right there watching as the last drop of blood fell.

# Chapter Thirty-one

## Lincoln

**HEARTBEAT**
Performed by The Fray

**I**T **TOOK LONGER THAN I WANTED** for Katerina to respond to me, giving me a bitter taste of my own medicine, knowing this was exactly how my family felt when waiting for me to get back to them. I killed the time by pulling from the internet as many images as I could find of the mural at The Tea Spot. I enlarged them, printed them out so all the details were easy to see, and gathered the supplies I needed.

When my phone rang, I picked it up expecting it to be Katerina, but it was the contractor who'd remodeled my house and was handling the renovation at the gallery. He reminded me he was coming the next day to get started, and I swore to myself silently. It meant I'd need to box up my projects and move them from the studio upstairs to the house.

But it would have to wait as I was anxious to get back to Willow. The sun was already warming the streets with a midday glow, proving I'd already been away from her for hours. So instead of packing, I grabbed the single box of supplies I'd put together for the mural and headed out the door.

I'd barely stepped outside, and the two hulking men in the black garb more reminiscent of special forces than the Secret Service had just flanked me, when my phone buzzed again.

"Lyrica, I'm a little tied up. Can it wait?"

"She looks like Sienna."

I barely resisted the urge to toss my phone. My tone was sharp and brutal when I replied. "She does. But I'll say the same thing I've said to my mom and anyone else who brings it up, I'm not with her because of how she looks or doesn't look. Willow and I have already discussed it, and we're okay. I won't let anyone upset her by bringing it up, are we clear?"

She didn't speak for several seconds, and I paced outside the gallery, waiting as my irritation grew and my need to get back to Willow surged.

Finally, she said, "It's just… I know you, Lincoln. I can hear it in your voice. The protectiveness you feel. You have this overwhelming need to shield everyone in your life. It's how Felicity got her claws into you. Now this woman shows up, looking like the lost love of your life, and I can't help but worry for my friend."

If she knew just how much more was going on than the photos, she'd worry more. But telling Mom about Willow's witness protection and the notes was one thing because my parents' resources might be able to help. Telling Lyrica would only make her increase her worries.

I inhaled deeply, letting some of the irritation fade. "I'm good, Lyrica. Honestly. I'm actually letting things go and moving on." Even with everything that had happened this week, even with Sienna reappearing, there was still truth in those words. It had taken Willow showing me the light for me to see I'd been stuck, relishing in the remorse as if it was the penance I had to pay. But really it had just been a selfish way to hold myself back, keeping even my family and friends at bay. "I can see a happy life with her."

And I could. At least I could see the beginnings of it. Slow Saturday mornings lost in each other's skin. Laughter. A heavenly bliss that smelled and tasted like Willow. We just had to find a way to cut the strings of our pasts trying to pull us back so we could focus on the new threads weaving us together.

"You deserve to be happy, Lincoln," she said softly. "You've always deserved it."

How many times had she told me she didn't blame me for getting shot? How many times had I agreed but not believed it?

"You deserve it too," I told her.

"I do," she said.

"Are you happy with Merci?"

"She's my current chapter. I don't know if she's the rest of my book yet." The day she'd broken up with me, Lyrica had told me, *Our life is supposed to have different chapters with different arcs and different people in them. It gives us the experience we need to realize when we've found the ending we want to keep. You're not my ending, Lincoln, but I'll always love the chapters that had you in them.*

"Willow isn't just a chapter I'm breezing through. She's my ending," I told her.

She made a sound of surprise. "I'm really, really glad. When do I get to meet her?"

I snorted at the request that mirrored Mom's, and I gave her the same "soon" response before ending the call.

I picked up the box of supplies, gave the two bodyguards a nod, and then jogged across the street, hoping to get back to The Tea Spot before anyone else interrupted me.

When I walked in, the café seemed even more packed than normal. Not quite the crowd that had been there to see Willow's food art, but it was definitely buzzing. The air was full of a restless chatter that spoke of the drama that had occurred as much as coffee and scones.

Hector saw me, gave me a wave from behind the counter, and hollered, "Willow went home with Erica."

I couldn't help the beat of sheer panic that flew through me. I debated dropping the box and racing to the cottage just to ensure she was still there. Even knowing Willow didn't want to go, that she wanted the chance for her and her mom to build a life here, I wouldn't blame Erica, or the Marshals, for insisting they leave.

My hands gripped the box so tight, the edges bent.

She wasn't gone. Willow would never disappear without

saying goodbye. And I wouldn't be an obsessive asshole who couldn't give her the space she needed to figure things out with her mom. I wouldn't be Felicity no matter how strongly the need to see Willow and protect her raged.

No, I had to trust Axel and his team would discover a way to end this for them—for all of us—before anyone forced her hand.

So instead of storming out of the café, I stepped over to the wall, set out my supplies, and used painter's tape to hang the images I'd printed out. While I worked, I felt eyes on me. It wasn't the skin crawling sensation I'd had all week, but more the curious sensation of people who recognized me. I hadn't worn a baseball cap or glasses again today, but I wasn't sure a disguise mattered anymore. My secret time tucked away here had come to an end.

I ignored the looks, trusted the two bodyguards to watch my back, and started drawing.

I'd already sketched the animals and part of the woman by the time Hector joined me. "You don't have to do this, Lincoln."

"I want to. It'll never be the same, but it'll be as close as I can make it," I said. When I looked up, his normally grinning face was lined with concern.

"You know what's going on with them. With Willow and Erica?" he asked.

"I do, but it isn't my place to say."

"You hired those men." He glanced to the one leaning up against the wall only a few feet away. "To keep them safe."

"Yes."

"Thank you." His voice was deep with emotion. "It means more to me than I can say. More than even this." He eyed the mural, throat bobbing. "And that means a whole hell of a lot."

His employee, who always seemed one step away from falling apart, called his name. Hector rolled his eyes to the ceiling, patted me on the back, and then set off for the counter without another word.

My phone rang, and maybe because I was distracted, or

maybe because I was still waiting to hear from Katerina, I answered once again without glancing at the number. "Hello."

"I was just crawling out from under the psycho label you hung around my neck, Lincoln, and now you've got people hunting me down? Accusing me all over again?" Felicity's voice was sharp and brittle. Nothing like the happy, warm voice she was renowned for using in her movies and interviews. It was one of the things I'd learned about her first. That she could carve knives in you with a simple tone and a smattering of words. That she got off on doing just that.

"You hung that label around your own neck, Felicity."

"I saw what I wanted and went for it. I did everything I could to get it. If I were a man, people would be cheering me on, patting my back, and saying good job. Because I'm a woman, I'm called unhinged."

"The fact that you had someone break into my home, my computers, and my phone said that, not because you're a woman," I snapped.

"Whatever. Just call off your hunting dogs. There's nothing here for them to find."

"I swear on all I hold holy, if you have anything to do with what's going on right now, I'll do everything in my power to make sure your career is over for good. You won't even be able to get a gig for a backwater television commercial."

"I have no idea what's going on with you!" she hissed.

"Someone's leaving notes, using your words. The ones you tossed out about me not deserving the fairy-tale of you. Who else would write them?"

"You don't deserve me. Just like Rex Carter didn't. Just like that shitty director who just rejected me for his stupid part doesn't deserve me," she ranted before inhaling sharply, and calming down some. "I'm done with you, Lincoln. I want nothing to do with you. Please leave me out of whatever this is and let me be."

A dark chuckle escaped me, "Feels pretty crappy, doesn't it? To want out of something. To want to move on and have someone dragging you back kicking and screaming?"

"So, this is some sort of twisted payback?" she demanded.

I pushed a hand through my hair in exasperation. Felicity had a way of tearing away my nice and making me show the ugly I didn't even know had lived inside me before she'd entered my world. "No. Just like you, I want to move on. I don't want to go back, not for revenge or any other reason. If you say you had nothing to do with this, I'll try to believe you. But, like you were always telling me, you're a really good actor. Lies are what you do for a living."

"Leave me alone, and I'll leave you alone."

She hung up, and I ran a finger along a brow before hitting Axel's number. When he answered, I said, "I just got a call from Felicity."

"Doesn't surprise me. She was pretty wound up when I talked with her. She insisted she hadn't made contact with you in months, which we know is a lie. Then, she went on and on about how she didn't give two shits what was going on in your life before saying if you brought the past back up and the media got wind, she was going to sue you for slander and take every dollar you had."

"You think this is her?"

"I think we can't close the door completely yet, but I'm working on it."

But a little voice inside me wasn't sold that what was happening here had anything to do with her. I'd thought earlier that if it wasn't Felicity, the other option would be terrifying, and I felt a tremor of that fear run through me once more. If we marked off all the boxes, and the only option left was Aaron, it would cost Willow her entire world and would ensure Felicity's words came true for me. Because losing Willow would wipe away any chance I'd ever have for a happy ending. That third strike would be merciless and last a lifetime.

# Chapter Thirty-two

## Willow

**YOU BETTER BELIEVE**
Performed by Train

**WHILE *I* WAS IN THE KITCHEN** working on miniature lemon meringues I planned to top with gold leaf, our camera app went off at the same time the doorbell rang. My pulse skittered happily, wildly even, because I knew immediately who it was. The security team wouldn't let a threat close enough to ring the bell, and I'd known Lincoln would eventually show up. We'd spent an intense weekend together, and our bubble may have burst, but the pull toward one another hadn't gone anywhere.

Mom looked up from her laptop, saw my hands full, and rose to answer it.

Lincoln had barely stepped inside, had barely said hello, before she was hugging him.

She whispered something quietly, and butterflies winged around in my chest at the sight of them together. His eyes met mine over the distance. He winked and the fluttering inside me turned into a frenzied delight.

"You promised not to embarrass me," I called out.

Mom let Lincoln go and said, "It's a pleasure to meet you in person."

"The pleasure is mine, Mrs. Earhart."

"It's Erica, please."

Mom led him to the kitchen, and the look in his eyes as he got closer caused every part of my body, soul, and mind to light up. Happiness. Love. Desire. We'd been apart mere hours, but it felt like it had been a lifetime. I literally ached to be near him again. I wanted to keep him. To keep this. The pain of not knowing if I could, regardless of Mom's insistence we weren't leaving, was harsh and sharp.

But when he didn't stop at the counter, coming right to me and kissing my temple while Mom watched us like a hawk, it took the pain and doubts and sent them sailing.

"I missed you," he said. And with those three little words, I fell in love all over again.

My smile was ridiculously large as I replied, "I missed you, too."

"My heart just exploded," Mom said. "Have you had dinner, Lincoln?"

"No. After the food Willow made this weekend, I was greedy for more of hers."

Mom chuckled. "It's a good thing my blood pressure is steady, otherwise you'd have me swooning. You'll join us then?"

"I'd be honored."

The pleasure inside my chest grew even more until it was almost buzzing around me. Lincoln was responsible for bringing it back. He thought he was all dark shadows and torment, but he had his own light that shone brightly when he let it.

"I made baked manicotti," I said. "It has a few more minutes,"

"With a sauce from scratch instead of a jar," Lincoln teased.

I was happy to play along. "As if. No other kind of sauce exists."

He swiped a finger into my meringue, sticking it in his mouth, eyes closing as he savored it. My insides ignited at the simple, seductive move.

"Don't put your fingers in my dessert!" I scolded, but my words were missing the heat required to be a true reprimand.

"Take a seat, Lincoln," Mom interrupted, patting the stool next to her. "I've never had the chance to interrogate a boyfriend of Willow's before."

His smile disappeared, which I hated, but he moved around to sit beside her.

"I'm pretty sure you know more about me than I know about myself," he said with a casual shrug.

"You mean how you like to party?" she asked. Even though she'd put on her serious face, I knew her well enough to know she wasn't truly upset by this fact, but Lincoln didn't.

"My love of dancing has often been misconstrued as a love of partying," he said. "And even those days of losing myself in a rhythm on a dance floor seem to be trailing behind me."

"I see. I was sort of hoping you'd shove my girl out in the world. Make her behave a bit more like a twenty-three-year-old instead of a forty-three-year-old."

"Mom!"

"Dancing and wild parties it is then," he said with a chuckle.

But we all knew it wasn't going to happen. Not only because that wasn't who I was or who Lincoln was but because of the threat hovering around us.

"Kiddo, do me a favor. Go get my wooden music box from my room and bring it to me."

My eyes narrowed. "Why?"

"Because I want something out of it and because I need a moment with your beau."

"Mom."

"Willow."

We locked eyes, and in them I saw her determination, but also a little plea, and so I gave in. I wiped my hands, rounded the corner and fist bumped her shoulder. "Be nice or I'll never forgive you.”

She just laughed.

In her bedroom, I went straight to the dresser where the music box always sat, only to find it wasn’t there. Frustrated, it took me several minutes before I discovered it tucked in her bedside table. I’d just stepped back into the hall when her words to Lincoln had my feet skidding to a stop.

“The Marshals can’t find Aaron.” She said it matter-of-factly, but I recognized the fear in her tone that matched the same fear in me.

Lincoln’s response was a singular, feral snap, “What?”

“Someone looking like him was playing the part. They think he’s been gone for days and that he might have skipped off to some non-extradition country.”

“I got confirmation that Poco is the one who sold the photographs to the press, but it’s unlikely he sent the notes.” I could hear the self-recrimination in his voice, and it was confusing. This wasn’t on him.

I didn’t want him to see this as something he’d failed at. Something else to blame himself for. Maybe I should let the Marshals take me away. Mom could stay here. Aaron didn’t care about her, he just hated me. But would he hurt her, thinking he could use her to find me? Would he hurt Lincoln? Hector? The thought of leaving any of them ripped me apart all over again.

Any decision I made left me feeling like a coward.

“The Marshals have given us forty-eight hours to decide whether to relocate or leave their protection,” Mom told him.

I couldn’t see them. Couldn’t see their faces, but I knew what would be on Lincoln’s. Anger. Determination. That love we hadn’t said.

“I swear to you, Erica, no one is going to hurt her. No one. I’ll protect her with every ounce of muscle and intelligence I have. I’ll spend every last dime at my disposal to hire the best people to keep her safe.” It was a fierce and protective vow I loved as much as I loved him.

Mom let out a shaky exhale I could hear all the way into the hall. "I'm glad to hear that's how you feel. But if we walk away from the Marshals, that's permanent for us. We won't be able to go back."

She was asking him for things she didn't have a right to ask. Things Lincoln and I hadn't even discussed and seemed ridiculous considering the limited time we'd known each other, and yet couldn't be denied.

His sincere response of, "You won't have to. I'll always have someone there watching over you," finally forced my feet to move.

I stepped between them at the barstools, setting the box down in front of my mother and nailing her with an irritated frown.

"Mom, stop." I turned from her to Lincoln. "Whatever decision we make isn't on you. It will never be on you. If we decide to walk away from witness protection, the responsibility for that is on us."

His eyes narrowed, and his arms snaked out to wrap around my waist.

"I can almost hear you screaming how ridiculous this is in that beautiful head of yours," he raised a brow that promised payment, but he was serious as he said, "I meant it when I told you I wasn't going anywhere. That promise I just made your mom, it's only the truth. Whether you steal my heart and walk out of my life or not, I will always make sure you're safe."

"Lincoln—"

"Besides, there's a chance this may have nothing to do with you. This actually may be about me."

I shook my head, and he stopped it by pulling me to his side so he could look at both my mother and me as he said, "The notes and the damage to the café could have been someone Felicity Bradshaw hired."

"The actress?" Mom asked incredulously.

"I don't know if you heard, but I had to get a restraining order against her. She hired someone to follow me, break into my computers and phones. I'd thought things with her had finally calmed down. But the wording of the notes, the fact that they came after Willow once she'd been seen with me…"

I hated to even think it was true. I didn't want Lincoln to carry one more burden. If something happened to me, and he thought it was his fault, it would destroy him.

I grabbed his hand. "How could she have found out about us so quickly? We've barely been seen together."

"If she had someone following me again. Remember the gray sedan? The guy I ran into downtown?" His throat bobbed. "If it's her, I promise you, she'll wish she'd never heard of me or you by the time I'm done with her."

"Even if it is her, this still isn't on you."

Mom reached around me to squeeze Lincoln's arm. "Listen to me, Lincoln. You're not responsible for her obsession any more than we're responsible for the Viceroys' hate. If we take on that responsibility, we give them power over us. This easily could be Aaron Vitale wanting revenge. Not only for his brother dying, but because his entire world is crumbling due to the RICO case. All we can do is be as safe as possible. We can protect ourselves, but what I won't allow is for Willow, or anyone in a relationship with her, to take on that hatred and evil as if they could have controlled it and failed. From what I've heard, from what I can tell, you're a good man. I know my daughter is a good human. Let that goodness surround you and not their darkness."

The oven timer went off, and I moved away from them with reluctance to pull the manicotti from the oven. The smell of basil and tomatoes filled the air along with melted mozzarella. The toasting of the cheese was flawless, the mix of colors making a vibrant picture. It would have brought more pleasure if the heaviness in the air wasn't so strong.

I set it on the stove to rest and turned to the rosemary bread I'd baked, slicing it while Mom pulled the strawberry-walnut salad I'd tossed earlier from the refrigerator. Lincoln asked what he could do to help and when we both told him to just take a seat at the table, he did.

Wine glasses were filled, plates loaded, and we'd all sat down when the reality slammed into me. Mom and I weren't alone. We had a guest. *My* guest. A man I *loved.*

My heart kicked fiercely, spinning and soaring and sending the heaviness of our discussion skyward.

This. I wanted to keep this. The pleasure of having the people I cared most about seated around a table with me. The only thing that would be better is if Hector and Shay were there too.

New determination filled me. I'd have that. I'd have it all.

I might not know how yet, but I would keep this life and this beautiful man.

They were mine and I refused to let Aaron or Poco or even Felicity send them from me.

While we ate, Mom and Lincoln chatted amiably, sharing the ins and outs of their lives in a way that sent more thrills through me. I wanted them to know and love each other as much as I loved them.

Mom talked about the kids winning at State, and he talked about the gallery and his dad's election. By the time we'd cleared our plates, it felt like we'd been doing this for months if not years.

"I've never had better manicotti," Lincoln said. "I see what you meant about the garlic. I didn't miss it at all."

"Don't get her started," Mom said, lips twitching. "We'll be hearing about how America brutalizes authentic cuisine for hours."

I rolled my eyes, but Lincoln just said. "I'd be happy to listen to Willow talk for hours."

"Wow," Mom said, fanning herself with her hand as a full smile took over her face. "You really are too much." She pushed away from the table, carrying her empty plate to the sink. "I'm going over to Hector's. When I talked to him earlier, I told him I'd be by after dinner."

My eyes locked with Mom's. They hadn't really been able to talk earlier because he'd been busy at the café. While I hoped their conversation didn't end in a broken heart for her and joblessness for me, I also had to believe that Hector saw the truth of us past all the lies.

I got up and gave her a hug, and told her the same thing she'd told me earlier. "It's going to be okay."

She hugged me back. "You're right. It is. I can feel it."

She opened the music box on the counter and pulled two envelopes out.

"After Willow's dad was diagnosed with FFI, and he knew he wasn't going to live long, he decided to write letters I could give her at the important moments in her life." Mom's voice choked. "He'd intended to write a whole cart full of them, but these are the only two he'd finished before he was killed."

My eyes filled automatically as much from the flash of grief in Mom's expression as her words. She'd never even hinted I had letters from Dad waiting for me.

She hesitated and then handed the first envelope to Lincoln rather than me. My eyes widened, watching the envelope with longing as Lincoln took it solemnly. Then, she turned and handed me one as well. "Don't read yours until after Lincoln reads his." She kissed my temple. "I'll leave the two of you to show each other some of that goodness I was talking about while I go get some of my own."

"Mom!"

She chuckled again. "I love that blush, kiddo. Love it and love Lincoln simply because he gave it to you." She winked at him and then walked over to the door to grab her keys and purse. "I'm sure one of the Marshals will be following me, but the private security should stay here."

"There's more than enough to go around," Lincoln insisted.

"Thank you for protecting my girl."

"It's an honor to do so."

"Yes it is, but I'm glad you agree." Mom's reply was quick, her face happy. "You might just do after all. Regardless of your big life and your big family. You might just do."

She didn't give him a chance to respond. She went out into the night, and silence fell behind her. Lincoln stroked my heated cheeks with gentle fingers, sending delicious waves of desire swirling through me.

But not even the unrelenting need for him could distract me from the letter sitting in my hands from my dad. All I wanted to do was tear it open and read it. To get a piece of my father back, but Mom had said to let Lincoln read his first, so I waited. Anxious. Giddy. Desperate.

As if understanding my feelings without us saying a word, Lincoln tore his open and read. His face was serious, thoughtful but not upset. When he was done, he folded it up and put it away.

I gasped. "You're not going to let me see it?" Disappointment leached into every syllable.

He met my shocked eyes with tender ones. "I'd give you just about anything you asked for Willow but not that. He asked me not to. He asked me to keep it between us, and I think you'd rather I keep that promise to him than give it to you."

I wasn't sure if it was true. I was greedy for more words from my dad. I hadn't heard anything from him in six years. Longer, if I considered how little he'd said to me that last year. And when he had spoken, the words had often been twisted by the FFI into things he never would have said.

Lincoln leaned in, wrapped an arm around me, and nudged my shoulder with his chin. "Open yours."

So I did with hands that shook.

*My darling Wendy,*

*I'm hoping you'll have read a few of my notes by now. Your college acceptance, graduations, your first real job, and many more. But I want you to know these two letters, the one for you and the one for the person you chose to give your heart to, were the first ones I wrote. Because finding and keeping love is the most important thing about living. Out of all the wishes I've had for you, this was the most important one—that you love and be loved in return.*

*Don't ask your guy to disclose what I wrote to him. Allow me to have this private conversation with him just as I would have if I'd been there in person. A father has things he wants to tell his daughter's partner, so please trust that I gave him words of wisdom as well as gratitude for accepting your love and giving you his.*

*Now, let me give you some of the same.*

*Your mother and I may have named you Wendy because of our shared love of Peter Pan, but I want you to know, as your father, I don't want to see you with a Peter or a Hook. None of the men in that story are good enough for you. What I hope for you is that you'll find a Robin Hood. Someone who is willing to sacrifice everything for his Maid Marion. Who puts life and soul on the line to claim his place at your side. A man who thinks of others more than he thinks of himself.*

*If that isn't who's with you right now, drop him like a hot potato, kiddo, and go find someone who is all of those things. Because that's what you deserve. Nothing less.*

*But if I know you at all, you'll have found your Robin Hood because your light and your joy, along with your compassion and kindness, will have drawn him to you.*

*I don't doubt that darkness will do what it always does and try to cast shadows on you from time to time. In life, you will always find Prince Johns and Sheriff of Nottinghams and just damn fate trying to take greedily what isn't theirs, trying to break you and your spirit. But you have the strength in you to best those assholes, kiddo. You are courageous and brave, and while I don't want you to have to face any of them on your own, you can and you will.*

*And if, by chance, you get stuck in the dark of night for a few moments, remember that being lost in the moonlight isn't so bad. It's never pitch black. The moon and the stars both give off a bit of light. And if you're lucky to have someone solid and good at your side, it'll be easier to find those bright spots together. I hope the person you've given your heart to is that person for you. The one you can count on like I've always counted on your mom.*

*From the day you were born, you've always made me proud. But from here, when I can't be at your side, I want you to know that the best gift you could ever give me, the best way to continue to make me proud, is by enjoying your life to its fullest. Chase every dream, appreciate every smile, hold tight to every delightful moment, and love with every piece of your soul. If you do that, you'll have made me the happiest parent in this world and beyond.*

*Remember I am with you always,*

*Dad*

I couldn't stop the mix of sad and happy tears that escaped. I missed him so much I thought it might drown me, but I was also thrilled I'd received these few extra words from him. I wanted to make him proud by doing just what he asked. Living. Loving. How did I do that when the shadows were so close these days? So much evil and darkness around every corner. The stars were hard to see, weren't they? The moonlight was hidden beyond a thick fog layer as well as the normal black of night.

Then, I looked at Lincoln, shining in his own way after his repeated traumas, willing to extend a hand and help those he loved and cared about, and I knew Dad was right. If you had someone at your side, you could find those little sparks of light together. I'd found my Robin Hood even if Lincoln only saw himself as a vampire sucking me into his dark vortex.

Before I even had a chance to say a word, Lincoln pulled me from my chair onto his lap, placed his mouth on mine, and offered me his soul. Solace bled from his touch but also hope. The sweet comfort only lasted a few seconds before the hunger, the soul-deep craving erupted over us once more.

Mouths and hands began searching, flaming, taunting. I lost myself in the pleasure of it, tumbling headfirst into the heady sensations of love and want and need, feeling him fall with me. His palms slid under my shirt, and the skin-on-skin sensation was all it took to have me gasping and trembling.

When he broke our kiss, a little whimper of a protest escaped me. His lips traveled over my jaw and along my neck, nipping and tasting. A moan immediately followed my whimper, and he smiled against my collarbone, sending joy rippling through me with such strength it pushed at the darkness and the sadness that remained.

I dragged myself away, and it was his turn to protest with a deep growl. I held out my hand, and when he took it, I led him down the hall.

"Your mother going to be okay if dawn breaks and I'm here?" he asked.

"I'm not even sure she'll make it home herself after that little speech she gave."

"Still. There's no one at my place. A much bigger bed than that full size in your room. An entire house to lose ourselves in." He nipped at my ear and whispered, "Remember the table. The way I made you—"

I cut him off with my lips on his before breaking away to say, "Fine. Take me home, Lincoln. Let me grab a bag, and then you can take me home."

His eyes lit up, happiness practically dripping from them. "I like you using that word."

"What word?"

"Home."

The wild flutters in my chest returned. I hadn't even realized I'd used it. But I felt it. The cottage was where Mom and I lived. It had been a cage of sorts. One with love and caring inside it, but I'd been bound here not only by the Marshals' rules but by my own limitations. Lincoln's house… I could choose to be there. I could let love and hope fill me there.

I kissed Lincoln fiercely again, seeking his warmth. His beauty. His strength. We were both panting as he practically carried me to my room. "Sweetness, I need you to pack up whatever you were planning before I change my mind and use that tiny bed to show you how little space I need to make your body scream."

I'd never expected to have this. To have some gorgeous man saying these tender, steamy things to me. The fear of what was coming after us and the unknown of the FFI tried to push its way in, but I forced it out. Shut the door on it. Locked it. This was worth it. This time finding the stars and moonlight amongst the dark, reveling in these feelings, watching the smile spread across his face instead of the grumpy glower, was all worth it. I'd try to do what my dad had asked by living and loving in every moment I had with Lincoln.

I pulled a duffel bag from my closet and stuffed a pair of pajamas I wasn't sure I'd use and a change of clothes inside before going across the hall and shoving some toiletries in it as well. When I came out, Lincoln was waiting. He took the bag from me, twined his fingers in mine, and then led me home.

# Chapter Thirty-three

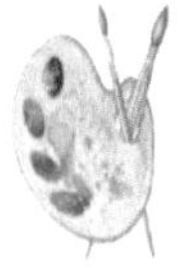

## Lincoln

**SUPERMAN (IT'S NOT EASY)**
Performed by Five for Fighting

*I'D SLEPT FOR THREE HOURS AFTER* losing myself in Willow, but it was only one in the morning by the time the ants came crawling. Fully awake, I stared at her tucked up against my chest, face calm and serene even though I could still see the remnants of the tears scattered across it.

Both Willow's parents had asked me to protect her. And even though Erica hadn't specifically asked if I loved her daughter, it had hovered beneath her other requests. She'd asked the same thing as Willow's dad had in his letter. Was I in it for the long haul? Did I love her enough to guard her heart like it was my own? Would I sacrifice my happiness for hers?

And the answer to all of it was yes.

Before my limbs started twitching so much that I woke her, I eased out of the bed. When she rolled over and hugged the pillow, I almost tore it out of her hands and slid back in. I felt right when I was twined with her, and I despised my body's inability to stay.

I dragged to the love seat with my sketchbook in hand, letting the moon light up the page for me. I drew without thought and found flowers flowing from my fingertips. Lotus blooms in different shades with so many different meanings, but always emerging from the depths of the mud and dark waters to open in the light.

*The lotus represents purity and rebirth and rising from challenge.* I barely glanced over to where Sienna paced by the window. When I didn't answer, she continued, *It's you. And her. And the gallery. Passionate souls, endless love, and new beginnings rising from the muck around you, clean and bright and beautiful. You can have it, Lincoln. You're almost at the finish line. Or maybe the new starting line? I don't know.*

She was right, as always, about all of it, but also that it would be a good name for the gallery. The Lotus Gallery. "Why are you here?" I demanded in a harsh whisper.

*To keep you from doing something you think is all noble and good and losing everything.*

"I won't lose her."

*You won't.*

"Lincoln? Who are you talking to?" I twirled around at Willow's sleepy voice.

I threw Sienna an annoyed look and then turned my back on her to join Willow in bed.

"Myself. My demons."

I heard Sienna's snort from behind me, but didn't acknowledge her.

"Go back to sleep."

"It's almost time for me to get up anyway."

I kissed her with force and heat and intensity. I kissed her because I was afraid that for some reason, somehow, I wouldn't be able to continue kissing her for much longer, even when my heart knew she was mine and I was hers. And maybe I was kissing her to prove to Sienna I knew what I was doing, so she could just scurry back off into the ether. But mostly, I kissed Willow because I didn't have another choice. She was too tempting. Too beautiful. Too everything I needed and wanted in my life.

Willow smiled against my lips and then pushed on my chest. "I need to get to work."

She didn't *need* to work because I could take care of us

both, but I couldn't imagine Willow ever not working. She enjoyed what she did too much. Her baking was as much a part of her as my painting was a part of me. So instead of spending another hour convincing her to stay in bed, I let her go with reluctance.

We got ready for our day together, and then I walked with her to the car and drove with the Marshals and Axel's team to The Tea Spot. When the team gave the all clear, I went inside with her.

"I'll see you after work," I told her, placing a kiss on her temple.

"At some point, you'll need to stop doing this," she said.

"What?"

"Following me along everywhere."

"I'm not doing it because I think I can protect you more than the men I've hired." When she rolled her eyes in challenge, I huffed out a laugh and said, "Okay, I'm not doing it completely for that reason. I'm doing it because I'm awake and I love spending every moment I can with you before our day pulls us apart."

It wasn't the I love you she deserved yet. But I felt like if I told her now, when it was too soon, she'd toss that word ridiculous at me again, and blame it on my need to protect the women in my life. She wasn't wrong. But those weren't the only reasons. So I'd hold on to the words a bit longer. Until the timing was better. Until the shadows weren't lingering over us.

It gave me one more incentive to end this quickly.

"I don't know how to respond when you say things like that," she said honestly. "Your words are beautiful and breathtaking and—"

"Don't say it, Sweetness. Don't say the R word because there are too many people who might catch us in the middle of me issuing a penalty for saying it."

She snorted. "Go paint something."

I chuckled and taunted back, "Go bake something."

And then I left with the music of her laughter following

me.

When I got to the gallery, I sketched out the lotus image and words for the gallery sign, until the contractor's team showed up. Then, I boxed up most of the supplies I'd just uncrated in the last week, and wrangled Axel's men into taking it and all my uncompleted projects to my house.

I'd just finished resetting everything up in one of the guest rooms, when Axel walked in with a grim expression on his face.

"Some college kid was paid by some guy to bring a note to Willow at the café. We intercepted it before it got to her, and we're working with the kid to identify him. So far all we know is that he was an average height man with brown hair, a beanie, and sunglasses."

He handed me a note that read, *Your part in this fairy-tale is to die.*

A growl escaped me as my rage grew. "Fucking Felicity!"

"She's still in LA," he said. "And we haven't identified any payments from her to another source."

I yanked my phone from my pocket, found the unknown number from the day before, and hit dial.

When she greeted me with a snippy "What?" I almost lost it.

"Call them off. Call them off or I swear to God, I'll find you and pull you apart limb by limb."

"I told you, Lincoln, I have nothing to do with whatever is going on with you." But I heard the hesitation. Heard the spike of something close to fear.

"You really want to end up in prison? You want people to die because of some goddamn obsession? Because you didn't get what you wanted from me?"

"I didn't do anything!" she shouted. She inhaled sharply, calming herself like she always had in the middle of an argument. "But I may know who's behind this. Sort of."

"Of course you do!"

"Not because I hired them! Just listen to me for two seconds."

"I'm putting you on speaker so the head of my security can hear," I told her. "Just fucking tell me the truth!"

I turned up the volume as Felicity said, "I told you I was being stalked, and I was, even though you didn't believe me! He said he was the only person who deserved the fairy tale of me. And after what happened in St. Micah, he said you didn't deserve any fairy tale at all when you'd caused so much pain to me and others. He swore you wouldn't get a happy ending."

"Those were your words. You said those to me!"

"I was so pissed at you and scared. And when you didn't seem to give a shit what was happening, I tossed the same ones at you."

"That was months ago!"

"I got another note earlier this week. He said he'd kill you for rejecting me as a way of proving how much he loved me. He insisted I belonged with him and only him."

"And you didn't tell me," I hissed.

"I didn't know you'd declined Secret Service protection. How was I supposed to know you'd left yourself vulnerable?"

She twisted it back on me. As if this was my fault, and maybe, because I was already thinking similar thoughts, her arrow landed home.

"Who is it?" I demanded.

"I don't know. My manager just threw the most recent note in a bag with all the other hate mail I'm getting *because of you*."

"So because you're angry and getting some ugly letters, you figured it was okay not to warn me? For me to be killed? For people around me to be hurt?"

"No! I just thought the letter was all bluster."

I didn't believe her, and I was positive Axel didn't either if the anger in the man's eyes said anything. Felicity Bradshaw would have been happy if I'd turned up dead. Whether or not she'd virtually pulled the trigger by hiring someone was a different story.

"This is Axel Garner, Lincoln's security," Axel said. "We need anything you still have. A photo of the letters for now, but

I'd prefer to have the actual ones sent to me. I'll give you the location to mail them."

"You'll have to talk to Richard, my manager. He has it all now."

"Give me his number," Axel demanded.

She rattled it off, and after he'd stepped aside to make the call, I said, "You're responsible for this." Maybe it was the truth or maybe I just wanted it to be true, so I wouldn't have to shoulder one more regret.

"I didn't do this," she insisted. "So please, can you keep me out of it? My career can't handle another hit."

A sound of pure fury erupted from my chest. "Your career? How about my life? How about Willow's life?"

"Who's Willow?"

Her voice turned icy. She didn't care. She'd never really cared, which was why I'd never felt anything for her in return. Felicity Bradshaw was a shell. An empty human being who wouldn't know a true emotion if it hit her in the face. It was also why the pinnacle of success she longed for would forever be out of her reach.

"If something happens before we catch this guy, it's on you," I snarled, and then I hung up.

Axel came back into the room. "Her manager confirms she's been getting creepy notes for several years, and that the latest one came earlier this week."

I refused to feel guilty for anything related to Felicity. If she'd had an actual stalker, it should have given her even more reason not to stalk me. But I was also sure that in her head, Felicity could twist the two events so they weren't anything alike.

When I said nothing, Axel continued, "He also said he hadn't shown Felicity the image that came with the note. But he forwarded it to me. It's a picture of you and Willow with Xs on your faces."

Every nerve ending and muscle in my body tightened as I looked at the picture of Willow and I dancing on the street outside the cottage. The intensity of my anger almost frightened me. The lack of control I felt, shaking me almost as much as the fury itself.

Through the haze, a thought snuck in. If Poco was the one sending the photographs to the media, was he also Felicity's stalker? That made absolutely no sense. No matter how small the world was, there was no way it was *that* small.

When I said as much to Axel, he agreed.

"The phrasing of the notes is almost the same as the words she tossed in my face," I added. "Whether she picked them up from her stalker or the other way around, she's involved somehow."

"We're fairly certain Poco isn't the one leaving the notes based on the timeline and what we've dug up on him. He may have sold some photos he took, but there could easily have been someone else who saw the two of you together."

"The guy in the sedan." Even as I said it, I remembered the car had buzzed past Willow and me the day we'd danced in the street. "Willow insisted it wasn't Poco's car."

"Let's go pay him a visit," Axel said.

"You're willing to take me with you?" I said with more than a little shock. My Secret Service detail wouldn't have let me anywhere near Poco or Tall Paul's place.

Axel gave a curt nod, "I know if the woman I cared about was being threatened, I'd want to confront the asshole suspected of doing it. Besides, if Poco is somehow involved, seeing you might set him off, and I can use that to our advantage."

I pocketed my phone and followed Axel out to a waiting SUV. The man was so big he made the driver's seat look like a go-cart chair. He hid his golden eyes behind dark sunglasses and tucked his shorn hair under a baseball cap. Once again, I'd left my disguise behind, but if Axel wanted me to be recognized, I didn't need one. The damn disguise obviously hadn't done its job like I'd promised Willow anyway.

As we headed toward the outskirts of town, Axel said, "Marshal Service told me they gave the Earharts forty-eight hours to move or exit the program."

My entire being tightened. I wasn't losing her. I'd promised Erica I'd protect them if they left, and I would. "As much as I'd hate for this to be about me, it would be better than the Viceroys showing up at their door. You got any ideas on that front yet?"

"I've got some men hunting Aaron Vitale down now that he's skipped town. Trail went cold in Texas. I'm thinking he headed over the border, planning to go south from there. Either we'll find him or the Marshals will."

"Yeah, and then what?"

"Willow has nothing to do with the RICO case. She can't cause him any more damage, in fact, coming after her now could actually put a nail in his coffin. I'm not sold she has anything to worry about from him, and the Marshals agree. They're just taking precautions because that's what they do."

Precautions that would rip her away from me.

Axel drummed his hands on the steering wheel, looking almost as frustrated as I felt.

"We haven't been able to get a license plate or ID on the gray sedan. Neither your security system nor the Earhart's have it at a good angle. I've got my team working with Detective Muloney to gain access to the cameras for the businesses along Main Street. We're hoping to catch something from one of those."

"What's taking so long?" I grunted.

Axel snapped back, "Forty hours, Lincoln. That's how long I've been on this job. We've established a perimeter around two properties, increased the cameras at the Earharts, established a twenty-four-seven security detail, bartered with the local police, negotiated with the Marshals, and all but eliminated Poco Malta from the mix. If you've got a problem with how we've performed, find another company, but I can guarantee you no one else could have achieved what we have in forty fucking hours."

He was right. I wasn't even sure the Secret Service could have done more.

I gritted my teeth and said, "I know. Your team has hit the ground running. I appreciate it. Let's just get this box marked off so we can focus on the Felicity angle."

Axel pulled into Flat Mike's parking lot. The building was an old metal warehouse that had been converted to a bar. A row of Harleys was lined up out front, and even this early in the day, heavy metal music poured from the place so loud I could hear the riffs while sitting in the SUV.

"Let me do the talking," Axel said, shooting me a warning look. "And don't take a swing unless you're ready for us to get the crap beat out of us. As good as I am, there are at least twenty bikers in there willing to fight for no other reason than getting to hit something. They won't give a shit who you are."

"They might actually swing harder because of who I am."

Axel's lips twitched, and we both got out of the car and headed inside.

The haze of cigarette and marijuana smoke was thick, turning the darkened interior into a black hole. Add to it the booming music, the smell of beer and sweat, the volume of bodies shoved into the place, and it was enough to disorient me for several seconds before my eyes and senses adjusted. By the time I did, we had at least two dozen people staring in our direction. Large men in mechanic uniforms and equally burly men in leather who lounged at the booths, the bar top, and pool tables.

Only a handful of women were mixed in amongst the men. Two carried trays, wearing skirts so short they almost shouldn't have bothered. The others sat at booths drinking. They looked as rough and burly as the men sitting with them.

Axel strode toward the bar, and the man serving pints behind it. The bartender's face glowed in the light of a neon beer sign above him, turning him weirdly demonic and making me think of my unfinished painting sitting next to the angel I had barely started.

"Paul, right?" Axel asked. The man's large shoulders tightened for a brief moment before relaxing again. He wasn't bulky, but he was at least six and a half feet tall, if not more.

Seemed like he'd earned his Tall Pall nickname the old-fashioned way.

"Who wants to know?"

"Axel Garner, Garner Securities. I'm looking for Poco."

Paul poured a pint and slid it toward Axel before filling another he sent in my direction. "Have a beer."

"We're not here for—" I started just as Axel said, "Sure."

He sat down on a stool, pulled a roll of cash from a pocket of his jacket, and made a big show of unwinding a couple of twenties before setting them on the bar. Contrary to everything I'd ever learned about self-defense and protection, Axel sat with his back to an entire room full of people as if he didn't care that they might come at him. I slid onto the stool next to him, twisting so I could take in at least half the room. My shoulders were tight, body tense and ready for anyone who might attack.

"Poco was taking care of some business for me. He'll be back soon. If you tell me why you're looking for him, I might be able to help you." He looked as rough and hard as his clients, but his voice was smooth and educated, seeming to contradict what Hardy had told me about him.

"He's been harassing my clients, selling images of them," Axel said calmly, all business. "We need to come to an understanding before things get out of hand."

"This about what happened at Hector's place?" Paul asked.

"And more," Axel said.

Paul's eyes landed on me, taking me in. "No Secret Service detail today."

"Do I need them?" I grunted out, and Paul's lips twitched.

"Depends."

"Your employee hasn't learned a very important life skill," Axel commented, drawing Paul's eyes back to him. The man leaned against the counter behind him and crossed his arms over his chest.

"Yeah? Which one is that?"

"No means no."

Paul's eyes narrowed ever so slightly. "You telling me Poco attacked a woman?" He shook his head. "No fucking way. He knows I won't tolerate that shit. I have a mom, a sister, a daughter. No one lays a hand on them. No one lays a hand on my employees either."

"How about Hector's employees?" Axel asked.

Paul moved fast, smacking a hand on the counter and leaning in with anger sparking in his dark green eyes. "Shay? He went after Shay?"

"No," I grunted out.

"The blonde then. Nice ass. Small tits."

My fists clenched, and I leaned in too so that our faces were closer together. "Watch what you say."

Paul laughed and eased back. "Poco was always a sucker for a sweet little blonde. But he knows my rules. Knows he's out altogether if I catch wind he's assaulted a woman. If she said something happened, she's lying."

"Believe me, he forgot that rule the other night in the cemetery. I was there. I saw it with my own eyes, and if I hadn't intervened, he would have hauled her away," I stormed.

Paul's eyes turned thoughtful. "The cemetery? What night was this?"

"Early last Tuesday. Like two a.m., kind of early," I said.

"Did he have a shovel?" Paul asked.

I shrugged. Hadn't Willow said he'd had one? "Maybe."

The song ended and nothing replaced it. The silence was both a relief and a deafening scream. In that quiet, the door to the back room slammed shut, and I turned to see Poco walking in. He took one look at Axel and me at the bar, and his beady eyes narrowed impossibly further.

Paul called out, "Hey, Poco, you been selling pictures of Hector's baker to people?"

Poco scoffed, heading toward us with a sure gait not matched by his eyes that darted around. He halted with his hands shoved into his jacket several yards away. "Why the hell would I do that?"

I was almost ready to push off the stool, stalk over to him, and shove one of his pictures down his throat when Axel put a hand on my arm and gave me a barely perceptible head shake.

"How about leaving stupid-ass notes on people's doors?" Axel demanded.

The beady-eyed creep looked legitimately surprised by that question, but it was Paul who grunted out a protest this time. "I'm not sure Poco would know how to write a note, would you?"

Anger flitted over Poco's face before it disappeared.

Paul moved out from behind the bar. "When I asked you, you told me you hadn't been by the cemetery in months."

The beady-eyed man glanced behind him at the couple of behemoths now blocking the door before he replied, "Haven't."

"Interesting that these two insist you attacked Hector's baker there just a few days ago."

"That's a bunch of bullshit," Poco grunted.

Paul lifted a chin in the direction of two behemoths, and they closed the distance, blocking Poco's retreat.

"We'll just have to see about that." Paul stopped near Axel and me. "He won't be bothering you or the blonde again. You have my word. Now, I think it's in everyone's best interest if you see your way out."

Axel rose and dropped two more twenties in the pile on the bar. "We appreciate your time and consideration."

I followed Axel, and as I did, I whistled the same sick tune Poco had been whistling when he'd been following Willow. Near the door, I turned back and saw Paul towering over the slimy little man while shoving him toward the back. When my eyes met Poco's for the briefest of seconds, they were full of hate but also fear.

A wave of satisfaction roared through me as Axel and I stepped into the bright sunlight. I knew what was going to happen to Poco. Or I had an idea that it was going to be brutally painful. He might even die, and I wasn't sure what it said about me that I didn't care. He'd terrified Willow. Had his hands on her. Been paid money for photographs that could have blown up her carefully guarded world. In my book, he deserved everything he had coming.

# Chapter Thirty-four

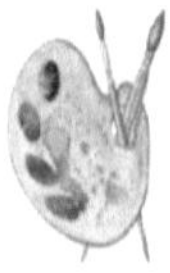

## Lincoln

**YOUR GUARDIAN ANGELS**
Performed by The Red Jumpsuit Apparatus

*AS WE DROVE TOWARD TOWN AND* The Tea Spot, it settled in that Poco wasn't the one leaving the notes. That left Felicity, the Viceroys, or some unknown we hadn't identified.

"One down," Axel said, and the satisfaction in his voice had a chuckle escaping me.

"Thought you said you weren't a hit squad."

"*We* aren't." He looked over his glasses at me and winked.

The tension in my chest eased ever so slightly. Special Agent Hardy wouldn't have walked out and left Poco to his just rewards. As much as I admired and respected the former head of my detail, I knew he was too honorable of a man to let someone die, and he would have been too enticed at the thought of bringing down a bigger fish by catching the small one to let Poco go. He would have hauled the man in for questioning, and then tried to cut him a deal in order to get him to turn on Paul so the Secret Service could take the whole organization down. But Axel had shown me he only cared about what I'd hired him to do, which was to protect Willow and end whatever was happening. It proved to me I'd hired the right team.

As we entered the alley behind the café, Axel's com beeped, and one of his men said Willow was on her way out to us. I got out of the car and strode toward the door.

She was beaming when she emerged, and it stole my breath. Baking had put that smile there. Creating food for others brought her the same joy creating my art brought me. It was who she was down deep. If she had to relocate, and could never bake again professionally for fear it would tie her to this version of herself, it would rip a different piece of her soul away than having her father taken away had.

I refused to let that happen.

I'd just pulled her hand into mine when tires screeched to a halt behind us and a loud pop sounded through the alley. The air by me sizzled and cracked. And all chaos let loose. The Marshal behind Willow screamed, "Shots fired! Shots fired!"

I heard but didn't register Axel and the other bodyguards yelling out commands as I reacted on pure instinct, pushing Willow to the ground and shielding her with my body.

Return gunfire burst around us, the bodyguards and the Marshals aiming in the direction of the street. One thought mixed in with the rage that consumed me—I wanted him dead. If he fucking hurt Willow, I'd find him and end him with my own hands. I desperately needed to scan her body and make sure she wasn't hurt, but I didn't dare move. Not until the gunfire stopped.

In those awful seconds, the truth hammered me as hard as my heart beat against my rib cage: our world had crumbled a bit further.

Men swarmed over us as wheels squealed against asphalt.

"Get them inside!" Axel hollered, and then I heard his SUV burning rubber out of the alley, giving chase to whoever had driven up and shot at us.

The security team all but picked us up and carried us into the café as sirens wailed in the distance.

A comm unit on one of the men erupted with Axel's voice demanding status.

"Clients secured," The man replied. "What's the status of the shooter?"

"I have a gray sedan in sight. The Marshals are right

behind me."

The gray fucking sedan. Knowing I could have stopped this sent anger and disgust curling through me. If I'd only approached the goddamn car when I'd had the chance.

Willow's uncontrollable shaking had me pulling away enough to search her body for blood. For wounds. To reassure myself she wasn't hit.

She scoured me with tortured eyes, combing me for the same damn reason.

"That sound, Lincoln!" Her voice was strained and terrified. "God… that night… I could feel the bullets in the air. Just like this… coming for me. For us."

I tucked her into me, so tight it felt like it might fuse our skin and bone.

I wanted to be in the car with Axel. I wanted to pull the shooter from the sedan and pound him. I wanted to destroy whoever this was for making her relive that night. For jerking her back to that damn closet where she'd almost died. Where a fucking speaker had come between her and death. Where she'd tried to save her dad with her own hands.

Instead, all I could do was spew words I hoped to somehow make true. "We're okay, Sweetness. You're safe. I've got you. You're safe."

A loud, unhappy protest from the line of men behind us drew our attention to Hector trying to get through. Willow tore herself away from me, heading toward him, and the men let him into our circle. Hector hugged her to him, glaring at me over her head as if I was the one who'd pulled the trigger. As if I was the one who'd caused this.

And damn it, I just might be.

Willow stepped away from Hector and turned panicked eyes on a man wearing a US Marshals vest. "My mom?!"

"She's okay. Her detail reported in. Everything is calm at the school."

"I want to see her!" Willow demanded.

"Both of you are in lockdown until the sedan is found," the

Marshal said.

Hector squeezed Willow's arm. "I'll go see her. Right now. I'll make sure she's okay and that she knows you are too."

She nodded, shoulders sagging. "Okay. Th-thank you."

"Don't thank me. We're family, Willow. That's what family does."

As Hector hurried from the room, his words stabbed at me. Because it was true and also because I didn't want this family to be taken from Willow if she was forced to run and hide again. I hadn't kept my promise to Erica. I hadn't protected her daughter. I wasn't doing a good enough job. Not even close. Maybe we needed to head to some secluded island. Some place far, far away from all of this. I could hide forever if I needed to. My family would hate it, but I'd make the choice if it was the only solution.

But damn it, neither of us should have to run. That's when the anger hit all over again. A fury that made me want to punch someone until my knuckles were raw. I slammed my hand down on the steel counter, and silence settled over the kitchen. It felt as heavy as the weight pulling me under.

All the eyes in the room turned on me. But only one pair mattered.

Willow took in a huge breath and then let it out. In two steps, she'd reached me. She fisted my T-shirt and rose up on her toes to look into my eyes.

"Stop it," she insisted. "This isn't on you."

I surrounded her with my arms, dipped my face into her hair, and inhaled the sweet scent. We were okay. We'd continue to be okay now that Axel was chasing down whoever had done this. I knew with a certainty I couldn't explain that he wouldn't stop until he had the man either in cuffs or dead on the ground.

Between Axel and me, we'd make sure she stayed safe. I wouldn't be in the passenger seat when the truck slammed into us. I'd be driving this time, making sure I was the one who took any more hits that came. No one else.

Willow squeezed me as tight as I'd squeezed her before,

fusing us together. Her voice was firm and solid, no tremble in sight, when she repeated, "Stop." She shifted so she could take my face in her hands, forcing me to meet gray eyes that flashed. "My mom was right last night. None of us can take responsibility for evil and hatred. This isn't on you."

"You were almost shot!" My voice clogged.

"But I wasn't. Because you hired Axel and his team to take care of me. Because *you* took care of me."

"I love you." It just poured out of me before I could stop it. She deserved to hear it when there wasn't an audience, when we weren't holding on to each other for dear life with men milling around, comm units screeching, and a sense of foreboding in the air. She needed to hear it when romance was the only thing that existed—candles and champagne and dancing that led to a long night tucked together.

Just as she went to speak, to say those three words back, a woman stormed into the café, wearing a US Marshal's windbreaker and her hand resting on the butt of the gun at her hip.

"Thank God you weren't hit," she said. "This is exactly why we need to relocate you. The situation is out of control."

The rumble of disagreement was almost out of me before I caught it.

I wanted Willow safe. I wanted her to live more than I wanted to keep her with me.

When Willow didn't respond, the Marshal turned to me, assessing me in a way that made me feel like a teen caught sneaking in a window, before she extended a hand, saying, "Deputy Marshal James. I'm the Earharts' handler."

I shook the hand she'd offered but didn't offer up my name. I didn't need to.

The Marshal's phone rang, and she picked it up with a grunted, "James," and listened for so long I thought I might lose my patience. Finally, she grunted out some acknowledgement and then hung up. "The suspect crashed and almost went into the Potomac."

It took several long seconds for the words to finally register, and when they did, the relief that coursed through me caused my ears to ring so loud I almost didn't catch her next words. "He's unconscious and being taken to the hospital. Axel says the vehicle is full of clothes and wrappers, as if the man has been living out of the car. It's being towed to the police yard. It might take a while to go through it all, but it looks like we've caught him."

Was it over? God, please let it be over.

My arms flexed around Willow as hope shot through me, heady and unrestrained. Maybe, just maybe, I'd actually be able to keep her.

When I looked down into her face, her eyes were glossy, and she was biting her lip in an attempt to hold back tears.

A shimmer in the hallway brought Sienna. I wanted to snarl at her to go away, to step back from this moment and let me just have it, but she was shaking her head violently and saying something that, for the first time ever, I couldn't hear. I didn't know if it was because of all the people in the café's kitchen, or because of Willow tucked up next to me, or because of the buzzing in my ears. When I clearly didn't understand her, she threw her hands up and paced, frustration eking from her.

"What is it?" Willow asked, and I dragged my eyes from Sienna's to a pair of concerned, gray ones.

"Nothing."

"Lincoln—"

"Really. Just my past tugging at old scars. We both had our worst moments slapped in our faces today. But all I am feeling now is grateful. Grateful and relieved."

She stared at me for a moment, as if deciding how much to push me. How much to let her own past spill into what was happening now. How much to let those old wounds bleed into our present…our future. "Take me home, Lincoln."

I swallowed hard, her words almost undoing me. I wanted my home to be a safe haven for her, and I could only hope, with one car crash, it would be. That this was over.

We'd survived again. She'd survived. But what would I have done if that bullet had hit her? I couldn't even think about it. I closed my eyes and kissed her softly, thoroughly. I let the warmth of her sink into me. The delightful scent of her. The peace I found when I was next to her.

She was safe. We'd made it through this storm.

The man responsible was caught.

We were going to be okay.

We were alive and here and in love.

I had to focus on that. It was what truly mattered.

When I opened my eyes, Sienna was there again. Glaring at me. Talking. Gesticulating wildly.

And for the first time ever, I truly didn't want to hear her. I didn't want to be haunted by the failings of my past. I wanted to finally hand over my guilt about not being the one who'd died that day when the truck hit us. If I had been, I wouldn't have been here to push Willow into living a full life. I wouldn't have been here to show her the joy that came from this, from being joined in every part of our body and soul, and she deserved that. She deserved the happiness of this moment. To focus on our present where life and love filled us.

So, I rotated our bodies, putting Sienna behind me, and headed for the door.

Willow was the only thing that mattered.

# Chapter Thirty-five

## Willow

**_INSIDE YOUR HEAVEN_**
Performed by Carrie Underwood

**_ONCE LINCOLN AND I GOT HOME_**, we tucked ourselves into his study, closed the door on the security team, and lost ourselves in another heated kiss. It felt different than any of the ones before. It felt as if Lincoln was kissing me so he wouldn't remember anything that had happened. As if he needed to *feel* our hands and bodies seeking and soothing and loving so he wouldn't feel anything else. And I gladly and willingly gave it to him because I didn't want either of us to think about what could have happened. I didn't want to remember the sound of the shot that had brought me straight back to Dad bleeding out on our living room floor.

We were alive. There should be no guilt in that. His or mine. We'd survived. We'd lived.

The relief I felt at knowing the man who'd done it had actually been caught bloomed large and strong. I didn't care that he was hurt. Didn't care that he might die. Perhaps I should have felt bad about it, but I didn't. If he died, it meant I wouldn't have to live through another four years awaiting a trial.

I was tired of being on the receiving end of violence. Tired of waiting to see evil punished. And I was tired of dragging remorse around with me. Lincoln and I continuing to hold on to bags of self-blame wouldn't honor anyone who'd lost their lives instead of us…because of us.

So, I let myself rejoice in Lincoln. In the touch of our mouths and hands and souls. In the three glorious words he'd uttered in the café kitchen that I hadn't been able to repeat yet.

I'd just torn my mouth away from his, determined to say the words right then and there, when our phones started ringing—and they didn't stop for hours.

We spent the afternoon fielding calls—from Axel, the Marshals, and our families. Hector told me not to come in the next day and then handed the phone to my mom. She said Hector had demanded she stay the night with him in a high-handed but sexy way, and it had ripped a laugh from me. But afterward, she'd gotten quiet and serious and asked if I was okay. I was surprised how honest I could be when I said I was. She told me she'd come by Lincoln's in the morning. While I talked to Mom, Lincoln's parents and sisters sent frantic messages that turned into long conversations I could tell were pure torment for someone who hated being on the phone.

But after the relief, the outpouring of love, and the adrenaline crash, a new concern started to flicker to life. This one was entirely about Lincoln because, as the afternoon turned into night, he kept sending scowls to the corners of the room, as if he was chasing away the boogieman. I didn't understand why he wasn't feeling as relieved as I was. I didn't know what was causing his brows to remain furrowed and the air around him to remain broody.

This chapter was closed. It was behind us. Wasn't it?

Was his reaction just the remnants of runaway endorphins? Aftershocks?

I'd started to tell him a dozen times that I loved him, needing to say the words as a comfort to us both, but every time he darted a glance to the corner of the room, it stopped me. Something was still eating at him. A shadow had surrounded him. One that seemed to be sucking him back into the black vortex I'd thought we'd escaped.

By the time we fell asleep with me tucked up against him, I thought maybe he'd started to come around, as his shoulders loosened and the furrow relaxed. But when I woke without his arms around me, I panicked, until the scratch of a pencil on paper drew my eyes to where he sat propped up against the headboard. He had a sketchpad in hand and a look of concentration on his face as his pencil moved over the page in the moonlight streaming in the window.

"How long have you been awake?" I asked. He looked up at me, hand freezing. Backlit as he was from the moon, it kept his eyes shadowed, hiding his thoughts from me.

"A while," he said. "Did I wake you?"

I shook my head. "No."

"Once I'm awake, once I get an image in my head, my body can't remain still," he said apologetically. "Normally, I get up. But I didn't want to leave you. I'll try not to wake you if it happens again."

I sat up, the sheet fell away, and Lincoln's eyes fell to my naked chest.

I closed the little distance between us, took the sketchpad and pencil, and tossed them aside before saying, "I don't care. Wake me up. Didn't you just tell me yesterday that it simply means we have more minutes together? We have a lifetime together now. For as long as this body gives me..." I trailed off, instantly feeling bad I'd brought up the FFI and the mutated gene. But maybe this was what he was still worried about—now that the physical threat had been removed, it brought my internal one into full focus.

He ran a hand over my arm and up along my collarbone and then cupped my neck. Goosebumps erupted at his touch. The very best kind.

"About that," he said.

I didn't let him finish. A moment of alarm had me preventing him from saying what Chad had said. That he couldn't take the leap. That knowing I might die early was just too much. So I kissed him, lips sliding over his, tongue seeking pleasure. And just like I'd hoped, the fire we never seemed to fully quench burst into an inferno, stalling all talk, all thought.

Until he pulled away, grabbed my chin, and stopped me

from continuing my onslaught.

"Listen. My mother has contacts—or maybe it's my dad and she's using them, who knows. Regardless, she contacted a lab in California, and they can send one of their scientists here. To us. They can test you for the mutated gene."

Shock rippled through me. "What?"

"I don't care if you have it, Willow. I want every single moment with you, no matter what that looks like. So it wouldn't matter to me if you were ever tested, but I don't want you to live with the uncertainty. I don't want it hanging over you."

My stomach tensed, flight instincts rushing through me. Mom and I hadn't officially told the Marshals we were leaving, even though I was positive it was where we'd landed. But the thought of being tested after years of hiding, years of being as quiet as possible, years of trying to blend in instead of standing out, only made the panic grow. It was mixed in with these new concerns I had for Lincoln and a larger concern that knowing the truth brought. Because if it came back that I had the mutated gene, Lincoln and I would have different decisions to make. A life to live or not live. A risk to take for both of us. Could I hurt him that way? Could he accept the burden of knowing I might die?

But what if I didn't have the gene? What if the test freed me? What if it gave me the gift of a true forever with Lincoln? Glorious decades without dreading the moment the gene ruined everything.

He frowned at my silence. "I should've asked…"

My eyes caught on the sketch Lincoln had been working on. It was me again, eyes closed as they'd been in the drawing this weekend—another Sleeping Beauty. It was fitting in many different ways because I did feel like I was coming awake…coming alive for the first time since Dad had been killed.

The alarm that had wrung through me disappeared, replaced with a sure resolve I promised myself I'd finally keep.

"What you see… This girl…" I tapped the page and shook my head, emotions clogging my throat. "You said I brought you into the light, woke you up out of a dream. You did the same for me. And now that I'm awake, I don't want to go back to sleep or into hiding or play it safe. I have a list in my journal I thought was full of small joyous experiences I could have while still living within the witness protection rules and with the unknown of the FFI. But I don't want small anymore, Lincoln. I want big. I want huge, overwhelming joys that mean taking all the leaps I can. Sometimes I'll fall, but it's worth the risk. The idea of getting to keep you…of building a life together…that's what I want."

He wrapped his arms around my waist and tugged me into his chest, kissing my temple. "First, you're not a girl. You're a woman who's got more strength and fire and courage than pretty much anyone I've ever encountered. And you weren't sleeping. It's more like you were waiting for the right time to step fully into your life. We both were. The asshole leaving the notes was wrong. We *can* have a happily ever after." He kissed my cheek, my neck. "Don't you feel it?"

I nodded. Because I did. I felt the pleasure, the peace, the hope all twined together, expanding and filling every piece of my soul. "Thank you, to your parents and you, for figuring out how to get the test done. It's a beautiful gift."

His eyes went behind me once again, as they had repeatedly in the last day, and I turned my head in the same direction with a spike of worry returning. Nothing was there except the shadows of the room. I turned back to him. "What is it?"

When I'd asked him that before, he'd said it was his past haunting him. I'd understood that. Hearing the shots had thrust me right back to that awful night. I'd felt the vibrations of the bullets hitting the speaker all over again. Seen my bloody hands pushing at the bullet holes and all the wounds I couldn't heal on my father. But whatever was bothering Lincoln felt different. It was as if he was expecting to see someone—or actually seeing someone. Goosebumps trailed over my skin.

"Is someone there?" I asked.

He pulled me tight. "No. It's just us here. Just us and our future."

But for the first time since he'd sauntered into the cemetery and demanded Poco let go of me, I wasn't sure I believed him. Something had drawn his gaze. Something was still worrying him. A tiny trickle of doubt seeped in before I pushed it aside.

I'd live in each moment like Dad had said. Savor every one of them.

And I'd start right now.

I moved, straddling Lincoln, and his eyes landed fully on me, going dark with that look of love and passion and hope I so adored seeing in his eyes. His body was hard beneath me, aching to be rejoined just like mine was. I shifted so I could take him deep inside. His nostrils flared, his hands tightened on my hips, and then we were moving. The pace was almost frantic, wildness rippling around us as if we were proving to ourselves, the world, and the fates that we were here. We were alive. We'd survived. We'd have a huge, beautiful life.

We'd live, damn it. We'd live.

My nails dug into his shoulders. Our soft pants and pounding hearts filled the room. Nothing existed but the delicious beauty of him inside me, becoming one with me, and taking me right up to the edge of the abyss that awaited us.

"I love the feel of you," I said, gaze locking with his. "I love everything about this. About you. I love you."

His body went completely still. The cobalt of his eyes turned dark and stormy once more. Midnight skies of passion.

"Say it again," he demanded.

"I love you."

"Forever. You and me, Willow. Forever."

For the first time in what felt like hours, I smiled. "*Ridiculous* to say forever when we barely know each other."

He grunted in protest, hips slamming into mine and making me gasp with pleasure.

"We've already proven what happens when you use that word in regard to us."

I met his intense look with a solemn one. "I want it, Lincoln. I want whatever the length of my forever is to be spent with you. *Ridiculous* or not. It's what I want."

"Then take it, Sweetness. Take it all. Take whatever you want."

Staring down at the gorgeous man who'd somehow, miraculously, become mine, I did what he asked. I took and took and took until we were both murmuring sensual words of love and gasping carnal words of lust. Until our bodies trembled from extreme pleasure instead of fear. And as I hit the peak and went over the edge, he took the leap right with me.

♪ ♪ ♪

We didn't make our way downstairs until the sun had already crept over the horizon, and the birds were bursting with song outside the windows. When we walked into the kitchen, Axel and Deputy Marshal James were there, sipping from plain take-out cups that didn't have The Tea Spot logo on them.

"What do we know about the man in the sedan?" Lincoln asked as he went about fixing tea for us.

"Ryan Jennings. Age thirty-five," Axel said. "He has a history of mental health issues. We believe he first met Felicity when she was in a facility herself as a teen. Their time there overlapped."

Lincoln looked surprised. "How'd you find that out? She said she'd had her records cleansed of any hospital stays."

Deputy Marshal James snorted. "Nothing is ever really gone. And digging is part of our job."

"Did she hire him? Ask him to do this?" Lincoln asked, and I could hear the guilt in his voice that I hated because none of this would ever be his fault.

"We don't believe so," James said.

"From what we can gather, as Ryan is still unconscious, he lost his job at a Hollywood studio last year and has been living in his car ever since. He was ticketed in D.C. for parking and sleeping overnight near one of the monuments around the time Felicity and you were together last summer. In addition to the notes on his phone, there were handwritten journals in the car.

We haven't gone through them all, but enough to know he was angry and obsessed. Some of the pages are love letters to Felicity, others are angry notes to her for being with you, and even angrier notes to her for ignoring him. Some vow to get revenge on you for hurting her. There are lots of pictures and news articles about Felicity and some of you, Lincoln. But no more photos of you and Willow besides the one he'd already sent to her," Axel said.

"It's over, then?" I asked, my voice wavering.

"For the most part. The only open question at the moment is where he got the gun. With his mental health issues, no state would grant him a gun license, and it's hard to see him having the right connections to get one on the black market." Axel and Deputy Marshal James exchanged a look.

"What?" I demanded.

"It's a Glock with an aftermarket switch attached. Two magazines with thirty bullets each." Some of the relief I'd felt spun away, a cold shiver creeping up my back.

"What's a switch? Why is any of this important?" Lincoln asked.

"Switches allow a shooter to literally switch back and forth from single shots to automatic. It's a favorite adaption made by many street gangs," Axel explained.

"It's what Danny and Roci used." My voice sounded hoarse and hollow. Lincoln reached over and grabbed my hand, and the warmth of it, the strength of it, grounded me.

"We don't think it's connected to the Viceroys," James explained quickly. "There's no evidence linking Ryan to them, and it doesn't look like he's ever been to Chicago."

"You think he followed me here from D.C.?" Lincoln's voice was dark.

"Yes."

I felt the shudder that went through him. He'd grounded me when I'd started to panic, and now it was my turn to do the same. I pushed at the frown between his brows and then squeezed his hand. "We're taking our future back, Lincoln. No more regrets. No more living small. We have you and me and our big futures. You promised. Forever. You and me."

He hesitated for a mere second before wrapping me in his arms and kissing the top of my head. "We'll put it behind us, Sweetness. It's over. All of it."

♫ ♫ ♫

Because it was the only way I knew how to show my gratitude, I made Lincoln run to the store so I could make breakfast for the entire security detail and the remaining Marshals. I made enough food that it probably could have fed another twenty people. So, when Mom showed up with Hector, there was plenty for them as well.

I hugged each of them and then asked, "Who's at the café?"

"I shut the doors for the day," Hector said. "Hung a sign that said family emergency."

"Hector! No!"

He looked at me with serious eyes and said, "I'm not upset, and you shouldn't be either. If I've learned anything in this life, it's that love and family come first. Those are the only things you can leave behind. The only things that truly matter."

He pulled me into another tight hug before dragging my mom into the embrace with us. When I saw the sweet smile they shared, I nearly swooned.

"I can see you've decided to stay," Deputy Marshal James said with a resigned look at the three of us tangled together.

One glance at Mom's glowing face had closed the deal for me. We'd found happiness here. I was done letting evil have even one more minute of my time. The ugly feeling in my chest that wouldn't stop beating…I'd bury it. Bury it in the past with this Ryan guy as we said goodbye to the Marshals.

When we nodded with stupidly happy smiles on our faces, Deputy Marshal James said, "Well, crap. I guess it was bound to happen to me at some point." She headed toward the back door. "I'll send the paperwork for you to sign. It might take a

365

few weeks, as government paperwork tends to move at a snail's pace, so it'll give us time to make sure things have really settled down here."

Then, she walked out without waiting for our response.

Mom's arms around me tightened, and her joy all but leaked into me. It filled me with hope that I could truly be the princess after the credits rolled, after the bad guys were banished.

"Take a walk with me?" Mom asked.

I nodded, and we headed out the back door. For some reason, I made my way to the cemetery gate, and Mom joined me. She wrapped her arm through mine as we walked amongst the quiet of the tombstones.

"We've earned this, Willow. I want you to live every moment from this day forward with only peace and happiness accompanying you."

"Same, Mom. I want the same for you." And to prove to her and myself I was embracing this new life, I told her about Lincoln's mom sending a scientist from the lab in California to us. "The doctor will be here this week."

"How do you feel about it?" she asked, eyes searching mine.

"Relieved."

"Really?" She seemed surprised.

"Knowing won't change what I have with Lincoln, but it prepares us. And I won't have the weight of the unknown hovering over me."

She tipped her head into mine and then let go, spinning around to eyeball the graveyard.

"I'll never understand your fascination with this place."

I took in the ornate carvings, the statues, the sweet words embedded in marble and granite. I still believed these people needed to be remembered, still hoped my dad's grave was visited by someone occasionally, and I'd still come here and celebrate these people who'd come before us, but I also wanted to look for the future and the new beginnings rather than the past.

Aaron was still out there. Who knew where? But he had far more important things to worry about than getting revenge on me. And I couldn't live, waiting for his shadow to block the sun.

"Let's go home and plan a huge dinner to celebrate closing this chapter of our lives and starting a new one," I said.

"I love that idea."

When we slipped back inside the house, Lincoln wasn't in the sunny kitchen anymore, but Hector was still there. He rose from the table with a goofy grin on his face. "Don't you both look beautiful. Happy."

"We are," Mom said. "Because of you. Because of Lincoln. Because we finally get to live our lives."

He pulled us both into a hug. "I love you both."

Happy tears filled my eyes. For me. For Mom. For him. I squeezed them to me. We had more people in our lives who could be targeted as we stepped away from the Marshals, more people who could be hurt, but I believed Lincoln when he said he'd protect us. I believed now that we could protect them together, so I wouldn't let worry sneak in.

"We're family," Hector said gruffly. "We already were, but Shay agrees. We'll be like the damn Brady bunch, except with only two kids instead of six."

"Maybe we'll have six grandkids," Mom teased.

And the thought lodged itself inside me like a beautiful dream you want to keep after waking. I tried not to get my hopes up. Tried not to think about having a family with Lincoln—babies with his blue eyes and wavy locks. Cupcake drives and parent-teacher association meetings. The thought of kids had always been an impossibility. But it dangled in front of me now as something I might just be able to have. A reality shimmering around the corner.

I'd let the doctors test me, and we'd deal with the results together.

I'd forget about Aaron and the Viceroys.

I'd do what we all were yearning to do. Live in the now. Live fully. Live with joy and love and hope, banishing the darkness.

# Chapter Thirty-six

## Lincoln

*LOVE DON'T DIE*
Performed by The Fray


***THE HAPPINESS THAT DRIFTED AROUND THE*** large wooden table I'd bought in hopes of having just these kinds of moments at it kept pushing light through Sienna's shimmering figure every time she appeared. I wasn't letting her in, which was frustrating her. But I wanted nothing more than to concentrate on the family sitting before me. It was different than the one I'd imagined, but it was all the more perfect because Willow was there, and it was her family. Just thinking about the times my family would be there too made the smile already on my face grow.

The doorbell rang, and I didn't pull my phone from my pocket to open the app and see who it was. I simply left the laughter and chatter of the kitchen to answer it.

The smile was still embedded on my face when I opened the door to find my mother glaring. She shoved her phone at me. "You haven't responded all day! I've heard nothing about the man who was chased down. Nothing about how you're handling all this!"

The bit of wild in her pale-blue eyes was the only proof of how upset she truly was. The rest of her seemed completely serene. Her cherry-wine hair was perfectly coifed without a hair out of place, and her forest-green suit was pressed straight on her tall frame. Behind her, two of her detail stood with blank faces, their sunglasses shielding their eyes, and suits stretching across wide shoulders. On the curb, two dark SUVs sat with more men inside them.

Mom brushed past me, still waving her phone. "I swear, Lincoln, if I have to ask the Secret Service to ping—"

A burst of laughter from the kitchen cut her off.

She turned wide eyes to me. I reached for her, pulled her to me, and hugged her tight. "Good to see you, Mom."

At first, the shock held her stiff before she hugged me back and then pushed away. "You have company?"

"Willow and her family are here."

Mom's face shuttered. "I see."

She started toward the kitchen, and I grabbed her elbow and held her back. "I love you."

She lifted a brow. We knew it—had said it to each other many times—she just hadn't expected those words to be my lead-in.

"But I'm telling you right now, if you go in there, thinking she's Sienna, thinking I'm with her because of it, and you upset her, I'm going to ask you to leave."

She stared at me for a long moment, assessing just how much I meant those words. Finally, she said, "You look tired."

"I always look tired."

"You've been through a lot. All over again. I don't like it."

"That wasn't her fault. We know now it was more mine than hers," I said, but the full measure of the guilt that normally surrounded me didn't follow me today. I was learning to let it go. To live. To be happy. To reach for the joy that existed here. And maybe that was why I'd blocked out Sienna every time she'd appeared since Ryan Jennings had shot at us. I wanted— no, needed—to let her go.

"This wasn't your fault either. It was Jennings's fault. Maybe even Felicity's, but not yours," Mom said quietly. We let that settle between us before she added, "Introduce me to the woman you love, Lincoln. Let me love her too."

Those words, her simple request, shot pleasure through me. Pleasure I was reaching out for with both hands. I wasn't sure what I'd do with it after so many years of not letting myself embrace it fully. So, I did the easiest thing, which was to lead her into the kitchen where our appearance in the archway brought silence among the people gathered there.

Willow and Erica had held a small party at the house as a way of celebrating their new life—our new life together. Hector and Shay, other workers from The Tea Spot, Detective Muloney and his family, and some of Erica's teacher friends had all been there. Willow and Erica hadn't told anyone but Hector and Shay about witness protection and their former lives, but it was still clear to everyone in attendance they were celebrating new beginnings.

The party had ended early, as everyone had work and school the next day, leaving just Hector, Erica, and Shay behind. Before the doorbell had rung, I'd been itching for our remaining guests to leave so I could be alone with Willow.

I wanted to dance with her in the moonlight and feel her body pressed against mine. I wanted to slowly remove her skirt and T-shirt and run my hands over all that smooth skin until it was puckered and flushed under my touch. I wanted to bask in the beauty she surrounded me in.

But now, with my mother having arrived, it would be even longer until the two of us were alone.

Everyone at the table scrambled from their seats as if "Hail to the Chief" had played. I made the introductions, and Mom shook hands and greeted everyone with her typical grace until she reached Willow. Instead of a handshake, she pulled Willow into a fierce hug. Willow's surprised reaction was much the same as mine had been when Erica had done the same thing to me the day we'd met.

Mom let her go, wiped at her eyes, and said, "It's a pleasure to meet all of you."

"We were just finishing up, but there's plenty of food left. Can I fix you a plate?" Willow asked.

"Thank you, but no. I'm still working off a fundraising

luncheon."

For a moment, an uncomfortable quiet settled over the room as everyone assessed each other. It was Erica who spoke first. "Thank you for arranging to have Dr. Gellar come out next week. You don't know how much it means to us."

The two moms eyed each other, and I thought my mother probably had a pretty good clue what it meant. We'd lived through test after test when I'd been a kid as they'd tried to figure out why I couldn't sleep, and some of the potential diagnoses had been scary.

I was as grateful as Erica that the scientist had called and said she'd be coming out so soon. We'd have the results before the end of the month. Just knowing that seemed to have made Willow's spirit glow impossibly brighter.

Hector cleared his throat and turned to Erica, saying, "I think it's time Shay and I head home. I'll call you later."

"You don't have to leave on my account," my mom said.

He shook his head. "I've got an early rise tomorrow as I've given Willow the rest of the week off."

"What?" Willow's eyes took in Hector's face with a frown.

"I need your next food art piece. People are clamoring for it, and I don't like customers leaving my shop unfulfilled. Do your thing, come back on Sunday refreshed, and bring your desserts and art with you."

"Hector!" she protested.

He patted Willow's shoulder. "I need to do this for you. *You* need to do this for yourself."

He and Shay bid everyone goodbye, and Erica said, "I'll walk you out."

As they moved down the hall, I reached for Willow, bringing her to me and kissing her temple while my mother watched with curious eyes. "Let him do this for you, Sweetness."

She elbowed me. "Did you arrange this with him just so I wouldn't leave the house?"

I chuckled. "No, but I like the idea of you here, concocting your art while I'm upstairs creating mine." Now that I'd brought a large portion of my supplies home with me due to the construction, I wasn't sure I'd take any of it back. I loved the idea of being here while Willow and I both created our art.

"You're really painting that much?" Mom asked.

"Too many pieces, actually. But I'm nearing completion on a duet." The angel and the demon were almost finished. The cemetery scene with Willow at the center was close as well, but I was still hanging on to that one for some reason. Holding back. Waiting for a missing detail. It would come to me. It had something to do with the broken-winged angel. Something I hadn't quite put my finger on yet.

Mom pulled a chair out and sat. "I'm a little at a loss for words."

"You?" I winked at Mom. "Impossible."

"Smart aleck," Mom said with no heat, lips twitching.

I chuckled and drew Willow back to the table, and once we were sitting, I shifted so my knees tangled with hers, so I was touching her as much as I could.

My mother watched, looking from me to Willow again before saying, "I'm sorry I'm staring. It's just that you really do look so much like her."

"Mom," I warned.

She waved me off. "I don't mean to upset anyone, and I don't expect Willow to be her. I have twins, for heaven's sake. I know two people can look alike and be complete opposites. It's just a shock of sorts."

Willow tensed, and I took her hand, rubbing it. Trying to soothe her. Trying to reassure her I wasn't with her, didn't love her, because of Sienna.

"One of the things I've always adored about my son is the way he gives himself completely to the love that enters his life. It's always been fast and furious but so fully embraced," Mom said, and I made a strangled noise of protest she ignored. "Over the last year or so, I was worried he'd lost that ability. I'm happy to see he hasn't."

"Mrs. Matherton, I know it's ridiculous," Willow said, and my hand squeezed her hip. There would be retaliation for that word, and she knew it, but she just shot me a coy little smile before she turned back to my mother. "It seems impossible to me that in mere days—hours, really—I've gone from not knowing Lincoln to being unable to imagine my life without him."

"Please, call me Cordelia. And the truth is, I know how ridiculous it can feel. I fell in love with Guy over a weekend," my mother said, and I raised a brow. I'd heard the story many times, but it wasn't something she readily shared. The press had a version of it they'd gotten from old friends of the family, but whenever Mom was asked about it, she usually clamped her lips and said nothing.

"You did?" Willow's voice held surprise.

"He had so much charm I accused him of having inherited selkie powers from his Scottish ancestors, luring me in with a single glance. I'd never seen myself as married with kids. I certainly had no interest in being a politician's wife, and even in college, that was always Guy's goal."

"What did you want to do?" Willow asked.

"I wanted to be Madonna. Or maybe an actress. I was thinking of skipping out on the rest of college and heading to Hollywood. Then I fell in love, and my life changed."

Willow laughed. "I'm sorry. That's not funny. It's just…I can't imagine Madonna being our first lady."

"Well, here I am." Mom's lips curved upward, tossing her shoulder and hair like a pop star.

Willow giggled, her body relaxing, and mine did as well. I was amazed all over again at how right she felt there, not just at the table in the home I'd renovated, imagining family around it, but also with my mom. Before, it had simply been my parents and siblings in those hopeful fantasies I'd had about this house. Not once had I imagined my own wife and kids at the table, and yet now I saw the possibility of them around every corner of the Colonial. Little Willow mini-mes. Boys with wavy hair and blue eyes who started a ruckus. Maybe half a dozen of them. I supposed I needed to talk to Willow about it and see what she wanted, but I knew enough to wait until we had the results of her tests. She wouldn't even entertain the thought of children before then.

But I already knew what the results would be. Sienna had told me. I shot a glance at the sulky ghost in the corner before ignoring her again.

Erica came back into the room, looking a bit tousled, a smile curving her lips. She sat at the table, glancing between us as if testing the air, and when she found it relaxed, her shoulders eased as well. "I'd just been trying to convince my daughter to come out of her shell a bit more, and then she surprised the hell out of me by finding and falling for Lincoln."

My mom's face turned stoic and assessing. It was a defense mechanism. Years of people coming at us, thinking they could use us to get to Dad.

"I found her, truth be told," I grumbled.

"And I'm glad you did," Erica replied with a sparkle in her eye.

We chatted for almost an hour about nothing really. Little anecdotes exchanged by mothers about their children that attempted to embarrass one or both of us but just left me feeling loved. Then, when the dark had fully descended and the moon had risen the two women rose to leave, almost in unison.

While Willow stepped outside onto the sidewalk to say goodbye to her mom, mine held me back at the door. "Shannon and Henrik are going to want to meet her, and it's going to be harder on them than it was me."

I hadn't thought about it—hadn't had time to think about it—but she was right. Seeing Willow so closely resembling Sienna and being part of my life was likely going to hit Sienna's parents in the chest every time they were around us. I hated it would cause them pain, but there was no way I'd give up what I had with Willow in order to make them feel better.

"I'll call them tomorrow, see if I can set something up for all of us to get together, and hopefully prepare them," Mom offered.

"You don't have to do that," I said. "I can call them myself."

"It'll come better from me. I'd like to do it for you."

I said nothing as Willow came back up the path. Before I could reach for her and pull her into me, Mom intercepted her. She gave her another hug before leaning back to meet Willow's eyes. "Can I ask a favor of you?"

"Of course, anything," Willow replied automatically.

Mom laughed. "Don't ever say that without knowing the favor. But in this case, perhaps you could encourage my son to carry his phone more? And maybe convince him to actually pick it up when his mother calls. This way, I don't have to ping his location and come stalking down here just to hear from him."

I shoved a hand in my pocket, narrowed my eyes, and repeated what I'd told Mom multiple times before. "I can't help it if the damn thing isn't attached to me like a third hand."

"I don't expect it to be, but I would like it if you looked at it once a day and responded." She kissed my cheek and stepped toward the two special agents who'd been waiting for her. Once she was ensconced in the SUV and both cars had pulled away from the curb, quiet filled the night behind her. The low hum of the crickets and the hoot of a faraway owl were the only sounds.

I closed the door behind us, locked it, and set the alarm.

"She's so down to earth," Willow said as she started toward the kitchen.

I grabbed her hand and tugged her toward the stairs.

"I need to clean the mess," she said, half-heartedly resisting me.

"And it'll still be there tomorrow."

"But it'll be gross. It'll take me ten minutes."

I turned, picked her up, and slung her over my shoulder. She laughed, hitting my back playfully as I said, "Payback is a bitch, Sweetness. I think you used those off-limit words several times tonight, and at least one of those times, you did it on purpose. You knew what would happen."

I didn't bother turning on the lights as I set her down in my room, and yet I could still see the smile she was wearing—that same coy one from earlier that thrust heat into my veins.

"Maybe I like the punishment," she taunted.

Instead of ripping her clothes off, as part of me wanted to do, I went to the side table and turned on the music app on my phone. The song I chose was slow and sultry, and when I turned back to her, confusion had drifted over her face. She'd expected me to tear her clothes off too.

I pulled her into my embrace, moving so our bodies met the sensual rhythm filling the air. I placed a hand on her back, pushing her into me. My other hand fisted in her hair, tugging it back so I could see her face, the beautiful arch of her neck. My feet moved, my hips thrust, and my mouth lowered to that pale column, trailing hungry kisses up and down it.

She shivered.

I let the beat drive me. As I slid her top up and over her head, my motions were as unhurried and measured as the music. I twirled her out and spun her around so when she returned to me, her back landed to my front. My hands could continue the dance along her body, slipping down to her waist and the skirt that had haunted me all damn day. I tugged until it fell over those round hips and pooled at her feet. Only then did I lift her, guide her to the bed, and continue my slow pursuit of her pleasure.

Each lick and stroke and kiss matched the beat that filled the room. Every time she got close to peaking, I stopped, slowed down, and moved my hands away before starting the onslaught all over.

"Lincoln." The beg in her voice tempted me to give her what she wanted, but I loved seeing her like this too much. On the edge, writhing and arching. Giving herself to me. Knowing she was mine and only mine.

"Punishment, Sweetness."

She tugged my hair until I lifted my gaze to meet stormy eyes.

"It's *ridiculous* because you're punishing yourself too,"

she said breathlessly.

I growled, locking her wrists in one hand as my mouth nipped and sucked, and my other hand brought her closer to the pleasure she sought. She arched, a sweet little whimper escaping her, and all I could think was how beautiful she was. How I wanted to paint her this way, how I wanted—

*Lincoln!* The frightened, hurried voice came from behind me.

My body went rigid.

Willow felt it, her eyes opening to search mine.

For two seconds, I ignored the voice like I'd been ignoring her all day.

*Lincoln, he's coming! He's coming!*

I turned, finding Sienna's gaze, desperate and wild as she searched the room.

*Hide!* she shouted.

"Lincoln?" Willow's voice was confused, hazy from lust, calling me back.

"Who?" I demanded of Sienna.

*The man. The man who wants to kill Willow!*

Confusion and alarm slammed through me. The man was in the hospital, unconscious. He couldn't be here. And yet Sienna was terrified.

"Where is he?"

"Lincoln, who are you talking to? What's going on?" Willow asked just as Sienna said, *He's inside. He killed the man at the back door. He shut off all the power. Your alarm was cut.*

Rage stormed through me, accompanied by a wash of fear. Who the hell had come for her? For us? And even then, the trepidation struck, knowing who it was. Knowing that the evil bastard had finally come for her.

I rolled off the bed, throwing Willow's clothes at her.

"Get dressed," I hissed quietly.

"Lincoln! What's going on?" Willow demanded.

"Quiet! Stay quiet." Where could I hide her? Where wouldn't he find her? I turned to Sienna. "Where is he?"

*Kitchen*, she said.

I dragged Willow into the hall, stepping around the board that creaked, but Willow hit it, and I winced as the noise echoed down the stairs. As quietly as I could, I opened the door to the guest room and the pile of Katerina's boxes. I pushed Willow behind them.

"Stay here. Stay down," I said.

"You're scaring me. What is it?" she demanded. "Who are you talking to?"

"We don't have time for this. Someone's here. In the house. Promise me you'll stay here." My unsteady gaze met her frightened one.

"Not if you're heading into danger. I won't let you face it alone."

My lungs squeezed tight. The idea of Willow being hurt was too much for me. "Please. Do this for me so I don't see another woman I love injured…killed." My throat closed with emotions. "Just stay. We don't have time to argue."

I left her, hoping to all the gods she stayed right where I'd placed her amidst a sea of boxes. At the door, I looked back, only mildly reassured that she was momentarily safe.

The music I'd turned on using the rechargeable speaker in my room turned from a sensual beat into the crescendo of an opera, leaking into the hall where Sienna paced. She glanced over the banister.

*He's searching downstairs. He has a gun.*

I went to the room closest to the stairs where I'd set up the studio the day before. I grabbed a can of turpentine—it would slow him down if I tossed it in his eyes—and then sought out my grandfather's switchblade that I'd been opening boxes with.

Back at the open door, I heard the bottom step creak.

My fury grew. He'd killed one of the men I'd hired. He dared to come after Willow. I didn't care who he was or why he'd decided to come after her now, but this would end. This would be over.

I quietly unscrewed the cap on the turpentine.

A shadow reached the top of the stairs. He edged along a wall, and even in the dark, I could see the gun he held. Black. Evil. I couldn't make out his face. He blended in with the shadows, but as he eased along the wall, opposite the doorway, I sprang, tossing the turpentine just as he turned at the sound.

A hiss escaped him, and he scrubbed at his eyes, but he didn't let go of the gun. Instead, he squeezed the trigger. Nothing but an innocuous puff filled the air—a silencer keeping it quiet. I barely had time to realize the bullet had gone wide before he was aiming it again. I charged, shoving the arm holding the gun up, and another bullet hit the ceiling, causing plaster to rain down over us.

I punched him in the face, but it released my hold on his arm with the gun, and he clocked me in the temple with the butt. Stars burst along my vision. I staggered back, swung wildly with the switchblade, and felt it catch on his hand, slicing through the cloth and skin. He grunted in pain, surprising us both when he dropped the weapon. I was mid-swing again when he kicked out, landing a foot in my stomach with enough force that it sent me whirling into the wall with a crash.

He lurched for the gun, picking it up and twirling to aim it in my direction.

Sienna was screaming. Words I couldn't concentrate on because I had one chance to fix this. To end it. If he killed me, he'd find Willow, and I couldn't allow that to happen.

With a snarl of fury, I ducked my head and rushed him.

The gun went off. I felt the burn as the bullet sliced into my arm, but my feet continued to propel me forward. Just as I was about to ram into him with my good shoulder, I saw Willow had emerged from the bedroom right behind him. Her face was determined and scared, and she had nothing but a goddamn lamp in her hand to defend herself.

I didn't have time to check the trajectory of my feet, and the force I slammed into him with shoved us both into Willow, sending all three of us tumbling to the floor.

# Chapter Thirty-seven

## Willow

### *MAGIC*

Performed by Kelly Clarkson

***MY ENTIRE BODY WAS SHAKING AS*** I crouched behind the boxes. Flashbacks to hiding in a closet tried to drag me under. Would the boxes protect me as the speakers had? What would protect Lincoln? He'd gone out to face some unknown assailant with nothing more than his fists.

Where was Axel's security team?

How had the intruder gotten inside?

I couldn't stay here. Couldn't let Lincoln face this alone.

As I moved, the solid object in my skirt pocket banged against my hip.

My phone!

I pulled it out and almost dropped it as my hands trembled. I was afraid to call 9-1-1. Afraid to talk and be heard. Instead, I texted Axel.

Something slammed into the wall outside the room, and I jumped. Lincoln! I leaped forward, searching the room for anything I could use as a weapon.

I'd just yanked a candlestick lamp from the wall as a body emerged through the closed door—shimmering through it as if the solid wood didn't exist. I almost dropped the light before instinct had me swinging at the woman with the lamp. It sliced through her as if she was made of nothing but air.

*He's going to kill Lincoln! You have to help!*

I heard the words in my head rather than aloud, and in shock, I nearly lost my hold on the light again.

The reality of what I was seeing sent my blood thumping in a cadence that left me breathless. She was a ghost. A figment of imagination and yet standing before me. My twin wearing a black lace dress. I knew instantly who she was. What she was. But I couldn't stop to analyze it. Not when Lincoln needed help!

I raced toward the door, and when she didn't move, I slid through her. It was like stepping into a cold shower. Shivers crawled up my spine as I eased open the door.

A man was standing right in front of me with his back to me and a gun in his hand. He had it pointed across the landing at Lincoln. I screamed, "No," just as Lincoln plowed toward him. A quiet huff sounded, jerking Lincoln's body as if he'd been hit.

In desperation and horror, I rushed forward, intending to bring the lamp down on top of the gunman's head. But Lincoln's momentum propelled him into the man, forcing them both into me, and we all tumbled to the floor, landing with me on the bottom and knocking the breath from my lungs. I couldn't shove the man off me, couldn't do anything with their combined weight holding me down.

"Drop the gun, or I'll slice your throat open." I hardly recognized Lincoln's voice. It was darker than I'd ever heard it. Deadly and cold.

The man fought against Lincoln's hold, elbows nailing me in my stomach. I shoved at the gunman using every muscle I had, but it was useless until they rolled off me, consumed with their own struggle.

Blood trailed on the wood planks, and when I saw it staining Lincoln's shirt, a tortured wail escaped me.

I stretched my hands out, frantically searching the floor for the makeshift weapon I'd lost in the fall.

The blare of sirens broke through the sound of their fight

and the pounding of the opera music.

Help was here and yet too far away. I watched in horror as the gun tipped toward Lincoln once more. Lincoln jabbed at the man's neck with a pocketknife. The gunman stilled as blood oozed from the wound, and eyes full of hate landed on me. Eyes and hate I knew. That I'd encountered once upon a time in a courtroom. Ones that matched the hate his brother had revealed as he'd shot my father.

"The bitch doesn't deserve to live," Aaron gasped. He shifted the gun so it pointed at me, and as his finger pressed onto the trigger, Lincoln dragged the knife across his throat. A mixed sound of strangled pain and disbelief escaped him, his blood spraying across Lincoln.

I finally found my feet, stumbling toward them and kicking at the gun so it went flying across the hall.

The front door slammed against a wall as Aaron's body went limp.

Even in death, his eyes still glared, still shot out evil and hate.

I shuddered, falling to my knees next to Lincoln where he'd rolled off Aaron. I used my hands to push against the blood soaking his shirt. "You're hit. God, you're hit. Don't die, Lincoln. Please, don't die."

I increased the pressure on the wound, and he grunted in pain. His free hand circled my wrist. "Alive, Sweetness. I'm alive."

Boots stormed the stairs.

"He's wounded!" I shouted as my gaze first met Axel's and then, close on his heels, Deputy James's.

"We need an ambulance," Axel spoke into his two-way. "Two down inside. One more out back."

James went to Aaron, checked his pulse, and shook her head.

Axel tried to pull me away from Lincoln.

"The blood. I have to stop the blood," I told him through tears.

"You've done a great job, Willow. A really great job. Now, let me see him."

Lincoln squeezed my wrist again. "Let him in, Willow. Let him in."

Sirens grew closer. More feet pounded up the stairs. More bodies emerged.

As I fell back and to the side, my eyes landed on the blood on my hands. Too much of it was the same again. Too much like that awful night. When I looked up, my gaze landed on the woman who'd come into the guest room, slipping through walls. She was pacing at the end of the hall, glancing back and forth between Lincoln and me. Her eyes were so real I could feel the weight of them on me. And yet no one else even registered she was there.

I looked down at Lincoln to see he was watching her pace just as I'd been.

And I suddenly knew.

It was Sienna he'd been seeing all along.

Chills raced up my spine.

What had Lincoln said to me all those days ago? That he'd thought she'd returned to haunting him? What had Felicity told the media? *He sees ghosts.*

The burning in my chest grew.

Sienna had saved us tonight.

She wasn't really there, and yet somehow she was, and she'd saved us.

The EMTs asked me to step back even farther, but Lincoln reached for me, gripping my hand with his good one. "She stays," he growled out.

They checked his vitals and tore his shirt to get a better look at the bullet wound. "I think it just winged the deltoid, but we won't know if it hit bone or a vein until we get you to the hospital. It's good you're awake. Try to stay with us."

"Somebody turn the lights on," James snapped.

"He cut the electricity from the main line down the street.

The whole street is out," Axel responded.

"Then where the hell is the music coming from?" the Marshal demanded, heading toward Lincoln's room.

As the song cut out and a heavy silence descended, a new fear rose through me. Mom. Alone in the cottage.

When James reemerged from the bedroom, a tortured cry leaped from my throat, "Mom!"

"She's fine, Willow. She's at Hector's. She went there as soon as she left here."

I wasn't sure why that knowledge was what started the tremors. Adrenalin. Relief. But when I looked down at Lincoln, covered in blood from him and Aaron, the shaking only intensified.

Shadowed in the weird light of the flashlights, two EMTs arrived with a stretcher and made their way to Lincoln.

"I can walk," he said, and using me and the wall, he attempted to stand and wavered. It was Axel on his other side who stopped him from falling.

"Nothing wrong with letting them take you out on the gurney," Axel barked.

"I leave this house on that thing and someone photographs it, it'll spread that I overdosed. Walk me out. Then, call my mother before she hears it from someone else."

Surrounded by the security team, the Marshals, and EMTs, we were led to the back of the waiting ambulance. Lincoln climbed in, and I stepped up after him. Finally, he lay down on the gurney. His face was white. Whiter than I'd ever seen it. Whiter than the ghost who'd stepped out of nothingness to warn us.

The ambulance moved, racing down the darkened street.

My hand clutched Lincoln's good one as the EMT checked his vitals again, hooking up wires and pads. Panic filled me. A deep, unyielding fear. I couldn't lose him. Not now.

Lincoln squeezed my hand. "Willow, look at me." My eyes met his, and I saw the anger there that blended with a strange sort of relief. "I'm okay. I'm alive. You're alive. We're okay."

I choked out. "You're shot."

"Was that Aaron Vitale?" he asked. "I'd seen his picture, but I wasn't sure."

"Yes." I nodded to reinforce it.

Lincoln's eyes shut. "Good."

The machine he was hooked up to beeped wildly, my heart seeming to keep pace with the frenzied beat as I called his name.

His lids snapped open. "I'm here, Sweetness. Just a bit tired."

When his eyes shut again, I demanded, "What's wrong?"

"He lost a lot of blood," the EMT said. "He isn't dying. His body is doing what it needs to do, shutting down so it can heal."

I wasn't reassured, but as the monitor continued to blip, and Lincoln's chest continued to rise and fall, I held on to his hand and murmured words of reassurance and love, hoping it would be enough.

♫ ♫ ♫

They wheeled him directly into surgery, and I was shown to a waiting room. For a brief moment, I was alone, until Sienna appeared again, shimmering through the wall and pacing around the room. Which was when I saw the wound at the back of her head, the missing part of her skull. My stomach lurched once more.

For a long time, she didn't say anything, just meeting my gaze with a steely one. Just as she opened her mouth to speak, the doors of the waiting room flew open, and my family ran in—Mom, Hector, and Shay.

Mom had me in her arms before I could say a word, holding me so tight I could barely breathe. Then, more people showed up—Axel, James, and their men.

James wanted my statement. She wanted to know how we'd known Aaron was in the house.

My gaze strayed to Sienna. She was standing in the corner

now, tracing a finger over a brow in much the way Lincoln did.

I swallowed, body shaking as I told them Lincoln had heard something, which was basically the truth. He'd heard Sienna, but I wasn't telling them that. Couldn't tell them that. They'd think we were both off our rockers. But I told them everything else I knew. How he'd had me hide. How I'd heard them fighting in the hall and came out with the lamp.

The door opened again to reveal men in black suits with Secret Service pins on their lapels.

Behind them, Lincoln's mom appeared with her eyes wild and worried, and after her, the president of the United States walked in. His face was grim and dark, but he looked so much like Lincoln that it hit me in the chest. Those bright blue eyes matched his son's perfectly.

Silence took over for a second, and then Cordelia rushed toward me, grabbing my hands that were still covered in Lincoln's blood. "Tell me what they've said."

I swallowed over the lump in my throat and told her what the EMT had told me.

Relief washed over her. "Thank God."

She held my hand with one of hers and then reached for Guy Matherton's with the other. He moved in, wrapping his arm around her shoulder and kissing her temple. How many times had Lincoln done the same to me? A fist squeezed my lungs.

"I've sent Daringfield to find out more," the president told his wife.

His eyes found mine, serious and assessing but mostly just worried.

The tears I'd held back finally came, streaming down my cheeks like a heavy rain. "I'm sorry. I'm s-so s-sorry."

My mom was there, on the other side of me, pulling me from Cordelia's hold. "This isn't your fault, kiddo. This isn't on you."

"He came for me. He came for me and shot Lincoln!"

I turned into her, face to her shoulder, while she ran a hand up my back like she had hundreds of times in my life, attempting to comfort me. Just like she had the night Dad had died.

"Let's get you cleaned up," Mom murmured.

And again, it was just like that night, when I'd been covered with Dad's blood.

Tremors ransacked my body.

I let Mom lead me down the hall to a single-stall bathroom. I washed my hands and looked up into the mirror to see blood on my neck and face. I scrubbed at those as well. My shirt was covered with it. Mom unzipped the sweatshirt she was wearing with the logo of Cherry Bay's high school and held it out to me. Underneath it, she had on only a pajama top.

"Put it on," she said when I didn't move.

I pulled off my T-shirt and slid into the sweatshirt, immediately cocooned in her warmth and smell. Reassurance. Comfort. But for the first time in my life, it wasn't her solace I sought. I wanted Lincoln's arms. I wanted Lincoln's soft words soothing me.

"He's going to be okay," Mom said.

I nodded. He had to be.

I needed a minute. A minute alone to gather my thoughts. To pull myself together and stop the torrent of tears.

"I need to pee."

Her eyes narrowed. "I'll just be outside. If you don't come out in five minutes, I'm coming back in."

The door closed behind her, and I sank to the floor. I wrapped my arms around my knees and rocked. It was over. It was over, but Lincoln had been shot.

*He's too stubborn to die from a bullet to the arm.* The voice in my head had me whipping my gaze up. Sienna was leaning against the wall, arms crossed. I couldn't see the wound at the back of her head from this angle, just the face of a surly, teenaged girl who looked spookily like me.

"I don't understand," I said, keeping my voice quiet so Mom didn't come storming in and demand to know who I was talking to.

Sienna shrugged. *Me either. I'm just here when I'm needed. He needed me a lot in the beginning. In those first few years, I was almost always around. The trouble he had sleeping got worse. I think he maybe got an hour or so every other day.*

"Wouldn't seeing you make that worse?"

She shrugged. *I don't make the rules. I'm just sent, so here I am.*

"You saved him tonight."

She looked up at the ceiling and back. *I was sent to save you both.*

"Thank you."

She tilted her head, as if listening to something. *That's my cue. You're good for him, Willow. Maybe even better for him than I ever could have been, because I took the love he gave me for granted. As a teen, when you receive that much love, you just think it's supposed to be yours. That it's always supposed to be that way. But you... You know differently. You know how rare and precious it is. How it can be gone in the blink of an eye. Make sure you live every day as if it might be the last.*

Then, she was gone.

# Chapter Thirty-eight

## Lincoln

**CHANGING TIDES**
Performed by The Fray

*I KNEW THE MOMENT I CAME* awake it had been drugs that had pulled me under rather than anything natural. I'd been on the receiving end of drug-induced sleep too many times in my life, and I hated it. It took me a few seconds longer to register the pain in my right arm and the smell of antiseptic that flooded my senses along with the steady beeping rhythm of the heart rate monitor.

A weight laying on me had me dragging my eyes open to find Willow asleep with her head on my chest and her lips slightly parted in sleep. She'd squeezed herself into the hospital bed along my left side. At least I hadn't been shot in my drawing arm.

I raised my good hand and stroked her soft, moonlight-colored hair.

She stirred immediately, leaning up on an elbow as she said, "You're awake!" She scanned my face, running a hand along the scruff on my jaw. "Thank God."

"I told you I wasn't dying," I grunted. My voice was hoarse and scratchy.

She rolled out of the bed, and I tried to grab her hand to stop her, but pain shot through me. I must have let out a sound, because she whirled back around, eyes wide. "You're hurting.

I'll get a nurse."

"Water," I rasped.

She pulled a tray over with a pitcher on it, poured water into a plastic cup with a straw, and brought it to me. I sipped at it, feeling like a five-year-old instead of a grown-ass man, which made me snap at her. "I don't need you feeding me."

Instead of being hurt or angry, it made her lips curve upward. "If you're growling at me, I really know you're going to be okay."

She put the cup down, leaned in, and kissed me softly. When she went to move away, I put my good hand on the back of her head and held her there, deepening the kiss. I let relief and love wash over me. She was alive. I was alive. Aaron was dead.

I'd killed a man.

I didn't feel an ounce of sorrow for having done it. I'd do it again to keep her safe. Do it again to keep any of the people I loved safe—but especially her. Still, the weight of it wasn't something I took lightly. Scales would be balanced at the end of our time on this earth, and this would be something I owed.

When I tried to tug her closer, pain ripped through me again, and my grunt made her pull away.

"Let me get the nurse. You need more pain meds."

"Don't need anything except you."

When she grinned, it made the pain all but disappear.

"Your parents are here. Down the hall. I told them I'd get them when you woke."

"I figured they'd be lurking around somewhere."

Her face turned serious, and she squeezed my hand. "It was Sienna."

When I met her gaze, it wasn't freaked out or judgmental or concerned. Instead, it was somber and almost serene. Still, a force of habit had me clamping my jaw tight and saying nothing. It was Willow who continued. "I saw her too."

My brows raised.

"Not at first. At first, I was confused because I didn't know who you were talking to and why you were freaking out. But then, when you were fighting with Aaron, she came into the guest room and told me you needed help."

"I used to think she was a hallucination brought on by the drugs they gave me for the insomnia. Then, I thought it was my guilty conscience imagining her. I thought we both needed closure. When her parents gave me her trust fund to open the gallery, I thought it was what we both needed to move on. And when she disappeared, I was sure of it. But she came back last week, and I didn't know why."

"She said she came when she was needed—or rather, that she was sent when she was needed. She hung around after we got to the hospital, making sure you were okay. She told me to make sure I didn't take you for granted like she had."

I shook my head. "She never took me for granted."

Willow shrugged. "Those were her words, not mine."

I didn't want to talk about Sienna. She was my past. This stunning, brave, quiet woman in front of me was my future. A future we'd almost lost. My chest tightened, and I squeezed her hand. "You were supposed to stay hidden."

"This won't work if we aren't on equal footing, Lincoln. We protect each other. We face everything together. That's how my parents faced life. From what I've seen, I think it's how your parents face theirs. We won't last if you treat me like a fragile thing needing your protection, and I want that forever you promised. I want it so badly I can taste it, can't you?"

"It tastes like you. Like browned butter and sugar."

"Funny, I think it tastes like you. A little bit bitter and quite a bit demanding."

"Smart-ass."

"I love you," she said, and my heart lunged so hard the monitor burst into a chaotic rhythm. She smiled at the sound before turning that beaming light on me. "Get better so I can take you home."

"You're moving in with me," I told her.

She huffed out a laugh. "Is that equal footing? You issuing commands?"

"Can't be equal if we're not under the same roof," I told her. "And I want to get married."

She sat beside me and ran a finger over my brow. "Some proposal that is."

For a second, I felt bad for having let it slip out like that, but then I just shrugged. "I'll give you romance once they get this ridiculous sling off me."

"Hmmm. Does this mean I get to punish *you* for using that word?"

"We'll punish each other." I tugged on her arm, making her wobble, and she landed back on my chest. Sharp agony arrowed through me, but I didn't care. I kissed her fiercely with determination and promises in every slide of our mouths.

She drew back, the soft, beautiful smile I adored filling her face.

"I'm serious, Willow. I want to get married—tomorrow, if I can make it happen. I want to start forever right now."

"Fast and furious." She shook her head and let out a little laugh. "I think we should probably wait until you can stand. Maybe get rid of the bandages."

"Is that a yes?"

"You didn't really ask, but yes, I'll marry you."

More relief washed over me. Together. Forever. I could do that. I would do that.

♫ ♫ ♫

They kept me for two damn days in the hospital. My parents hovered, the media tried to sneak in, and the authorities came and went with multiple questions. But by the time I got home, by the time Axel was going inside to clear the house ahead of us, Willow had moved her things from her mother's cottage into mine, which made coming back a true homecoming for me.

The bodyguard who'd picked us up from the hospital with Axel drove the SUV right up to the back door in order to avoid the media that had flooded Cherry Bay. Axel stepped out of the house and said, "You're clear. We've got men out front and out back, but the press has mostly stayed at the end of the street. They've been respectful, even when your parents were staying here."

Willow started toward the door, and the hands we had tangled together tugged at her as I held my ground. She looked back at me, puzzled. I gave her fingers a little squeeze, saying, "Go on in, Sweetness. I want to talk to Axel for a moment."

She darted worried eyes between us but then did as I'd asked.

Silence settled for a moment while I watched Axel's man standing near the garage, scanning the surroundings behind mirrored sunglasses. Another man had stood there just days ago and lost his life in the dead of the night.

"Your man…the one who died…I'd like to do something for the family."

"We've taken care of them," Axel said, lips tight.

"I imagine you have, but for my own sake, I need to do something too. One of the news articles mentioned he had kids, right?" When Axel nodded, I said, "I'd like to start a fund for them. They can use it for college or trade school or to start a business—whatever they need for their future."

Axel's throat bobbed. "That's generous of you."

"He lost his life protecting mine. Protecting Willow."

"You protected yourselves better than we did," Axel grunted, and I saw the remorse I was so familiar with echoed in his eyes.

"I don't know who it was that first said it, but if someone really wants to kill you, they'll find a way, right? Hate and evil keep coming until it wins or is stopped. You stopped Jennings. I stopped Aaron. I think we can call it a draw."

I couldn't see his eyes behind his sunglasses, but I felt them on me, weighing what I'd said, weighing me.

"I'll send you his family's details." He ran a hand over his shorn head. "Just so you know, Jennings died. Never regained consciousness, but we believe he got the gun from Aaron."

"What? How?"

"In Jennings's journals, he wrote about a man approaching him who wanted the same thing he wanted—you and Willow dead. The man gave him the gun, and from the way Jennings described him, it had to be Aaron."

"How did Aaron find us?"

"Poco."

I cussed under my breath, and Axel continued, "After his brother died, Aaron posted a wanted ad on the dark web for Willow. Poco saw it and had cashed in on it even before he sent the photos of the two of you to *The Exhibitor*."

"You arresting him?"

"No one can find him. Whatever he was shoveling in the graveyard must have had him digging his own grave with Paul," Axel replied. Knowing eyes met mine as we both remembered Paul and his men taking Poco into the back room. Maybe it was another scale I'd have to balance at the end of my time on this earth, but it felt fitting to know he'd suffered.

Axel stepped away and said, "If you need anything, anything at all, you call me."

He gave a chin nod to his man at the garage and then strode toward the street and the half dozen black SUVs waiting there.

When I walked into the kitchen, it smelled like sugar and spice and everything nice. It smelled like Willow. A pink box sat on the counter, lid opened, and when I glanced inside, I saw she'd finished another piece of food art. Stunning golden foliage littered the surface of a garden path with a starry sky over the top of it.

"You finished your Gustav Klimt?" I asked.

"More like art inspired by him. I found the print online, and it spoke to me more than his actual work."

"The gold is stunning combined with the blue. It's beautiful, Willow." I closed my eyes and let the smells run through me. Berries. Butter. Vanilla. "It's decadent. Too pretty for anyone to eat."

She waved at more pink boxes stacked behind her on the counter. "I have the individual desserts over there."

I eased toward her, wrapped my good arm around her waist, and drew her into me. "You've been busy."

"I couldn't sleep, even after you sent me away each night."

"I know how to fix that."

"Do you?" she asked, eyes twinkling with humor and a flare of heat that my body responded to automatically.

"Beds are good for two things. Sleeping and sex. I think we'll do both."

I twined my good hand with hers, tugging her toward the stairs just as my phone rang. My mother's tone. I felt around in my pockets and came up empty. I turned to look down at Willow in surprise as I heard her answering it.

She talked with Mom for a second, letting her know we'd just walked in the door and that I'd call her back. Then, she shoved the phone into the pocket of The Tea Spot sweatshirt she was wearing.

"You're answering my phone."

She looked chagrined. "Someone needs to be in charge of it. She's been worried, and she's right—you're really bad about picking up."

"I answered every time *you* called or texted." Her cheeks turned that delightful shade of pink I so adored. "Bedroom, Sweetness. Right now."

I took off for the stairs at a jog, hauling her with me.

"Lincoln. Slow down. You're still healing."

"Hasn't anyone told you? Sex is the best medicine. Heals all things."

She laughed, but as soon as the bedroom door shut behind us, she was helping me remove my clothes and the stupid-ass sling. I sat on the bed and watched as she shed her layers. The weak sunlight coming through the closed blinds turned her into a hazy mirage, just like a Klimt or Seurat painting, and yet incomparably more stunning because she was real. Because she was Willow.

She moved to stand between my legs, beaming at me happily.

And in that moment, I knew what the painting of her in the cemetery was missing.

The Willow in the painting needed wings. She was a broken angel, growing back her wings and carrying a sword. A golden sword to avenge the wrongs of the world. The wings would sparkle. The sword would be full of gems. And the entirety of her would shimmer in the moonlight.

Banishing evil from the night, she'd bring the peace and serenity of daylight.

I settled my good hand on her hip, thumb moving in a lazy circle as I looked up at her.

"From the moment I saw you in the cemetery, I knew you were a work of art. But having you here, like this, naked, hungry for me…" My body reacted to the heat flashing through those gray eyes. "You're a masterpiece, Willow. I understand Picasso now when he said art is a lie. Because I could spend the rest of my life trying to capture the essence of you, and it would never show the truth."

She straddled me, sliding over me in one swift move that had me stunned all over again. Her mouth collided with mine, proving she felt the same insatiable need I did. The need to be joined. To belong. To be together.

"Don't worry, we have forever for you to try," she whispered in my ear.

"Even forever won't be enough, but let's get started on it anyway."

And we tipped over into my new favorite place. My last favorite place. Joined with her.

# Epilogue

# Willow

***YOU PICKED ME***
Performed by A Fine Frenzy

***I WAS FUTZING WITH THE TRAY*** of my miniature desserts on a table below the painting when an arm wrapped around my waist and pulled me into a strong chest I knew as well as my own. It had only been twelve weeks since I'd moved in with Lincoln, and yet, it felt like we'd been together years already. We were working hard on that forever we'd promised each other.

He kissed the spot below my ear, sending flares through my body, shock waves of desire I had to rein in with other people in the room. I glanced toward the opposite wall where Lyrica and Trinity were talking, hands waving as they nudged a painting this way and that.

Trinity's work was full of a beautiful and whimsical realism. Magnificent, even. But the art that spoke to me most was this one on the wall above the tray. Cherry blossoms filled the air like a misty fog, and between the floating petals, the face of an angel peeked out. Me, but not me. It wasn't the face I saw in the mirror every day, but it was somehow what Lincoln saw when he looked at me. The demon in the painting next to the angel was dark. I saw pieces of Lincoln in it, but also Aaron and Poco and even Ryan Jennings, who I'd never met but who'd still hunted me. I hated that Lincoln saw himself there, but I thought, maybe, every day, he moved further and further away from the demon and more toward the angel.

"The smell…the toasted-sugar smell tangled with the ripe berries…it's perfect, Sweetness. Exactly what I wanted," he said.

The opening for the gallery was mere hours away. I was nervous for Lincoln and Trinity, but also for me because we were combining my food art with their masterpieces. People would taste while they browsed, combining the visual and olfactory senses. The music piping through the gallery's speakers added to the auditory, sweet fairy-tale songs and moody villain ballads. Every sense would be on alert. Taste would be explored once the food was served. Only tactile senses were missing, but I'd have Lincoln for that. I'd have his hand resting on my lower back, guiding me, his fingers tangled with mine while we stood side by side.

We'd face the fans and the critics together.

Like we'd done everything else since I'd moved in with him.

"This dress is going to kill me before the night is over," he said, trailing kisses up over my jaw, and my eyes darted over to the other women in the gallery. "It's perfect. Magical. Just like the paintings, but all I can think about is sliding you out of it."

Pleasure coasted through me at his words. Grateful and so damn happy he gave me them so easily. I was awed by the miracle of Lincoln in my life, feeling this way about me and adoring me in just the way I'd always longed to be.

I hadn't chosen my signature pink for the dress tonight. Maybe I'd needed to stand out from the woman in the cemetery, who was on the wall upstairs, who wore cotton-candy pink while her wings grew back and she banished the dark with her sword. That woman was strong and brave, seeking retribution as she held back the shadows. But she was also serious, somber, and sad. And that wasn't me these days. I was happier and much more fulfilled.

So, instead of pink, I'd worn a green dress that landed somewhere between sage and pistachio. A dress that danced with life, the gauzy overlay floating over an underskirt that clung to me. The top was tightly fitted with heart-shaped curves over my breasts, showing skin I rarely displayed. I'd fallen in love with it the moment I'd tried it on when Mom and Shay had taken me shopping.

I turned in Lincoln's arms, straightening the collar of the white button-down he wore under a richly colored, brocade vest. The pattern on the vest was intricate—ivy and lotus flowers made of silver and gold thread. Whimsical and real, just like the art he'd hung on the walls.

"This completely fits the vibe of the gallery," I said, patting his chest.

"You fit the vibe of the gallery," he responded. He kissed me, tenderly and yet with that passionate force that always existed between us.

"Are you two love birds ready to open the doors, or are you going to neck all night?" Lyrica called out.

Lincoln chuckled, color bloomed over my skin, and we turned to find the two women watching us. Lyrica was in blood-red silk, her warm skin blazing beneath it, while Trinity was in black lace that reminded me of the dress Sienna had appeared to me in. I wondered if Lincoln noticed it too. Regardless, neither of us mentioned it. We rarely talked of Sienna, and neither of us had seen her again since the night Aaron had attacked us.

"Open the doors," Lincoln said.

Lyrica rolled her eyes at his command but went to unlock the doors while Trinity and I pulled back the curtains from the windows. A crowd had gathered. My family. Lincoln's sisters. People from all over town, the state, and farther. Lincoln Matherton was opening a gallery, and that drew people like gnats to watermelon.

The hours went by in a flash, people in and out, buying art, tasting food, laughing, and joking. Trinity was glowing, Lincoln was smiling, and I was thrilled every time I caught someone eating one of my miniature desserts and murmuring in delight. Even after having created several art pieces for Hector, and having people buy and eat my treats for several months now, I was still unaccustomed to seeing their pleasure when they tasted something I'd created.

A rustle of bodies at the back of the gallery turned into Lincoln's parents as they came through the alley door. Secret Service had been in and out of the gallery all day and now there were almost as many of them in attendance as there were guests. His parents beelined for Lincoln, hugging him and me with warmth before greeting his sisters the same way and then turning to Trinity to fawn over her pieces.

Katerina caught me by the arm as Lincoln took his parents upstairs to see the angel in the cemetery.

"Give them a moment," she said.

While I hadn't met Katerina in person until she'd flown into town two days ago, I'd started chatting with her while Lincoln was in the hospital. Getting a better response from me than she ever did him, she just started texting me directly, and we'd found ourselves talking about everything and anything. I loved Shay like a sister. She was a friend and family, but in some ways, I was already closer to Katerina than I'd ever been to Shay. Maybe because I was finally letting myself open up to people again, or maybe because Katerina pushed herself through any doors you tried to close. Maybe it was both.

Juliette, on the other hand, I barely knew. She was quiet and reserved. So opposite of her sister and even her moody brother. Sometimes, I wondered if it was on purpose. If she chose to be invisible whenever she was standing next to their fiery energy.

What I did know was that Lincoln worried about both twins constantly these days, but especially Katerina since she'd let her Secret Service detail go. Lincoln had hoped he'd get to the bottom of it when she flew in for the opening, but I wasn't sure they'd had a moment to talk alone yet.

"Lincoln is sure something is wrong with you," I told her.

She rolled her eyes, but they shifted down and away. "I was working like a demon to finish the movie. I have weeks more to spend on the editing floor. I haven't had the time to respond as much as I usually do. Tell him he's just getting a bit of his own medicine."

She said it with the normal, flippant attitude Katerina always had, but my instincts, like Lincoln's, told me it was something more. Different.

"You know he'll always have your back," I said softly.

Katerina met my gaze and held it. She let out a soft sigh, as if she'd been holding her breath for too long. "I know. And I promise if I need him, I'll tell him. For now, everything is fine."

I would have pushed more, but the music stopped, taking the atmosphere so important to Lincoln with it. I turned, ready to head to the stereo system in the corner, and my feet stalled as I saw him on the stairs, looking down at me with a microphone in his hand.

"Lyrica demanded I say something," he said, waving at his friend. "And if you know Lyrica at all, you know you don't disobey." Laughter floated through the gallery. "So, thank you for coming to the opening of The Lotus Gallery tonight. Thank you for letting Trinity Carerra and me unlock a door for you into a world where magic and mythical creatures really do exist, flitting next to us whether we see them or not."

His eyes searched the room and stilled when they came to rest on me.

"When I first came to Cherry Bay, not quite a year ago, something in the air, something about the cobblestones and light and the woodlands on the outskirts spoke to me. Called to me. I didn't realize it at the time, but it was simply destiny walking me home and bringing the magic into my life I'd been missing. It brought all of you and a new take on art, but more important than anything else, it brought me Willow."

As an entire room full of people turned to look at me. I squirmed, fighting the instinctive reaction to duck my head and hide.

The days of being invisible, of needing to be invisible, were behind me. Everywhere we went now, people photographed Lincoln and me. Our pictures were regularly in the tabloids. Part of me hated it. The piece of me that had been told to hide in order to keep safe sometimes still panicked. But whenever I really started to go over the edge, Lincoln would grab my hand, run his fingers along my palm, and I'd be centered again. I'd find home again.

"I made a mistake with her," Lincoln said, and my chest tightened, even as his blue gaze burned me with its love. "You see, after I'd been shot and was lounging in the hospital on painkillers, I did something stupid. I gave her a promise and demanded one back, but I didn't give her the charming moment she deserved. So, Willow, if you could come up here now, I want to fix that. I want to make it right."

My feet grew roots, binding me to the floor.

Katerina nudged me, and Lincoln's eyes beseeched me.

But it was Guy Matherton, who I hadn't even realized had come to stand on the other side of me, who got me moving. He winked, lips turned upward in a smile that matched Lincoln's, and said, "Perhaps you shouldn't leave my son stranded up there while he attempts a grand gesture."

My eyes widened, but then I was moving, unsteady on heels I was unaccustomed to wearing as I weaved through the crowd. When I reached the base of the stairs, Lincoln held out his hand and helped me up the final steps until I was next to him. He set the microphone down, dug in his pocket, and came up with a tiny velvet box.

"Forever is what we promised each other that day, Willow. But here, in front of all our loved ones, and a good chunk of the town we've made our home, I wanted to ask you appropriately, with not only love in my heart but with the romance you deserve, if you'll do me the honor of becoming my wife."

He opened the box, and I stared at the ring—a bright-pink diamond surrounded by an infinity symbol.

Happiness bubbled through me so large it felt like a mountain was trying to shove its way out of my chest. We hadn't talked about marriage since that day in the hospital. Not once. He'd said he wanted it to happen as soon as possible, and then we'd said nothing. I hadn't been upset. I hadn't even really thought about it because we'd been content playing house, getting to know each other, learning each other's moods and likes and dislikes. He'd been busy getting the gallery ready and painting multiple pieces, many of them with my face or shape, and I'd been busy working on my food art and how to make enough miniatures at a price that turned a profit for Hector and me.

We'd been busy. Happy. In love.

It had been enough.

Especially once I'd gotten the news that I didn't carry the FFI mutated gene. Once I knew our forever could be longer than I'd ever thought I'd have, life had been nothing but bright stars and bright moments.

I looked up from the ring to Lincoln's shining blue eyes and the smile that was mine and mine alone. The one that had stolen my heart before I'd recognized what was happening.

"We're already in forever, Lincoln. You've already given me everything I never knew I couldn't live without. Every day, you give me romance. Love and joy. Sliding a ring on my finger won't change that, but I'm thrilled to do so. Thrilled to give you the happily ever after you so deserve."

I threw my arms around his neck and kissed him.

Cameras flashed.

And I knew what would be in the tabloids tomorrow. My lips smooshed up against his.

But I didn't care.

Because for today, tomorrow, and always, I wanted people to see this was who we were. A couple joined by fate and love but also the magic of an entire town.

♫ ♫ ♫

**Want to know what's up with Katerina and just what Axel will have to do to protect her** from the shadows that followed her to Cherry Bay? Stay tuned for her HEA coming in 2025 from LJ Evans.

**Want a bit more of Lincoln and Willow before they disappear?** Catch them on their wedding day in this <u>Bonus Epilogue available for FREE with a newsletter subscription</u>.

# Lost in the Moonlight Bonus Epilogue

https://bookhip.com/VWSHFAW

If you want more Cherry Bay suspense stories with a hint of the supernatural, check out this excerpt from the standalone, single-dad romantic suspense *AFTER ALL THE WRECKAGE*.

# After All the Wreckage

# Chapter One – Rory

### *AM I ALRIGHT*
### *Performed by Aly & AJ*

*IF PANIC ATTACKS COULD HAVE BABIES,* I'd be having *quintuplets*. The thought landed in my chest as I pulled my royal blue Honda Rebel into a tiny spot on the street outside my dad's office. It was the last place I wanted to be for more reasons than I could count. Some of those reasons were petty, full of old grudges and teenage hurts, and some were deadly serious.

The deadly part was why I'd swallowed my pride enough to come.

I slammed my foot on the kickstand and swung my leg over the seat before standing in my thick-soled Harley-Davidson boots and pulling off my helmet. I dragged the hair tie from my ponytail, slung it around my wrist, and ran a hand through the dark brown strands.

When I turned toward the small but expensive building that held Bishop Investigations & Security, my reflection caught in the two stories of glittering glass. I cringed, knowing neither my bike nor my appearance would help my cause today. My black jacket was naturally distressed with spiderweb cracks along the leather, and the hole in my black jeans was from a tussle with a cheater I'd been following rather than any designer styling. They'd be the first of many things my father would pick at today. A few more additions to the long list of my mistakes. But two could play at that game. After all, I had a list of his that I could recite too.

I shoved my shoulders back and strode through the doors. The inside of his office was professional and cold. Decked out in steel and gray leather, the lobby was elegantly arranged to impress Dad's clients. As if the surroundings screaming wealth proved he could get the job done rather than the fact he had a good interior designer. But the truth was, as much as it irked me to admit it, Dad always got the job done. Whether the client liked what he found was an entirely different story—one I knew firsthand.

My eyes drifted to my wrist and the black-and-blue fingerprints that had turned darker throughout the day. I tugged the cuff of my jacket down, clamping it against my palm with my fingers. If Dad saw the marks, any chance of asking him for the favor I'd come for would be lost. And I needed him to come through. For the first time in almost a decade, I actually needed my father.

I hated it.

At the desk, the latest receptionist in a long string of Georgetown grad students sat waiting. Each of them used their time with his company to launch a litany of justice and law enforcement careers. His name on their résumé was an exclusive D.C. insider's gold star that opened doors. Too bad I'd never been offered a chance to earn one. Maybe he'd known I would have rather been boiled in acid than sit at that clear glass desk answering his phones.

"Rory," Chanel greeted me with a snip to her tone. Her gym-toned legs below the hem of a gray pencil skirt crossed as she swiveled toward me, purple Prada pumps dangling from her feet. They were the only sign of color in the stark space. She fit into Dad's image perfectly whereas I looked like I'd been dragged in from the biker bar on the edge of Cherry Bay—the town I called home after leaving D.C. a few months ago.

"Dad in?" I asked her, trying to keep my voice light and even.

Her gaze flitted over me briefly, barely withholding her judgment, but I could hear it anyway. The silent *How on earth is this Sutton Bishop's daughter?* Because the only thing I'd inherited from the blond-haired dynamo in a suit who was my father was the cleft in my chin. He was tall with a square face and wide shoulders, whereas

I was almost all Mom with honey-toned Italian skin and a lithe, short frame. Dad's green eyes screamed their color even over a distance while the tiny bit of jade that flashed in my brown ones was only visible if you were close enough to kiss me.

Not that I'd been kissed lately. It had been so long, my lips and vagina thought I'd abandoned them.

"He has twenty minutes before he has to leave for lunch on the Hill," Chanel said primly.

It was exactly what I'd hoped for. Dad spent more time wining and dining D.C. bigwigs these days than he did investigating. Although, maybe that wasn't much different from when Mom had been his partner. Back then, he'd brought the business in and she'd executed it… or I did. Right up until the divorce split them down the middle and me along with it.

As I headed for the stairs, I tossed a jab over my shoulder. "Dad has dining with sleazy politicians down to a science. They should give him the oil prospector of the year award."

"First, not all politicians are sleazy. Second, you're one to judge. How's it going swimming with the cheaters?"

My foot stalled on the first step, and when I looked back, her eyes were narrowed. I almost laughed at her quick retort, but then I wondered if her defense of Dad came from a sense of loyalty that went much deeper than an employee-employer relationship. I wondered if Dad had tucked this receptionist into his bed a time or two… or more.

It made me want to heave up the cold mac and cheese I'd called breakfast.

I didn't respond, turning back around to take the stairs at double time.

His office door was open, the low hum of his voice audible if not the actual words. He didn't have an assistant guarding the entrance. He didn't believe in having one. The fewer eyes and hands on sensitive information, the better in his opinion. And if for some reason the nearly perfect Sutton Bishop did need help, the highly paid receptionist downstairs would be tasked with it.

Dad had his chair turned toward the enormous windows looking out at the dome of the Capitol Building. I knocked, and he swung around to take me in. His eyes narrowed ever so slightly before a tight smile appeared on his lips.

"I'll have to call you back," he said into the phone, pausing to listen to the response. "I'm telling you, you're worrying over nothing, Roland. I'll see you tonight."

He hung up and watched as I moved to stand next to the pair of straight-backed chairs in front of his steel desk. The chairs weren't designed for comfort. Dad didn't want people to dally in his office any more than he wanted them lingering in his personal life.

Handsome and brimming with charisma, my father could have been a politician as easily as he'd become a private investigator. He could charm his way into just about anywhere… and anyone. It was a skill Mom said I'd inherited from him, and sometimes, I wasn't sure if it was a compliment or not.

"I'd love to say it's nice to finally see my daughter again, but I'm confident you didn't drive into D.C. on that asinine bike just to visit dear old Dad," he said dryly with a pointed look at the helmet under my arm.

I tossed it on the chair as he came around the desk to draw me into a one-armed hug. A catch and release he'd once shown me how to do while fishing. The nonchalance pricked at old wounds I couldn't afford to let show.

A wisp of pine from his cologne combined with a hint of smoke from his occasional cigar wafted over me. I was dismayed by the temptation to hold on to him longer, to use his strength to buoy me up. To once again be the little girl he'd beamed at when she'd handed him the proof of a certain congressman sleeping with a prostitute. Proof that had cost the man his reelection and his wife.

I gritted my teeth and stepped farther away. If I allowed myself to drop my shield even briefly, the weight I was carrying might slip off and I'd never be able to pick it up again. I wasn't even twenty-three yet, but I had both lives and a business resting solely on my shoulders.

As he leaned up against his desk, he scanned my outfit, his look lingering on the fresh cut and red skin visible through the hole in my jeans. I grabbed the cuff of my jacket extra tight, ensuring it stayed firmly in place.

"To what do I really owe the pleasure?" he asked.

I regretted the cold mac and cheese all over again.

Now that I was here, I didn't really want to make my request. I took a few seconds to run through the numbers in our bank accounts once more. Then, the image of Mom lying in the bed at the long-term care facility settled cruelly in my chest. Her skin was paler than ever before, and her eyes were always shut as a feeding tube, a host of cords, and beeping machines kept her alive. I forced back an unexpected rush of tears. I couldn't afford them any more than I could afford the damn hug to undo me. Tears never solved anything—the saying should have been monogrammed on our Bishop family crest.

"I need a loan," I told him.

I knew better than to ask for money straight up. Dad believed in earning what you got. Struggle built character. It was the one and only thing my parents had agreed upon after the divorce.

Dad crossed his arms over his chest. "How much and what's it for?"

If I said I needed it to cover the added expense of Mom's new facility in Cherry Bay, he'd object. He'd made it very clear he disagreed with keeping her on life support after the doctors had recommended shutting it off and the insurance had stopped paying because of it. But if I said I needed cash to cover Marlow & Co. bills, he definitely wouldn't give it to me. He'd be happy if the business Mom had created after divorcing him disappeared. One less competitor.

After my mistake in high school—getting suspended and almost expelled for stunning a drug dealer in the boys' bathroom—he and Mom had pretty much switched sides. Once he'd seen me as an integral part of their business, now all he saw were my errors.

Because neither of the real reasons I needed the money would sway him, I gave him the fake one I'd come up with on the commute into D.C. "I want to get my master's."

I tried to keep my face impassive through the partial lie. I'd once planned on going to grad school before applying to the FBI, but these days those ideas seemed like Neverland dreams, and I was out of pixie dust. After missing the spring semester because of Mom's accident, I'd transferred from Georgetown to Bonnin University in Cherry Bay where I was weeks away from squeaking out a bachelor's degree. Even though it was less expensive, I'd still had to take out a loan as every penny from the sale of Mom's D.C. condo had gone toward keeping her breathing.

Dad's eyes narrowed as if he was attempting to read me. My face remained stony, but I made the mistake of shifting ever so slightly on one foot, and he caught the small movement.

"You've applied and been accepted to grad school? Where?"

He wasn't buying it. Why had I humiliated myself like this when I'd already known it was a futile effort? Mom's face flashed in my head again, and those fricking tears I never let out threatened once more. I grabbed my helmet and headed for the door before I further humiliated myself.

"Never mind. Forget I was even here," I said.

"I didn't say I wouldn't give you the money. I just want to know the truth."

Gripping the chin guard of my helmet with one hand, I waved at him with the other. "Why does it matter? Your daughter needs a loan. I'm not asking for a handout. I'm not asking for anything I won't pay back. You set the terms, and I'll meet them."

The second he strode toward me with anger flashing in his eyes, I realized my mistake.

He grabbed my arm, demanding, "Who hurt you?"

"It isn't important." It was embarrassing was what it was. A stupid wardrobe malfunction that had let the cheating bastard lay a hand on me.

"Damn it, Rory-girl! How many times do I have to repeat myself? You aren't cut out for this business. You're going to end up dead just like your mother."

"Mom isn't dead!" I growled back, pushing him away from me and taking a step into the hall.

He sighed, the sound full of frustration and sadness. "She is, Rory. Even if, by some miracle, she comes out of it, she'll be a shell of a person. She won't ever be Hallie again."

"Just because you've given up hope doesn't mean Nan or I have," I hissed. "And Mom didn't die because some asshole cheater came after her. She crashed into the Potomac."

I stomped toward the stairs.

"Because someone messed with her car's computer."

As his words sank in, my feet stalled. My heartbeat sped up, doing triple time, as I whirled around to face him. "What?"

He rubbed his forehead. The regret and exasperation on his face were a clear message he'd let something slip he'd never intended for me to hear. I'd repeatedly asked the detective in charge of Mom's accident for the cause, and Muloney had told me they'd never know for sure. There hadn't been another vehicle involved. She'd just gone over the edge and into the river. A submerged tree had pierced the right side of her head, and she'd drowned before the rescue people got to her. They'd resuscitated her, but she'd never woken up. She'd gripped my hand a few times, her lids had fluttered open and closed, but she'd never really been cognizant.

And now it had been eleven months… Eleven months I'd survived without her. But it felt like twenty years. An eternity in which I'd lived in some alternate version of what had once been my life.

"Who told you that?" My words were garbled as pain and fury roared through me. He didn't respond, and it only goaded me further. "I can't believe you! You told Muloney to cut me out? You're not her next of kin. You don't get to make any decisions about her. You lost that right when you divorced her. Like it or not, I'm the one who's responsible for her now."

"Except you want my money to keep her alive."

"That's not what it's for."

"Isn't it?" he demanded, brow rising again. "I know you've gone through the tiny profit you got out of the condo, Rory. I know you've had to change facilities more than once. This bullshit idea about a master's degree? You and I both know it isn't what the money is for."

God, there were times I hated how good he was at his job. He really knew everything. He always had. It was why clients flocked from all over the Northeast to his doors.

"Keep your damn money. I'll do this alone, just like Mom and I have done everything else for the past ten years, and I'll figure out why someone wanted her dead while I'm at it."

"I don't want to lose my daughter *and* my wife."

"Ex-wife. Your latest girlfriend would hate to hear you call her that."

He blew out an exasperated breath. "You're not cut out for this, Rory," he repeated. "It's my fault you started down this path. I can admit I was wrong. I never should have asked you to do any of the things I did, and Hallie should never have let you coerce her into picking up where I left off.

"Jesus, look at you." He gestured toward me. "You're battered and bruised, racing around town on that deathtrap, for what? An idea that you can be some real-life Veronica Mars? Real detective work isn't anything like that goddamn show."

Each syllable was a hit to my already bruised psyche. Scars and scabs hidden deep in my soul started to bleed. Veronica had saved me. And ever since Mom's accident, my life had taken on an even more decidedly Veronica-like vibe. She'd stayed to help her dad after he'd gotten sick just like I was helping Mom. She'd gone back to running the family PI business, and I'd done the same. The clients and money I brought in weren't nearly enough, though. I was doling out more each month than I was bringing in, and Nan didn't have any extra cash to offer. She was barely getting by on Pop's widow's pension.

I swallowed hard, striking back the only way I could with words I wasn't sure were true but would hit home anyway. "At least Keith Mars loved his daughter. Fake show. Real love. The complete opposite of this." I waved a finger between us and then turned on my heel and headed down the stairs.

He followed me to the railing, calling after me. "Rory, don't leave like this."

I didn't respond.

"You know there are a lot of companies who would give someone with your computer skills a hiring bonus. If you're looking for money and don't want it on my terms, at least consider it. You need to leave this business behind and concentrate on what you *are* good at."

Chanel was pretending not to watch the show as I stormed past her desk, but I saw the smirk, and it only fueled the rage inside me. I wished I could slam the door to the building, but all it did was swing back and forth.

As I stalked over to my bike, the realization that Dad might be right caused bile to hit my throat. Maybe I did need to get some eight-to-five desk job in some corporate office peddling my computer skills. Not because a buckle had gotten caught in a trellis and the cheater had pulled me from it by my wrist, but because a job in a corporate office would pay a helluva lot more than my handful of clients.

But then Dad's slipped admission came back. Someone had messed with Mom's car! Someone had done this to her on purpose. There was no way in hell I'd let that go. I'd borrow money from Tall Paul, the biggest loan shark I knew, before I'd just walk away.

Just like Veronica Mars had once said, this was where I belonged. In the fight. It was who I was. And I could guarantee whoever had done this would regret it.

As I pulled on my helmet and merged into the heavy traffic of D.C. at lunchtime, I wondered how much Dad had paid Baloney-Muloney to keep the truth from me. Was Dad investigating it on his own or was he leaving it to the tiny force that made up Cherry Bay's police department?

If Dad had any information, I'd find out. I had a backdoor into his network that he was clueless to. I'd find out what he knew, and if it was nothing, there were other doors I'd start banging on—or hacking into.

Dad was right about one thing. I'd die before I let anyone get away with this.

# Chapter Two - Gage

### *BROKEN*

*Performed by The Guess Who*

*I* TAPPED MY FINGERS ALONG THE edge of the Pathfinder's steering wheel, trying to push down the impatience I felt sitting at the back of the car line in front of Cherry Bay's only middle school. I had a long list of things to get done at the bar, which meant I barely had time to manage picking Monte up and getting back to the apartment before opening.

The car in front of me inched forward, and I did the same thing as I scanned the sea of tweens sidling down the sidewalk past the car. No copper-topped waves in sight. Had Monte worn a baseball cap today? I couldn't remember. My younger brother did more often than not. He hated his red hair. Hated the curls more. Hated that kids teased him about being Orphan Annie's twin brother. How the hell they even knew who she was beat me. I'd had to look it up.

"Bubba, I have to pee," a tiny voice from the back seat whispered.

*Shit.* I glanced in the rearview mirror, meeting Ivy's gaze. My sister's pale blue eyes were just like our mother's, but at the moment, they were wide and desperate. A look I wasn't sure I'd ever seen in Demi's. I'd seen fanciful, whimsical, and even clouded, but never desperate. More often than not, Demi's were strangely serene, even in the face of my anger.

Ivy wiggled in her seat, and panic filled my veins. I definitely didn't have time for a bathroom accident. Didn't have time to clean the car seat, the car, or tame the shamed tears that would flow. It wasn't her fault. What three-and-a-half-year-old hadn't had an accident or two?

"Hold tight, Ives," I ground out.

I flipped on my blinker, zipped out in front of a car in a way that earned me a loud honk, then cut off another car before it could block the driveway of the school's parking lot. After sideswiping the orange cone set up to keep people out, I pulled up along the sidewalk near the flagpole in front of the nondescript square building.

I was in the red zone, but I didn't care as I jumped from the driver's seat and jogged around to help Ivy unbuckle even as she protested. Holding her tightly to my chest, I ran toward the bathrooms outside the gym—smelly spaces I knew well from when I'd attended the school a lifetime ago.

I skidded to a halt outside the boys' and girls' restrooms, debating which to use.

"I don't know if I can hold it," Ivy's small voice squeaked out.

Her alarm raced through me. I rushed into the boys' room. When I didn't see anyone standing at the urinals, I sent a silent thanks to the universe. Two stalls were empty. I'd barely set her on her feet before Ivy was jumping up onto the seat. I winced, trying not to think about what was on the toilet. It wasn't like middle school boys were known for their hygiene. But the look of pure gratitude on her face eased the chokehold that had taken over my chest.

Her ponytail was askew. Little wisps of curls had escaped, surrounding her elf-like face dusted with a light sheen of freckles. If there was anything in my life that could make me feel like a failure, it was her damn hair. How did other parents do it? Every time I picked Ivy up from preschool, all the other girls seemed to have their hair still perfectly assembled—neat and tidy—while Ivy's seemed to come loose the moment I put it up.

How was I, at twenty-seven, even in a position to be thinking of a little girl's hair and where the nearest bathroom was? My life was so far from where I'd imagined it would be that there were days the simple weight of it was like an anvil sitting on my shoulders. I was living the wrong life. With that thought came the spike of anger and frustration that usually followed it. Fucking life. Fucking Demi.

Once Ivy was done, she leaped off the seat, and her face burst into a smile so bright it felt like heaven was shining a beam right down on us. It took every thought I'd just had about living the wrong life and all the rage, and zapped it away. She was worth it. She and Monte both.

"All better?" I asked.

She nodded, slipping her tiny fingers into mine, and we made our way out to the sinks where we both washed our hands. With our damp palms joined, we made our way back to the SUV as Ivy tried to skip. She looked like some malfunctioning robot, but it made my lips twitch upward for the first time all afternoon.

I was definitely going to be late now. But I had help at the bar. River would be there, and he'd pick up the slack by unloading the delivery. Audrey would handle the setup inside, and between the two of them, they'd shoulder the tasks I hadn't been able to get to. It would be fine. It always was.

When I got back to our gray Pathfinder, I lifted Ivy into the back seat and watched as she struggled to buckle up. She was extremely proud of being able to do it herself and would get frustrated if I tried to help. It took her five times as long as it would have if I'd done it, but it all came down to that old saying about teaching someone to fish… No one ever mentioned how much patience and energy it took the teacher to do so.

I hopped into the driver's seat and moved to a spot that had opened up near the school's front office. I left the car idling, pulled my phone from my pocket, and shot Monte a text.

*ME: Ivy had to use the bathroom. We're parked in the lot.*

A couple minutes went by, and the number of kids wandering past dwindled. The vehicles in the car line beyond the sidewalk started to fade. Still no sign of my brother. He knew the timing was tight from pickup to the bar opening, so he usually did his best to get out quickly. I flipped my phone over to see there was no response.

*ME: Hey? Did you have practice today?*

I had his basketball schedule taped to the refrigerator, logged into the calendar on my phone, and burned into my brain. But that was the other thing I'd found out the hard way—nothing was predictable with kids.

The principal meandered down from the head of the car line, picked up the cones in the driveway, and set them aside. Three kids tagged along behind him, backpacks weighing them down, phones in hand, and walking while texting in the way teens did despite the warnings that it could be dangerous.

An inkling of something that wasn't quite fear but close hit me in the chest.

*Nothing is wrong. Everything is okay.*

It was a mantra I lived by these days.

Except last night Monte hadn't slept, and neither had I because of it. His eyes had been shadowed this morning, a sense of despair clinging to him as he'd shoveled in the eggs and toast that his growing body demanded.

"What's the point of even having the visions, Gage?" he'd asked. "I'm useless to stop whatever they show me. Nothing I can do. Nothing you can do. We've both tried."

*What if he'd gone on his own to D.C.?* That singular thought caused more alarm than any kind of pee accident could.

While waiting for his response, I shoved my hand through the pitch-black of my thick waves. I looked nothing like my brother and sister. They were all Demi—strawberry-blond strands with pale eyes and soft white skin that showed off their freckles. I was Dad from my dark hair, gray eyes, and square chin down to my skin that always carried a hint of tan year-round.

As the minutes ticked away, my anxiety grew. I stabbed out another desperate message.

> *ME: Please tell me you didn't go to D.C. I'm at the school. Ivy is about two seconds from melting down.*

It wasn't Ivy who was having the meltdown. It was me. But Monte would do just about anything for our little sister. When she'd first been born, he used to crawl into bed with me for comfort whenever she was crying, even when it was just a normal *I'm hungry* type of cry.

My phone buzzed with a reply from Monte, and relief washed through me.

> *MONTE: I went home with India, remember? I'm spending the weekend with her to work on our science project.*

My relief was quickly replaced with guilt. Had he told me and I hadn't paid attention? I'd been so focused on his vision, sleeplessness, and growing restlessness that I might have missed him telling me.

*ME: Are you sure that's a good idea with everything happening?*

*MONTE: It'll keep my mind off it for a while.*

In my gut, I knew the truth. He was doing this for me as much as himself. He didn't want me hovering over him, worrying. But it was my job to protect him, not the other way around.

I put the SUV in gear and backed out of the spot, heading toward the bar.

The asphalt roads at the edge of town quickly turned into cobblestone streets in the town center. The first village in Cherry Bay had been founded in the late 1700s, but the college that had been built on the bluff overlooking the Potomac in the 1940s was what had put us on the map. It drew students and academics from around the globe.

I hooked a right at the alley between two stone buildings that would have been perfectly at home in a medieval English village and headed into the small parking lot at the back. The Prince Darian Tavern had been in my family for over two hundred years. It had first been a post inn, and now it was a bar and restaurant with a two-bedroom apartment and extra storage space above.

While Dad had leased out the restaurant several decades ago, the tavern had been run by a Palmer since its inception. Between the renovation loans I hadn't known he'd taken out and the pandemic closing us down, we'd been almost wiped out financially. After Dad had died, I'd had to sell the house, and we'd moved into the apartment that he used to rent to college students. We were squished together in a space crowded with furniture that didn't fit, but I refused to get rid of those last pieces of our family history. Selling the Victorian we'd grown up in had been painful enough.

I parked the Pathfinder and waited with gritted teeth while Ivy fumbled with her buckle. My gaze journeyed to the next parking lot over, and my heart skipped a beat at the sight of a dark-haired woman. I could practically feel the energy vibrating from Rory Bishop as she headed toward the doors of the Cherry Bay Police Department. The aura of brave confidence was the same as it had been when she'd been fifteen. A self-assurance that mimicked the fictional heroine she'd worshipped back in the day.

Lithe and edgy in all black, I was hypnotized by the way she moved. Unable to draw my eyes away from her.

How long had it been since I'd seen her? How many miles, years, and traumas had filled the space between us?

I was just about to call her name when Ivy jumped out of the car and landed on my foot. It turned any sound that would have emerged from me into a deep grunt, and I had to catch my sister as she wobbled and balance myself at the same time. When I looked back over to the station, Rory was gone, and something a bit like sadness filled me.

Which was ridiculous. I didn't even know Rory anymore. I'd barely known her as a teen.

I pushed aside any thoughts of her, stepped around the wrought iron staircase leading to our apartment, and headed for the rear entrance of the bar with Ivy's hand in mine. A delivery truck had its door rolled up, and as I'd expected, River was already unloading it on his own.

His wide shoulders flexed as he hefted a case of vodka onto his shoulder. His height and build along with his shaved head, pierced nose, and plethora of tattoos intimidated most people. They had no clue his aura radiated nothing but kindness when all they saw was a scary giant.

River had been working for my dad since he'd been in college himself, and decades later, he was still here. Although I was pretty sure that had more to do with not abandoning me and my siblings than because he needed the job. Not when his art was in high demand around the country.

"Sorry we're late," I offered before looking down at my sister. "Go into the office and get a snack from the snack drawer and your coloring books from the shelf. I'll be in after I help River."

"Can I have a chocolate cwinkle?" she asked, eyes wide, knowing I normally didn't let her have sweets this close to dinner. But with my nerves feeling frayed after the scare I'd just had at the school, I didn't feel like arguing with her.

"Yes, but only one," I said, narrowing my eyes at her.

She grinned and then took off down the hall, her messed-up hairdo bouncing around her.

"Hey, Squirt! Don't I even get a hello?" River grunted after her.

She waved her stuffed otter without ever looking back as she hollered, "Hi, Uncle Wivuh!" her R's lisping into W's.

"I expect a hug later."

I grabbed another case off the back of the truck, hauling it to the storage room above the bar. The dark interior stairs were small and groaned with age, but they were smooth and stained to perfection. Everything in the building might be old, but it wasn't shabby. Dad had made sure of it, and I'd picked up where he'd left off.

While River and I unloaded in silence, my thoughts kept drifting back to the brown-haired dynamo I'd seen next door. A piece of me longed to go back in time to when I'd known her. When I'd had nothing to worry about but internships and college tuition. To a time when I'd been adored by a girl who I'd known would take the world by storm and set some guy's heart on fire.

Last I'd heard, she was at Georgetown, but I vaguely recalled some mumblings late last year about her mom being in a car accident. I hadn't paid much attention to the talk because Rory and her mom hadn't lived in Cherry Bay for almost a decade. Plus, I'd been hip-deep in another of Monte's visions and finalizing the paperwork on Ivy's and Monte's adoptions. I'd barely been able to breathe at the time, let alone think of a young girl from my past.

But now I couldn't shake the image of her.

Why was she in town? Was she visiting her friend Shay, whose family owned the Tea Spot across the street? Or was she visiting her grandmother? Regardless of why she was there, I didn't have any more time now to let my thoughts dwell on her than I had a year ago.

I signed the receipt from the delivery and walked toward the tavern's office. I pushed open the antique wooden door with its beveled glass to find Ivy at a claw-foot table that had been there probably since the tavern had first opened. She was on her knees in a burgundy brocade armchair, draped in a mosaic of color from the stained-glass window that made her seem like one of the paintings of our ancestors hanging on the walls in their gilded frames.

When I got up close to her, the mirage broke, and a chuckle rumbled through my chest. She was covered in chocolate from forehead to chin. It never failed to surprise me how quickly and absolutely she could become a mess when eating. She'd need a full body scrub before dinner.

Which reminded me, I needed to call our babysitter and beg her to come over. I'd expected Monte to be home to watch Ivy, which only reconfirmed I hadn't known my brother would be at India's. Unease settled in my chest once again—a worry I couldn't shake. I was an Olympic champion at worrying these days.

I pulled my laptop from the old captain's desk on the other side of the room and brought it over to the table. I kissed the top of Ivy's head as I set it down in front of her. "Give me a few minutes, Ives, then I'll take you upstairs for dinner. Do you want to watch something while you wait?"

She nodded. "Scooby-Doo?"

Her addiction to the cartoon made me smile. "Sure."

I loaded the streaming service, started an episode, and then looked at her chocolate-covered face and hands. "Don't touch the computer. And wash your hands when you're done with the cookie."

She nodded absently, already watching Scooby and the gang as they scurried over the screen in the opening song. I stepped away, watching her with regret curling through me. She was loved and cared for, but she didn't have a normal childhood. Then again, none of us had been allowed one. Not with Demi in and out. Not with the abilities she'd branded us with.

But we had each other, and that was all that really mattered.

**Keep reading *AFTER ALL THE WRECKAGE* now**

**FREE in Kindle Unlimited**

**https://geni.us/AATWLJE**

# Acknowledgements

I'm so very grateful for every single person who has helped me on this book journey. If you're reading these words, you *are* one of those people. I wouldn't be an author if people like you didn't decide to read the stories I crafted, so THANK YOU!

In addition to my lovely readers, I need to acknowledge these people:

My husband, who never ever lets me give up on myself, even when the battles seem endless. Your sacrifice, your strength, your laughter is what gets me through the dark, guiding me home.

Our child, Evyn, owner of Evans Editing, who remains my harshest and kindest critic. Thank you for helping me create my stories and driving me to be a better human. Love you, kiddo.

My parents, sister, and in-laws who listen to me gripe about publishing and then cheer me on as if I'm the greatest writer on earth. Thank you for making me feel loved and valid every single day.

Michelle Fewer, who patiently reads, uplifts, and plots without judgment and so much grace. Thank you for giving me your time, energy, and love.

Jenn at Jenn Lockwood Editing Services, Karen Hrdlicka, and Stephanie Feissner who have been on this journey with me since nearly the beginning and continue to have faith in me no matter how far apart we get pulled. Your edits and proofs are always the perfect polish that my words need.

The entire group of beautiful humans in LJ's Music & Stories who love and support me. I can't say enough how deeply grateful I am for each and every one of you.

The host of bloggers who have shared my stories, become dear friends, and continue to make me feel like a rock star every day. Thank you, thank you, thank you!

All the independent authors, including Stephanie Rose, Erika Kelly, Kathryn Nolan, Lucy Score, Hannah Blake, Maria Luis, Annie Dyer, Aly Stiles, and AM Johnson, who have shown me that dear friends are more important than any paralyzing moment in this wild publishing world, thank you for being by my side.

All my ARC readers, who have become sweet friends and true supporters. Thank you for knowing just what to say to scare away my writer insecurities.

Leisa C., Rachel R., and Stephanie F. Thank you beyond words for being the biggest cheerleaders, partners, and friends I could ever hope to have on this wild ride called life.

*I love you all!*

# About the Author

Award-winning author, LJ Evans, lives in Northern California with her husband, child, and the three terrors called cats. She's been writing, almost as a compulsion, since she was a little girl and will often pull the car over to write when a song lyric strikes her. A former first-grade teacher, she now spends her free time reading and writing, as well as binge-watching original shows like *Wednesday, The Mentalist, Veronica Mars,* and *Stranger Things*.

If you ask her the one thing she won't do, it's pretty much anything that involves dirt—sports, gardening, or otherwise. But she loves to write about all of those things, and her first published heroine was pretty much involved with dirt on a daily basis, which is exactly why LJ loves fiction novels—the characters can be everything you're not and still make their way into your heart.

Her novel, **CHARMING AND THE CHERRY BLOSSOM**, was *Writer's Digest* Self-Published E-book Romance of the Year in 2021. For more information about LJ, check out any of these sites:

www.ljevansbooks.com

FaceBook Group: LJ's Music & Stories

LJ Evans on Amazon, Bookbub, and Goodreads

@ljevansbooks on Facebook, Instagram, TikTok, and Pinterest

# Books by LJ

## Standalone

### *After All the Wreckage* — Rory & Gage

A single-dad, small-town, romantic suspense

He's a broody bar owner raising his siblings. She's a scrappy PI who's loved him since she was a teenager. When his brother disappears, she forces aside years of pining and family secrets to help him.

### *Charming and the Cherry Blossom* — Elle & Hudson

A contemporary romance with hints of magical realism

Today was a fairy tale. I inherited a fortune from a dad I never knew, and a charming guy asked me out. But like all fairy tales, mine has a dark side, and my happily ever after may disappear with the truth.

## The Hatley Family Standalones

### *The Last One You Loved* — Maddox & McKenna

A single-dad, grumpy-sheriff, romantic suspense

He's a small-town sheriff with a secret that can unravel their worlds. She's an ER resident running from a costly mistake. Coming home will only mean heartache…unless they let forgiveness heal them both.

### *The Last Promise You Made* — Ryder & Gia

A single-dad, grumpy-cowboy, romantic suspense

He's a grumpy rancher who swore off all relationships. She's a spitfire undercover agent who brings danger to his life. Not even a common enemy can force them to trust each other. Desire is an inconvenience. Falling in love is absolutely out of the question…

### *TLDYS* — Sadie Hatley's HEA

A single-dad, grumpy-cowboy, romantic suspense

Coming February 2025

### *Perfectly Fine* — Gemma & Rex

A fish-out-of-water, celebrity romance

He's a charming, A-list actor at the top of his game. She's a determined, small-town screenwriter hoping for a deal. They form an unexpected connection until heartbreak ruins their future. Available on Amazon and also FREE with newsletter subscription.

exposing all his secrets.

### *Branded by a Song* — Brady & Tristan

## A single-mom, rock star romance

He's a country-rock legend searching for inspiration. She's a Navy SEAL's widow determined to honor his memory while raising their daughter. Neither believes the intense attraction tugging at them can lead to more until their futures are twined by her grandmother's will.

### *Tripped by Love* – Cassidy & Marco

## A broody-bodyguard, single-mom romance

He's her brother's broody bodyguard with secrets he can't share. She's a busy single mom with a restaurant to run. They're just friends until a little white lie changes everything.

### *The Anchor Novels: The Military Bros Box Set*

## The books + an exclusive novella

*Guarded Dreams, Forged by Sacrifice,* and *Avenged by Love* plus the novella, *The Hurricane*! Heartfelt reads full of love, sacrifice, and family. The perfect book boyfriends for a binge read.


# The Anchor Suspense Novels

### *Unmasked Dreams* — Violet & Dawson

## A second-chance, forced-proximity romance

As teens, Violet and Dawson had a sizzling attraction they were forced to deny. And five years later, forced into living together they discover, nothing has changed—except the lab she's built in the garage and the secrets he's keeping. When she stumbles into his covert op, Dawson must break old promises to keep her safe, and once he has her at his side, he isn't sure he'll be able to let her go.

### *Crossed by the Stars* — Jada & Dax

## A second-chance, forced-proximity romance

Family secrets meant Dax and Jada's teenage romance was an impossibility. A decade later, the scars still remain, so neither is willing to give in to their tantalizing chemistry. But when a shadow creeps out of Jada's past, seeking retribution, it's Dax who shows up to protect her. And suddenly, it's hard to see a way out without permanent damage to their bodies and souls.

### *Disguised as Love* — Cruz & Raisa

## An enemies-to-lovers, forced-proximity romance

Surly FBI agent, Cruz Malone, is determined to bring down the Leskov clan for good. If that means he has to arrest or bed the sexy blonde scientist of the family, so be it. Too bad Raisa has other ideas. There's no way she's just going to sit back and let the infuriating agent dismantle her world…or her heart.

# The Painted Daisies

Interconnected series with an all-female rock band, the alpha heroes who steal their hearts, and suspense that will leave you breathless. Each has a HEA.

### *Swan River* — *The Painted Daisies* Prequel

## A rock-star, small-town, romantic suspense cliffhanger

The Painted Daisies are an all-female rock band and beloved family. With their star on the rise, life seems perfect until darkness strikes. When the group's trouble points to the band members' hidden secrets, it'll take every ounce of strength they have to unravel the mystery. Available on Amazon and also FREE with newsletter subscription.

### *Sweet Memory* — Paisley & Jonas

## A broody-protector, second-chance romance

The world's sweetest rock star falls for a troubled music producer whose past comes back to haunt them.

### *Green Jewel* — Fiadh & Asher

## An enemies-to-lovers, single-dad romance

He did it. She'll prove it. Her body's reaction to him be damned.

### *Cherry Brandy* — Leya & Holden

## A forced-proximity, bodyguard romance

Being on the run with only one bed is no excuse to touch her…until touching is the only choice.

### *Blue Marguerite* — Adria & Ronan

## A celebrity, second-chance, frenemy romance

She vowed to never forgive him…not even when he offers answers her family desperately seeks.

### *Royal Haze* — Nikki & D'Angelo

## A bodyguard, on-the-run romance with a morally gray hero

He was ready to torture, steal, and kill to defend the world he believed in. What he wasn't prepared for…was her.

# My Life as an Album Series

### *My Life as a Country Album* — Cam's Story

## A boy-next-door, small-town romance

This is tomboy Cam's diary-style, coming-of-age story about growing up loving the football hero next door. She vowed to love him forever. But when fate comes calling, will she ever find a heart to call home? Warning: Tears may fall.

### *My Life as a Pop Album* — Mia & Derek

## A rock star, road-trip romance

Bookworm Mia is trying to put years of guilt behind her when soulful musician Derek Waters strolls into her life and turns it upside down. Once he's seen her, Derek can't walk away unless Mia comes with him. But what will happen when their short time together comes to an end?

### *My Life as a Rock Album* — Seth & PJ

## A second-chance, antihero romance

Recovering addict Seth Carmen is a trash artist who knows he's better off alone. But when he finds and loses the love of his life, he can't help sending her a host of love letters to try to win her back. Can Seth prove to PJ they can make broken beautiful?

### *My Life as a Mixtape* — Lonnie & Wynn

## A single-dad, rock star romance

Lonnie's always seen relationships as a burden instead of a gift, and picking up the pieces his sister leaves behind is just one of the reasons. When Wynn enters his life just as her world is disintegrating, their mixed-up pasts give way to new beginnings neither of them saw coming.

### *My Life as a Holiday Album* – 2$^{nd}$ Generation

## A small-town romance

Come home for the holidays with this heartwarming, full-length standalone full of hidden secrets, true love, and the real meaning of family. Perfect for lovers of *Love Actually* and Hallmark movies, this sexy story intertwines the lives of six couples as they find their way to their happily ever afters with the help of family and friends.

### *My Life as an Album Series Box Set*

## The 1st four Album series stories plus an exclusive novella

In the exclusive novella, *This Life with Cam*, Blake Abbott writes to Cam about just what it was like to grow up in the shadow of her relationship with Jake and just when he first fell for the little girl with the popsicle-stained lips. Can he show Cam that she isn't broken?

# Free Stories

Get these novellas, flash fiction stories, + bonus epilogues for
FREE with newsletter subscription at:
https://www.ljevansbooks.com/freeljbooks

## *Perfectly Fine* – A fish-out-of-water, celebrity romance

He's a charming, A-list actor at the top of his game. She's a determined, small-town screenwriter hoping for a deal. They form an unexpected connection until heartbreak ruins their future. Also available on Amazon.

## *Swan River* — A rock star, small-town, romantic suspense *prequel*

The Painted Daisies are an all-female rock band and beloved family. With their star on the rise, life seems perfect until darkness strikes. When the group's trouble points to the band members' hidden secrets, it'll take every ounce of strength they have to unravel the mystery.

## *Rumor* – A small-town, rock star romance

There's only one thing rock star Chase Legend needs to ring in the new year, and that's to know what Reyna Rossi tastes like. After ten years, there's no way he's letting her escape the night without their souls touching. Reyna has other plans. After all, she doesn't need the entire town wagging their tongues about her any more than they already do.

## *Love Ain't* – A friends-to-lovers, cowboy romance

Reese knows her best friend and rodeo king, Dalton Abbott, is never going to fall in love, get married, and have kids. He's left so many broken hearts behind that there's gotta be a museum full of them somewhere. So when he gives her a look from under the brim of his hat, promising both jagged relief and pain, she knows better than to give in.

## *The Long Con* – A sexy, antihero romance

Adler is after one thing: the next big payday. Then, Brielle sways into his world with her own game in play, and those aquamarine-colored eyes almost make him forget his number-one rule. But she'll learn… love isn't a con he's interested in.

## *The Light Princess* – An old-fashioned fairy tale

A princess who glows with a magical light, a kingdom at war, and a kiss that changes the world. This is an extended version of the fairy tale twined through the pages of *Charming and the Cherry Blossom.*

www.ingramcontent.com/pod-product-compliance
Lightning Source LLC
Chambersburg PA
CBHW022256310726
48973CB00001B/89